# Empire of the Gods

PATRICK D. CATLETT

"Empire of the Gods," by Patrick D. Catlett. ISBN: 978-1-63868-186-1 (softcover).

Published 2025 by Virtualbookworm.com Publishing Inc., P.O. Box 9949, College Station, TX 77842, US. ©2025 Patrick D. Catlett. All rights reserved. No part of this publication may be reproduced, stored in a retrieval system, or transmitted in any form or by any means, electronic, mechanical, recording or otherwise, without the prior written permission of Patrick D. Catlett.

# Contents

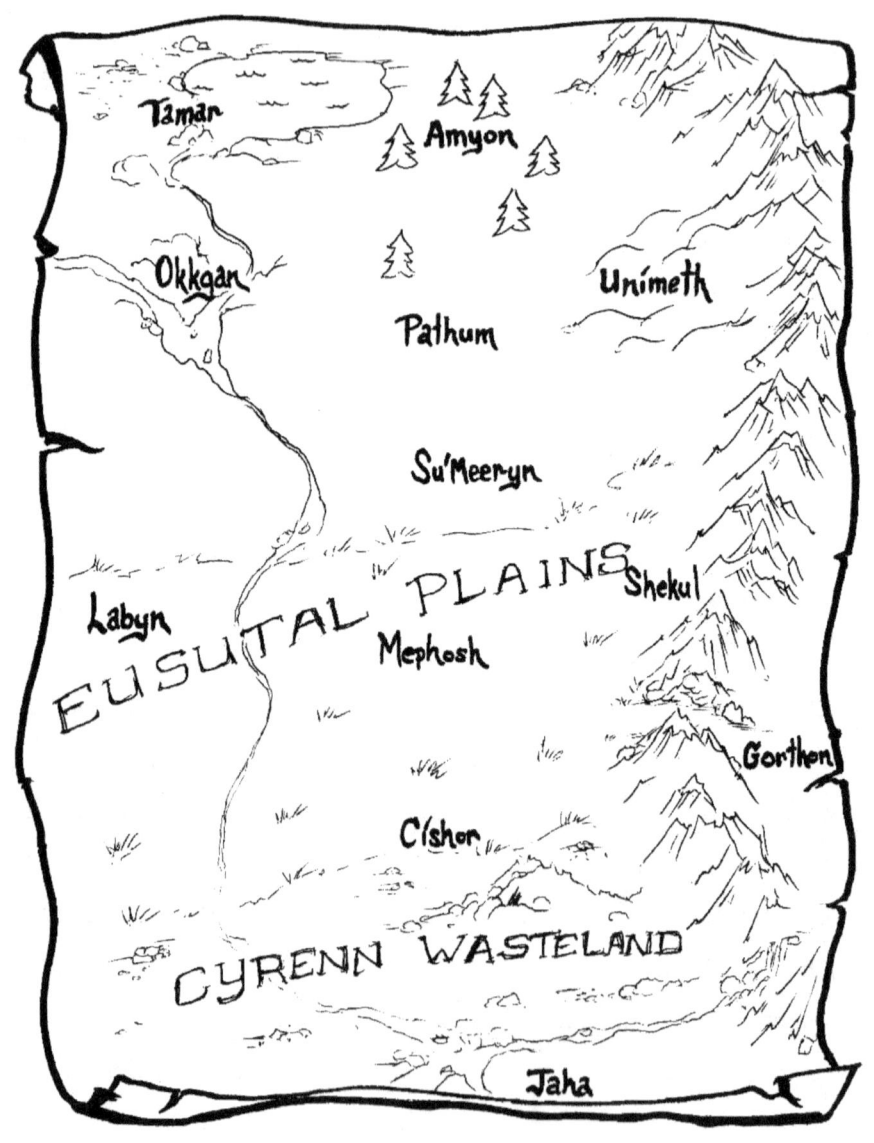

# Prologue

THE KING AMBLED SLOWLY about his personal chamber. Each step seemed to awaken a different ache in his aged body. He gingerly sat in one of the plush chairs and turned longingly to the portrait that hung directly across from him. Though he could no longer see her very well, he had memorized every inch of his beloved wife's image. She was still young when the painting had been completed, and her beauty seemed to radiate off the canvas. He hardly ever noticed the scar or her marred ear. Despite his protests, and those of the painter, she had staunchly refused to have them removed from the portrait. "This is how I look," she would say, "and that is what I want to see in my portrait." She had not just been a remarkable woman, she was the most remarkable person he had ever known. She had died over a decade ago, and yet the portrait still brought tears to his eyes whenever he gazed upon it. But the king refused to feel sorry for himself. He had lived longer than anyone he had ever known; the queen had too, for that matter. He would not be sad that he remained alive. He had even outlived all their children. He did not dwell on that either. Most of his children had been blessed with full lives, so there was no reason to mourn. He did have his grandchildren, and even a great-grandson. What more could a king want?

He shifted in the chair as his hips were becoming numb. While he felt some relief, that just emphasized other aches. Yes, he had almost constant pain, but that was to be expected at his age. He did not know exactly how old he was, but he guessed it was approaching ten decades. He glanced at the stump where his arm had been. He knew of others who had lost limbs in battle and had continued to experience pain from where that limb had been, but he had never heard of anyone whose pain had lasted for the rest of their life. However, he would not complain about that either. So many others had died in battle, and yet he still lived. A little pain was more than a fair tradeoff for all he had seen since the battles to liberate his kingdom.

He looked towards the door, waiting expectantly for it to open. Although it was extremely blurry, he assumed it remained closed as he had not heard any movement. Unfortunately, he could not rely on his hearing, which was even worse than his vision: just another price of living to this unheard-of age.

A new twinge from his hip caused him to shift again, but this time the pain did not slacken. He had vowed to never complain, and he knew he would soon be given respite from all his ailments as something within his being told him that his life was marching towards its conclusion. There was nothing specific that he could point to, but it was just a sense that became greater with each morning that he still awoke. He did not dread that day, but he also did not look forward to it.

While his debilitations kept him in his room, he was still the king. His mind remained sharp and this was an important task he needed to complete.

Eventually the door did open, and he watched as the small shape approached. While he could not make out the appearance, he knew it was his great-grandson. With a smile on his face, he motioned for the boy to join him. Jaleph sensed a bit of apprehension from the child as he sat in the adjoining chair. He knew the boy loved him, but he also knew that children found it uncomfortable to get too close. The king did not blame them. They had no experience being around someone as ancient as he was, and it made them uneasy. That made this meeting so important as the boy was his great-grandson, and he would most likely be king some day. He would have to get used to dealing with uncomfortable situations.

"I'm pleased you could join me, my boy," Jaleph said, reaching his hand out to the child.

The boy reached back and squeezed his hand. That gesture increased Jaleph's confidence in his great-grandson since Hellet was able to push past his apprehension and touch the withered flesh. The boy had already learned much at his young age.

"How are you grandfather?"

"I am as well as can be expected, but I don't know for how much longer. I feel my life is coming to an end."

"Don't say that!" Hellet said loudly, leaning forward to make sure the old man heard him.

"It is the way of things. I've lived much longer than I ever thought possible. So don't be sad. But there are a few matters I want to discuss with you."

Hellet sniffed then wiped his nose with his forearm, and Jaleph thought he say a tint of red in the boy's eyes. Yes, it was most fortunate that Hellet was the son of the oldest prince. Jaleph was certain he would make a wonderful king. "What do you want to tell me, grandfather?"

Jaleph hesitated as he tried to distinguish the boy's features. Despite Hellet's very young age, it had been clear to all who knew him that he possessed an inner strength. For whatever reason, Hellet already exhibited great maturity and wisdom. Jaleph understood that Hellet's gifts gave him a confidence in his bearing, not seen in others. And the king knew that these gifts would serve the boy well.

"You are a wise boy, Hellet, smarter than anyone your age, or older for that matter. You know that you are destined to be king of Su'Meeryn someday, and I am confident that you will be a fine monarch. However, you need to realize that there is more to being a king than just wisdom. I would not say that I was the wisest king, and I was very impulsive in my youth, especially before I lost my arm." The king paused momentarily as his eyes absently turned to his stump.

"There are two lessons that I want you to take to heart," Jaleph continued. "As I said, everyone knows that you've been gifted with wisdom, but a king must not take only his own counsel." Jaleph stopped to take a deep breath as his remaining hand had seized up, and bolts of pain shot up his arm. With a sigh, he forced his fingers to straighten.

"You must have good people around you," the king continued as he turned his dim eyes back towards the portrait. "Kieran was the wisest and most compassionate person I ever knew. I was more than fortunate to have her as my wife and queen. I would not have been half the king I was without her at my side. I also had my close friend Wander." The king chuckled briefly. "We didn't always agree, and we argued much. A disagreement between us forced him to leave Su'Meeryn, and his loss was a great burden to me. He was irreplaceable, and I should have never let it come to that." He paused again at the memory of losing his old friend, but he had dealt with that regret decades ago. "You must have people around you who are comfortable enough to argue with their king. Do you understand me?"

"Yes grandfather."

"Promise me that you will heed my advice."

"I will grandfather."

Jaleph tried to look into the boy's eyes, and though he could not see clearly enough to read Hellet's expression, he knew the honesty and sincerity of his great-grandson. Hellet meant what he said, at least for now.

"One more thing that I always want you to remember, you will be king and the sovereign of Su'Meeryn someday. However, never forget that the king should actually be a servant. You must serve your people, it should not be the other way around. If you follow these two pieces of advice your kingdom will thrive, and your people will love you. What more can a king ask for?"

The boy leaned over and wrapped his arms around the old man. Jaleph could not remember the last time Hellet had embraced him, and his eyes teared up. "I will grandfather. And I promise you this, I will name my first son after you to always remind myself of this promise."

"You are a fine boy, Hellet, graciously gifted by the creator. You shall be a great king."

# chapter 1

TRAVYN ENTERED THE ROYAL HALL of Pathum with a feeling of unease. It is a rare occasion to meet one's future spouse, and he had no idea whether he would find her pretty or homely. He had heard conflicting reports regarding her appearance, so he did not know what to believe.

He thought he had been spared the fate of a prearranged marriage when his father had died, but being the youngest offspring, he quickly realized that he still had little say in his own fate. His brother Orrin was not yet king as, for whatever reason, their grandfather refused to die. It was not that Travyn disliked Jaleph, but he always found the old man to be fairly self-righteous. Yes, he had heard all the stories about his grandfather's exploits, but he still found Jaleph patronizing whenever they interacted. Travyn had no use for the king's religious babblings; however, at least it was not Jaleph who had commanded his marriage to the princess of Pathum. He had Orrin to thank for this misery.

The king and queen of Pathum sat on their thrones while he strode towards them. The room was lined with dignitaries and royal guards, but the sight that immediately caught his attention, and caused him to stutter-step for a moment, were the three wolves sitting on the floor to the left of the king. Travyn had viewed images of wolves in various works of art, but he had never actually encountered one. The size of the beasts shocked him; they were larger than he would have expected; however, despite their sinister reputation, the animals seemed extremely docile.

Nevertheless, his eyes remained transfixed on the animals as he continued to approach the throne, so he did not even notice the girl who sat on a chair stroking one of their necks. When he reached the thrones he stopped, tearing his eyes from the wolves to address the monarchs of Pathum. "Greetings from Su'Meeryn. I am prince Travyn. I am here to escort your daughter, the princess Dellea back to my home, as agreed, to be my wife."

"I am Marken, king of Pathum. Welcome, Travyn," the king responded then took a long drink from the mug before him. "And my wife Bryon," he added, motioning to his left. Travyn nodded to the queen, then his gaze followed the king's back towards the wolves. There he finally noticed the young princess as she stood from her small chair and approached. The wolf she had been stroking looked annoyed when she removed her hand, but then it just yawned and sprawled out on the floor.

When Travyn was finally able to examine his bride-to-be, he was somewhat relieved, but not pleased. She was of average height and very boney, almost appearing sickly. Her thin red hair had a tinge of orange and hung in unruly strands around her clean yet bland face. Yet, she was still young and might develop more distinguishing features in time.

Dellea's squarish, almond eyes slowly surveyed him as she approached, which made him uncomfortable. When he thought he saw a similar reaction in her gaze to how he felt, he became annoyed. How dare she judge me? Not the best start but it could have been worse, he told himself. Dellea glanced back at her parents then returned her attention to him. "Welcome, husband," she said flatly.

Travyn reached out and took her hand, gave it a quick kiss and released it. "It is my pleasure to meet the princess Dellea. My family is grateful that the king of Pathum has consented to this marriage. The great king Jaleph looks forward to even stronger ties between our two kingdoms," he recited the memorized words, pleased with himself at how well he had performed them. Despite his marvelous presentation, Dellea's face remained frozen with the look of disappointment, which Travyn found infuriating. She should be thankful that she was allowed to marry such a fine man.

"Very good," the king stated as he stood from the throne. "Now let's proceed to the feast. I wish to get to know my future son." The king took Travyn's arm and led the prince of Su'Meeryn from his hall. As they walked, Travyn looked back for his fiancée, but instead of following them, the princess was returning to the wolves. The beasts rose with her approach, and they followed her in the opposite direction as she exited the chamber.

***

Travyn sat at the large table with Bryon to his right and Marken to his left. It was a cavernous room filled with smaller tables before them, and a celebratory clamor filled the air while nobles and dignitaries enjoyed the meal. Through the commotion, Travyn could barely make out the music of the minstrels situated along the walls. Mounds of cooked meats and roasted potatoes rested on the tables along with a rainbow of fruits and vegetables. Goblets of wine were raised in honor of the betrothed as Travyn took another long swig from his mug. A moment later, he glanced over and noticed that Bryon ate very little and was only drinking water.

"So, how old are you son?" the queen asked as she placed her container back down on the table.

"I shall be twenty years this summer," he answered before taking a bite of a carrot. The taste surprised him. It was not that he hadn't had many carrots before, but there was some spice that had been roasted into the vegetable that made it the most delicious carrot he ever had.

"That's good," replied the queen. "I'm sure you shall make a fine husband for our daughter."

"How old is she?"

"She is three years younger than you," Marken answered gruffly before taking a large bite of the slab of meat that dwarfed his plate. He then grabbed his massive, jeweled-adorned mug and took a deep mouthful of ale.

"And where is Dellea?" Travyn asked, "and the prince? I was told Dellea has a brother."

The king huffed angrily then took another long drink. The queen rose from her seat and searched about the hall. "Where is that girl?" she asked quietly. Though he was not sure, Travyn wondered if he heard a trace of fear in Bryon's voice, but he quickly dismissed the notion. Travyn was an excellent judge of character, and there was certainly nothing to fear during this celebration.

After a few moments Bryon returned to her seat when the princess and her wolves entered the hall from the rear. As Dellea approached the table, she motioned with her hand and the animals stopped and sat at the side of the table, eyeing her expectantly. Dellea then waved to a servant who entered with a large tray covered with three chunks of raw meat. Dellea took the tray before turning back to the wolves. They were stretched out on the floor, but their eyes never left the princess. She waited a moment, which confused Travyn. What was the point of making them wait? The animals remained motionless during the long pause; finally, the princess slowly handed each their portions, stroking their heads as they ate. She watched them finish their meals before joining her family and Travyn at the royal table.

"How many times have I asked you not to bring those creatures into the hall?" the queen asked, and Travyn caught the tone of both aggravation and exasperation. The king muttered something angrily amidst his chewing which Travyn was unable to decipher.

"They are my friends," Dellea responded quietly.

"At least they will finally be gone," the king spat before taking another hearty drink.

A frown crossed Dellea's pink-flushed face but, she then turned her attention back to her plate and mumbled, "I see my brother hasn't come."

"You need not concern yourself with Dorren," the king rebuked her, then his yellow teeth ripped into a large turkey leg.

"And what of you, Travyn?" The queen's question turned his attention away from the king and his bride-to-be. "Tell us about yourself."

Before Travyn could reply, a servant refilled Marken's tankard. The king took another deep swallow and banged the goblet on the table causing large drops of the bitter liquid to fly into the air. The mood at the table was confusing to Travyn; why were they all not celebrating? While he was not looking forward to this marriage, he certainly did not possess the animosity he was feeling around him. "I'm the prince from Su'Meeryn," he eventually answered.

Dellea laughed at his words, and Travyn could not tell if it was out of genuine mirth or condescension. "We are aware of that," Bryon continued patiently. "You wouldn't be here if you weren't. But since you are to be husband to our daughter, we would like to know something more about you than just your position in Su'Meeryn's court."

"Enough!" Marken bellowed. "We are not here to interrogate our guest. They will have plenty of time to get acquainted after the wedding. Now is the time to celebrate!" He slammed his hand on the table, his face turning red. "So celebrate!"

The queen jumped in response to the outburst, and Travyn was also taken aback. He looked at Dellea, who seemed oblivious to her father's fury. She just turned her head to the wolves, and Travyn followed her eyes. He noticed that the animals had sat up and were gazing at the princess, with stains of the devoured meat around their jaws. When Dellea's attention returned to her plate, the wolves relaxed back onto the floor.

"Well, we will be in Su'Meeryn soon, so I at least have that to look forward to," the princess whispered, almost inaudibly.

The tension in the room pressed against Travyn's skin like a boa constrictor gripping its prey. His gaze returned to his meal, but his appetite had completely vanished. He looked back at Dellea whose hands seemed to tremble while she took a tiny bite of a pepper. He had no idea what to do. Glancing over, he saw that Bryon was gingerly pushing her food about her plate before taking a sip of water. Peering out into the hall, he saw the nobles and dignitaries continuing with their meals, ignoring his table.

With a loud crash—startling Travyn—Marken angrily banged his utensils and goblet about the great table. "Let's enjoy our meal!" he barked out in a slur. Travyn noticed the girl flinch, and she set the pepper back down on her plate. Her head dropped, and she turned her attention back to the wolves.

What has Orrin gotten me into? Travyn thought as the anger he felt towards his brother for arranging this unfortunate pairing multiplied. A prince of his stature should not be subjected to this type of spectacle.

# chapter 2

A clap of thunder rolled through her room while Dellea sat frozen on her bed, a tear running unchecked down her thin cheek, the feeling of loneliness engulfing her. Her possessions were strewn about the room as she was unable to begin the process of packing her belongings. A flash of lightning was quickly followed by more thunder and then the pounding of heavy rain. Dellea sat quietly and listened to the storm. The rainfall pelting the ground down below her window was soothing, but it could not relieve her anxiety.

It was not that she had a desire to remain in Pathum as with each passing day, her father was becoming more belligerent than the last. He rarely left the royal hall, and his giant mug was always filled with ale. She had never cared to be near him; even when she was younger, he had always been demanding and mean-spirited. But as the months and years passed, he had become even more aggressive. She knew he hated having her wolves around—which increased his ire, but at least he had not ordered them away, or worse. However, the fact that he had acquiesced on this one matter did little to endear him to his daughter.

Her older brother was not much better. Dorren had not even bothered himself to attend the betrothal feast; he was probably passed out somewhere in a drunken stupor. Her brother drank as much as their father—maybe more. When he was not carousing in a pub or brothel, he spent his time with the nobles, preparing himself for his eventual coronation. Though the siblings rarely spoke, when they did, it was clear Dorren hated Marken almost as much as she did. During the rare times her brother was with his family, he would dwell on his plans to find the most profitable bride for their kingdom. However, Dellea was certain that Dorren was just making excuses so he could cavort with the daughters of the Pathum nobility. Dellea found her brother's actions disgusting. She had heard all the rumors; he was using his position to sleep with as many of the young maidens as possible. He had no interest in marrying any of them. Dellea could not understand how her brother had convinced Marken to delay his marriage so long, but eventually he would be forced to marry. Dorren was prolonging that outcome as long as possible, but she, unfortunately, did not have that freedom. When the delegation from Su'Meeryn had arrived with the proposal from Prince Orrin, Marken had gladly and eagerly accepted without discussion.

Even Bryon was not an ally for Dellea. Her mother had problems of her own as she was often the victim of Marken's drunken furies. Dellea knew that the queen needed to be careful in how she approached her father, but Bryon coped by simply ignoring his outbursts. Dellea wanted to feel some sympathy for her mother, but it was difficult to find any empathy when Bryon remained silent in the face of the king's rages against their daughter. Dellea knew that with her awkward demeanor, she was not an ordinary girl, but that fact was no reason for the constant abuse. Had her mother even attempted to speak up in defense of her daughter, Dellea would have been overjoyed, but that was not the case. She had no friends or allies in the castle. She had nobody—nobody except her wolves.

So Dellea had no wish to remain in Pathum; unfortunately, the thought of marrying Travyn and moving to an unknown city was equally appalling. She saw nothing appealing in the prince from Su'Meeryn, and by moving there, she would be surrounded by strangers. And so she found herself paralyzed on her bed, listening to the rain. She hated the thought of leaving, but she also dreaded the thought of staying. It was a misery, and she wondered if she would be able to endure it.

A soft knock roused her, and she slowly stood to open the door.

Her mother entered with a manufactured smile upon her face. "You haven't even begun packing, Dellea."

"No," the princess responded, turning away, quickly drying more tears from her face. She hoped that her mother would offer some comfort, but she knew it would not happen.

"Well, it's a good thing I came," Bryon replied, either oblivious to her daughter's pain or simply ignoring it. "We need to make sure you are ready to leave, otherwise your father will be very unhappy."

When isn't he, Dellea thought bitterly. Bryon squatted down onto the floor and began sorting her daughter's garments. The princess came up beside her, but rather than helping, she tentatively placed her palm on the top of her mother's hand. Bryon stopped for a moment and tilted her head towards Dellea but did not lift her eyes to look at her daughter. During that pause, Dellea hoped her mother would speak to her, offer her a reassuring word. Instead, Bryon pulled her hand away to continue gathering the clothes. "Why aren't your servants helping?" was all the queen said.

"I wanted to be alone."

Bryon paused and looked out the window. Then she said, "We need to get moving."

Dellea reached over and grabbed the pair of trousers she always wore when she took the wolves around the castle. She clutched the fabric to her chest as she moved back onto the bed; those solitary hikes were the only pleasant memories she had of her home.

She noticed that the rain outside her window had stopped; the brief storm had passed. There was nothing that would delay her embarking to Su'Meeryn. Her hands shook, and her chest tightened as she felt her anxiety growing. She stood back up and began to help her mother pack her belongings. The decision had been made, and she could do nothing to change it. She would be leaving Pathum in the morning. At least she would be away from her family.

✳✳✳

The ground was still damp from the previous night's rain as trumpets sounded a regal call. Banners unfurled while Marken, Bryon and Dorren climbed atop the dais. Dellea glanced towards her family while she mounted her horse, a turmoil of mixed emotions swirling within her. Bryon had wanted the princess to ride in a wagon, but Dellea refused. She did not think she would be able to coax the wolves to join her in the carriage, and she did not want them traveling amongst the horses without her nearby. She had made sure they were fully fed before they prepared to leave, but she still did not want to take any chances. The wolves sat patiently as Travyn rode up next to her. He eyed the beasts warily before turning to his fiancé.

"It is a marvelous day for a ride, isn't it?" he asked. "You must be very excited to be coming to Su'Meeryn with me."

Is this man a complete fool? she thought. Travyn knew she was leaving her home for an unknown life. Why would she be excited? While she was trying her best to hide her apprehension, was he not able to see at least some concern on her face?

"Are you sure we need to take these animals with us?" he continued. "I don't know what use they can be."

"Yes," she responded quietly.

Travyn looked back down at the beasts, unsure how to respond. He then kicked his horse and returned to the front to the group to join the soldiers from Su'Meeryn.

The trumpets blared again, and Dellea heard the banners fluttering above while she passed through the castle gates. As the company started to move forward, Dellea looked back towards her family one last time. Dorren had already vanished and Marken's smile appeared to be an expression of relief, happy for the disappearance of a burden. Bryon's face displayed sadness, but Dellea had to wonder if that was sorrow at losing her daughter, or that there was now one less distraction for the king's anger to fall upon.

Dellea reminded herself she was happy to be leaving, but would Su'Meeryn be any better? While she hated everything about Pathum, at least it was the life she knew. Now she would be alone, surrounded by strangers, which was terrifying, and married to a man—though they had just met—she could barely tolerate. At least she had her wolves.

# chapter 3

THE QUEEN'S FUNERAL WAS A COLORFUL, BUT SOLEMN AFFAIR. The great hall overflowed with the nobles and dignitaries of Mephosh as well as the royal family. The king sat alone on his throne, pretending to scan the chamber. But his daughter knew it was only for show. Naren's failing vision had left him nearly blind, and he rarely ventured out in public anymore. Ellaniya wondered if anyone outside her family knew of the king's condition. Naren was far from being considered an old man, but whatever sickness was stealing his vision, it was also ravaging his body. Now that her mother had succumbed to her illness, Ellaniya was certain that her father would soon follow.

Ellaniya stood stoically at the side of the hall, attempting to hide from the eyes of the attendees. She watched as the nobles milled about. Although she could tell that some were truly saddened by the death of their queen, many clearly feigned their sorrow. As much as she wanted to, she could not be angry with the hypocritical nobles; she was experiencing the same ambivalence herself. While she did not harbor animosity towards her mother, she despised what had become of Mephosh since the glory days under Queen Lynna. During Lynna's reign, Mephosh had been the most powerful kingdom in the land. Yes, Lynna had made some mistakes, and the conflict with Su'Meeryn and the northern kingdoms had weakened Mephosh, but as a student of history, Ellaniya knew there was more to the demise of their kingdom than just those battles. Lynna had done much to rebuild her power following their last terrible defeat, and as a result Mephosh had remained strong. While Lynna had been the greatest monarch in the history of Mephosh, she had made errors. And those errors led to the kingdom's decline after her death. But the largest culprit was that damned book that began circulating amongst the masses following the final battle with Su'Meeryn.

*The Book of Sul,* she hated even thinking about it. Yes, Mephosh had been weakened by their defeat against Jaleph and Su'Meeryn, but after the death of Lynna, it was that book that had fostered their true decline. Despite her losses, Lynna had always remained true to her faith in the gods. She had done all she could to stop the spread of the book. Her hatred of Sul had been singularly focused, and she severely punished anyone who had any dealings with his book or the heretical religion. Most people in the kingdom did not know how to read, so if anyone was found reciting the book, that person was immediately executed.

Since Lynna never had an heir, her death had been a tremendous tragedy. The kingdom had been thrown into turmoil following her demise. While all the nobles were prepared for the eventuality, it still did not make the succession easy. There had been much controversy when Ellaniya's family had been selected as the new royal line. Her family had succumbed to the heretical teachings of Sul, and there had been serious debate regarding the religious implications of that decision. But the nobles' cowardice was made evident. They had ultimately decided that building better relations with their neighboring kingdoms was more important than maintaining true worship. Once her family had taken the throne, the power of Mephosh had declined even further. The worship of the false religion took precedence over strengthening the army. As such, Mephosh was no longer the dominant kingdom in the region.

No, Ellaniya did not hate her mother, or her father for that matter, but she despised the abandoning of the true faith, and she was certain things would only get her worse. Her father was useless, but he would likely be dead soon. The problem was her younger brother. Pharen was a weak-minded follower of Sul's religion. He cared not about rebuilding their power; his only concern was his religious studies. Once he became king... well, she could not envision how bad things would become. And just because she was born a girl, there was nothing she could do about it.

"How are you?" A concerned voice from behind stirred Ellaniya from her musing as she turned to see the teary-eyed face of her brother.

"It's a sad day, Pharen," Ellaniya replied, attempting to feign sorrow.

Pharen wrapped his arm around his sister's shoulders and dried his face with his free hand. "Father is taking it hard; I worry about his health."

"Yes."

The prince stood quietly, waiting for Ellaniya to continue. When she did not, he added, "Father's faith is strong, and I pray this will not be his demise."

"If you say so."

"Ellaniya, I don't know what else to do with you," Pharen's voice quivered. "I wish you shared our faith. It was Mother's dying wish."

It took enormous effort for Ellaniya to suppress her anger. What to do with me? How dare he? She was not the one in need of assistance. It was the arrogance of her father and brother which required correction. They were the cause of Mephosh's decline, but there was no point to continue that argument. She had debated religion so many times with Pharen that their discussions had become comically redundant.

But what could she do? Pharen was an even greater fanatic than their father. He would take the throne, and she would be married off and likely not even live in Mephosh. Thankfully, any thoughts of marriage had been delayed due to the queen's illness, and there would likely be no discussion while Naren's health was so fragile. However, if the king were to die soon, the crown would pass to Pharen, and she would be subjected to her brother's misguided decisions. She could not bear that thought, as he would certainly select another heretic to be her husband. It was a terrible dilemma, but at least a decision had not been made yet. She still had time.

"I pray that somehow I can convince you of your error," he said as he gave her a squeeze before returning to their father's side.

Soft, mournful music continued while the guests began to exit the hall. Ellaniya watched them leave with a mixture of emotions. She was sad that her mother was dead; in a way she had loved her, but Ellaniya was angry as well. While she may not be the heir to the throne, she still had some power as the princess. Ellaniya still had time. Now, she just needed to figure out how to use that power.

✳✳✳

Ellaniya sat in her personal study the following day, reading one of the sacred texts of the gods when a knock sounded. With slight irritation at the interruption, she gently set the tome down, stood and opened the door.

The princess found Pharen in the entry, still looking despondent. "I figured you would be here." He looked at her books, and Ellaniya saw an expression of frustration and disgust cross his face.

"What do you want?"

"There is news from Su'Meeryn. Prince Travyn is to marry Dellea of Pathum. We need you to travel there as the representative from Mephosh."

Su'Meeryn, she thought; can this get any worse? "Why don't you go? You are the heir to the throne. You would be a far better representative than me."

"With father's health as it is, I need to be here, in case…"

You disregard me until I'm needed, Ellaniya wanted to say, but she held her tongue. "Very well," she eventually replied, "now leave me be. I'll return to my rooms presently."

Pharen nodded then quickly spun about, clearly happy to not have to continue the conversation.

Ellaniya angrily returned to her seat. Her lips curled under her teeth, clenching to the point of pain before she forced herself to relax. The last thing she desired was to leave the kingdom at this time. She did not want to interrupt her studies, plus her father would likely be dead soon. She still needed to devise a plan to thwart her brother's desires for Mephosh. This was the worst possible time to leave, but she had no choice. And to make her torment complete, she had to travel to the kingdom she loathed.

Dropping to her knees, she quickly offered up a prayer to the gods. She asked them to bless this miserable trip and, if they so desired, to make it a fruitful journey. With her prayer completed, she returned the book to the shelf and stomped out the door and made her way to her room.

# chapter 4

THE SIGHT OF THE THREE WOLVES WAS EXHILARATING and terrifying to Hellet. He had heard rumors about his future aunt upon Travyn's return, but he was unprepared for the sight of the beasts. They were both magnificent and frightening at the same time.

"Go over and pet them," Neffy suggested with a grin and a nudge against the prince's shoulder.

Hellet turned to his large, young friend. "Why don't you?"

"They're not going to be in my family."

Other than a few servants, the royal hall was empty except for the two boys and the wolves. It was odd seeing the creatures in the hall, but Hellet had heard that Dellea wanted them nearby while she settled into her new home. Soon the animals would be relocated to a secure area within the stables.

Hellet looked at his friend, who was still smirking at his own clever remark, then turned back to the creatures. They were strewn out across the floor, presumably sleeping, though he was not certain. Obviously, the beasts were not dangerous, otherwise they would not be in the castle, unattended. Neffy gave his friend another push, and Hellet shot him an irritated scowl, which just made Neffy's smile broader. Fine, Hellet thought. Without further hesitation, the boy marched up to the wolves.

Their size was even more impressive once he stood next to them. His eyes traveled over their bodies and, even through their thick fur, he could see the power in their muscles. "Impressive, aren't they," he heard a voice say from the shadows. He was surprised by the comment, but he fought off the urge to jump back. A skinny, red-haired girl emerged from the darkness, and he knew it had to be Dellea. "Who are you, and why are you disturbing my friends?"

Hellet glanced down; the wolves had raised their heads at the sound of Dellea's voice, but when she did not acknowledge them further, they settled back onto the ground, closing their eyes. "They hardly looked disturbed," he stated.

The prince thought he would get a laugh, or at least a smile from the girl at his remark, but her expression remained unchanged. "What about my other question? Who are you?"

"I am Hellet, your soon-to-be nephew."

That comment brought a slight grin to Dellea's face. "Nephew, huh? You're not much younger than me."

"True, but the fact remains."

The girl's head tilted to the side while her eyes fully examined the boy. "How old are you?" she asked sharply though Hellet could tell that Dellea feigned the aggravated tone in her voice. He wondered at that. Why would she feel the need to put on such a show?

"I am fourteen, soon to be fifteen," he stated defiantly, arching his back, and he noticed the trace of a grin cross the girl's lips at his gesture.

"Fourteen, huh? I would have thought older."

"I've been told that many times," Hellet responded truthfully.

"So, you're the one they're making so much fuss about," she stated.

"I suppose so."

"My marriage is being delayed until after your party. Well, I can at least thank you for that!"

Before Hellet could consider the girl's words, he heard Neffy's voice from behind, "Get on with it!"

"With what?" Dellea asked.

"I was going to pet the wolves," answered Hellet.

Dellea let out a chuckle. "I wouldn't advise it."

"Why not? Clearly they're not dangerous."

Dellea stood straight as a pole, arms crossed across her thin chest with a strand of orange-tinted hair covering one of her almond eyes. "They don't like men."

"That's not a problem as I'm not a man yet."

This time Dellea did laugh at his jest. Rather than respond she just motioned towards the animals before taking a step back, her arms now at her hips.

Hellet felt his heart racing while a trembling hand reached down. The beasts glanced up at him as his fingers reached the first animal's head. The wolf's blue eyes peered into his and Hellet instantly knew the beast sensed his hesitation. He tried to push the trepidation aside as his hand passed through the fur. He had no idea what he had expected, but the fur was rougher than he would have thought.

When he moved to the second animal, the first wolf slowly stood. Hellet again pushed aside his nervousness and stroked the next beast.

That one also stood as he turned to the third; it was stretched out on its side, so the prince dropped to his knees to stroke its belly. Before stopping, a cold nose started sniffing the back of his neck, and he felt the moisture of a tongue across his cheek. The licking continued as a second tongue found the other side of his face. Next, large paws pushed on his shoulders, and Hellet was forced to the ground. He was terrified for a moment, but the licking continued at a frantic pace. The fear quickly evaporated, and laughter escaped from his lips. But as soon as it did, a tongue entered and probed the roof of his mouth. He rolled to his side, giggling in delight while three tongues continue to seek his mouth. His hands covered his face as the laughter continued to burst from between his fingers.

"That's enough," he heard Dellea say, and the wolves begrudgingly stopped their harmless attack and returned to the floor.

Hellet stood, wiping his face on his sleeves, the laughter finally ceasing, and he caught sight of Neffy. His friend was staring at him, mouth agape, dumbfounded by the scene he had just witnessed. He then turned his attention to Dellea. The girl stared at him with her hands still on her hips. Though her expression was difficult to read, Hellet figured she was annoyed that her wolves had responded so well to him. However, he sensed a streak of pleasure as well. "I guess they like you," she stated bruskly.

"Apparently."

She looked at him for moment, and Hellet awaited another comment. But she said nothing more. Finally, she turned back to the wolves and motioned for them to follow her from the hall with Hellet's gaze lingering on her as they disappeared into the darkness.

Once the girl and her animals were gone, Neffy approached his friend. "Well, that wasn't what I expected," he said.

"Me either," Hellet replied, then they also exited the chamber.

***

"I wish you weren't making such a fuss over this," Hellet said while taking a drink of water from the goblet resting on the table next to his plush chair.

"Grant me this one indulgence," his mother replied. "Of course I know a boy's sixteenth birthday is traditionally the biggest celebration, but it has been a trying year."

Hellet offered Jenna a sympathetic smile. How she had kept her joyous nature after the death of another child during the winter was astounding to Hellet. He had been her first born, but, since then, all of her other four children had died of various ailments at an early age. Hellet did not remember the first two, but the recent death of his baby sister had been extremely traumatic. Jenna's pregnancy and childbirth had been miserable, and nobody knew if the newborn would survive. However, the child had begun to grow and get stronger as the months went by, so his family thought they were past the state of worry. It seemed like a cruel twist of faith when his sister took a fever, and in a matter of days, she too had died.

His father had taken the loss of his last child even harder than Jenna. The final tragedy of the death of his baby girl had been too much for him. While Orrin's demeanor had not changed through all the tragedy, Hellet sensed a difference in him. It was as if his father had become a shell of the man that he once was. While Orrin was still a good father, and Hellet felt he would still be a good king, he was troubled to see that deep seed of sadness in Orrin.

Jenna's ability to maintain her joy was a wonderful model for Hellet. She had suffered more than any other person he knew, but she had not allowed her suffering to bring her to bitterness. Everyone who came into contact with her still loved her for her wise and caring nature.

"If this will help make you happy, who am I to question it?" he stated.

"I appreciate you giving me your permission," Jenna replied in a mocking, but playful tone as she ran her fingers through her now gray hair. It was not so long ago that her full mane displayed deep, rich textures of browns and black, but all the suffering his mother had experienced had stolen the fabulous colors. However, she remained a striking woman. He did notice that there were a few more lines in the soft skin of her face, but they did not detract from her penetrating dark eyes. She still carried some extra weight from her last pregnancy, but it seemed that was slowly disappearing. While she was not a vain woman—she rarely wore cosmetics and only a sparse amount of jewelry—Jenna did take a great deal of pride in her appearance. She knew she would soon be queen, and she wanted to look the part.

"Neffy and I met the wolves and Dellea, and it got me thinking, who will I marry?"

Jenna sighed then took a sip of wine. "Your father and I have spoken much about it, but it has not yet been decided. I'm hoping it will not be just a political marriage, like Travyn's. You are a special boy, Hellet, so I think it is only right that you have some say in this, unlike your uncle. Unfortunately, Travyn does not have the judgment to make wise decisions."

"He's not so bad," Hellet said.

Jenna placed her wine glass down and offered her son a smile. "You see the good in people, my sweet boy, but I'm afraid you don't always see the complete picture."

As much as Hellet loved and respected his mother, he was somewhat annoyed at her statement. While he may be young, he was not naïve. He understood that his uncle was slow and had issues with pride, but he felt that some of the blame fell on his family and how Travyn was often treated. His father would sometimes lose patience with his brother, as would Jenna on rare occasions. However, any annoyance he felt evaporated as he looked into his mother's eyes. "I've spent more time with him than most."

"You will learn as you get older," replied Jenna. "You may be wise beyond your years, but you lack experience. Never lose sight of that. Your intelligence needs to be tempered by experience. I have spent time with Travyn too."

"Agreed, but your scope is limited."

Jenna took another sip of wine before continuing, "I know you are aware of your gifts, my boy, and that is good. It's important that we know our strengths, but you must also understand your shortcomings. As I said, you still lack experience. Make sure that you remain humble. If you let pride get the best of you, you could end up being a terrible king."

Hellet pondered his mother's words which reminded him of the time when Jaleph had called him to his room those years ago. It was sobering to hear a similar warning from his mother. He had been told by so many for so long that he was a remarkable child. With his mother's influence, he had managed to not let the praise turn him arrogant, but he realized that he needed to remain vigilant. He desperately wanted to be a great and wise king for his people one day, and it was good to be reminded that well-meaning intentions would not necessarily result in success. "Of course, mother, as always, I thank you for your sage counsel. Now, on to other matters. Let's plan the party. But please, don't embarrass me."

Jenna offered her son a wicked laugh before regaling him with her grandiose plans.

# chapter 5

TRAVYN SAT IN HIS ROOM, SULKING, LOOKING OUT HIS WINDOW. He took a deep breath, trying to enjoy the moment, and he could almost taste the aroma of the royal garden. It was still early in the spring, and most of the flowers had not yet bloomed. But the few that had provided a pleasant contrast of pinks and yellows amidst the hues of dark green from the various, meticulously trimmed bushes.

It was an amiable scene, but it was not enough to vanquish his aggravation. He glanced about and the sight of a few maidens tending to the bushes only increased his frustration with his brother. A prince of Su'Meeryn should not be forced to marry such a homely girl, and the time he had spent with Dellea during the journey back to Su'Meeryn only reinforced his opinion. While not ugly, Dellea was far too skinny and plain. Clearly a prince of his stature deserved a much better wife. Was his brother playing a cruel joke on him? All the years of torment culminating with this betrothal? Was Orrin laughing to himself while sitting in his chambers? And with Hellet's birthday approaching, the focus of the kingdom was turned to the young prince. Travyn's marriage had almost become an afterthought. While he had no desire for this wedding, he most certainly warranted attention from the royal court.

He took a bite of one of the strawberries that had been left at his door. It was still early in the season, so the fruit was hard and bland. Rather than swallow it, he spit the half-chewed berry out his window and tried another. That one tasted only slightly better. Now he could not even get satisfaction from his favorite food. What a misery his life was: first Dellea, and now this? He deserved far better.

His mind drifted back to his fiancé. While he was not attracted to her, he also decided that he did not like the girl at all. She was clearly selfish, and he found her mannerisms odd. She did not talk much, and when she did, her responses were short and curt. Then there were those damned wolves she was so obsessed with. He had no use for the beasts, and he did not like the way they looked at him when he was near her. No, he was not happy at all.

Travyn tried another strawberry, but that one was sour, so he threw it and the rest—along with the bowl—out the window as well. He was about to storm away when he heard the sound that he had been both dreading and anticipating for years. A bell began to ring within the castle; a few more joined, then more from around the city. It could mean only one thing: Jaleph had finally died.

While he was not happy that his grandfather was dead, he was relieved to know that his wedding would now have to be further delayed to accommodate the funeral. Once his brother was crowned, Travyn could petition him to stop the marriage, and ask for a more suitable bride. There was no guarantee that Orrin would agree to the change since he had arranged the betrothal in the first place, but perhaps there would be a possibility. He looked back down at the garden, hoping to get another glimpse of the maidens, but they were gone.

What started out as a torturous morning, had shifted in an instant. He still might be forced to marry the strange girl, but perhaps he had a chance to avoid that misery. There would be the funeral, followed by Hellet's birthday festivities; certainly Orrin would not cancel the celebration of his only surviving child: the favorite son of Su'Meeryn. Would the delay of the wedding provide him time to find the words to sway his brother—the new king? Travyn was certain he would find a way. Hellet was not the only clever one in the family after all. Now, if only he could find some ripe strawberries.

# chapter 6

JALEPH WAS DEAD. Ellaniya did her best to mask the pleasure pouring out from her soul, but she did not know if she was successful. Good riddance, was all she could think. She knew the history between their two kingdoms, and the dead king had been instrumental in the defeat of Mephosh all those years ago. If not for his blow that had blinded Sul, none of the subsequent events would have happened. Mephosh would likely still be the dominant kingdom in the land, and the heretic religion would have been crushed.

Two royal funerals in such a short time, she thought. But she did not face the same internal struggle as she did at her mother's. She was thrilled with Jaleph's demise.

She remained in the back of the hall watching as all the dignitaries passed by, wiping away tears from their mournful faces, and she had to bite her lip to keep a smile from forming.

"Not going to pay your respects?" The voice beside her was startling, and Ellaniya wondered how she had not seen the young man approach.

As she looked him over, she noticed that despite his youthful appearance, his tan hair was already beginning to thin. His torso was thick with muscles, but she noticed a bit of fat emanating from his gut. It was not much but just enough to be visible. His face was plain with oval, mud-colored eyes. He was dressed like royalty, but she did not recognize his face. She assumed he must be from Su'Meeryn as those who had accompanied the princess from Pathum had already returned home, and dignitaries from other kingdoms could not have arrived so soon. "And who are you?" she asked, ignoring his question.

The eyes gazing back at her squinted a trace, and Ellaniya could tell the young man was annoyed that she did not recognize him. "I am Prince Travyn," was his curt reply.

"Ah, the happy groom-to-be." Travyn's eyes narrowed even more, and she caught the trace of a sneer cross his thin lips; evidently, he was not pleased with his forthcoming marriage.

"So it would seem."

Ellaniya paused for a moment to consider the prince. Though she had never wanted to visit this vile kingdom, she sensed a possible opportunity. While Jaleph's death was certainly a pleasant surprise, it was, in fact, inconsequential. He had been ancient and sequestered in his chambers for years. This day was inevitable. She initially thought the delay of the wedding ceremony would be a further annoyance since she would have to prolong her visit to this retched place, but now she was not so sure.

"Forgive me for saying, but you don't appear pleased with your future bride." Ellaniya was concerned that her statement might have pushed too far, but she decided to take the risk.

If Travyn was taken aback by her comment, he exhibited no sign of that. "Ellaniya, I believe?" The girl nodded. The prince tried to hide it, but she saw that he was looking her over. Ellaniya knew that she was not considered a beauty. Her young body resembled that of any other girl recently entering womanhood. Her face was round and surrounded by dark, unruly hair. Due to the difficulty in managing it, she kept her hair cut short, far shorter than any of the other women in the court. But her one captivating feature were her eyes, they glowed a sparkling purple deep within her soft, white skin. From the rumors she heard regarding the girl from Pathum, she knew her appearance was a step up from Dellea. While Travyn was not particularly attractive himself, that was not her concern.

"You are a perceptive woman," he continued. Ellaniya was surprised at his blunt words, but she was also pleased. She sensed a weakness in the young prince, and she was hopeful she would be able to use it to her advantage.

"Royalty does have its disadvantages at times," she said, lightly taking his forearm. The gesture had the desired effect as she saw his face brighten.

"That is true," Travyn replied, motioning to a nearby bench. Ellaniya wrapped her arm through his as they made their way to the seat.

"Do you get many dignitaries from Mephosh here?" she asked, not caring what his response would be since the question was designed merely to guide the conversation. Of course, as a princess of Mephosh, she would be aware of the dealings between their two kingdoms, but, based on her initial impression of Travyn, it seemed unlikely that he would consider this.

"Not really. The troubles between our two lands are in the past, but the memories still linger."

"Yes, it is the same back home. I wish we could all get past our history and move on," she lied.

"That would be nice."

"I can see that you and I are in agreement; we seem to have much in common." Ellaniya feigned a sigh and made the decision to probe the prince further. "With that knowledge of the past, it seems a union between Pathum and Su'Meeryn might not be the most beneficial plan at this time."

Travyn looked at her with a mystified expression on his face, and she could not believe that he was unable to follow her train of thought. While normally this level of ignorance would be unappealing to the princess, her pleasure with the discussion was growing. She chastised herself for doubting the wisdom of the gods; clearly, they knew what they were doing by orchestrating her visit to this horrible kingdom.

"I hope I'm not being presumptuous, but I wonder if marrying you off to the princess from Pathum is the best strategy for your fine kingdom," she elaborated.

"Exactly!" Travyn practically bellowed. "Why can't my stupid brother see that?"

"Perhaps a bond between our kingdoms may be a wiser choice." Travyn's blank expression showed that he still was not following her. "Maybe you should marry someone else."

"Exactly!" he repeated.

"There are other options," she stated as she sighed again. The conversation was going better than she could have ever imagined, but she needed to find out one more bit of information first. So, Ellaniya considered her next words carefully. She placed her hand on his thigh as she pushed herself up to a standing position. Gazing at the coffin across the hall, she said, "Your grandfather was a remarkable man. I have heard much about his tremendous exploits. He was instrumental in establishing the faith in Su'Meeryn."

"I suppose so."

"That faith is strong in Mephosh now," she continued as she sat back down beside him, their thighs touching.

"I don't think that's the case here lately," Travyn responded.

"What do you mean?"

"Well, the faith was extremely important to Jaleph and Kieran. But she died long ago, and Jaleph hadn't been outside his room for a few years. After all his children died, it seems those who remained didn't care much about religion anymore."

"Oh, that's too bad." She had to force the words from her mouth. And she knew that Travyn's response would be critical if she were to continue down this path.

"If you say so. I don't have much use for religion. I never saw the value in it."

Ellaniya had to suppress the grin that threatened to blossom on her face. "To be honest with you, I agree. It seems that religion has done nothing but cause problems. Look at the history of our two kingdoms."

"Exactly!" Travyn exclaimed for the third time as his palm went to her knee. Ellaniya did not know whether it was a conscious movement, but she did not care. She immediately placed her hand on top of his.

"I was right, we do have a lot in common," Ellaniya continued. She noticed him glance down at her hand with a wide smile on his face. "My family has just started the discussions about my own marriage," she continued. "As I think on it, perhaps there is a better solution for both of our lands."

"What is that?" he asked.

She had to pause to keep a look of disdain from forming on her face. How stupid is this man? "Maybe you and I should be husband and wife."

A look of dawning comprehension grew on Travyn's face, and she saw traces of pink begin to flush his cheeks. "With Jaleph dead, I was planning on talking to my brother about the current arrangement," he said excitedly. "Orrin had ordered my betrothal to Dellea, which I never wanted. She's terrible. I'm sure I can make a strong argument for a marriage between us!"

Her fingers lightly stroked his hand. "If you think that's wise," she purred.

"Oh, I think it's very wise."

This time Ellaniya allowed her smile to emerge. While she had no real desire to marry this man, she was certain she would be able to manipulate him for her plans. She did not know yet what those plans might be, but being joined to a prince of Su'Meeryn—and one who was so malleable—seemed to be a perfect start to re-establishing the gods to their rightfully place. If Travyn and she could convince their families to order this marriage, she might be well on her way.

# chapter 7

THE SCENT OF WILDFLOWERS TICKLED HIS NOSE as a light breeze ruffled the brown hair which hung far below his shoulders. He dropped his forearms to the cold stone of the parapets watching the black and gold banners flutter around him. The air was crisp in the early spring morning, but Tollan enjoyed the brisk feel against his face. The sun sat low in the sky, partially blocked by fluffy white clouds. He inhaled again, enjoying the flowery scent, when a chirping distracted him from the aroma. He glanced to his left and saw a half dozen jays darting from the trees, chasing away a large hawk. Tollan smiled at the arial mobbing as the hawk retreated from the attack.

Below him, the castle was beginning to stir awake. Merchants were arriving in their shops, and he saw the fire of a blacksmith's kiln blaze upward. It was later than normal for the day's activities to begin, but Labyn had partaken in raucous festivities the previous night. Tollan's smile broadened at the thought as the celebration had been for his wedding to the beautiful lady Adira.

Despite the late night of revelry, Tollan had not been able to sleep much. Just before dawn, he had carefully risen from bed, so as not to disturb his new bride and went down for an early breakfast. After finishing the meal, he began to walk around the castle. Most of the hallways were deserted. The few individuals he ran into offered friendly nods to the prince as they went about their business.

He had made his way to the top of the castle wall, but, unfortunately, had missed the sunrise. However, the clouds still had traces of pinks and purples, so it remained a beautiful sight.

With the hawk now gone, the jays had returned to their nests, but the chirping continued. Tollan rested his chin on his forearms, his eyes peering out to the east as the sun continued its assent. Though he could not envision a more idyllic scene, his thoughts were troubled.

"Why?" he asked himself as he stood up straight and stretched his arms out. Why should he be perplexed? He was heir to the throne of the mighty kingdom of Labyn. He was son to Gorhum, a kind and much-loved king, and he had a lovely new wife. Despite knowing each other only a short time, the couple had bonded quickly and easily. While the marriage had been arranged by Gorhum and Adira's father, Tollan had offered no reservations. He had gladly consented to the marriage, though his consent had not been required.

So, why the melancholy? He turned away from the castle wall and made his way back to the stairs with chastising thoughts. Despite how he tried to fool himself, when he was honest, he knew the reason for his angst. It was fear. He knew he would be king one day, and that thought terrified him. He loved his parents, and he loved his home, but he did not want to be king. He did not want to rule.

Tollan was the only child of Gorhum and Wynyth. The royal couple had had tremendous difficulty conceiving, and their one pregnancy before Tollan had resulted in a still-born brother. With many tears, the king and queen worried they would never have a child and heir. However, after many prayers to the creator and countless sacrifices at the temple, Wynyth, late in life, miraculously conceived a second time. Not wanting to risk another still-birth, the queen had remained in bed for her entire pregnancy. When Tollan had been born healthy, the entire kingdom celebrated. He was the answer to his parent's prayers and the hope for continued prosperity for the kingdom.

It was a heavy burden which Tollan did not know he could bear.

Tollan wanted to serve his people—he was not a selfish man, but how could he ever measure up to his father's example? Gorhum was the greatest king in the history of Labyn—or so Tollan had been told. While the prince had no idea if that was actually true, Tollan had no reason to doubt it. And there was the fact that Tollan had always been viewed as a miracle child. How could he ever be expected to measure up to such impossibly lofty expectations?

While still vibrant, his father was getting older. How much longer would Gorhum live? A few more years; a decade—maybe two? Unless something were to happen to Tollan, he would be king someday, and the thought terrified him.

With a deep sigh, Tollan descended the stairs and made his way back to his chambers and Adira. He wanted to tell her of his troubling thoughts and fears, but despite the love that had quickly grown between them, he still did not know her very well. And he did not want to concern her with his reservations.

He quietly opened the door to their room and found Adira still asleep. Tollan dropped into a chair and gazed at his beautiful bride. He rebuked himself again for his gloom. He was one of the most blessed people in all of Labyn; what right did he have for this dejection? But though his thoughts and concerns might seem petty, he knew he could not simply will his feelings away.

Adira stirred and her olive eyes opened. When her sleepy gaze rested upon him, she smiled. She sat up and long, cascading golden locks flowed down her body. Adira reached for her husband, and Tollan joined her back in their bed, his brooding thoughts briefly forgotten.

# chapter 8

THE ROOM FELT HOLLOW AND COLD. Yes, it was adequately furnished and decorated, but that did not change her feelings. Dellea wrapped a blanket around her skinny body as she sat up in the bed. She was emotionally drained from all the activities the prior day with Jaleph's funeral, which was unlike any funeral she had previously attended. While the old king was beloved by his people, it was difficult to mourn the passing of such an ancient man. Besides, nobody outside of his family had seen him much over the last years as his age did not permit him to move about the castle. While there had been many tears due to Jaleph's passing, there had also been a sense of celebration regarding the long life of such a great man.

As a princess of Pathum, and soon to be member of Su'Meeryn's royal family, Dellea had attended all the events of the ceremony. But, as always, being surrounded by strangers only increased her anxieties which compounded her loneliness. The delegation that had brought her from Pathum had left prior to Jaleph's death, but what did that matter? None of them were her friends. Truth be told, she had no friends, even back at home. Her father barely tolerated her, and her mother was too afraid of the king to stand up for her daughter. Her self-absorbed brother was a slightly better companion than Marken. But that was only when he was not engaged in some dalliance or recovering from a night of heavy drinking. She had nobody. Nobody that is except her wolves, and the thought of the creatures brought a slight smile to her sad face.

She slowly rose from the bed and donned a dressing gown. With a sigh, she crossed the room to look out the window. The countryside of Su'Meeryn spread out before her, but the spring-time beauty did not register in her brain. Though her eyes peered out, her vision did not focus. She shivered a bit from the early morning breeze and regretted not bringing the blanket with her. Dellea felt empty.

Her betrothed came to mind, and the thought increased her angst. Travyn clearly did not want to marry her, and she did not blame him. Dellea knew she was different from most other girls; why would anyone want her? But the fact was that she did not want to marry him either. He was clearly dim-witted and proud, but at least he did not seem mean-spirited, like her father. However, how would it be—married off to someone who did not want her?

Dellea's chest heaved while moisture formed in her eyes, but then her thoughts returned to the wolves. Although Dellea had protested when she was not allowed to bring them to her room, she could not be angry with the decision. She understood that others would not feel comfortable with wolves in the castle, but no one knew the beasts as she did. Her mind drifted to the day when she had stumbled upon them during one of her hikes through the forest. The three pups were huddled by the blood-covered bodies of their mother and two other siblings, whimpering and shaking. They were so small and helpless that she could not just leave them. She had considered waiting to see if their father would return, but even if he had, he would not have been able to nurse them. She wondered what had caused the death of the other three, but what did it matter? Her decision had been made: she would not leave them to die. Her guards objected to taking the pups; however, she had forced them to comply. Despite her young age, they were obligated to obey, though they had faced her father's wrath upon their return.

It was a decision that she never regretted. She had nursed and raised those wolves, and they became her only friends. She had no idea how long wolves lived, and she dreaded the thought of what would happen once they passed away. But that was in the future, and she would enjoy them in the present.

Dellea then recalled the other day when Hellet met the wolves. She still had a hard time believing what she had witnessed. The animals had never shown warmth to any other person, and they barely tolerated men. The fact that she was the only one they loved had given Dellea a little sense of importance. So, she had been annoyed at the affection that they showered on the prince, but something in her had begun to warm at the memory of the encounter. Yes, he was younger than her, and she was promised to his uncle, but she found her thoughts drifting to him often. Despite his age, he gave off the impression of one much older. She thought of that encounter and how at ease she had felt. That never happened with her when meeting strangers, and she had even managed to talk to him without any of her usual discomfort. Dellea could see why everyone in Su'Meeryn was making such a fuss about the prince. He had such a captivating charisma. And though she had no desire to marry, she began to wonder how she would feel if she had been promised to a different prince of Su'Meeryn.

But, unfortunately, though she had not yet reached seventeen years, her father had deemed her old enough to marry, and to Travyn. As a princess, she had known that marriage would be required of her, and she had always faced that reality with mixed emotions. How could she ever be intimate with another person? While she was able to tolerate most people, she could not think of a single individual she truly loved. It was a sad reality to acknowledge, but it was true. Perhaps it was her defense against a world where no one loved her in return. She had always been respectful to the servants in Pathum, though she could tell that none held any fondness for her. Did she mistreat them? She was certain she did not; she was not overbearing and belligerent like her brother. But there had to be a reason their distance, and it likely was the same reason as all the others: they sensed her discomfort and assumed it meant that she did not like them. At least she did not have that issue with her wolves.

She went to her bureau and grabbed a plain shirt and trousers from atop the pile. After dressing, she left her room and headed towards the stables where the wolves were being kept.

As she walked down the hallways, she felt overwhelmed with trepidation for her forthcoming marriage. But her mind quickly drifted away from Travyn as she was filled with thoughts of Hellet.

***

Hellet's party was an event beyond anything Dellea had ever experienced. Spring flowers decorated every corner, and throngs of happy people filled the courtyard in all manner of dress. They danced to the fast-paced music from the exceptional musicians situated atop a large, ornate podium. It was a cacophony of sound and color that threated to overwhelm her senses.

Travyn had escorted her to the courtyard; however, after arriving, he had quickly disappeared into the crowd. But she could not decide which was worse, being in Travyn's company, or being left alone. Everywhere she turned, Dellea saw laughter and merriment. The people of Su'Meeryn were taking full advantage of the gaiety, and also the considerable amount of drink that was freely available. Every person in attendance was clearly enjoying the day. Everyone but her. She found the press of strangers suffocating, so she was unable to join in the revelry.

Dellea continued to watch the festivities while she slowly made her way towards the back of the courtyard. She figured it was probably best that Travyn had left her. With so much elation swirling around her, she would likely go unnoticed. Dellea would be able to sit back and watch for a while until she could make an early exit.

"There you are," she heard from behind. Startled, she turned around and was surprised and relieved to see Hellet. "Where's my uncle?"

"He left to get some ale, and I haven't seen him since."

Hellet gave a slow nod, and she saw a look of understanding in his deep blue eyes. She still marveled at his youth as he gave off the impression of someone twice his age. And his appearance also belied his years. He was of average height, and his body was slight, but his handsome face displayed a maturity she had never seen. Auburn hair hung to his shoulders with a few waves around the ears, but it was those eyes from which she could not turn away.

"You don't seem to be enjoying yourself," he commented.

"I don't really know anybody here."

"You know me."

"That's true," she replied as she noticed the tightness in her chest slacken. "And you are obviously a well-loved person in Su'Meeryn."

Hellet laughed. "This has more to do with my mother than me. Free food and alcohol, along with loud music, can make anyone's birthday look important."

This time Dellea laughed. "Granted, but I wonder if you are displaying some false humility. I've heard many people mention your name with admiration."

"Well, I haven't had time to disappoint anyone yet."

The overhead sun was warming her skin, but it was more than the bright rays that improved Dellea's mood. Hellet's eyes continued to regard her as if she was the only person at the party, and she wondered if that was how he actually felt or if it was a skill he had learned. She pondered why he was paying so much attention to her; he was such a handsome boy and the heir to the throne. Why would he waste his time with her, the awkward and plain girl from Pathum betrothed to his uncle? She could not understand it, yet, as she stood beside him, she felt her comfort growing, despite the chaos swirling about.

Dellea continued to stare into his eyes, searching for the right words to say, but nothing came to her. The warmth from the sun seemed to fade as she felt her anxiety returning. Would her awkwardness put off Hellet, like all the others?

"Come," he said as he grabbed her hand. "Let's go see my mother."

Before she could reply, they were darting through the crowd, hands still clasped together with Hellet pulling her along. She felt his skin against hers and was saddened when they reached the podium and he let go. "Here she is."

"Hello Dellea," Jenna said warmly. "It's nice to see you again. How are you settling in?"

"Fine, thank you," Dellea replied.

"We are to be sisters soon. How are you feeling about that?"

Dellea glanced about, trying to push away the clamor of the party. "Travyn seems nice," she replied.

Jenna looked at her but did not respond further. Her gaze began to scan the crowd, and she waved when she found what she was searching for. A few moments later, Travyn approached with a young lady sporting short hair and purple eyes.

"Hello Travyn. Who might this be, and why aren't you with your bride-to-be?" Jenna asked.

"This is Ellaniya from Mephosh, I've been showing her around," he responded.

"Oh yes, please forgive me, princess," Jenna continued. "The past few days have been very hectic. How could I forget you? But Travyn, don't you think you should be with your fiancé?"

"I am a dignitary of Su'Meeryn, and I've been escorting the princess of Mephosh," Travyn replied sharply.

"It's nice to meet you, Dellea," Ellaniya stated, and Dellea noticed Ellaniya gently push Travyn's arm to guide him away from the podium and back into the crowd. Had she felt any affection for Travyn, Dellea would have been annoyed. However, she was just happy to see him leave as she turned back to Hellet and his mother.

Before Jenna could say anything further, two large boys barged their way in and accosted Hellet, pushing both Dellea and him away from the podium. She recognized one as Neffy, but she did not know the other.

"There he is, our birthday boy," the second one said. His speech was slurred, and he reeked of ale. He looked to be a few years older than Hellet, but he was of immense size with a thick, barrel chest and huge arms. Dellea wondered if he would be able to smash a boulder with his bare hand. "What happened to your idiot uncle?" the young man asked. "I just saw him."

"How many times do I have to tell you not to speak of him that way, Darus?" Hellet responded sternly.

"Bah!" He's a dolt!"

"He is your prince, and you need to show him some respect."

Darus said nothing more, but he took a long drink from the chalice he still held in his hand as streams of the sour liquid ran down his cheeks.

"And how are you, Dellea?" Neffy asked. "My sympathies for your upcoming marriage." Neffy's words were also a little slurred, though not nearly as much as Darus'.

"Dellea?" she heard a soft voice from the other side of Darus, and the princess noticed a beautiful young lady who had been hidden behind the two large men. She wore a cobalt dress that flattered her exquisite curves, and ebony hair rolled down her back in long curls. Full red lips were surrounded by soft white skin, and her green eyes sparkled in the mid-day sun. "So, you're the wolf girl."

"Dellea, may I introduce you to Perrin," Hellet interjected. "She's the daughter of one of the nobles of Su'Meeryn. And she's a *friend* of Darus."

"Friend!" Darus blurted as his free hand grasped Perrin's shoulder and pulled her in for a ferocious kiss. "I'm going to marry her!"

"That's still to be decided," Hellet replied.

"Bah!" was his only reply, and he again raised the chalice to his mouth. A look of grave disappointment crossed his face when no liquid spilled out. "Come Neffy!" he roared. "More ale!" Darus grabbed Neffy by the neck—his mug falling to the grass—and led him away.

"Those boys," Perrin said as she turned to follow the pair. "I better make sure they don't get into any trouble. But I do want to talk with you some more, Dellea!" And with that, the beautiful girl also disappeared into the crowd, leaving Dellea alone again with Hellet.

"Your friends?" Dellea asked dryly.

"I guess Darus didn't make a good first impression."

"That lovely girl wants to marry him?"

Hellet chuckled. "Don't judge him by this meeting alone. He's a good and loyal friend."

Dellea felt her pulse quicken, and she immediately regretted her words. She had taken a strong dislike to Darus and was afraid that her unsolicited judgment may have soured Hellet to her. But she was put at ease when Hellet continued.

"He can be a lot to take in at times, and he's pretty drunk. So, I understand your reaction."

"What did you mean about the marriage not being decided?" Dellea continued, feeling an enormous sense of relief at Hellet's response.

"Perrin's father is only a minor noble. As Darus is a good friend of mine, he holds a high standing in Su'Meeryn. It isn't clear if his father will allow the marriage."

*Why can't we marry who we want?* she thought, looking into those warm, blue eyes. "Why does marriage have to be so difficult?" she asked dejectedly.

"One of the burdens of royalty," he replied. Hellet then took her hand again and led her to the side of the courtyard. The music and dancing continued but it was somewhat quieter as they sat on a bench.

"Where is your father? I didn't see him."

"Oh, he's around somewhere, probably sharing drinks with the nobles."

"Jenna doesn't mind being left along?"

"While my mother planned much of the celebration, she just enjoys sitting on the podium, watching the people of the kingdom having a good time," Hellet answered.

"Your family seems pretty small," Dellea pointed out.

After a deep breath, Hellet told her of a trade mission to Unimeth Orrin and his brothers had taken years before. They were ambushed by brigands, and his uncles had been killed; only Orrin survived. Travyn had not been on that expedition as he was too young at the time. He then told her of his two aunts who had both died during difficult pregnancies. And there were his siblings whose graves lined the back of the garden. Only Orrin, Travyn and he remained of the line of Jaleph. He mentioned how all that death had changed his father. There was now a deep sadness in the king-to-be which he could never fully hide.

Hellet's heartbreaking story left Dellea speechless. How could she respond to all the suffering Hellet and his family had experienced? She wanted to offer some comfort, but she did not know how. What should she do?

"I know it's a sad tale, but we must move on, right? What about you? Tell me about Pathum," Hellet continued after a pause, as if he could sense her agitation.

Dellea then told him of her home and family. She was surprised how easy it was to talk to him and how open she was about her struggles. She had never been so honest with anyone in her life. What was it about Hellet that put her so at ease? As she talked, his eyes never left her. For the first time in her life, she felt safe and comfortable around another person.

As she was finishing her tale, describing a particularly annoying story about her brother, Neffy burst in and grabbed Hellet. "You're needed to conclude the celebration, birthday boy!" Neffy announced.

Hellet stood and began to follow his friend. He turned back and offered Dellea a shrug of his shoulders as Neffy and he headed back to the podium. While Dellea watched Hellet climb the steps, she felt both a longing and a despair. For the first time in her young life, she found herself enjoying the company of another person even more than her wolves. But how could that be? And besides, soon she would be married to his uncle.

Atop the podium, she saw Hellet standing alongside Travyn, and, for some reason, the princess Ellaniya was there as well. Dellea realized that she should also be up there too, but Hellet had allowed her to remain on the bench, alone. Apparently he could tell that she would not want to stand on the podium in front of everyone, and that kind gesture drew her to him even more.

The music grew in volume as the entire courtyard began to sing to Hellet. Despite the distance, she could see Hellet's face flush, but she also saw Ellaniya place her hand on Travyn's forearm. Rather than feeling annoyed at the insolence of the princess of Mephosh, the gesture gave Dellea a glimmer of hope. Might there be a chance for a change in plans?

# chapter 9

THE CORONATION HAD NOT YET TAKEN PLACE; however, Orrin had already begun sitting on the throne. It was certainly a breach of protocol, but nobody said anything to the soon-to-be king. Blood-shot eyes peered out from behind the thin strands of brown hair hanging in front of his face like the dying embers from an unattended fire. Travyn wondered how his brother could be comfortable with his unruly hair, but he really did not care. In fact, he hoped that Orrin was uncomfortable. Any discomfort the prince might feel brought pleasure to Travyn. He despised his brother. As the oldest of Jaleph's grandsons, Orrin had always exhibited an ugly hubris with regards to his family, and that pride had only increased after the last of Jaleph's children died.

But it was more than just his brother's arrogance that brought about the ire of Travyn. Orrin had always been unrelenting in his bullying of his younger brother—all those nasty comments and condescending sneers. While Orrin had never physically accosted Travyn, the verbal assaults were far worse than any beating that Travyn might have endured; the years of constant humiliation remained an ongoing source of aggravation.

Orrin had made certain to belittle him at every opportunity; he had insisted Travyn train with the sword even though he struggled. Travyn was certain that Orrin found merriment at his rudimentary skills with a blade. Why force his youngest brother to endure such embarrassment? What cruelty! And what difference did it make if he was not able to read? He could survive just fine without books and scrolls.

Even though he had always struggled with his lessons, Travyn knew he was smarter than his relations. But it was a different type of intelligence than that of those around him. While Travyn did not do well with his schooling, his intelligence was displayed in other areas. He was an excellent horseman and an exceptional wrestler as he was stronger than most boys.

In addition to all his other gifts, it was his ability to read the emotions of the people around him that he truly relished, much as he had done with the princess from Mephosh. While he had taken an immediate dislike to Dellea and her obvious selfishness, Ellaniya was completely different. Travyn had sensed her strong affection and could tell she held a pure and burning desire for him. And that desire was clearly not marred by any other ulterior motives. How refreshing it was to be sought after just because of an attraction.

He loathed having to come before his brother to plead his case, so he was grateful that Ellaniya had agreed to accompany him. This meeting was of utmost importance, and he needed to take advantage of every available resource.

"What can I do for you two?" his brother asked. Though Orrin's tone sounded genial, Travyn was certain he heard animosity in that husky voice.

"Brother," Travyn began with his prepared speech, "things have changed since you arranged for my marriage to Dellea of Pathum. Ellaniya and I wish to appeal to you as you will soon be king. Might you consider another option?"

"What has changed?" the king-to-be asked as his red eyes shifted to Ellaniya, "and to what option are you referring?"

Is he really that dense? Travyn thought. Shouldn't he be able to tell by the two of us standing in front of him?

"As his highness can certainly deduce, perhaps a different union might be more beneficial to Su'Meeryn," Ellaniya interjected smoothly before Travyn could speak further.

Orrin's eyes narrowed as they shifted back to his brother with what appeared to be aggravation. Travyn grew a nervous, wondering what had brought on this new ire. His mind raced, trying to form words, but nothing came out.

"If you can present a more desirous match for my brother's union, I'll consider it," Orrin replied.

"As you are aware, the relationship between Mephosh and Su'Meeryn has not been strong for several generations," Ellaniya continued. "What better way to strengthen that bond than through marriage?"

"Why him?" Orrin asked bluntly, not even looking at Travyn.

"She likes me!" Travyn blurted out, pleased that he found the appropriate words to support their case.

Ellaniya gently placed her hand on his forearm. "If I may. We met at the funeral of your grandfather—such a great man." She sighed before continuing. "Though it was a solemn occasion, we had a pleasant conversation. I don't want to overstep my position, but it just felt right. He's a…" Travyn listened eagerly for Ellaniya's next words, but her voice trailed off.

"And what of your father? How would he react to this suggestion?"

"I'm certain if the newly crowned king of Su'Meeryn requested his daughter to join this fine family, my father would be very pleased. With the recent passing of my mother, such a blissful union would brighten his day," Ellaniya answered with a sweet smile.

Orrin gazed back at Travyn then took a deep breath. "If this is what the two of you want, I suppose it would be fine. It does make sense, but first I must discuss the matter with Dellea. I want to make certain that this change of plans does not cause problems with our neighbor to the north. Dellea's father was eager for your pairing."

"She will be pleased with this decision," Travyn stated confidently.

"If she is, and her family is in agreement, you have my blessing."

"Thank you, Orrin," Travyn responded, and he thought he saw a sneer on his brother's face. Yes, his pride is only growing, he thought, but perhaps it did not matter after all. Before either of the men could speak further, Ellaniya's hand, which still rested on his forearm, gently turned him around and led him from the hall.

Yes, the death of Jaleph could not have come at a better time.

***

The bench in the courtyard was chilly, but the air was warming nicely as the day progressed. Travyn and Ellaniya sat quietly under the spring sun while the flavor of the ripe strawberry exploded in Travyn's mouth. It brought him almost as much delight as Orrin's blessing to cancel his engagement to that awful Dellea. Springtime was his favorite season as that was when the first strawberries in the royal gardens ripened, and he loved nothing more than indulging himself with his favorite fruit. Unfortunately, their color reminded him of his brother's eyes, but that did not bother him on this day. Soon he would marry the princess of Mephosh, and he would finally find some joy in his miserable, tormented life.

Droplets of juice trailed down from the corner of his mouth as he chewed on a few more of the sweet berries. He offered the plate to Ellaniya, and she regarded him with what could only be lust in those violet eyes.

She shook her head, content in watching him enjoying his treat. Travyn brought the plate to his nose and inhaled the fragrance before scarfing down the final berry. "When should we wed?" he asked.

"It has not been completely confirmed yet, Travyn. We first need to receive the approval of Dellea's father," she said. Her expression stiffened somewhat, and Travyn knew it was due to the delay in their union.

"Dellea will be happy with Orrin's decision," Travyn assured her.

"That may be, but it's her father we need to be concerned about." Her face hardened a bit more, and Travyn felt sympathy for the girl. She could not wait to join him in the marriage bed.

It was all baffling to Travyn; why must everything be so difficult? Why should the king of Pathum's thoughts have any influence on his marriage? If Marken did have an objection to this change, Travyn was certain he would be able to sway the king's opinion. Who better to argue his point than himself? With his ability to read others, he was confident there would be no problem.

Travyn smiled to himself then directed the grin to his future wife. "It will all work out," he stated assuredly, then he commanded a servant to bring him more of his favorite fruit.

# chapter 10

"SO, YOU ARE THE ONE I HAVE TO *THANK* FOR THIS," the old stable keeper said as Hellet and Dellea entered the stables. Wairren was a large and dark-skinned man, though not to the degree of the other people of Gorthon Hellet had met. He was the son of the prophet Wander and served as the last remaining cleric in Su'Meeryn, when he was not running the stables. He was tall and muscular despite his age, but the years were creeping up on him. Hellet knew Wairren would need to retire from the stables soon, but after the death of his last daughter, Orrin had made it clear that he would no longer subsidize Wairren's religious practices. Once Wairren was unable to continue the strenuous work, Hellet doubted the old man would be able to earn enough profit as a cleric to sustain himself. However, Hellet was certain that Jenna would be able to sway her husband. Fortunately, it was not yet an issue as Wairren still displayed a vigor that astounded Hellet. "Those wolves are more trouble than they're worth."

"They are honored guests of the royal family, and you will treat them as such," Hellet immediately shot back with a chiding but soft tone.

"Honored guests don't normally tear apart the wood in my stalls," Wairren scowled, but he then turned to Dellea and offered her a wink. Hellet looked at the girl, and he saw an expression of bewilderment and concern on her face. It was a sad thought that she was so unfamiliar with playful banter.

"I'm certain that you are taking proper care of them," Hellet continued, hoping to put Dellea at ease.

"Of course, my prince," Wairren replied. "They are making a mess of things, so I've made sure that they're always fed. But they don't like being locked up, and they seem to like me even less."

"They are not used to being confined," Dellea agreed. "They need to get into the wilderness as often as possible."

"Take them out as much as you like. I don't appreciate the way they look at me," Wairren responded. "Let me bring you to them."

After a short walk, Hellet began to hear whines and whimpers as Wairren opened the gate. Before Wairren could get out of the way, Dellea rushed in and was assaulted by the animals. It remained a strange sight to Hellet, watching the huge beasts knock the slight girl to the straw-covered ground and those tongues assailing her face. She laughed while the whines increased in intensity. Slowly, Dellea pushed the rambunctious faces away and lifted herself up as Wairren closed the gate behind him with a trailing string of 'humphs'.

The whines, which had died down, resumed once the wolves made their way over to Hellet, all three tails waging at frenzied speeds. Despite the pleasant initial meeting Hellet had with the animals, he still felt apprehension as they approached. The whining stopped, and the wolves began to sniff the air around him, and after a couple soft yips, large paws from one of the creatures lifted to his shoulders as his face was assaulted by a forceful licking. Hellet chuckled as he scratched the animal behind its ears. The wolves then returned to Dellea and stretched out at her feet. Dellea too plopped down and began to pet each one.

Hellet watched the scene with delight. He still found the whole scenario a bit absurd: this fragile girl in command of the three large beast that were so feared by most people. She displayed a large smile—something he was not sure that he had ever seen before—while she stroked their fur.

What was it about this girl that captivated him so much? Her features were not anything that most people would classify as beautiful; her appearance could only be described as plain, and she certainly had trouble being around other people. Despite all that, he had sensed a confidence in her the day they first met. He remembered how shocked she was when the wolves had taken to him so quickly. But why should that attract him to Dellea? He did not know, but what he did know was that he felt a bond with her.

He pondered her engagement to his uncle, and through the times they had spent together, he could tell she did not want to marry Travyn. That was understandable. While Hellet did not harbor the same ill feelings towards Travyn as most others, he was not oblivious to his uncle's shortcomings. As they were not far apart in age, the two had spent much time together when they were younger. Travyn seemed less obtuse when they were alone, but his over-inflated self-confidence was always close at hand.

51

Hellet thought of his birthday celebration and how Ellaniya had commandeered Travyn's attention. What little interaction he'd had with the princess from Mephosh left the impression of a confident and intelligent young lady. It seemed odd that she had gravitated to Travyn, but that unexpected development presented him with a possible opportunity.

"How do you like living in Su'Meeryn?" Dellea asked, still petting the wolves.

Hellet looked at her, thinking it was an odd question. "What do you mean?"

"Do you like it here?"

"It's my home," he said.

"I know that, but do you like it here?"

Hellet regarded her. She was obviously content being in the presence of her animals, but he sensed an agitation under her surface. "I have no complaints, but I don't really have anything to compare it to. We have fine people here in Su'Meeryn."

After a pause, Dellea quietly said, "I hate Pathum."

Hellet tried to look into her eyes, but she lowered her face, and he noticed that her hands had stopped moving. Two of the wolves looked up, but then they dropped their heads back down and closed their eyes. Hellet knew it had taken a tremendous act of courage for her to make that pronouncement, and he wondered how he should respond. He began to fully realize how traumatic this engagement had been to her. She had no desire to marry his uncle and was obviously uncomfortable moving to an unknown kingdom, but she also did not want to remain in Pathum. What a terrible dilemma to have forced upon oneself. He began to understand just how lonely Dellea was, and her relationship with the wolves was making far more sense to him.

The silence remained like a heavy fog in the stable as Hellet considered his reply to her declaration. He wanted to comfort and reassure her, but how? "Regardless of what happens, be assured that you will always have at least one friend here." He wanted to ask her about why she hated her home, but he also did not want to press her. He figured she would offer more if she wanted to, and he just wanted her to feel safe. When she did not look up, he decided he had made the proper decision.

Her hand went to her face as she wiped away what had to be tears, and for whatever reason, he felt his attraction to her grow. He wondered at this; was it just that he felt sorry for her, that he wanted to protect her? No, it was more than that. He knew she was awkward, but he was discovering that there were reasons for her insecurities. What did it matter anyway? Did he need to define his feelings?

"You said the wolves need to get out. What did you do with them when you were back home?"

Dellea finally raised her head, and though her eyes were still a little red, there was no trace of tears. "I would take them on hikes around the castle. So long as they were fully fed, they would not go off to hunt."

Hellet walked over to her, and the wolves stirred. He reached his hand down to her and helped her up. "Well, let's take them for a hike around Su'Meeryn."

A slight smile emerged on Dellea's face as they led the wolves out from their stable. Shortly thereafter, the pair were hiking around the castle with the animals trotting behind. Neither said much, they were just enjoying the activity and being out on a lovely spring day.

They continued down amidst the scent of blooming wildflowers, and Hellet thought he saw a bounce in Dellea's steps as she watched the wolves sparing with each other and careening through the brush. It gave him pleasure to see Dellea enjoying herself, but he wondered how long it would last if she had to marry Travyn.

Hellet dropped back a couple steps, watching Dellea as she strode in front of him, and he thought of his eventual marriage. He knew that Orrin had brought it up numerous times with Jenna, but she had always rebuked him claiming Hellet was too young. However, Hellet knew it was more than just his age. After all the tragedy Jenna had faced, she was not ready to lose her son to another woman. But at some point that would have to change. He would be of age in two years, and plans would need to begin soon.

Dellea looked back at him, her face alight with pleasure, while the wolves continued to dash around, and Hellet decided that he had a plan for his future. His mind went back to Ellaniya and Travyn at his party. Perhaps things could work out well for all of them.

# chapter 11

THE RED EYES STARING THROUGH THE SLENDER STRANDS of hair were disconcerting, but Dellea saw no trace of malevolence on the bony face. Gaunt fingers which protruded from black sleeves absently stroked the arm of the throne. Orrin's head tilted to the side and a small clump of hair fell across one of his strange eyes. While she felt apprehension in Orrin's presence, it was soothing to have Hellet beside her.

"How, may I attend you, Majesty?" Dellea asked.

"I am not king yet; the coronation is still being planned." Despite Orrin's soft tone the girl still felt uncomfortable.

"My apologies," she mumbled.

"No matter," said Orrin. "But I'll get right to the point. My brother has made a request of me. He asked that I cancel the wedding of you two as a marriage between him and the princess of Mephosh was proposed. Now, I am under the impression that you, personally, are pleased to hear this; however, I'm concerned how your family might react."

Dellea's emotions swirled in her head. The news was better than she could have envisioned, but it also brought about a huge problem. If she did not marry Travyn, there would be no reason for her to remain in Su'Meeryn, and she would have to return home. She could not determine which would be worse: marrying Travyn or leaving. "I..." she stammered, trying to buy time. Her father would not take this news well as she was certain he was happy to be rid of her and the wolves. "I..." she started again, but she still had no idea how to respond.

"If I may, father," Hellet interjected as he stepped forward. "Perhaps, there is a happy solution to this problem. The marriage can be canceled, but Dellea could still remain here and join Su'Meeryn's royal family. There is one other member of our family not yet spoken for."

"You!" Orrin blurted out. "You're too young, and your mother would kill me."

"Of course, the marriage would not take place immediately. It would have to wait a couple years, but that would not matter. It would still solve the problem." Hellet then turned to Dellea. "If the princess would consent, she could remain in Su'Meeryn as your ward until the time of the marriage. That would give her plenty of time to acclimate and learn all about our family and the kingdom."

Dellea was amazed once again at the maturity of the boy. He had surmised the situation in short order and devised a plan that could solve all her problems: she did not have to marry Travyn, and she could remain in Su'Meeryn. She had to admit she had felt a closeness and attraction to Hellet, but she had never considered the possibility of marriage to the young prince. While he was not yet of age, she was not much older than him, and she had never been in a hurry to marry anyway. She always knew she would have to wed at some point, and she could not conceive of a better mate. As she looked back at Hellet, a smile pulled at the corners of her mouth.

"What do you say, Dellea?" Orrin asked.

Dellea's head nodded as she was finally able to form words. "I find the idea appealing, and I'm certain that my father will agree. Better his daughter is married to the heir to the throne than the prince."

Orrin glanced back at his son with a look that Dellea could not decipher. "Very good. I will discuss this with his mother, but I see no reason that there will be an issue. This seems to resolve everyone's concerns, so it's a good day. Now if you will excuse me, in addition to preparing for the coronation, I need to tell my wife that her boy is going to be married." Despite Orrin's sinister appearing features, Dellea saw a trace of fear in those red eyes. But before she could probe his expression further, he rose from the throne and exited the hall.

Other than the guards, Dellea was left alone with Hellet. The boy grinned at her, and for the first time in a long time, though not in the presence of her wolves, she did not feel lonely.

✱✱✱

Orrin and Jenna stood upon the podium for their coronation as regal music emanated from the musicians behind them. Hellet was to the right of his father with Neffy and Darus on either side of him. Travyn and the princess of Mephosh were perched to the left of Jenna. A smug smile covered Ellaniya's face; Dellea wanted to be annoyed by the expression, but she could not be. If Ellaniya wanted to wed Travyn, all the better. That decision had allowed her to become engaged to Hellet which grew more appealing each passing day.

Wairren placed a glistening crown over Orrin's thin hair during a crescendo in the music. A slight grin etched his mouth as those scarlet eyes glistened under the high sun. Dellea had spent some time with the royal couple after Hellet had proposed his solution to the wedding problem, and she found that she liked them well enough. Though a bit overbearing, Jenna was a kind enough woman. She found Orrin friendly but stoic; however, that was understandable after all the sorrow he had endured. Despite that, he was nothing like her father. While he did enjoy his frequent mugs of ale, she never saw him drunk. He clearly loved Hellet and was treating her like a daughter. While she found her future parents pleasant, she still felt uneasy around them; she did not know why, but she only felt comfortable around Hellet. Hopefully that would change in time.

As Wairren then crowned the queen, Dellea saw Darus give Hellet a shove on the shoulder followed by a laugh. How are those two friends? She thought. Neffy was scarcely bearable, but she found Darus to be obnoxious and extremely annoying.

"There you are," she heard from behind her as the ceremony continued. "I've been looking everywhere. Why aren't you on the podium?"

Dellea turned around to see Perrin approaching. She had been thankful when Hellet had said that she need not join them on the dais since she had no desire for all these stranger's eyes to be on her. However, being alone in the crowd was almost as bad; at least she did not have to talk to anyone, until now.

"Hello Perrin," Dellea replied, ignoring the question. While Dellea had seen Perrin a few times, she had never appeared as stunning as she did this day. A rose-colored dress contrasted perfectly with her black hair and creamy skin. The tastily applied cosmetics amplified her natural beauty without being too ostentatious, and a silver chain sparkled in the sun displaying an elegant sapphire. Dellea assumed that Perrin was doing all she could to impress Orrin and Darus' father since the marriage between Perrin and Darus had still not been agreed upon. Though it remained a mystery why such a beautiful girl would want to marry that louse.

Perrin wrapped her arm around Dellea's and began to lead her away. "Come, they're going to be at this for a while. We don't need to stand around." Dellea was dragged through the crowd while the music softened until they reached the back of the courtyard. "Now, we are finally alone," Perrin said as she pulled them both down onto a bench. "We haven't had many opportunities to talk. I'm so thankful that you and Hellet are to wed, and you won't be subjected to that awful Travyn. As I'm hopeful that Darus will soon receive the approval to marry me, we are going to become close friends."

Hopefully! Dellea almost blurted out. How could anyone be hopeful to marry that obnoxious jerk? She appreciated that Perrin was making an effort to get to know her, but Dellea had no idea if she wanted to get close to her as Dellea questioned her judgment for a husband. Plus, Perrin seemed somewhat self-absorbed and overly exuberant, which she found unnerving.

When Dellea did not respond, Perrin continued enthusiastically, "My father says that there has been much talk about you in the royal court. Everyone is so intrigued by the 'wolf girl' and those wolves. Come now, tell me everything."

The term 'wolf girl' annoyed Dellea. Was that how she was thought of? Was she known only by her extraordinary pets? However, she realized it was to be expected. People did not know her, and what else was there for them to say? She looked at Perrin and saw only curiosity on her companion's face, but how was she to respond? The wolves were an intimate part of her life, and this was not something she wanted to share with anyone, except Hellet.

"I don't think we should be back here," Dellea finally responded, changing the subject. "The ceremony will be ending soon, and we will be expected to be present."

Perrin gave Dellea a knowing look then a slight tap on the knee. "Of course, I should not be selfish and monopolize your time. Let's return." She grabbed Dellea's hand and escorted her back to the base of the podium.

When they arrived, the ceremony had concluded and Hellet was on the ground looking for her. Dellea heard a call from the side and Perrin dashed over and was swept up in Darus' arms. Neffy gave Darus a hearty pat on the back as the three disappeared into the crowd.

"Perrin commandeered you I see," Hellet noted.

"Yes, she wanted to hear about the wolves."

Hellet's head tilted to the side as he brushed a strand of hair away from his bright blue eyes. "She means well, but she's pretty... vivacious. I guess she would have to be if she's going to marry Darus."

Dellea wanted to question him regarding his comment, but she thought better of it. Darus was his friend, and she was afraid of alienating Hellet if she said the wrong thing.

When Dellea remained silent, Hellet continued. "I'm sure you two will be able to become friends, in time. I know this all difficult for you."

It was remarkable to Dellea that Hellet always seemed to know exactly what to say and always with such compassion in his voice. She marveled at what had begun as a miserable move to Su'Meeryn had turned into such good fortune. This remarkable young man wanted to marry her; she still wondered if she would wake and find this all to be a dream. But she knew it wasn't. Without another word, she wrapped her hand around his forearm as he guided her to the hall and the coronation feast.

Could her life get any better?

# chapter 12

THE HEAT OF THE SUMMER DAY felt stifling as the small contingent headed south from the castle towards Mephosh. While Ellaniya had not wanted to travel to Su'Meeryn—as she still bore a strong hatred towards that kingdom and its people—her trip had surpassed any of her expectations. However, despite the positive developments, Ellaniya was still pleased to be leaving that despicable land. If all continued to go well, she would be married to Travyn soon, a prince of Su'Meeryn who was so easily manipulated. But her desire to leave Su'Meeryn was tempered by what awaited her at home. She adored her homeland, but the future still troubled her. Her idiot brother would only make things worse once he took the crown. There remained much for her to do.

She glanced over at Travyn, who was riding beside her. He looked towards her and smiled as he stuffed a strawberry into his mouth, and she forced herself to return the gesture. It was difficult to believe, but her fiancé was even more of a dullard than her brother. But in this case, that fact was to her benefit. She did not yet know what her ultimate plan would be, but the possibility of being married to Travyn provided intriguing possibilities.

How her father would react to her request was a bit of mystery, though she did not anticipate he would reject the idea. The king and queen had begun discussing the marriages of their children prior to her mother taking ill, but when it became clear that the queen was not healing, all those talks had stopped. Ellaniya was certain her father would agree with the union with the royal family of Su'Meeryn, and Once Ellaniya's future was secure, Naren would be able to focus strictly on his son.

Everything seemed to be falling into place. She would just need to figure out her next steps once the betrothal was secured.

***

The sickly king rubbed his eyes, trying to get a good look at his potential new son. Even though she despised the faith of her father, Ellaniya still felt some concern for his failing health when she saw the grimace of pain Naren failed to hide. Pharen stood behind the king with a look of worry on his face as a long cough escaped the king's throat. If Naren were to die soon, making any changes in Mephosh would be even more difficult than they would be now. Pharen—with his overly pious, misguided faith—would be a disaster as king.

"Tell me about yourself, Travyn," the king wheezed.

"Your strawberries are even better than the ones back home!" Travyn exclaimed as he finished the last piece of fruit that had been brought for him. "They're sweeter!"

"I am gratified to hear that you are pleased with our fine produce," Naren responded patiently, "but I need to know more about you before giving my blessing to this proposed union."

"Our marriage would bring Mephosh closer to Su'Meeryn," Ellaniya interjected. "Hasn't this always been a desire of yours?"

"Of course," the king replied, "but I'm not pleased having this sprung upon me, especially so soon after your mother's death."

He coughed again, and Pharen placed a hand on his father's shoulder. "If I may, while this might have been a breach of protocol, I believe Ellaniya is correct. A union between the royal families of Su'Meeryn and Mephosh will do much for both kingdoms. We all know our past, and a marriage will go far to make sure we avoid potential future hostilities. Also, I hear the faith is in decline there. A joining of our families might give us an opportunity to reverse that trend; however, I know my sister will not agree with my sentiment."

Though she despised her brother, Ellaniya was pleased that Pharen was agreeing with her—at least he thought he was. He would be strongly opposed to the marriage if he understood Travyn's limitations and her true intentions.

"Enough!" Naren barked. "I may be ill, but I am not a fool. I understand the politics, but, before she died, I promised your mother that I would do my best to find suitable mates for both of you. Now, I want to hear from Travyn."

Travyn slowly lowered the plate from which he had been licking the last remnant of juice, his eyes appearing over the edge. "I am a prince of Su'Meeryn," he responded.

"Yes, and?"

Travyn turned to Ellaniya with a look of confusion, and she stifled a laugh. He had to be the most ignorant person she had ever met, and she prayed that the gods would reward her for this great sacrifice of marrying him. "Tell my father of our meeting," she prodded.

"Ah! I was to be married to that horrible girl from Pathum. I don't like her, and she's not pretty. Then I met Ellaniya. We began to talk. She's very caring and warm, and beautiful. It was immediately clear that we both loved each other. My marriage to Dellea was delayed when Jaleph died, and that gave me the time to convince my brother to cancel that marriage and approve this one." When Travyn completed his soliloquy, his chest puffed up, and he glanced about with a look of satisfaction.

Ellaniya knew the meeting was progressing poorly, as she thought it might. While Naren was king, he was also a father. With his failing health, she was afraid he would be less concerned with the politics of her marriage, and that he would not be willing to marry off his daughter to some idiot. Her mind raced; she needed to find a way to appease his doubts.

"Father, if I may," she began. "Our honored guest is tired from the long journey here, and he's a little nervous meeting the king of Mephosh and his new father.

"We talked much when we met, and there was an instant attraction between us. I was hesitant to hope that anything might come of it as he was promised to the princess from Pathum, but love will not be stopped. It was clear to me that he would not be happy with marrying that girl. I met her, and she is a strange one. Why should he be subjected to a life of misery when a different union would be better for both Mephosh and Su'Meeryn?

"You promised mother that you would find me a suitable husband. Well, he stands before you. I love him and he loves me. How often do politics and love come together so perfectly? I beg you—no, we beg you. Give us your blessing."

When she had finished her speech, Ellaniya stood quietly, supremely pleased with herself. She knew she had articulated a perfect argument for Naren, and it did not hurt that Travyn had remained silent. She looked from her father to Pharen. Her brother's expression seemed to indicate disapproval—as if he sensed some deception, but he said nothing.

Naren pushed himself up from his chair with a wheeze, and he shambled over to Ellaniya to hug her. "If this is what you really want, I find no fault in it. You have my blessing."

Ellaniya wrapped her arms around his bony back to return the embrace, and she felt a true affection that had been absent since she was a little girl. It was a pleasant feeling that her father was simply concerned with her wellbeing. While, she had deceived him, what did that matter? She was getting what she wanted, and it did not hurt the king. "Thank you, father," she said, "you will not regret this." As she turned away, she caught a glimpse of Pharen, and she hoped she was able to hide the smirk that threatened to form on her lips.

As she was exiting the king's chamber with her fiancé, Travyn asked, "Are there any more strawberries?"

***

The premarital banquet was attended by all the nobility of Mephosh. Despite his young age, Hellet was sent as the representative from the Su'Meeryn royal family. Dellea had accompanied him, but there were no wolves to be seen.

As the hour started to become late, and with much ale having been consumed, Travyn jumped atop a table and bellowed out his love for Ellaniya until a few guards, not so gently, guided him back to the ground. He had already pronounced his devotion to her on multiple occasions that night, but his pleasure meant nothing to her. However, she figured it was good that he was happy with the arrangement. His infatuation would just make him easier to control, though she was still deciding how to best take advantage of the forthcoming union.

"Ah, the happy bride-to-be." Ellaniya turned away from Travyn, towards the unfamiliar voice and spotted a man she had never seen before. That was not unexpected as she did not know all of Mephosh nobility, but by his appearance, she would have certainly remembered him. He was an attractive man of average height with a strong physique. His thin face was unblemished without a hint of a whisker. Thin hair hung to his shoulders, and despite his youthful appearance, the hair was completely white. It was not the white of an aged person, rather there was almost a silvery glow to it. She had never seen a color like that before, and, if she had, she certainly would have recalled it. The man wore a white cloak that was bound at his waist with a silver belt. The cloak was open in the front, revealing a muscular chest that was completely hairless. "It's a pleasure to meet you." His soft gaze emanated a soothing aura which immediately drew Ellaniya to him.

"And who might you be?" she asked.

"A friend," he replied. He motioned to the corner of the hall, a request for her to follow him. While she would not usually obey the direction of a stranger, the draw of him increased as she glanced back and saw Travyn guzzling down another mug of ale.

62

With a nod, she allowed the man to led her away from the crowd. When they were relatively alone, he turned to her and continued. "This is good. I wanted to speak to you alone."

"You still haven't answered my question," Ellaniya pointed out. "Who exactly are you?"

The man just smiled warmly at her. "I have been an admirer of Mephosh for a very long time. And I know of all the troubles here."

"What troubles?"

"The troubles with which you are so concerned."

Though the cryptic words annoyed the princess, they did not quell his allure. What was this man getting at? "I know of no troubles. My forthcoming marriage will be a joyous occasion."

He let out a friendly laugh. "Yes, Travyn is an impressive individual." Ellaniya could not tell if her companion was being sarcastic. "But rest assured, I have the same desires as you."

"And what might those be?"

The strange man glanced about before turning back to her. She too looked around and saw nobody nearby who might be able to overhear them. "To return the gods to their rightful place," he stated.

His words jarred her. Ellaniya had never met anyone who shared her faith, but she remained hesitant. Was this some kind of trick? If it was, what would be the point? "How do you know what I want?" she found herself asking.

"I am far older than I look," he answered. "As I said, I have been a friend of Mephosh for a very long time, and I am the answer to your prayers."

Her mouth fell open, but no sound came forth. She had many questions, but she could not formulate them into words. What was happening, and what did this mean?

"You may call me Ut," the beautiful man continued. "And I am a messenger of the gods."

# chapter 13

THE HORSES GALLOPED AWAY FROM THE CASTLE, kicking dirt up from the path into the warm summer air. Despite Tollan's protests, no guards accompanied the pair. "I have no need for protection in my kingdom," Gorhum had stated. While it was true that the citizens of Labyn loved their king, Gorhum's stubborn refusal worried his son. Though Tollan's primary concern was for Gorhum's wellbeing, he also had a selfish reason: he wanted nothing tragic to happen to his father as he did not want to be king.

It had been several blissful months since his wedding, and the love between the young couple was deepening. Over time, Tollan had finally felt comfortable enough to confide his fears of inadequacy to Adira. Unfortunately, despite her best efforts to understand his concerns, Adira had a difficult time reconciling his trepidations. "You greatly underestimate yourself," she would tell him. "You're a kind and caring man. You'll be a fine king." While he appreciated her reassurances, his doubts remained.

When he was not with his wife, Tollan would spend his time with Gorhum, absorbing all he could about the ways in which his father ruled. He watched the king expertly manage the desires and requests of the nobility. Gorhum also often met with the tradesmen, merchants and traders of Labyn, and they would tell the king of their grievances and concerns. Gorhum did all he could to help them with their affairs, and his concern for all the citizens of Labyn was sincere and obvious. Even the most belligerent of his petitioners left his presence at least satisfied that the king had heard them and would address their concerns. It was a marvel to watch. Though Tollan loved witnessing his father's diplomatic skills, there was a downside as well. He continued to wonder how he would ever be able to live up to Gorhum's example.

In addition to the studying with his father, the prince also spent time training with the expert swordsmen of Labyn. While he would likely never be considered a master of the blade, Tollan was a diligent student and his skills continued to improve; he was becoming more than competent with his weapon. Apart from the times with Adira, he enjoyed his martial training more than anything else. He relished the feeling of sweat rolling down his body after a strenuous session, and it was one activity in which he did not have to worry about comparisons with the king. Due to their long period of peace, Gorhum had never been forced to wield a weapon.

When the horses reached a small creek, Gorhum signaled for a stop. The pair dropped from their steeds and allowed the horses to drink from the creek as they watched a school of silvery fish dart by. After the animals were satiated, Tollan tied their reins to a nearby tree and sat on the grass next to his father, bathed in the warm summer sun.

"News from Mephosh that the princess has been wed to Travyn of Su'Meeryn," Gorhum said before biting into a pear he pulled from his pocket.

"He's the one that's a fool?" asked Tollan.

"That's what I'm told." Gorhum scowled at the taste of the pear and tossed it over to the horses.

"Wasn't he supposed to marry the girl from Pathum?"

"Yes, but that was before Jaleph died. There must have been some change in plans."

Tollan thought about eating the pear he had brought, but he decided against that after seeing his father's expression. Instead, he took a swig of water from his wineskin before commenting, "I wonder if you should have sent someone to Su'Meeryn for the funeral."

"I would have, but by the time we heard the news, the service was likely concluded."

Tollan sealed the wineskin as he stood from the ground. "I'm worried that Labyn has been isolated from the other kingdoms, father. Do you think that's wise?" he asked as he reached down to the king.

Gorhum grasped his son's hand as he slowly rose from the ground. "There was a lot of strife between Mephosh and Su'Meeryn in the past, as you know. Labyn managed to stay neutral, and that is my preference. So long as we're not threatened, I see no reason to involve ourselves in the matters of the other kingdoms."

"I understand," Tollan replied as they walked back to the horses.

"Is there something bothering you, my son?"

"Why do you ask?"

"Your face looks troubled, and you don't seem to be yourself."

Tollan stopped and turned to the king. How could he answer that question? He wanted to tell Gorhum of his concerns and fears, but what could he say? He was receiving all the training that was available, so what more might Gorhum be able to offer the prince? Why bother the king with his petty troubles? "I just wish you'd keep some guards with you," he replied.

Gorhum turned to his son and placed his hands on Tollan's shoulders. "I appreciate your worry, but what kind of king would I be if I wasn't safe in my own kingdom?"

"A safe king. You'll never be able to please everyone, father."

Gorhum turned and dropped his arm around his son's waist, and the pair moved back towards the horses. "We've had no conflict in decades. The workers and merchants are satisfied. Labyn is prospering which keeps the nobles happy. We expelled all the pagans long ago and the temples are full of true worshipers. What is there to be concerned about?"

As Tollan grasped his reins he watched a kingfisher dive into the creek and emerge with a fish in its beak. "There could be some disgruntled, angry person that you don't know about."

After mounting his steed, Gorhum turned to Tollan. "If that were the case, I have plenty of others to protect me. Now, enough of this, let's return to the castle." With a kick from its rider, Gorhum's horse jumped into a gallop.

Tollan just shook his head as he watched his father speed away. He climbed into his saddle hoping, his father was correct. The thought of something happening to the king was extremely troubling. Tollan did not want to lose his father, and he also did not want to lose the king. He knew he was not ready to assume the throne—if he ever would be.

Rather than galloping back to the castle, Tollan kept his horse in a slow trot. He was in no hurry to reenter those walls as Adira was spending the day with his mother, and he would not see her until later in the evening. So he decided he would take his time and enjoy the peace he felt in his solitude, untroubled by his inevitable future.

# chapter 14

THE CROWN STILL LOOKED STRANGE SITTING ON HIS FATHER'S HEAD, but it did mute the sinister appearance of his gaunt face and those red eyes. While most others might not be aware, Hellet knew that Orrin's features did not match his demeanor. The only person Hellet could remember his father being short with was Travyn. But it was hard to fault Orrin for those times as it was always Hellet's uncle that, unwittingly, brought on the abuse. Hellet had seen his father's attempts to include his younger brother in various activities and to help him when he struggled; however, Travyn's belligerent behavior never made things easy for Orrin.

It was not Travyn's stunted intellect that was the problem, it was his pride. Maybe it was because he felt so inferior that Travyn put forth his blusterous, arrogant face. But, whatever the reason, Travyn's conduct was taxing on them all.

Even some outside the royal family found occasion to tease the young prince. Hellet had to routinely rebuke his friends, especially Neffy, regarding their harsh words towards his uncle. Neffy had advanced quickly in his martial training while Travyn lagged far behind, and that just angered the prince. So Travyn would often attempt to belittle Hellet's strong friend. "You have to ignore him," Hellet would say. "I know he's a problem, but he is a prince, and he really isn't so bad. We can't have you acting that way with him." Neffy would just shrug an acknowledgement, but Hellet knew that the problem would resurface. Neffy was not a patient boy, and he could only take so much.

Hellet pushed those thoughts aside as he approached the throne. Orrin's smile at his son was a bit brighter than normal, and Hellet figured it was because Travyn had agreed to stay in Mephosh for a time following the wedding. It was certainly unprecedented for the groom to remain in his bride's homeland, but nobody in Su'Meeryn complained. Everyone in the family was happy for a break from Travyn, if only for a brief time.

While it was clear that most people disliked Travyn and avoided him when possible, Hellet did not share those sentiments. Yes, he was well aware of Travyn's short comings, but still he was fond of his uncle. The times they spent alone had generally been pleasant. Travyn always wanted to wrestle (the one thing he was good at), but Hellet usually refused. As Travyn was older, larger and stronger, Hellet could never win. The few times he had agreed to a bout, Travyn was always gentle, except once when Neffy and Darus were present. That time he was very rough and took far longer to score the pin then was needed. Hellet left with many bruises and never agreed to another match, but Hellet had forgiven his uncle for that occasion. He knew what prompted the change in Travyn. Feeling inferior is a dangerous emotion, and Hellet refused to contribute to Travyn's insecurities. He had vowed to himself to always be pleasant to his uncle.

But what made matters worse was all the praise that Hellet received from the nobility and everyone else. While Travyn struggled mightily in his lessons, Hellet had quickly caught up then passed him. It made Hellet uncomfortable: all the acclaim he received, especially in Travyn's presence. How many times had others remarked regarding his maturity at such a young age? Hellet once brought his concerns to his father regarding how Travyn struggled with all the praise he was receiving, but Orrin had mumbled something that Hellet did not understand and sent him on his way.

So, he had done what he could to encourage his uncle, but he was afraid it had not been enough. In fact, Hellet doubted Travyn was even aware of all his nephew had tried to do for him. While he did recognize Orrin's pleasure at having a break from Travyn, he did find it a bit distasteful.

"Did you and Dellea enjoy your trip to Mephosh?" Orrin asked.

"Yes, father, and I do believe it was beneficial as I was able to ascertain that the faith remains strong there. Much stronger than here."

Orrin's eyes seemed to glow a deeper red at that comment. All the tragedy that their family had suffered had taken a toll on Orrin, and he showed less and less religious concern as time went on, despite the protests from Jenna and his son. Hellet and Jenna often discussed the matter, and Hellet was told it had not always been that way. The death of his siblings and all his other children had made Orrin bitter. He loved and cherished his son and was thankful that he had a clean heir to the throne, but each subsequent death had chipped away at this faith until it had completely disappeared within his bitterness.

"You don't foresee any problems once the king dies?" Orrin asked.

"No. His son's faith is stronger than his. I had many chances to talk to the prince, and he is committed to peace. His only goal, once he is crowned, it to strengthen the faith in Mephosh, and that is expected to be soon. Naren is not well."

Orrin sighed, as Hellet knew he would, but, despite his father's doubts, Hellet had brought good news to the king. A peaceful change in monarchs in a former adversary was important for Su'Meeryn. "And how did Dellea handle the trip?"

"She did fine, I suppose. I encouraged her to speak to some of the ladies, but she mostly stood at my side. It was difficult for her being away from the wolves, and she was concerned about them, but she knew they were being well cared for."

A short grunt escaped the king's mouth. "I'm sure they were happy to see her return. I was told they were pretty agitated in her absence and caused considerable damage to their stall. None of the servants were anxious to feed them. It's good we have plenty of meat." He shook his head slightly. "It is a strange thing."

"Yes, but they make her happy."

"That could be a problem in the long term."

"I agree," Hellet replied.

"Are you certain you want to go forward with this marriage, my son? It's not that I dislike Dellea, but she is somewhat… odd. If you were to request it, I could still cancel the betrothal. We could make other arrangements."

Hellet wanted to be angered at his father's words, but he could not find fault with Orrin for being concerned regarding his wellbeing. How could he explain his connection towards Dellea to his father when he could not find the words for himself? "I've never been more certain of anything," he stated empathically.

"I just wanted to make sure you were still certain after this trip with her," Orrin said as he rose from the throne and embraced his son. "I'm glad to have you back. Now, make sure you spend some time with your mother before attending to your studies. She still thinks you're too young for some of the tasks I assign, so she will greatly enjoy doting over you."

Hellet smiled at his father. "I know." It seemed that his mother was the only one in the entire kingdom who did not think of him as older than his years. Hellet assumed that all the pain she had endured contributed to her attitude towards him, but that just made him love her even more.

Her fawning nature often became tiresome, even occasionally annoying, but he could do nothing but forgive her.

**\*\*\***

"It's still hard to think that soon you'll be getting married," Jenna said as she lounged on the couch in her personal study.

"It won't be for a couple years," Hellet pointed out.

"Of course, but I still think of you as my baby."

'Nobody else thinks of me as a child." Hellet immediately regretted his response. He was afraid that it sounded accusatory, but Jenna had not seemed to notice.

"Despite what you might think, my son, I am well aware of your gifts, but it gives me pleasure that I don't have to dwell on those when we're alone."

"I know," Hellet replied as he sat next to her on the couch.

Jenna took the book that she had been reading and placed it on the table next to the couch then stretched her arms out with a sigh. "I'm sure your father asked the same question, but tell me, how did Dellea fare on the journey?"

"She didn't say much while we were in Mephosh, but she seemed happy to be with me."

"That's good, but you need to see to it that she makes other friends. She can't rely solely on you and those wolves. Nobody knows how long wolves live."

While Hellet appreciated Jenna's concern—much as he had done with his father—he had to fight back a festering annoyance. He was well aware of these issues, and while she was not saying it out loud, Jenna was implying a concern for Dellea if something were to happen to him. Her soft eyes reached into his and, as usual, he melted at her warmth. He could never be frustrated with her as her only concern was for him, and he again wondered how all the death she had experienced had not affected her like Orrin. He often wanted to ask her about that, but always decided it would be better to not broach that subject. "I'm doing what I can," he said. "Perrin seems to like her well enough, and it looks like Darus' family will be approving the marriage. If so, the girls will see a lot of each other."

"That's good, but I can't imagine that Dellea likes to be around Darus much, or Nefalel either."

"Neffy is behaving himself, and Darus... well, I'll continue to talk to him."

Jenna groaned slightly as she repositioned herself on the couch. "The years are starting to catch up on me."

"You are still young, mother, and one of the prettiest ladies in Su'Meeryn."

"What have a I told you about lying?" she replied, and Hellet was a little startled that her chide was not playful. "Now, unto our business. I want you to go meet with Wairren."

"I see him often, when I accompany Dellea to the stables."

"No, that's not what I mean. While I love your father, we both know that he has completely abandoned the faith. It is critical that you seek counsel from Wairren. We must make certain that our faith does not vanish from Su'Meeryn. It's time to add religious studies to your lessons. You are my son, my only surviving child. I've never asked anything of you before, but I do now. You are old enough to begin to take on this burden."

The seriousness in her tone was astonishing to Hellet, he could not remember ever hearing her speak in such a way. "I will, of course, do as you ask."

# chapter 15

IT FELT NICE TO BE HOME, at least what she now thought of as home. While it was still a foreign kingdom, residing in Su'Meeryn had become a far better life than being in Pathum with her father and the rest of her family.

The midday sun was hot against Dellea's skin as she sat on the small ridge watching the boys in their game. The wolves lounged around her, not anxious to move in the heat. Her hand absently stroked the neck of the nearest beast who seemed oblivious to her touch.

The game Hellet and his friends were playing was unfamiliar to her. It looked rather rough; there was a ball that was being passed around and a lot of tackling and yelling. Despite watching intently, she still had no idea what the objective might be. When she had asked if she could join in, Neffy just laughed and walked away while Hellet smiled and followed his friend into the fray. I guess that was for the best, she thought.

She watched as the boys darted about, chasing the ball, then some fell on the ground and rolled about until a cry of pain reached her ears. She stared into the melee, and the head of one of the wolves lifted for a moment too. She was relieved to see Hellet standing, looking down on the sprawled form of Darus. Before she had time to worry, Darus jumped back up, and the boys returned to their contest, any minor pain quickly forgotten.

She watched as Hellet continued to dash about within the group. Though she still did not know the point of the game, he clearly was not the strongest player out there. Neffy seemed to be dominating whatever it was that they were doing. Eventually, one of the other boys was hurled into the air. His landing on the ground with a hard thud apparently signaled the end of the match. Dellea heard much laughing but also some groaning as the boys began to disperse. Hellet turned his attention to the ridge, and she saw his bright smile as he waved to her. She returned the gesture but did not move. Hellet then turned back to his friends and the three of them sat down and began to chat. She saw Darus glance towards her a few times with what appeared to be an intimidated look at her animals, which was fine with her, and that made Dellea smile even more.

While the three boys continued to chat, Dellea's gaze lingered on her husband-to-be. She remained marveled at her draw to him. What was it about the young prince? Though he was still not of age, she could not think of him as a boy. His attractive features along with his intellect and maturity gave off the impression of someone older than herself, but those alone did not define the appeal. Actually, she rarely thought about his appearance. There was something more to him that she could not define.

With a feeling of joy, she stretched out on the ground—the wolves surrounding her—and she thanked the creator for these new-found blessings. While she had never wanted to marry Travyn, she had been consigned to the prospect as it would at least get her away from Pathum. But now? She could not have imagined such a pleasurable outcome. She would get to stay in Su'Meeryn and marry the wonderful boy who would one day be king. And Travyn would be a distant memory. Her life was progressing far better than she could have ever envisioned.

***

Back at the hall, the three boys were bragging to each other regarding their marvelous exploits in the game. Dellea sat quietly next to Hellet with a grin on her face. Hellet and Neffy had tried to engage her in the conversation, but she mostly just nodded; she did not have much to say. Dellea could tell that Neffy was starting to feel uneasy with her silence, but that did not bother her. The pleasure of being in this setting was all that mattered. She was happy and did not find any reason to disrupt the situation with words.

Whether Darus was growing uncomfortable, or just did not care, he stood from the table. "If you will excuse me, I need to meet with Perrin's family. It's looking like the marriage is going to be approved," he said happily.

"That's good news for you," Neffy commented, "but give my sympathies to Perrin."

Darus jeered at him, but Dellea could not tell if it was due to anger or was in jest. "She could do far worse," he replied as he glared at Neffy.

Neffy scoffed at Darus, waving him away, and Dellea heard laughing as Darus made his way out of the hall.

Neffy then stood as well. "I should also be on my way too," he said with a groan. "Probably should have refrained from the games today as

I have training." He paused as he took a deep breath, and a slight grimace crossed his face. "Well, we'll see how it goes."

"I'm sure you will be fine," stated Hellet.

"Thanks. I'll see you soon." He then looked at Dellea. "And you. I hope you enjoyed your day."

"It was very pleasant," Dellea responded.

"You weren't bored?" Hellet asked when they were alone.

"Not at all. We liked relaxing in the sun and watching."

"We…" Hellet began, but then he stopped himself.

"I still wonder sometimes why you are friends with them," Dellea said after a silent pause. "Especially Darus."

"He's kind of obnoxious, but he's a good, faithful man."

"If you say so."

Hellet took a drink, and Dellea noticed a slight wince. "My mother has arranged for me to meet with Wairren," he said. "As you know, he's the only remaining prophet in Su'Meeryn. He doesn't speak much anymore, but with Jaleph gone, she wanted me to meet with him. You should come."

"Of course."

***

As they made their way to the cleric's home, Hellet told Dellea about how Wairren's father had did much to reestablish the faith under Jaleph after the wars with Mephosh. Most people knew of Wander's fame from Sul's book, but what happened later in his life remained a mystery to Hellet. Wander had moved on after the death of his wife when Wairren was still a child, leaving his son behind. Hellet was never told why Wander had left, but Wairren eventually took on his father's work. As Jaleph aged, and Orrin assumed more control over the kingdom, Hellet's father had reduced the subsidies to the cleric. As a result, Wairren had taken work in the stables, continuing to preach whenever he could. However, those opportunities had lessened with each passing year. Fewer and fewer people remained interested in his sermons, and it had come to the point where even Hellet and Jenna rarely heard from him anymore.

Dust swirled as they entered the home of the prophet. Wairren sat at a small table, and a scowl formed on his face when he noticed Dellea. "I thought it was only you coming, Hellet. Don't I get enough of this girl at the stables with those damned wolves?"

"Are you complaining about doing your job?" Hellet asked without a trace of emotion.

"My job is horses, not wolves."

"Now it's both." Dellea could not tell if either of her companions were angry, but she immediately felt some discomfort.

"So, I hear you won't have to marry Travyn," Wairren said abruptly, turning to her, and Dellea was pleased at the change in subject. "I expect you are delighted with that decision."

Dellea nodded.

Hellet gently placed his hand on Dellea's wrist. "My mother thought I should meet with you and begin my ecclesiastical studies, and Dellea agreed to come along."

"Yes, your mother, the queen. She's a strong woman, but I have concerns about your father."

"What's wrong with my father?"

"How old are you now boy? I've lost track."

"Answer my question."

Wairren stood from the table, reached over and grabbed a staff that was leaning against his filthy wall. He spun it around and looked at the hunk of medal that adorned its top. He then slammed it on his table. "I said, how old are you boy?"

Dellea jumped at the sound, but she tried to remain stoic. She noticed a slight tremble in Hellet's lip, but it quickly disappeared. "I'm fifteen, as I'm sure you know. The kingdom recently had a huge party for me. Did you not attend?"

"What use have I for such revelry?" Wairren replied as he placed the staff back against the wall, then sat back down, motioning for the pair to join him. "Fifteen, eh? Still young but that is good. Now, your father. Orrin is a decent man, though he has not treated me very kindly, but I am aware of his issues, as are you."

"How do you know what I'm aware of?"

"Don't be so sensitive, boy. I am the son of Wander, the greatest prophet our land has ever seen. And I am the last prophet in Su'Meeryn. I have been granted the gift of wisdom, and I am aware of much." Dellea could tell that Hellet wanted to interject, but Wairren raised his hand to stop him. "My visions of late have been troubled and disjointed, so it's good that you have come. I was not sure what I was seeing until this moment." Wairren turned and peered at Dellea. "Having you here, girl, has given me clarity." Turning back to Hellet, he continued. "You will have a vital role for Su'Meeryn, but it will be a difficult road. Great hardship and sorrow will be your companion. I don't know the full extent yet, but there is an evil brewing. Su'Meeryn suffered much due to Lynna and Mephosh—all the wars and death, but what is coming will far surpass that. I see much sorrow and strife." Wairren paused as his mournful face regarded the pair. "I wish my vision was clearer, but it has just now begun to come into focus.

"You will need to be prepared." Then Wairren's eyes rested on Dellea. "Both of you.

"Stay close to your friends Hellet, you will need them as well." When the cleric stopped, Dellea felt the tension in the room; it clung to her as if she was an insect, trapped in a spider's web.

Wairren's dark eyes then went back to his staff. He gazed at the indistinguishable hunk of metal that rested at the top. "I don't know any more yet," he continued, still staring at his staff. "Keep up with your training, but maintain a watchful eye. Once I have more clarity, I will summon you again. Now, please leave, I must commit myself to prayer."

"That's it? What about beginning my studies?"

Wairren grunted at Hellet's comment. "Did you hear what I told you, boy?"

"I heard every word, but if you're right, wouldn't it be best for me to study with you?"

"Yes, I will need to teach you, both of you, but first I need to clarify the proper direction. For now, I need time to reflect. I need solitude."

"If you say so," replied Hellet with a shrug as he grabbed Dellea's hand and guided her from the small home.

As they walked away, neither of them spoke. Dellea was stunned at Wairren's dire proclamation, and she cursed herself for dropping her guard. Why should she have expected that she would finally be granted happiness after all the years of misery? Had she been given the delight of these pleasant summer days just to tease her? She glanced at her companion and thought of her wolves who were currently housed in Wairren's stables. She was happy, happier than she had ever been, but if the cleric was to be believed, all of his new-found joy would soon disappear. However, perhaps he was not correct, Dellea thought desperately. Perhaps Wairren was just an old fool. But, unfortunately, something in her told her that that was not the case. At least, if this trial was to come, she would not be facing it alone.

# chapter 16

THIS MAN WHO CALLED HIMSELF UT was an impressive person. Travyn had never encountered anyone like him before. He was a beautiful individual, but the aura of confidence that surrounded him was even more captivating. Like all the other people he had met, Travyn could instantly read the man's demeanor and motivations; Ut was certainly a person to be trusted. Travyn smiled to himself for his skillful perception as he and his new bride joined their companion at the table in Ellaniya's personal study.

"The gods are pleased that you have agreed to meet with me," Ut began. Ellaniya had previously mentioned Ut's connection to the gods to Travyn. While he never viewed himself as a religious person, he had quickly acquiesced to his wife's request for this meeting. Travyn wanted to do all he could to make his wife happy. And if this Ut could offer something to benefit his new bride, that was just fine with him. He stuffed a few strawberries in his mouth as he eagerly waited for Ut to continue.

"They have heard your petitions, Ellaniya, and they want you to know that they appreciate your devotion. They remember the glory of old Mephosh with fondness and are committed to seeing that former glory return. And I am to tell you, princess, that you will be instrumental in ridding the land of these heretics once and for all. But it will not be easy; the task can only be achieved at great cost. They want to make sure that you are up for the challenge. Are you?"

"Of course!" Ellaniya responded enthusiastically, her face beaming like a bright morning sunrise. Travyn's smile matched hers, immensely pleased to see his love's delight.

Ut's expression hardened, and his eyes bore into Ellaniya's. "Be certain of what you are saying, my dear. The tasks required of you will be difficult and bloody."

"I am fully committed to the gods and their desires," Ellaniya replied with determination etched in her voice.

Ut nodded to Ellaniya then his finely contoured face turned to Travyn. "And you, they have grand plans for you as well." Of course they did, Travyn thought, sitting up straighter in his chair—the sweet flavor of strawberries still lingering in his mouth. His head leaned towards Ut, anticipating the man's next words. "They want to see you on the throne of Su'Meeryn, and your reign extending far beyond."

"Yes!" Travyn bellowed.

"You will be greater than a king. They wish to see you as emperor."

"Yes!"

"But your task will be equally challenging. Much blood will need to be spilled to achieve their divine goals."

Travyn heard Ut's words, but they did not register in his mind. His thoughts had stopped—the throne of Su'Meeryn and the word emperor were all that he could contemplate. How it came about was of no consequence to him. He would finally be in the position that he deserved; the path that took him there was inconsequential.

"I serve the gods, and I shall do as they bid." Ellaniya's voice broke through Travyn's musings, and he attempted to focus on his wife. "But can you tell us more of what will be required?"

Ut sat back in his chair. His vision passed from Travyn to Ellaniya like a slowly flowing stream, and he did not respond immediately. Travyn began to feel uncomfortable in the expanding silence, wondering if the man was going to speak again.

"If the two of you are to rule Su'Meeryn and Mephosh, those on the thrones, and who are in line to take the thrones, will need to be eliminated," Ut replied. "Do you understand what I'm saying?"

Travyn turned to his wife. He saw her eyes constrict above a small sneer. "Yes I do. That will not be a problem for us." She turned to Travyn, and though her dark expression was a little frightening, it also excited him. He thought of his brother and the implication of Ut's words began to dawn on him. He had always hated Orrin, and if his brother needed to be killed, that was of no bother.

"I look forward to it," Travyn stated.

✳✳✳

Dinner had concluded, and Travyn was preparing to retire to his chambers with Ellaniya when Pharen sat down at the table next to them. Travyn was annoyed as he was anxious to take his wife to bed, and he did not particularly care for his pompous new brother. What was it about families that were so difficult? Aside from his nephew, Travyn liked none of his, and Pharen was no better. Ellaniya consistently complained about her brother, and her annoyance swelled Travyn's ire.

"I'm glad I found you two, I have someone to introduce," Pharen stated.

"Another one of your clerics?" Ellaniya quipped.

"No," the prince replied as Travyn wondered why Pharen had to constantly annoy Ellaniya.

"Then who is it? I'm tired."

Pharen looked up and waved his hand. Travyn turned and saw a dark-skinned man approach. "This is Vor," the prince stated. Travyn had heard of the men from Gorthon, but he had never met one. Vor was a large, muscular man with his hair cut so short that he looked bald. His face was lean, and almost triangular as the lines of his cheeks flowed down to his prominent chin. A sleeveless shirt revealed his huge arms. Travyn noticed many scars bisecting his rippling muscles. But the most striking feature of this impressive man was his golden eyes. They seemed to dance in the torchlight of the hall, as if scores of fireflies had been shrunk and absorbed into their depths. "He came to our land many years ago as a hired sword," Pharen continued. "He has served the kingdom with distinction. Since Rennal is advancing in years, Vor is being assigned as the new head of your guard."

Ellaniya's eyes traveled up and down Vor's body, and Travyn was pleased by the smile on his wife's face. He wanted to make sure that Ellaniya always had everything she needed, and her safety was his primary concern.

"It seems you've finally done something well, brother," Ellaniya said.

"Why do you always have to be this way? Perhaps you will be in a better mood tomorrow, and we can talk more then." Pharen sighed as he stood from the table. "For now, I will excuse myself." He then glanced at Travyn and gave him a nod as he walked away.

Why was it that Pharen must always find ways to aggravate his sister? Travyn was glad that the prince was gone and he would soon be alone with Ellaniya. As they stood to leave, he determined to himself that if Pharen did not learn to behave around Ellaniya soon, Travyn would have a hard discussion with him, regardless of his position of royalty.

"I am pleased to meet you," Ellaniya said to Vor as she followed Travyn from the hall. "You may escort us to our room, but I will want to talk to you tomorrow. I would like to hear more of how you came to Mephosh."

"As you desire, my lady," Vor said with a bow.

When they reached their chamber, Ellaniya flung the door closed behind them and ripped off her clothes. She dragged her husband to the bed, and Travyn experienced the most savage love making of his life. When it was over, he stretched out beside her, exhausted. Ellaniya seemed to purr as she curled up under the blankets before falling asleep. A wide smile remained on Travyn's face, content with himself with how he so masterfully satisfied his wife. She is indeed lucky to have me, he thought; who else could please a woman like that?

Turning onto his side he stared at Ellaniya's lovely face. Even in her sleep, an expression of delight remained on her delicate lips. He had a wife who clearly adored him more than anything, and with Ut's assistance, he would soon rule Su'Meeryn. What more could he want?

# chapter 17

ALTHOUGH HIS FRIENDS WERE OLDER AND STRONGER, Hellet was a far superior horseman than either. The three horses galloped around the countryside with Hellet in the lead, and he was enjoying the knowledge that he could best them in at least one physical competition. And he knew that they did not let him win due to his position as prince and heir to the throne. He could see the exasperation on their faces every time he prevailed which made his victories even sweeter.

When he reached the tall tree by the brook, Hellet sprung from his steed, turned and awaited his companions. He laughed when he saw the familiar looks of frustration as they too dismounted. Cupping his hands in the creek, he took a refreshing drink of the cool water before pulling out an apple from his bag for his horse. The three friends then leaned back against the tree and stared up at the hazy summer sky.

"So Darus, are you really getting married?" Neffy asked.

"It appears that way," replied Darus. "My father has finally agreed to the union. Perrin and I are ecstatic. I've never been happier."

Hellet found his friend's tone intriguing as Darus was rarely so forthright with his words. More often than not he would lace his statements with sarcastic barbs or feigned arrogance. To be as open as he was clearly displayed his eager anticipation. "When is the wedding?"

"That's still being discussed."

"I'm glad to hear it; we can't remain boys all our lives. And what about you?" Hellet asked, turning to Neffy.

"Marriage! Ha! You two fools might be ready for that misery, but I have too many girls knocking at my door to choose just one!"

Hellet knew better than to accept Neffy's bluster. They had been friends for as long as he could remember, and much like Darus, many of the nobles would be more than happy to match a daughter with Neffy. But Hellet knew that girls were not throwing themselves at the large boy.

When Neffy was not spending time with his friends, he was participating in his military training, so he had precious little time for cavorting. However, his parents would not allow him to ignore his marital obligations much longer.

"We should probably be getting back soon," Hellet stated. "I have more training to do."

"What kind of training this time?" asked Darus.

"Wairren asked to see me again."

"Wairren?" Neffy exclaimed. "Are you learning to shovel manure?"

"Dellea and I met with him a while back." Hellet hesitated while he considered how much he wanted to share with his friends as he did not want to worry them if nothing came of Wairren's dire words. He had only divulged them to his parents. Predictably, Orrin had just shrugged them off while his mother was far more concerned. Truthfully, Hellet did not know whether he himself believed Wairren, and he did not want to burden his friends with the ominous warning if nothing came of them. "With my father on the throne now, Wairren thought it would be best if we met now and then. He's still a prophet of the creator."

"If you say so, but what benefit could that old fool offer the prince of Su'Meeryn?" asked Neffy.

Hellet cocked his head to the side giving his large friend a knowing stare. "Some of us are still strong in the faith," he said softly. "Or at least we try to be."

Before Neffy could open his mouth to tease his friend further, Darus interjected. "If Hellet wants to waste his time with the Wairren, let him. It's no business of ours."

Hellet was used to being badgered by his friends; they were both older and Hellet was always good natured about it. But he was beginning to grow irritated with the pair. He was heir to the throne, and insolence, no matter how playful, could not be tolerated. "I will be king someday," he stated emphatically. "You two better watch yourselves."

Neffy and Darus were both startled somewhat by Hellet's stern words. Neffy chortled nervously while Darus attempted to hide traces of anger. Hellet rarely, if ever, spoke in such a manner, and his friends did not know how to respond.

"To the horses," Hellet eventually commanded. "Let's return."

The three friends rode back in silence as Neffy and Darus were still taken aback by Hellet's strong rebuke. While Hellet did not want to make his friends uncomfortable, he felt it important to remind them of his position. Yes they were all friends, but he was their prince, and it seemed they occasionally needed that reminder. He was not angry with them, as he knew they would always be loyal. However, the teasing did grow tiresome at times.

As the castle wall grew in size, Hellet knew the minimal tension they felt would disappear once they passed through the gate, and he would not have been surprised for the teasing to return.

When they reached the stables, Wairren was not present, and neither were the wolves. There was no reason for Hellet to seek out Dellea as she certainly was out with her animals, and Hellet was a little surprised when both his friends excused themselves without another joke regarding manure. As the hour had not yet arrived for his visit with Wairren, Hellet returned to the royal chambers.

***

"Where is father?"

"Merchants from the north have arrived, and they wanted to discuss increasing the trade between Su'Meeryn and Amyon," Jenna replied, as she stood up from the canvas she had been painting and motioned for Hellet to join her on the coach.

"It's coming along well," Hellet noted as he looked at his mother's artwork. "You've always liked sunsets, though I suppose it could also be a sunrise."

"It's adequate. Painting gives me something to do, but I don't think I'd ever want to hang my work on the walls."

Hellet wanted to disagree with her, but he knew it would just irritate Jenna. She hated being patronized, and they both were aware her skills as an artist were amateur at best. "You know, you could join father in his meetings," Hellet pointed out. "The queen doesn't need to be absent from negotiations."

"I could, and Orrin would not object, but he is far better at politics. Besides, some emissaries are uncomfortable dealing with women. I must admit, their discomfort would bring me some pleasure, but I don't want to make things more difficult for your father."

Hellet huffed at her comment. "I suppose you're right, but you offer much, mother."

"That I do, but I leave the politics to Orrin. There is more to running a kingdom than negotiations. Alliances must be built and cultivated—inside and outside the walls. Your father may be good at negotiations, but I am far better at developing friends, and allies. As you know, his appearance can be off putting which makes some people uncomfortable."

"You are wise," he said while making a mental note of her comment. It is important to know one's strengths as well as one's weaknesses. It is not prideful to recognize and acknowledge one's gifts. It would be foolhardy to ignore them. But it is of equal importance to be aware of weakness and surround oneself with others to fill those gaps. Hellet appreciated and valued his mother's wisdom, and it was an example that, while he may have advanced intelligence and maturity, he did lack experience.

"I hear your friend Darus is to be married."

"That's what he just told me."

"This is an example of what I'm telling you. It took quite a bit of maneuvering for Darus' father to agree to the marriage. He views your friendship with his son as of supreme value, and he wanted to wed Darus to the daughter of a richer noble." Jenna placed her brush down on the easel and offered her son a broad smile. "Negotiating and maneuvering are very different skills."

"Are you saying you helped to get him to agree?"

Jenna's smile grew wider. "Not everything needs to be political. Perrin is a lovely girl, and the two are happy together. Plus, I've seen how she's tried to befriend Dellea."

"Perhaps you are acting more political than you purport."

His mother's smile remained. "If Darus' marriage benefits you as well, all the better."

Hellet's grin matched his mother's as he reached over and hugged her. "I guess I see who is truly running this kingdom."

"Be careful what you say, my son. I know that was only a jest, but jests have ways of growing into rumors. Words matter, always remember that, and always be careful of what you say."

"You are right, as usual. Well, I've enjoyed our visit, but I should be on my way soon. Wairren will be expecting me. I'll let you return to your masterpiece."

He knew she would take his comment in the spirit it was intended, and Jenna did indeed chuckle at his quip with a knowing look. As they both stood, she kissed him on the cheek before giving him a shove towards the door.

# chapter 18

THE LEAVES AROUND THE CASTLE WERE STARTING TO SHOW the first traces of brown, and a refreshing crispness tinged the late afternoon air. With the sun beginning to set, a golden aura engulfed the princess's view. Ellaniya strolled down the path with her husband on one side and Ut on the other; he had become their almost constant companion since his arrival in Mephosh. She glanced at Travyn, and not for the first time wondered how her current situation had come about. While she certainly did not love him, she did not hate him either. Occasionally she even found his presence enjoyable, though it was a pleasure usually reserved for a favorite pet rather than a mate. Her thoughts then strayed to their love making. While it was not unpleasant, she desired more from her husband. She found no intimacy with Travyn and her mind often drifted to Vor when they were together in bed. But she resigned herself to the fact that the gods were finding favor with her for her sacrifices and decisions; in the end, all her choices would be worthwhile.

As they reached the tiny creek at which she and her brother had enjoyed playing when they were children, Ut stopped them. "Well, my young friends, it is about time that we put our plans in motion. We need to make the two of you rulers of Mephosh, and then Su'Meeryn. Once completed, we will be ready to begin establishing your empire, and enshrine the gods back to their rightful place of worship."

"I've been thinking about that," Travyn stated. "While I hate Orrin, I don't think I can kill the others Hellet has always been good to me."

Ellaniya thought she saw a flicker of irritation on Ut's face, but as soon as it surfaced, it had disappeared, and Ellaniya wondered whether she had imagined it.

"Please Travyn, we have discussed this," continued Ut. "You will be emperor of the entire land!"

"Yes," Ellaniya interjected. "My family needs to be eliminated, and so does yours."

"I know, but Hellet is good boy. I don't care for how the other's treat him—he's not that special! But I like him."

"He's next in line for the throne," Ellaniya explained with all the patience she could summon, "He must be purged as well. Sacrifices must be made."

"I know, but isn't there another way?"

"My friends," Ut said in a soothing voice that seemed to mirror the comforting bubbling flow of the creek, "there are a few things I need to say.

"Even before the defeat of Mephosh by Su'Meeryn, the gods were becoming displeased with the worship practices. They had grown tired of the animal sacrifices during the time of Lynna. The gods tell me that stakes must be raised to soothe their anger. In ancient days, their priests performed human sacrifices, and the gods now desire for that ritual to return. And it seems only fitting that the first of those are the royal families that have done so much to hinder their rightful worship.

"As for my second proclamation, they had instructed me to await the appropriate moment, and now is the time. Once the land is conquered and you two are established as empress and emperor, you will join the gods on high. You both will be made divine."

Ellaniya stared dumbfounded at Ut. Divinity? Was it possible? She had been studying the faith of the gods since she first found the texts hidden away in a dusty corner of the library of Mephosh, and she had wanted to serve them since she was a little girl. But could she actually become a god herself? Though she had her doubts, the words of Ut were intoxicating.

And human sacrifices? She had never come across mention of such in all her readings, but who was she to question a prophet of the gods? She looked at her husband and saw giddy delight on his face and all traces of uncertainty were washed away by Ut's sweet words. Travyn's determination had been forged like an ax in the hands of a master blacksmith—a tool ready to be used, and she knew he would do what was required of him, as would she.

They retreated down the short path, away from the creek to where her guards awaited. Vor stood still like a tall, strong tree; his expression barely changed at her arrival, but Ellaniya did notice the slightest hint of a grin. The thought of him taking pleasure at her return intrigued her, but now was not the time to consider such things. Or was it? She would need allies within Mephosh to accomplish their goals, and Vor would certainly be a fine ally to have. Ut had promised that Travyn and she would be secure once they assumed the thrones, but some extra precaution would not hurt.

As they strolled on in silence, Ellaniya thought about her father. With Naren's failing health, the thought of his killing had not weighed heavily on her. In a way, it would be a mercy, at least that is what she had told herself. But though his vision was continuing to fail, she noticed his coughing seemed to have subsided a little. Was he getting stronger? If his death was no longer imminent, she was forced to wonder if she would be able complete the task, though she had not voiced those doubts to Ut.

While killing Pharen would not be easy, she knew it too was necessary. She had no true desire to see her brother die, but his death was also required. Much like her feelings at her mother's funeral, she would not mourn as he must not become the next king of Mephosh. His rule would only hasten the decline of her home and push the gods even further away.

She glanced again at her husband as the small party hiked back to the castle wall. Travyn was stuffing strawberries into his mouth, his serene face displaying no turmoil regarding their plans. She wondered if she should envy his simple mind and his lack of an internal struggle.

Ellaniya then returned her attention to Ut who practically bounced along beside her. He remained an enigma. Why did she trust him so? She had no reason to doubt he had been sent by the gods as he knew so many of her petitions and desires. And everything he counseled was what she too desired. Though she had never considered becoming empress, certainly such a position would give her even more power to extend the true faith, and that is what truly mattered. With Mephosh returning to its rightful place of prominence in the region, she must keep sight of the ultimate goal: the restoration of the gods. And if she could join them one day? The thought of divinity caused her pulse to race.

If the gods now required human sacrifices, it only made sense that the heretic king and prince should be the first offerings. It would not be pleasant, and she did not look forward to it, but she knew it needed to be done. If the gods required a harsh task of her, she would not shrink away, and she looked forward to the ample blessing they would ultimately provide her due to her devotion.

"Damn," Travyn moaned as he finished the last strawberry and liked his fingers, unconcerned regarding what awaited them.

As they reached the portal, sentries cried out and the gate was lifted to allow their entry. Vor lightly grasped Ellaniya's elbow to steer her away from a small puddle as they passed through. She thanked him and he offered her a warm smile.

Ut's promise continued to roll through her mind. Yes, she would lose much, but what she would gain would far surpass that loss. She would not question herself any longer. The path was set, and she was ready to begin.

# chapter 19

A DRIVING RAIN POUNDED THE EARTH. The water was cold, but also hard—like sharp stones. How could water be hard? The relentless cascade of water assaulted her bare skin, leaving welts. Pain flowed inward from each appendage to her organs. Something was wrong; rain should not feel this way. Then suddenly the rain became snow, then shards of jagged ice. It continued to fall, assailing her quivering body. Tortured eyes saw nothing but ice.

The misery in her body was slowly replaced by a deep chill which grew to a freezing cold. But then the pain slowly returned, first to her arms then her torso. As it grew, it was like a jigsaw puzzle of agony. She wanted to drop to her knees, but the falling ice pushed against her body, forcing it to remain erect. It was overwhelming, how could one person endure such torment?

Then just as the misery grew to an unbearable level, it abruptly ended. The onslaught stopped, and all that was left was a vision of ice and snow: in every direction was a glittering white. The tundra stretched to the blue sky of the horizon. White and blue was all that was visible. Suddenly the sun jumped from the horizon and its rays blanketed the ground. Its warming rays burrowed into the snow as it all quickly melted.

Her skin—which had just been tormented by pain and cold—now only felt heat. Sweat flowed down her naked, bruised body and intermingled with the melting snow. As the white quickly retreated in the heat, shades of red became visible, then some gray. Shapes began to take form as the snow disappeared. Once all the snow had melted, her vision was clear. The shapes were bodies. Corpses littered the landscape. The ground was a gruesome display of twisted arms, legs and flesh. And blood. Everywhere was blood.

The horrific sight overwhelmed her, and she cried out. It was too much for her mind to process. The heat continued to intensify, but she barely noticed; she could process nothing but the ghastly vision before her. She tried to back away, but her foot would not move. She pulled and pulled, desperate to flee, but it remained stuck in place. Looking down, she realized a skeletal hand grasped her ankle. She cried out again.

"Dellea! Wake up!"

Her eyes flew open as her sweat-covered body trembled, and she saw a concerned Hellet staring down at her. "You were having a nightmare."

She bolted from the bed and wrapped her arms around his neck. "It was awful," she cried, her body still shaking.

"It was just a dream," he replied softly, his hand gently stroking her hair. "I apologize for entering your room uninvited. The servants said you were here, but you didn't respond to my knocking. I was worried."

She pulled away from him and dropped back onto the bed, hoping the visions of this dream would fade away like all others, but it remained vivid in her mind, bright like a mural. "I'm so glad you did, it was terrifying," she paused, forcing her body to stop shaking. "I was just going to get some rest while I waited for you, and I guess I fell asleep."

"What was the dream about?"

Dellea raised her head and looked at him. She was startled to see the concern on his face, and she wondered if this was the first time anybody showed any real interest for her wellbeing. Perhaps her mother did when she was younger, but if so, she had no memory of it. "If you don't mind, I'd rather not talk about it."

"If that's what you wish, I understand, but if you change your mind, I'm here for you. Do you need some time before we go to Wairren's?"

"Yes, I'd like to change and get some water."

"Certainly, whenever you're ready. I'll be outside."

She stood and grasped his hand as he turned to leave. He looked back and sympathy seemed to flow from those blue eyes like the melting snow of her dream. When the door closed behind him, she changed out of her damp garments that still smelled of the stables. After putting on a clean dress, she stood still for a moment, looking at the door. She knew Hellet was on the other side, patiently waiting for her, and her admiration for the young man grew.

***

Wairren glared at the pair with disdain. Dellea was somewhat relieved when the cleric's ire turned to Hellet. "Why haven't you studied the scrolls I gave you?"

"I did read them, but my father has been keeping me busying training in the affairs of the kingdom; he said I need to be prepared for my future. He's not happy with you instructing me and thinks it's a waste of time."

"You must convince him otherwise. He won't listen to me. Reading is not enough; I need you to study and meditate."

"I've tried to at night, in my room, but I'm always exhausted from all my training. I'm not able to concentrate, and I fall asleep."

Dellea turned to her husband-to-be and sensed his frustration growing. How many times had he come to her aid? Now she saw an opportunity to return the favor. "If I may. Hellet is correct. It seems Orrin finds any excuse to thwart his studies. But while Hellet may be hindered in this area, I am not. His parents treat me well, but they have little concern with how I spend my days. Why don't you teach me?"

Wairren's irritated look dissolved into an expression of bewilderment. He glanced at her, then back to Hellet. His mouth dropped open, but no words emerged. Instead, he placed but hands on the table and pushed himself up with a groan. He walked to his small window and peered out for a moment while Hellet and Dellea looked to each other in uncertainty. But before either could speak, Wairren returned to the table.

"It's an interesting notion," the prophet began. "I've been studying Naar's teaching my whole life, and your suggestion poses a bit of a dilemma."

"What dilemma?" Hellet asked.

"As you know, Naar is the oldest and wisest of all the prophets of the creator, and the basis of our faith comes from him. Most of his writings are straightforward, but those that are predictive are hard to interpret. There are mentions of battles against the evil one, but the protagonist is always male. I'm not opposed to teaching a girl, as I am not bound by our patriarchal society. However, I also don't want to waste my time."

Now it was Dellea's turn to exhibit her own anger. "What is that supposed to mean?" She had endured her father's ire for so long, and she was not willing to be humiliated by Wairren too.

"Relax girl," he said with no trace of apology in his voice, "it's just that I need to consult the scrolls more. I continue to be prompted with the sense of an evil growing that may danger Su'Meeryn. But I don't know whether or not this is what Naar foretold. But I do know that time is running short, and I still don't see clearly. And it doesn't help that the king is thwarting my plan by refusing to let Hellet study." He paused and turned to the prince. "Return tomorrow, both of you. If the king won't allow you to come, my boy, then just Dellea. I have much work to do."

"But why can't I—"

"Tomorrow!" Wairren bellowed, interrupting Dellea, and with a hasty goodbye, the pair left Wairren's hovel.

**\*\*\***

With the light fading, the two sat in the stable alongside the wolves, feeding the animals their dinner. Dellea gazed at Hellet. His soothing expression did much to relieve her tension from the meeting with Wairren as well as the images from her nightmare which remained intensely clear in her mind. "I want to take them out again tomorrow. Can you join me?" she asked. "Winter will arrive soon, and it will likely become more difficult to go out on hikes."

"Of course," replied Hellet. "We can wake early and feed them before dawn. We'll be able to get them out for a while and back before we have to start our day."

"That would be good," she stated as she stroked two of their heads while the animals curled up on the ground, their meals finished. The third, after seeing that Dellea was occupied, snuggled up to Hellet. Even though she had seen all the wolves' positive react to Hellet many times, it still surprised her.

"I've been meaning to ask, why haven't you ever named them?" Hellet asked.

Dellea remained silent as she considered the question. It was so difficult for her to be vulnerable with others, but she knew she could trust Hellet; however, that did not make offering her response any easier. "When I first saved them, I didn't want to. I did not want to grow too attached to them as I figured I'd release them once they were healthy and strong enough. But they had come to rely on me too much to be let loose. At least that is what I told others. I don't know if that's true. The reality is that I needed them—they were my only friends. But I had had them so long without names, I didn't see how I could at that point."

"Wouldn't it be easier if they had names."

"I suppose so. It's just…" She stopped for a moment and gazed at the boy sitting across from her. What she was about to share, she had never spoken to anyone before. But he would be her husband in just over a year, and they had been spending so much time together lately, that she felt she could open herself up to him. He was the first person who she ever felt comfortable with, and who seemed to be comfortable with her. "I never thought I'd tell anybody this. As a princess, I knew I'd have to get married someday, but I didn't think it would be a pleasant experience. The wolves are my companions. I know them, and they know me. I don't need names for them. In a strange way, not naming them makes them my own. It seemed if they were not named, nobody else would ever be close to them. Does that make sense? Maybe it doesn't…" She hesitated, then said, barely above a whisper, "I didn't think I would ever share my wolves with anyone." She paused again, and she knew her next words would make her even more vulnerable. "And then we met. They have accepted you into our little family, and I want to share them with you.

"Perhaps we should name them, together," she said quietly, with her head low, staring down at the straw-covered ground.

Hellet sat still when she finished, and the wolf beside him nudged his hand to start the stroking again. While Dellea thought she knew how he would respond, it was still anxious moments until his words reached her ears. "I thank you for that. I know you have unpleasant memories of your family and your upbringing. Perhaps you will share more of that time with me in the future. But for now, I'd be honored , to help you name them, when you're ready."

She wanted Hellet to say more, and the prince seemed to sense that. "Trust me," he continued. "The day my father agreed to our marriage was the happiest day of my life. I look forward to our wedding, and I am delighted that I am part of your life."

Tears formed in the corners of her eyes and began to roll down her cheeks. She knew that she was not a pretty girl and was so awkward around people, but, despite everything, the heir to the Su'Meeryn throne, this remarkable young man, wanted to take her as his bride. That fact brought her a joy that even the wolves did not. She wanted to throw her arms around him and kiss him, but she restrained herself. She could be patient; she cold wait. Again she felt a peace here in Su'Meeryn—with Hellet beside her—that she had never before experienced. If the only downside was waiting, she could easily endure that. She leaned back in the straw, each hand resting on the head of one of the beasts, a smile emerging on her face. But then Wairren's words returned to her mind. Would this all be for nothing? Would she end up suffering here even more than at her home? Perhaps, but maybe Wairren was wrong. He did seem confused on several matters.

If this peace was to be short lived, she would enjoy it while she could. Despite the cleric's warning, she told herself that the future was not certain. And if her future remained undetermined, perhaps she might be able to shape it as she saw fit. Certainly it was a possibility, but she remained under no illusion that it would become her reality.

One of the wolves then moved its head and a large tongue began to lick her face. While her future remained cloudy, at least her present was—for the first time in her life—pleasant.

As the weeks passed, Dellea continued to visit Wairren alone. Although Orrin had since forbidden Hellet to accompany her, he really was not missing much. Wairren spent most of their time rummaging through his scrolls, complaining how they made no sense. Naar had foreseen a dark time for Su'Meeryn, or at least what Wairren thought was Su'Meeryn. But then he would wonder if Naar was referring to a single dark time or perhaps two separate evil events. It was all very confusing, and she was becoming bored watching the cleric scratch his forehead in frustration. While she missed having Hellet with her during these visits, she took comfort in knowing he was not wasting his time.

It was a typical fall morning when she arrived at Wairren's home and experienced his usual bluster. "You're late girl," he chastised her in his now-familiar tone, but she had heard it so often, it barely registered to her anymore. "I need to get back to the stables after lunch. Someone needs to take care of your *pets.*"

"I'm sorry, I overslept. I had another nightmare."

Wairren's head shot up from the scrolls he was rummaging through. "What? Nightmare? Another? What're you talking about?"

Dellea had no desire to relive the horrific images, but with continued prodding from the cleric, she recounted her gruesome nighttime visions. She stumbled over her words as she recounted each terrifying detail. It was the third time she had the exact same nightmare, and this dream did not fade from her memory like all others.

"Third time! Why are you just telling me this now?"

"It was just a dream, a nightmare."

"Have you ever had a dream repeat itself? And so vividly?"

"No."

"This is very strange," he said as he stood from his chair and began to pace around the room. "Dreams can be important, especially ones like you're experiencing." He stopped pacing and rubbed his chin as his face scrunched up. "No, this is troubling indeed and seems to confirm my visions. Now, be on your way. I know you just arrived, but I need to be alone, and I need to return to the stables soon."

Dellea wanted to protest, but the seriousness of his voice stopped her. He began pacing again and did not notice her leave.

As she was exiting Wairren's home, she felt unsettled from his abrupt dismissal and the recounting of her nightmare, but then another misery came to her mind. She would have to prepare herself for the party of the formal engagement of Darus and Perrin. It was unusual that such an extravagant party would be given for a couple when neither were royalty, but Darus and his family were close friends of Orrin and Hellet, and Perrin came from a family of nobility.

As she entered the palace courtyard, the chaos of the preparations were palpable. She sensed the excitement around her; it engulfed her like the waters of a bath. But these waters were not of a pleasant temperature. She dreaded the thought of this party. She would be surrounded by people; most she barely knew—if at all. She was always uncomfortable around people, but a room full of strangers? That was terrifying. As for those she knew? While Neffy was tolerable, she did not like Darus at all. And Perrin? Perhaps they would be friends one day, but she was not certain. At least I'll have Hellet, she thought. If she ended up standing quietly by his side the entire evening, she could handle that. Maybe she would be able to make an excuse and leave early and head to the stables.

When she reached her room, she fidgeted about the small table with the few cosmetics she owned. She never had a desire to wear them in the past as she never had a person in her life she wanted to impress. Certainly her wolves did not care about cosmetics; therefore, she had no skill in their application. But for this day, she decided to give it a try—for Hellet. She knew it would not be important to him, but with all the kindness he had offered her, this was one way she could, perhaps, reciprocate. After several failed attempts, the reflection that stared back at her in the polished metal mirror looked presentable.

She grabbed the deep blue dress that had been left on the bed for her, pulled it on and returned to the metal mirror. It fell loosely and straight on her boyish frame, but she decided it looked nice enough. As she left her room to meet up with her fiancé, she anxiously wondered how he would react to her appearance. She had never felt this pretty in her life, and she hoped Hellet would feel the same way.

She was not disappointed after knocking on his door. When he opened it, his face told her all she needed to know. She saw the pleasure in his eyes as he said, "I was just about to come and get you."

"I couldn't wait to see you."

"You look lovely." He took her hand, and they strolled happily down the corridor.

Dellea wanted to thank him for the compliment, but she found it impossible to formulate words. Had anyone ever complimented her before? She could not recall. Instead of speaking, she squeezed his hand as they continued down the hallway.

Even if the next few hours turned out to be a misery, she knew she knew would survive as Hellet was with her.

# chapter 20

THE ENGAGEMENT PARTY WAS GETTING MORE RAUCOUS as the wine barrels emptied; however, Hellet did not join in. Being the prince, Hellet could have participated anytime he might have wanted, but he had seen the results of overindulgence often enough. He always found those scenes distasteful, so he never had a desire to partake.

Hellet did enjoy the time celebrating with his friends and the various nobles and dignitaries of Su'Meeryn, but he made sure that Dellea was always by his side. He sensed her discomfort—not that it was difficult to miss from the pained expression on her face—and made certain that she was never alone. A couple times he tried to include her in a conversation, but she remained quiet, so he decided he was better off letting her remain silent.

His frequent smiles at her and quick grasping of hands seemed to be all that she needed, and once he realized that, he found his own stress over her wellbeing evaporate. He knew this was not a scenario she was comfortable in, but with him at her side, she was managing well enough.

As the festivities wore on, Hellet decided that Dellea would appreciate a break from the clamor, and he guided her to a corner of the chamber. The pair was standing quietly along the wall when the king approached with a stern expression on his face. "You need to be mingling more." His eyes were an even deeper red then normal, and he had a slight slur to his words.

"We have been, but I needed a break," Hellet lied.

The red eyes turned from Hellet to Dellea than back again. Whether it was due to the liquor or compassion for his future daughter, Orrin's countenance softened. "Royalty requires its duties, regardless if they're pleasant."

"Of course, father. It was getting a little warm in there, and I wanted to get some water. Give us a bit, and we'll return to making our presence known."

Orrin turned again to Dellea with a knowing look, "Not too long," he said as he spun away, calling across the room to Perrin's father.

"Thank you," Dellea said quietly to Hellet.

"I better get a drink of water, so that I'm not a complete liar," Hellet responded.

As the evening was starting to wind down, the couple approached Perrin and Darus. "You two look happy," Hellet stated as he grabbed his friend's shoulder.

"Very happy," Perrin bubbled as she kissed Darus on his cheek. She smiled at Hellet then kissed Darus again as her face flushed. While the girl was obviously happy to be marrying Darus, Hellet could tell the wine was contributing to her giddiness. "We had such a wonderful evening! Please make sure to thank your parents for us!"

"I can't believe how lucky I am," Darus stated, staring at Perrin. His sincere words, with the lack of even a trace of a drunken slur, was surprising to Hellet. "The wedding can't come soon enough."

"Oh Dellea!" Perrin exclaimed when her blood-shot eyes turned to the girl, "I haven't seen you all evening. You look so beautiful." She then grabbed Dellea's hand and dragged her away from Hellet. "Come, let's leave these two alone for a bit. We need to gossip about our men!"

As Dellea was dragged away, Hellet could not help but laugh at the expression on her face. Her head was still turned to him with a look of both amusement and horror.

"I think your future bride has had too much to drink," Hellet pointed out.

"This isn't normal for her. But I figured, let her enjoy the evening."

"I suppose so."

Darus shot a disapproving glare at his friend, but the barb Hellet expected never surfaced. "She's happy, so I'm happy as well."

"Doesn't seem like you had any wine yourself," commented Hellet.

"Surprised?"

"Actually, yes. I figured you'd be comatose on the floor by now."

Darus let out a low laugh. "I did have a few sips, but I was busy talking to all the guests. And I guess I figured it would not be good if both of us were drunk."

Once again, Hellet was surprised at this friend's response, as Darus never seemed to be one who cared what others thought of him. "Perrin has had quite an effect on you."

A large sigh emerged from Darus' burly face. "I'm very fortunate. She's so beautiful, and the sweetest girl I've ever met." After a moment, he continued apologetically but awkwardly. "And you are very lucky too. Dellea is terrific."

"It's not a competition," Hellet said, but before he could respond further, they were joined by the queen, escorted by Neffy.

"There you two are, alone, without your ladies," Jenna stated.

"They went off to talk about us," answered Hellet.

"Really?" The queen replied, clearly surprised that Dellea was not with her son.

"You know, girls and gossip," said Darus.

"Do I?" the queen asked, her voice suddenly sharp.

Hellet chuckled to himself as Darus' mouth dropped, but no sound came out. His face turned a little pink in the uncomfortable silence, and Hellet wondered when his mother would release his friend from his misery, but her next response answered his question. "Are you telling me that men don't gossip?"

Darus began to stutter as his weight shifted between his feet, and the pink hue of his skin turned to a rosy shade of red. "Please mother," Hellet interjected, "don't torture poor Darus any further."

Jenna's face remained stern, but her reply was calm, yet authoritative. "Words have power, my young friend, as you have seen. I counsel you to always consider your words carefully." She then turned to Neffy. "Thank you for escorting me here, Nefalel, but I will leave you three friends alone and return to my husband. You can say terrible things about me when I'm gone." She kissed Neffy on the cheek, then her son. Standing before Darus, she put her hands on his neck and drew him close. "Remember," she practically whispered before kissing him too. As she released him, she grinned before leaving.

"Your mother is something," Neffy stated.

"Do you think she was really angry with me?" asked Darus.

Hellet considered for a moment. "Angry? No. Displeased with your comment? Yes. She does not appreciate flippancy."

"Ha!" Neffy barked. "If Darus wasn't flippant, he'd never have anything to say!"

"Alright, let's not go down this path," replied Hellet. "Tonight is the night to celebrate Darus—and Perrin. That is what we should be doing."

"Celebrate? Bah!" Neffy bellowed as he gave Darus a playful shove. "What's there to celebrate? Marriage? Why both of you want to be married at our ages is a mystery to me."

"Maybe because we've found the ladies that we love," and Hellet was again surprised at how measured Darus' response was.

"Love? I've got plenty of girls to love!" Neffy proclaimed as he waved an arm towards the dancers in the courtyard.

"I think you might be expressing some hyperbole, Neffy," Hellet stated.

"What do you mean by that?"

"Forget it," Hellet replied. "If we're all happy, we should be pleased for each other. There's no need for mocking."

"You're right!" Neffy bellowed. "Come, let's get a drink!"

"You go. We aren't drinking tonight," Hellet said.

"Suit yourselves. I'll go see if I can find a few more noble ladies to fall in love with."

As Neffy trotted away, Hellet turned his attention back into the hall. Across the room he could see Perrin gesturing emphatically to Dellea before bursting into laughter. From Dellea's body language, Hellet could tell she was uncomfortable, but it appeared she was managing well enough. "I am happy for you, Darus," he said, "and I'm happy for myself. I just hope Wairren is wrong with his predictions. Su'Meeryn has been at peace for generations. I would hate to see all this end."

"Wairren?" Darus scoffed. "End? What're you talking about?"

"Just some things he said to Dellea and me," Hellet answered, regretting that he had let the matter slip, especially on this day. He did not want to worry his friends with Wairren's vague warnings, especially since he was unsure if he believed them himself.

"Forget that fool. What does he know besides shoveling dung?"

Hellet took a deep breath then sat down on a nearby bench. He hoped Darus was correct, but he recalled the stories Jaleph used to tell him of Su'Meeryn after the defeat of Mephosh. Though the kingdom had suffered much, the faith grew and had been strong. Things were no longer the same, and Orrin did not seem to care. Were they being short-sighted by a lack of vigilance? Was Su'Meeryn becoming too complacent?

"You worry too much," Darus responded to Hellet's troubled expression, any thought of hardship unable to take root in his blissful mind. "You'll be king someday, and despite that, you've been able to choose your bride. There's no reason for this melancholy."

Hellet wanted to share his large friend's enthusiasm; however, Wairren's words remained heavy in his mind. And he did not want to offer anything further that might darken Darus' happy mood, so he decided it would be best to extricate himself from the conversation. "It's getting late. I better go rescue Dellea." Darus laughed and the two friends made their way over to their future brides.

**\*\*\***

The air of the early morning was crisp as the couple left the castle. The chill was a refreshing signal that fall was fast approaching. The wolves trotted merrily behind them, satiated with their bellies full of fresh meat.

"Any thoughts on naming them?" Hellet asked when they passed through the city gate.

"I'm still thinking about it, but nothing has come to mind."

They walked a little further then Hellet decided to ask the question that he had been dreading. "Forgive me for being blunt, but do you have any idea how long wolves live?"

"I've wondered that for a long time," Dellea responded without a hint of reproof. "I asked around Pathum, but nobody had any idea. No one had ever heard of a situation like mine before."

"I worry for you when those days arrive."

After a beat, Dellea replied. "I do too, but not as much now. I know it'll be hard, but at least I now have someone who will help me through it."

"We could always get you other pets when that day comes."

Dellea grabbed his hand and pulled it to her face. She gave him a light kiss on his palm then wrapped her fingers into his. "We shall see," was her reply. They then continued on in a pleasant silence as the rising sun cast a golden glow about the valley. One of the wolves strode up to Hellet's other side, and his free hand reached to its head, stroking the fur as they made their way from the castle. While Hellet longed for the day when they would marry, he could find no impatience in his soul. Yes, he wanted to marry Dellea and experience the bliss of the marriage bed, but could his future ever present a better day than this? How could it?

"Hopefully Wairren's wrong," he whispered. The only response from Dellea was a pleasant humming, so he figured she had not heard him. That was fine as there was no reason to trouble her further. While their future might be uncertain, for now, everything was perfect.

# chapter 21

"ARE YOU OKAY?" ASKED MAX as Tollan dropped his sword on the dusty ground and shuffled over to a nearby tree and sat down in the shade. "You were doing well."

Tollan grabbed a rag from his belt and wiped away his perspiration. Turning his head towards his dark-skinned friend, he repositioned his long tail of tan hair behind his back. "I know," he replied with a sigh. "It seems I was able to keep you at bay better than usual."

Max sheathed his own blade before joining the prince on the ground. "Then what is it?"

"How long have we been friends, Max?"

"As long as I can remember."

Max's family had been traders from Gorthon who had come to Labyn when he was still a small child. Tollan had been told that it was a rarity when people from Gorthon arrived as they seldom traveled far from their mountainous homeland. Unfortunately, Max's parents succumbed to an illness shortly after arriving, leaving their son an orphan. Gorhum had been deeply concerned for the plight of the orphan boy and made it his responsibility to see that Max was cared for. The king had approached the swordsman Jarret and his wife who willing agreed to Gorhum's proposal to adopt the orphan. As such, Max had been training with all manner of weapons his entire life, and since they were of similar age, Max and Tollan had become close friends.

"It's just…" Tollan stammered. He wanted to share his problem with his friend, but he was concerned how his wife might react to their issue being shared with another.

"What?"

"Well…" Tollan paused again. "I guess it's not breaking a confidence, Adira is just concerned that she hasn't conceived yet."

"Ah, I see. I hear sometimes these things take time."

"But it's more than that," Tollan continued. "You know my history; Adira is worried that it's me. She's concerned I inherited this problem from my parents and that we may never have a child."

Max turned to his friend, and Tollan saw the concern in his dark eyes. "That is rough, but there's no reason to think it'll be as difficult for you two as it was for them."

"I know," Tollan replied as he gently slapped his friend's thigh and stood up. But there was more to his concern than just Adira's worries. How could he tell his friend about his misgivings concerning his future? What right did he have to claim a burden to Max—or to anyone? He was a prince after all; he had no reason to complain. No, he would not share these thoughts; the only one he would confide in would be his wife.

Tollan took a few steps and grabbed his sword from the ground. "There's nothing I can do right now," he said. "Let's get back to it."

With a shrug, Max pushed himself up from the ground, unsheathed his blade and readied himself to continue their sparring.

***

Tollan had returned early to his chambers after finishing the training with Max, and Adira was not present. His plan had been to meet with his father who was going to be discussing some trade routes with a few of the nobles, but he was tired. And he was dejected. Was there really anything else he could learn from Gorhum? How many more meetings should he attend? Was there a magical number that would suddenly transform him into feeling competent? Was there any more knowledge he could acquire? If his concerns were not dispelled by this time, he feared they never would be.

After removing his sweaty clothing, he cleaned himself then flopped into a chair. He was sulking, but he was also angry. As usual, he was annoyed with himself that he could not get past this fear. He had no right for this melancholy with all the blessings at his disposal. He wanted to stand and peer out the window at the beautiful landscape of the kingdom, but that might disrupt his pouting. Since he was alone, he figured he had the right to pout all he wanted. He wanted to laugh at his own petulance, but his eyes were growing heavy from the intense sparring. Following a yawn, he was fast asleep.

"You're back early," Tollan heard as he was roused from his slumber. The light was still bright from outside the window, and it seemed to give Adira a glowing silhouette behind her white gown and golden hair.

"I was tired after training with Max," he replied as he stood and hugged his wife.

"You need to shave," she said with a smile as she gently pushed him away. "Your face is scratchy."

Tollan offered a chuckle; it seemed that Adira always found a way to soften his moods. "I'll make certain to correct this heinous problem tomorrow."

Adira ran her fingers through his long hair then dropped onto their bed. "Why didn't you meet with your father?"

"Why should I?" he responded as he returned to the chair. "What more is there for me to learn? I couldn't possibly count all the meetings I've attended."

"Then why are you still so concerned?"

"It's more than knowledge, Adira. Knowledge alone doesn't create skill."

"Of course not, my heart, but it is important, and you do have much knowledge."

Tollan took a moment and sighed, hoping to expel some of his frustration. "That may be, but all I've learned hasn't relieved my worry."

Adira rose from the bed and approached her husband. She bent down and gave him a soft kiss before grasping his hand. "Let's put this aside for now and join your parents for dinner. And, perhaps we will conceive tonight," she said as her smile widened.

"You are very wise."

# chapter 22

A STRONG GALE FROM THE NORTH BROUGHT A CHILL to Ellaniya as she wrapped the fur about her shoulders. It had been over a month since her last conversation with Ut and the pronouncement that her father and brother would be the first human sacrifices to the gods in ages. Ut had said he would have to leave for a time to make arrangements but that he would return soon; however, Ellaniya was growing inpatient. Was a month absence too long? Should he have returned by now? Travyn, of course, was of no help during this time. Though he seemed even more eager than she for their plan to start, he could offer her no comfort. She wondered how one person could be so anxious yet complacent at the same time. Travyn wanted to get started, but he would continually say that they needed to wait for Ut's return.

"All the strawberries in storage are gone," Travyn said as he came up beside her. "I'll have to wait until the spring for more."

"We all have sufferings to endure," she responded, confident that he would not notice her sarcasm.

Travyn nodded. "At least I'm here with you. I'm thankful that Orrin approved of us living here. It's the only kindness he's ever offered me. Mephosh is far more pleasant than Su'Meeryn. I don't suffer the abuse here that I did back home."

Ellaniya wondered about the comment. Though she had spent an unfortunate amount of time in that forsaken kingdom, while she was there, she had not witnessed the abuse that Travyn claimed to have experienced. But whether it was true or not, it was good for him to maintain that ire for what would be coming. "You will never have that hardship with me," she assured him.

His large arms wrapped around her, and he kissed her as the cool wind continued to buffet them. When he finally released her, Ellaniya gazed at her husband. While he was a dullard, he obviously loved her. Could she ever return that emotion? Affection had never been the reason for her to pursue the marriage. When she had first met Travyn, it seemed like he would present an easy way for her to influence the hated kingdom of Su'Meeryn. However, Ut's arrival had changed her plans along with the fact that they had been allowed to remain in Mephosh. But perhaps Travyn could still be useful. Besides, most royal marriages did not start with love. Marriage was a means to further power, if love developed later, that was just a bonus. Ellaniya never thought her parents truly loved each other. They were not miserable in their relationship, and they shared a mutual fondness, but she did not believe there had been love.

On the rare occasions when she and her brother would talk, if they discussed their parents, Pharen had vowed that he would not subject himself to a marriage such as theirs. He was not interested in furthering the power of Mephosh. He would say that he would find a girl strong in the faith and his wedding would never be political. But any discussions of either of their marriages had ended when their mother took ill. And now Pharen's desires were of no matter as he and their father would die before a betrothal could be made.

The plan remained an unpleasant thought, but she pushed her trepidation away for the moment. Ellaniya turned her attention back to Travyn, who was peering out at the trees in the distance—their leaves starting to show the first traces of autumn color. Her question returned, could she ever love him? No. A loving marriage would never be for her. But she had chosen this path. Could she have been happy? Was she deprived of happiness in order for her to serve the gods? She would never know, but she did not regret her decision. The gods would honor her sacrifices, and, besides, she did not hate her husband. At least she was not miserable.

"What should we do with the rest of our day, my love?" Travyn asked.

Before Ellaniya could reply, Vor approached them. He was wearing a thick vest, but despite the cool temperature, his strong arms remained bare. He nodded to the prince then said, "A message for you, my lady."

Ellaniya took the parchment from his calloused hands, and her gaze lingered in his golden eyes for a long moment. The message was from Ut. He wanted to meet with her, alone, outside the castle later in the afternoon. Travyn was not to join her.

"Is there a problem?" her husband asked.

"No, just a matter that I need to deal with." Ellaniya wondered if she should devise a more elaborate lie, but Travyn's face confirmed that was unnecessary.

"Should I come with you?"

"There is no need. You can have your lunch and maybe do some training after."

"I don't want to," he whined. "I'll never get any better with the sword."

Ellaniya had to suppress the annoyance that threatened to grow within her. She did not care what he did, but she also wanted to keep him occupied. "If not that, then maybe you can work with some of the young men. I'm sure many would like to learn from such a fine wrestler as yourself."

"That's a wonderful idea. I'll do that," and without another word, Travyn trotted away.

Ellaniya was now alone with Vor. He stood stoically beside her, his dark skin seeming to absorb the sun's rays. He was bound to her and required to follow her commands, and she wondered how far she might be able to push his loyalty. As Travyn disappeared from sight, she thought she might have to test that loyalty soon.

"Come Vor, I'd like to get lunch, then you can take me to Ut."

"Yes my lady." As he led her from the castle wall, she followed closely behind, her eyes drinking in his muscular body.

***

That afternoon, Vor and a handful of guards lead her from the castle. After a short trip, they approached the tree line and found Ut leaning against a sturdy trunk. As usual, he was wearing only the white tunic and silver belt, and the brisk air seemed to have no effect on him. As they approached, Ellaniya motioned for Vor and the other guards to remain behind.

"I wondered if I would see you again," she began. "I was growing concerned."

Ut laughed at her words. "That should never be a worry for you, my dear."

"Why did you want to see me alone? What about Travyn?"

Ut chuckled again. "Come now, do you think he is necessary? We are both aware of his traits."

Ellaniya was unsure how to take Ut's statement. Everyone who spent any time with Travyn understood him to be a fool, but none would openly say so. "What do you mean?" she asked, though she knew the answer.

"Let us walk," was Ut's only reply. He led her on the narrow trail through the trees, with her guards trailing at a respectful distance. "I needed to put a number of matters into place before we move forward with our plan. I have many allies, and I wanted to make sure that I selected the most appropriate ones."

"And what have you put together?"

Ut stopped and glanced up to the sky, and instead of answering her question, he said, "Are you aware that dragons once flew across this land?"

"Dragons!" she exclaimed with delight. "I've heard talk of them, but I assumed they were only myth."

"Oh, they are certainly not myth, my dear. They are intelligent beasts, perhaps not as smart as they think they are, but intelligent nonetheless. And they are quite arrogant; I've had dealings with them in the past." With a gentle nudge, he started the pair strolling again. "As I've said, I am far older than I appear."

"You'll be bringing dragons to our aid?" Ellaniya asked excitedly.

"Unfortunately no. Now is not the time. Perhaps in the future…" His voice tailed off, and he appeared to be deep in thought. This was odd as Ut always seemed fully prepared with his words. "It was just an example. But do not fret, they are not my only allies. All is now prepared; we can strike at the first opportunity."

"But I don't understand why you didn't want Travyn here," Ellaniya pressed.

"We must discuss what comes next. Once Mephosh is in your hands, what follows?"

"I assumed we would take Su'Meeryn. It would be only fitting after all the harm they've done to Mephosh and the gods."

"Yes, Su'Meeryn must pay, but should they be our next target?" Ut asked.

"Why are you asking me? You always seem to have an answer."

Ut nodded with a glowing smile crossing his handsome face. "You are indeed wise, my girl, but this is a partnership. We both know your husband is an imbecile. He will serve his part as a puppet king and emperor, but, beyond that, he is useless to us."

Ellaniya was shocked at the bluntness of Ut's statement. Of course Travyn lacked intelligence, and she had manipulated him to reach this point, but she did not dislike her husband. And if she was honest with herself—in a strange way--she did have some affection for him. Travyn would soon be king, and she felt Ut should be more careful. He may be a servant of the gods, but Ut was also her servant. However, that thought gave her pause. Was Ut in her service or was it the other way around? I guess it doesn't matter, she thought; all I care about is that we accomplish our mutual goal.

"So what happens after we take the throne?" she asked.

Ut stopped their stroll and turned to the princess. "First we will take Labyn; after that Pathum. Su'Meeryn will be encircled and will not stand a chance."

She smiled at the thought. How all this would be accomplished was unknown to her, but Ut was clearly confident. "You are certain we have the strength for this?"

Ut's head raised slightly, and his eyes seemed to sparkle in the sunlight. "Oh, yes."

# chapter 23

THE MORNING HERALDED THE HARVEST celebration in which offerings of thanks were given to the creator for the bounty of the season as well as the preparations for winter. For days, Mephosh had been preparing for the festivities, and a few small celebrations had begun prior to the final festival and banquet. People were coming and going through the gates, setting up the brown and gold cloth decorations and getting all the crops in order.

The scabbard dangled awkwardly from Travyn's belt. While he had always been skilled at wrestling, swordsmanship was a struggle for him. Ut had told him that he would need the weapon as it would be important to complete the sacrifice the gods demanded in order to solidify his position as king. When Travyn had pointed out his lack of skill with the blade, Ut had told him not to worry. And since Ut was such a trustworthy individual, Travyn had no problem putting his faith in the man.

The royal family sat in wooden chairs on the hastily constructed podium. Normally the king would offer up the opening prayer, but as his health was still poor, he allowed the prince that honor. Travyn heard Ellaniya mumble something under her breath, but he could not make out her words. He knew of her disdain for her family's religion, and he congratulated himself for perceiving her mood. But it would all change momentarily. He was not certain how the deed would be accomplished as Ut had told them he wanted to offer the pair a surprise. Travyn liked surprises. But Ellaniya's sullen disposition seemed strange as she did not appear anxious, and she was normally not a very patient woman. However, Travyn figured she was just looking forward to Ut's present.

It was wise that Ut had told him to start wearing the scabbard a few weeks ago and to participate in some combat training. Now it was not suspicious that he had the blade with him. What an intelligent man, Travyn thought; he's probably the smartest person I've ever met.

The courtyard of Mephosh was filled with farmers and merchants who applauded at the conclusion of Pharen's prayer. Then the music began as a selection of the final crops harvested were brought before the king. He accepted the basket with a slight bow of his head which sent a twinkling of colored lights dancing from his crown. He then passed the basket to a priest who placed the contents in an urn. Another priest approached with a torch and the offering was set ablaze: a sacrifice of thanks to the creator.

Travyn watched all this with a giddy delight. While Su'Meeryn had their own festivals, none of them met the grandeur of what he was witnessing. Once the offering was burnt up, even more musicians joined in, and the raucous song filled the air. All the citizens began to dance before the podium, and the laughter and merriment nearly drowned out the instruments. For the moment, Travyn was so enraptured with the festivities, he forgot what was to come.

The king was clapping his hands, and with Pharen's help he rose from his seat. His cloudy eyes peered towards the crowd, and with what strength he could marshal, he danced along with the music. Travyn saw Ellaniya's head turn to the side. He followed her gaze and his sight rested on the royal guards. They all wore their ceremonial armor, swords resting in their scabbards. Their eyes seemed to dance along with the throng, enjoying the spectacle. Vor stood in the front, and he gave a slight nod to the princess.

As the music reached a crescendo, a dozen men bolted out from the crowd. They reached the podium before the king's guards realized what was happening. Two of the guards fell instantly, victims of well-aimed swords piercing their throats. Blood from one of the guards burst from the back of his neck, spraying Travyn's body. The remaining guards reached for their own weapons, but before their swords could be unsheathed, blades crashed against helmets and breastplates. The assault was completed almost as quickly as it had begun, the half dozen guards strewn on the ground in puddles of blood. Vor stood over them, his sword dripping a trail of crimson onto the corpses.

With renewed vigor, the king sprung forward and placed his arms in front of his two children, as if that might save them. The attackers leapt onto the podium, with blades pointed at the king. It was then that Travyn realized that the music had ended, and the courtyard was deathly still.

The king stood defiantly, still attempting to protect his children as Ut emerged from the silent crowd. He clapped his hands and laughed in delight. "Very good!" he roared. "Yes, so very good indeed." He grabbed the smoldering urn and leapt effortlessly onto the podium, took a sword from one of the attackers and pushed the king's arm aside. When he handed the weapon to Ellaniya, Naren's mouth dropped. Travyn could not understand the change in his father-in-law's expression, but he just shrugged off his confusion.

"Today is the glorious day in which we finally put an end to this abominable heresy of the creator that was forced upon Mephosh by Su'Meeryn and The Book of Sul," bellowed Ut. "The gods are displeased that they have been forgotten for so long, and they demand sacrifices to quell their righteous anger. Not something meaningless like this," and he threw the urn into the stunned crowd. "In generations past, animal sacrifices sufficed. No more. They now demand the ultimate tribute."

Half the attackers stepped forward to restrain the king while the other half grabbed his son. Both struggled to break free, but it was of no use. "You may proceed," Ut continued.

Travyn watched as his wife raised her sword. He saw no pleasure on her face, but what only seemed to be determination. The prince screamed for mercy as he was pushed trembling to the ground. Ut just chuckled as Ellaniya placed the tip of the sword against his neck. "Please," Pharen whispered. Ellaniya hesitated, staring down at her brother. Her hands began to shake as the blade slowly drew away. The prince's sobs slowed for a moment, but then the blade returned to his skin. Pharen's body shook as Travyn looked to his wife.

The crowd began to murmur, and some started to approach the podium. But before any of the townspeople could come to the royal family's aid, scores of soldiers emerged from the buildings with their weapons drawn, and the crowd fell back.

"It must be done," Travyn heard Ut command softly. "This is the only way to appease the gods' anger."

Ellaniya's sweaty hands still trembled as she regripped the sword handle. The prince continued to struggle against the attackers holding him down, with pleading sobs escaping from his threatened throat. "Now!" Ut barked and Ellaniya drove the blade into her brother's flesh. His scream was cut short as his blood erupted into her face.

As the prince's body went limp, soldiers of Mephosh pushed through the crowd, attempting to reach the podium. Ut's troops confronted them while the townspeople finally fled the courtyard. Travyn wondered where Ut had secured so many men and how he had hidden them within the walls without anybody realizing, but that is what his new friend had promised.

Naren's soldiers fought desperately to save the king, but they were outnumbered and quickly surrounded. Ut's men fell on them like savages. Swords and axes rose and fell. The clash of steel and cries of pain filled the air as did the blood of the dead and dying.

The bodies of the Mephosh soldiers fell to the ground in heaps of quivering flesh. The gore rippled like a gruesome stew in a sinister cauldron.

"Kill those that fight on," Ut commanded. "Those that surrender and pledge themselves to the future king and queen will live."

After a short time, the fighting ceased, and all eyes turned back to the podium. The few soldiers who remained alive were on their knees, surrounded by blood and death.

"Now," Ut called forth, "the final sacrifice."

Travyn looked at Ut, then at Ellaniya. The final sacrifice, he thought, at last; I wonder what it will be. When Travyn did not move, Ut patiently took a step to him and pointed at his sword. Travyn looked down, then back at Ut, bewildered. When Ut pointed at the feebly struggling and weeping king, Travyn finally understood. And, unlike his wife, he would not hesitate.

The blade rattled from his scabbard as he spun towards the king, swinging wildly. The sword crashed down on the king's head, but it mostly caught the hand of one of Ut's soldiers. The man who had been restraining the king screamed as two of his fingers dropped into Naren's lap. The glancing blow of the weapon left only a trickle of blood from the king's hair. Naren cried out as he tried to break free, but two more of the soldiers grabbed him, holding him down.

With a huff of displeasure at his failed first attempt, Travyn repositioned himself and raised his weapon. As the blade hurled down, all the soldiers pulled away. The sword hit skull and the king collapsed. Seeing no more blood, Travyn struck again, then again. When the blood finally pooled around the king, Travyn nodded to Ut with satisfaction as the injured soldier shambled away, grasping his bleeding hand.

Travyn could not understand why Ut did not mirror his pleasure, but the deed was accomplished—the sacrifice complete. And Travyn had delivered the final glorious stroke. Those two who had tormented his wife for so long were now gone, and without his supreme skill and guile, this moment never would have happened.

Ut turned back to the courtyard and stared at the few people who were brave enough, or stupid enough, to remain. "I present the new king and queen of Mephosh, chosen by the gods. The blood that covers them is the sacrifice that appeases their anger. Now that Mephosh has once again received the gods' favor, the kingdom will reclaim its rightful place in ruling this land. Those who swear allegiance to Ellaniya and

Travyn will be much rewarded. Those that do not will meet the fate of the former king and prince."

Travyn felt the warmth of Naren's blood flowing down his arms and fingers. He dropped his sword and raised his hands to his face, and the red liquid reminded him of the juice from his favorite fruit. How interesting, he thought, pleased with himself at his revelation. He then turned his attention to the murmuring crowd as the witnesses to the sacrifice began to melt away.

Vor approached, grabbed Travyn's sword from the ground and stuck it into his belt. The dark-skinned warrior then came up to Ellaniya, who stood like a statute. Her body was stiff, but Travyn saw an expression of shock on her face. Taking the new queen's arm, Vor led her away from the ghastly scene. Ut's expression of disappointment as Ellaniya departed confused Travyn, but he shrugged it off as servants began to drag the bodies away.

As the murmuring slowly ended with the clearing of the courtyard, Travyn turned to Ut. "When do I get my crown?"

# chapter 24

THE MUSIC OF THE MINSTRELS FILLED THE COURTYARD as the performers danced atop the stage. Tollan smiled when he heard a huff of disapproval from Max. While his large friend had enjoyed the drama that just concluded, he did not care for the music, and dancing even less. Tollan gently released his grip from Adira's hand, and when she glanced over, he motioned towards Max. The princess gave him a knowing wink as Tollan stood. The prince tapped Max on the shoulder and gestured to his friend as he made his way from the canopy-covered seats. Max followed him into the bright midday sun, relieved to be fleeing the revelry.

"You need to learn to experience enjoyment, my friend," Tollan commented as the pair headed away from the crowded courtyard into the castle.

"I might say the same to you."

Tollan wondered at that comment. Max was well aware of the growing concern that Adira had yet to conceive, but was Max sensing his other frustrations? He thought he had been hiding his fears well enough, but now he questioned himself. Rather than engage in that subject, Tollan decided to broach another topic. "My mother told me this morning that the king has finally decided to assign you as his personal guard."

"Yes. I suppose he's had enough badgering from the two of you." Before Tollan could comment, Max continued, "but I agree. The king must be more serious about his safety. I'd prefer him to have a few more guards, but at least I will be with him when he leaves the castle."

"I agree. Let's go find my father and see why my parents weren't at the performance."

As the pair entered the palace, Tollan noticed nervous expressions on the faces of the guards at the door as well as heralds scurrying about. "What's going on?" Tollan asked.

"Troubling news from Mephosh, my prince, but I don't have further details."

Tollan and Max exchanged an anxious look before hurrying across the chamber floor and entering the royal chamber. Inside they found Wynyth, sitting alone, as a page was just exiting through a far door.

"Before you ask," the queen began, "I don't know. Something has happened in Mephosh and Gorhum is trying to ascertain further details."

Max stood before Wynyth as Tollan sat down next to his mother. She then nervously rose and approached Max. "I'm glad that you're here," she said as she wrapped her arm through his, "and that Gorhum finally agreed to have a guard. I couldn't have asked for better."

The king then entered followed by a herald. He stomped into the room and angrily turned to face the man. "If you don't have any more information, then leave us," he commanded as he waved the herald away.

When the four were alone, Gorhum dropped into a couch. He looked at the others as Wynyth joined him.

"What is it?" Tollan asked.

"The reports are confusing, but the king and prince of Mephosh are dead. Ellaniya and Travyn have assumed the throne. Some reports say that she killed her family, others indicate that they died of a sickness. We don't know what exactly happened, but one thing is certain: the pagan religion is being reestablished in Mephosh."

"The pagans!" Wynyth blurted out. "I thought we'd seen the last of them years ago."

"We all thought so, but the timing cannot be coincidental. Ellaniya must have always been a worshipper, since, as we know, Mephosh was the pagan bastion during Lynna's days."

"What do you intend to do, father?" asked Tollan.

Gorhum looked at his son then to Max. "I don't know yet, but this all seems far too suspicious to me. We will keep our spies around Mephosh and watch for pagans here in Labyn." He then looked back at Max again. "And before any of you can say it, yes Max, you can assign additional guards to me."

# chapter 25

THE COLD WINTER AIR MATCHED THE FREEZING in Ellaniya's soul. The blaze from the fireplace did little to relieve her chill. A couple months had passed since the harvest festival, but still she saw visions of her sword plunging into Pharen's throat. It was not that she regretted the death of her father and brother—or the guards for that matter. They had brought their fates upon themselves by rejecting the true faith of Mephosh. It was just that while she had fully supported Ut's plan, Ellaniya found she had not been prepared to carry out the grisly deed herself.

The memory of her body bathed in her brother's blood remained a frightful scene. She would often gaze at her hands—and though clean—she could still see the scarlet stains covering her skin. She was unable to confide in her husband, and when she had mentioned her struggles to Ut, he had merely laughed at her. "You will be fine, my girl," was his reply. "The gods will honor you for your obedience. You are now their most favored child and have a bright future in their eyes."

Since the assassinations, she had spent most of the time alone in her chambers. As the winter progressed, Ut had been absent more and more, and when he was around, he spent his time with Travyn, making sure Mephosh was secure from any of her father's allies. She was glad when Ut did arrive as she did not trust the new king with this task himself, and she found she had little desire to participate.

Despite his many pleas, Ellaniya only shared her bed with Travyn from time-to-time. She had initially hoped the love making might smother some of her anguish, but it only added to her melancholy as she felt no intimacy with her husband. And she remained troubled that she still had not conceived. She now controlled the kingdom, and she desired to forge her legacy—unlike Lynna—with an heir. The last time she did see Ut, she mentioned her frustration, but he told her not to worry; it was not yet time for her to bear children; they still had much to do. Ut had assured Ellaniya that the gods would grant her the blessing of motherhood once the empire was established, and her divinity was secured. Ut's promise did give her some solace, but it did not remove her grief.

On the rare occasions when she did leave her rooms, Ellaniya took it upon herself to oversee the rebuilding of the temple of the gods that had been destroyed after Lynna's death. She could find no architectural records of the former structure, but that did not matter as she wanted the new temple to far surpass its predecessor's splendor—another offering to the gods. While the temple remained under construction, the true religious practices were being performed in temporary locations. Since there were no clergy in Mephosh, Ut had brought in a few to begin the rebuilding process of the faith, and the queen would seek their counsel regarding the will of the gods when she felt up to it. She was pleased to see the proper faith flourishing, and while that did much to alleviate some of the burden of her blood-soaked memory, it did not eliminate it.

Her mind then drifted from the reestablishment of the true faith to her husband. She had to admit that the times they spent together were not unpleasant, but she did not look forward to them. He was always in a joyous mood when summoned to their chambers, but her thoughts continually shifted to the muscular, dark-skinned body of Vor, and his loyalty to her. When the subject had been broached of him regarding the plan to make her queen, he had offered no hesitation. He was bound to her, and he would do whatever was required. That promise was never far from her mind.

On one of the coldest nights of the winter, after rebuffing another request from Travyn to come to him, she summoned Vor to her room.

"How may I serve you, my queen?" the stoic soldier asked.

"Vor, you have proven your loyalty to me, so I will never question that. And I am certain you will never speak of what I'm to ask of you."

"I will always abide by your commands."

Her gaze drifted up his body to those golden eyes that captivated her so. "Your service to me has been exemplary, and I have treated you well, have I not?"

"Of course, my queen. I have no complaints."

A short laugh escaped from the queen's throat. "Even if you did, you would not admit it. But I do believe you." Vor's stance remained rigid, which was a little disconcerting to Ellaniya. "Relax Vor," and she motioned to a chair. "Take a seat."

"That would be inappropriate majesty."

Ellaniya wanted to be angered by his refusal, but she knew his response was only due to the honor in which he held her. "I can't have you standing as a soldier with what I'm about to ask you."

Vor's eyes remained transfixed on Ellaniya, then he relaxed his shoulders and allowed his body to slump a bit. "Does this please your highness?"

"It does." Ellaniya tried to continue speaking when she felt her nerves begin to overwhelm her. She had never approached a man as such before, but after all she had been through, she realized she had no cause for concern. Her life up to this point had been about service: service to her home and service to the gods. Even her marriage had been an act of service. She could not remember once making a decision strictly for herself, for her own pleasure. This night would be different.

She took a deep breath then finally continued. "I will be blunt. Perhaps you have seen the way I look at you; I have desired you since we first met. I have no love for my husband, and he brings me only minimal pleasure. I want you in my bed tonight, and any other night that I choose."

"You are a very desirable woman, majesty, and your glances have not gone unnoticed," Vor replied after a pause. "It is not my wish to disobey you, but I am concerned what would happen if you were to conceive. It would be clear that the baby was not Travyn's."

"You need not worry regarding that. I have been unable to conceive with my husband, and Ut has advised that I will not become pregnant until all our plans are completed. Now, come join me."

Vor hesitated for a moment, but then a smile crossed his face as he removed his scabbard and climbed into the queen's bed.

***

It would be at least another month before the spring thaw, so the kingdom remained tranquil and quiet. Spies from the neighbor kingdoms would have reported on the dreadful developments, but Mephosh spies had reported no troubling news from their neighbors. At Ut's suggestion, they had spread conflicting reports regarding Pharen's and the king's deaths, so Ellaniya figured there would be confusion over what had really happened. Either way, it was unlikely that the other kingdoms would expect any aggressive moves from Mephosh as whatever had really occurred was an internal issue.

Since she had been spending more time with Vor, Ellaniya noticed that her mood was improving, and she thought less and less about her father and brother. She was even granting Travyn an occasional audience when Vor was otherwise occupied. When she was not in her chambers,

Ellaniya would venture to the newly constructed temple or her library to continue her studies. With each passing day, the bloody visions of the murders faded a little more, but they never left her. Even the pleasures she now found in Vor's arms failed to erase the memories completely. Though her ongoing studies convinced her that the barbaric action had been necessary, the guilt did not disappear. And with each day that the guilt remained, her anger would grow at what had become of her. If only Mephosh had not turned away from the gods in the first place, the decisions she had made would never have been forced upon her.

Her anger grew, but it was not at herself. Her anger was directed towards the heretics and how they had caused all this misery. "They will pay for this," she told herself. Travyn and she would conquer all the lands and finally destroy the heretical teachings, and Vor would be at her side. And if the land would have to be bathed in blood to wash away the apostasy, so be it.

# chapter 26

THE ARRIVAL OF SPRING WAS ENJOYED by all the inhabitants of Su'Meeryn. It had been the harshest winter in recent memory, so the first thaws were much celebrated. Along with the beginning traces of buds on the trees and shrubs, the kingdom had also celebrated the wedding of Perrin and Darus. With Perrin's nobility, and the close relationship of the groom to the prince, the festivities had been almost a royal affair. While Su'Meeryn had much to celebrate, ill tidings threatened to dampen the joyous mood.

The news out of Mephosh had been troubling. It was unclear regarding what exactly had happened there. Reports told of the assassination of the king and prince at the hands of mercenaries, while others claimed the deaths had been orchestrated by Travyn and Ellaniya, which seemed unlikely. Still others reported the king and prince had both succumbed to a fever. Regardless of the true circumstances, Travyn and Ellaniya now ruled over Mephosh. Despite protests from his wife, Orrin had decided that he would not worry himself over the actions in that kingdom. After all, what kind of threat might his fool of a brother be? Mephosh had been severely weakened from their prior battles with Su'Meeryn and never fully recovered, so Orrin was not concerned over Mephosh posing a danger.

However, Dellea was not so sure. She had continued to meet with Wairren throughout the winter, and though nothing came of those meetings, the cleric persistently warned her of pending dangers and hardships. And he remained baffled by her frightful nightmares that continued to haunt her. When the disturbing news from Mephosh had been received, that only amplified his concerns. Whenever she questioned Wairren about how Mephosh was related to his supposed visions, he did not have an answer, but it seemed that each passing day increased his anxieties.

Despite the bitter winter and the perplexing times with Wairren, the past few months had been some of the best of Dellea's young life. With little to do but wait for the weather to break, she spent most of her days with the wolves and Hellet, when he was not busy with his duties. It seemed that with each week that passed, her fiancé grew and filled out a bit more. He was looking more and more like a man, and she longed for the day of their marriage. They still had not named the wolves as she never managed to think of anything appropriate. However, there was another reason: she was so satisfied with her life that she was afraid naming them might bring a change. And apart from getting married, she did not want anything in her new life to be altered, though it would be nice for her dreams and Wairren's predictions to end.

When they were not alone—or when Hellet was not training with his father—they would spend time with Darus, Perrin and Neffy, and those instances were barely tolerable for her. While she was beginning to find Perrin pleasant enough, and they were becoming quite friendly, she still did not like Darus. He was reasonably amiable when Perrin was nearby, but Dellea always found him to be condescending and insecure. The combination of those two traits created a very annoying person, and she continually wondered why Hellet and he were friends.

She did not dislike Neffy, but he was arrogant; he always seemed to be boasting over his skills with the sword or some other deed. She did not begrudge Hellet the time they spent with the others, as she knew he needed his friends, but she much preferred being alone with him, or for them to be together with the wolves. However, she often told herself that someday she would be queen, and she would need to get more comfortable in social settings, but that knowledge did not relieve her unease.

Though the air was somewhat warmer when Dellea and Hellet returned from a hike with the wolves, Dellea still pulled her cloak tightly about her attempting to fend off a chill. When they left the stables, Hellet went off to meet with his father and Dellea headed towards Perrin's home. It was not often that the two girls met alone together, and while Dellea would have preferred to be going to her room, she did not dread the meeting.

"It's nice to see you," Perrin said warmly as Dellea passed through the doorway.

"And you."

Perrin smiled at Dellea's response. "Are you certain?"

"What do you mean?" Dellea asked.

"Come now, my dear. I know you better than that."

Dellea was annoyed at Perrin's response as she found the statement *my dear* fairly patronizing. After all, she was only slightly younger than Perrin, but she decided to shrug off her irritation. "What do you mean?" Dellea asked.

"I have come to know you well. You don't like people." After a slight pause, she continued, "well, except for one."

"That's not true."

Perrin guided them to the table and handed Dellea a mug of tea. "It is not an accusation or an insult. I can tell that most people make you uncomfortable. But I'm hoping that I might not be one of them. We will be spending much time together in the future."

Dellea was only slightly surprised at Perrin's observation. She knew she impacted people negatively, but most thought it was because she was a disagreeable girl, not because she was always uncomfortable. She looked into Perrin's soft eyes. Part of her wanted to open up to her new friend, tell her how right she was. But that would just make her more vulnerable, which she was unwilling to do with anyone other than Hellet. Unfortunately, that led her to a predicament. Apart from agreeing with Perrin, she had no idea how to respond. "I like you well enough," she stated, which was true.

Perrin took a sip from her own mug and considered her guest. She remained silent for a much longer time than Dellea expected, which only increased her agitation. "I suppose you do," Perrin eventually said.

"How is Darus?" Dellea immediately asked, as she did not want another uncomfortable silence.

"He is well; he's drilling with Neffy." She took another sip of tea then continued. "You don't like him very much."

"No," Dellea replied, but then instantly regretted it. How could she be so stupid? While Dellea might be uncomfortable being alone with Perrin, Darus' wife was a perfectly nice lady. How could she blurt out that she disliked her husband?

Perrin laughed, obviously seeing the discomfort on her companion's face, and she placed a soothing hand on Dellea's wrist. "Don't fret, my dear," she said calmly and honestly. "I know he has this effect on most people."

"So why..."

"Why did I marry him?" Dellea nodded at Perrin's question. "Actually, you two are not so dissimilar. He too is uncomfortable around people, but his reactions are different. While you are awkward and ill-at-ease, he gets boisterous and pompous. When we are alone, I see the true Darus. He is a caring and loving man and husband. The fact that I see past his faults just draws us closer. I wish others could see him as I do. Perhaps someday."

Dellea had a hard time believing Perrin's words. Being compared to that bully annoyed her, but she had to consider Perrin's explanation. Why else would this beautiful daughter of Su'Meeryn nobility agree to marry that exasperating man? Yes, a union with Darus would bring her family closer to the king and Hellet; however, Dellea could see no trace of deception in Perrin's face. But regardless of the truth of Perrin's statement, what difference did it make? She was married to one of Hellet's closest friends, so they would be friends of a fashion. Plus, the fact that Perrin was not put off by Dellea's quirks was a good sign.

"You know him better than I do," Dellea conceded. "I appreciate you sharing this with me. Perhaps it will make things easier."

Perrin stood from her chair, walked to the other side of the table and gave her guest a ferocious hug. Dellea flinched at the physical affection, which was far more than she had even shared with Hellet, perhaps more than she had received in recent memory. While she appreciated the gesture, it only increased her unease. Maybe Perrin sensed that as Dellea did not return the embrace, and she quickly let go. "Well," Perrin said, "we will have plenty of time to get past this. Maybe someday we will look back to today and laugh, but for now, let's go shopping."

Without waiting for an answer, Perrin pulled Dellea up from the chair, and then led her by the hand, out into the sunshine and towards the market.

The two young ladies walked about the market, and Perrin chatted about so many topics that Dellea lost track. As it was one of the first nice spring days, the area was bustling with activity. Vendors bellowed out their sales pitches while customers haggled over prices. The scene was unnerving to Dellea, but if she must endure the chaos, she was pleased to have Perrin as her guide.

They stopped at a jeweler's table, and Dellea eyed a necklace with a leather band and a sparkling star-shaped pendant. When Dellea mentioned the idea of purchasing it, Perrin laughed at her calling it a trashy trinket and pointed out an exquisite broach of silver and gold. Dellea examined the broach; she found it gawdy, so she commented that it was too expensive. Perrin offered to purchase it for her, but Dellea refused. With a shrug of her shoulders, Perrin led her away from the table to browse elsewhere.

By the end of the afternoon, Perrin had purchased a dainty orange and silver scarf along with a pair of emerald earrings. As they headed away from the market, Dellea thanked Perrin for the lovely time together then headed straight back to her room. The day had so physically and emotionally exhausted her that she ate a quick dinner alone on her bed. Once finished, she stretched out, thinking of the necklace she liked. Why had Perrin called it trash? It was just a piece of jewelry. She liked it well enough. Perhaps she would return to the vendor and purchase it the following day; after all, what difference did it make what others thought? But she could not ponder the dilemma further as her fatigue overwhelmed her and she fell asleep.

***

She stood on a plain, alone. The sun was overhead, and its rays beat down on her. The warmth felt pleasing on her body, and when she glanced down, she saw that she was naked. Dellea wanted to cover herself, but she had no garments. The warmth then turned to heat, and her skin turned red and hardened. Her flesh began to crack, and she cried out in pain. Her head turned to the sky pleading for relief, but no clouds shrouded the blazing sun. Her misery increased as the blue sky turned a deep shade of purple. The sky continued to darken as the sun disappeared, but the blistering heat remained.

She dropped to her knees and wrapped her arms around her body, trying to block the heat, but the temperature continued to rise. Her agony grew as welts emerged on her skin. She cried out again as the sky above turned black. She could see nothing, but then she heard a rustling. The sound grew to a roar and drilled through her ears into her brain. She sobbed as a wind began to flow across her tortured body. The brisk breeze offered some relief from the grueling heat, but the wind intensified and beat against her blistered flesh. She screamed in pain, begging for the torture to end. Mercifully, the wind ceased, and the sky once again turned blue.

Despite the cloudless sky, a light rain started to fall, and it washed away the battered welts and all her misery. She fell onto her elbows and stared at her reflection in a puddle that had formed before her. The water rippled, distorting her image. When the rain stopped and the puddle was still again, her reflection had changed. Hellet's face was gazing back at her, but he was barely recognizable. His skin was covered by blood, and his expression was one of immense sorrow.

She woke with a shout, dripping sweat, and the bright light of the morning sun shone through her window.

# chapter 27

WHILE HE MIGHT NOT BE KING IN HIS HOMELAND, Travyn could not complain as Mephosh was the next best thing, and his loving wife ruled with him. If Ut was to be believed, soon he would rule over Su'Meeryn and—following that—the entire land. And the new king had no reason to doubt his closest friend. Ut had proven to be trustworthy, and there was no reason to begin questioning the god's messenger now. To have finally received a position of power—which he so richly deserved—was exhilarating.

He reached down and grabbed a strawberry from the basket by his side. The berries had ripened early, and they tasted sweeter than ever, but then everything seemed to taste better since he had received his crown—another benefit of monarchy.

Travyn glanced over at the queen's empty throne and was, as always, thankful that he had not been forced to marry that stupid girl from Pathum. The decision to cancel the betrothal had been the sole time Orrin had been anything less than cruel to him, but that one kindness did not erase the past. Soon Orrin and the rest of Travyn's family would join the former king of Mephosh as sacrifices to the gods, and that was just fine with him. He often thought on the day that he smashed Naren's skull. Though he had never killed a man before, the death did not bother him in the least. It was what had been required to put his wife and himself in their rightful place. The thought of killing again was of no concern. In fact, he looked forward to the day he looked into his brother's cruel red eyes as Orrin received his just due. He was just disappointed that the overthrow of Su'Meeryn would be delayed. He could not understand why Ut counseled patience. Well, at least he would enjoy the advantages of ruling while he waited; besides, the strawberries were delicious.

Other than the continual presence of his royal guards, the palace hall was empty. Travyn sat on the throne, peering up at the candelabras dotting the ceiling, wondering how they got there, when his wife finally entered the chamber. While he still found her beautiful—far more than Dellea—she had seemed disheveled and distant these past months, and Travyn was uncertain why. Perhaps it was the ongoing illness she was struggling with. Though she always appeared healthy, her ailment routinely kept her away from the marriage bed. So Travyn figured the lack of love making had much to do with her demeanor.

She sat on the throne and gave him a look he could not decipher while her hand tapped the arm of her royal chair. "Who are we meeting with today?" the king asked.

"I received a message that Ut was returning, and he wanted to see us first thing," Ellaniya answered.

"He is? Why didn't I get the message? I am the king."

"Of course you are, my husband," Ellaniya replied as she patted his wrist.

"That's right. Now, when will Ut be here?"

The queen took in a deep breath as her eyes slowly closed, then she let out a long sigh. "I don't know; I was just told this morning."

"Very well," Travyn replied as his eyes gazed about the hall. "Let's get on with it."

"We will, as soon as he arrives." Ellaniya's hand then reached up to his face and gently began to stroke his cheek. He sensed the desire in her, but he was afraid her illness would once again prevent her from joining him this night.

Travyn turned to her and smiled. He bent down and gave her a kiss before turning back to the chamber doors. "Are you feeling any better?" he asked. "Have the healers helped at all? I worry for you, my love."

"No. My ailment lingers, but I hope we can be together again soon."

"As do I." The pair then sat quietly for some time before the portals opened and Ut strolled in.

"Ah, what a pleasure to see my favorite royal couple," Ut declared enthusiastically with a clap of his hands as he marched towards the dais. "It has been far too long."

"Where have you been, Ut?" Travyn asked.

The handsome man's head tilted slightly to the side as his eyes darted to Ellaniya then back to Travyn. "I've been busy working on plans to further our mutual desires. The gods have required much of me. I am their servant, after all."

"And what might those plans be?" Ellaniya asked before Travyn could respond. "If I may ask."

A smile formed on Ut's face. "Of course you may, my dear," he replied softly. "Our plans have changed—"

"What?" Travyn interrupted. "What has changed? I'm still going to be emperor, aren't I?"

The smile disappeared from Ut's face as he turned back to the king. "The goal itself has not changed," he snapped. "We are just going to go about it in different fashion." Travyn's mouth opened, but Ut raised his hand to stop him before he could speak further. "Changes are coming in Amyon," the messenger continued in his normal, velvety tone. "The queen recently died, and the king is infirmed. I believe their son would be sympathetic to our cause. Ellaniya, I think you should travel there and make overtures to the prince. He could be a strong ally once the king is dead.

"As for you," Ut continued, turning to Travyn, "we need to start preparations for our next move. The gods have decided that our first objective is to conquer Shekul. It is a smaller kingdom than Labyn and will fall to our forces quickly."

"If I may, my forces aren't very strong at the moment," Ellaniya pointed out.

"Do not worry, my dear. As I have mentioned previously, I have many allies. I will supply a mercenary force powerful enough to overwhelm Shekul. Once conquered, the strength of Mephosh will grow, and then we conquer Pathum."

"Excellent!" Travyn bellowed as he sprung from his throne. "When do we attack?"

"Soon, but I want the queen to travel to Amyon first. They are the strongest northern kingdom. Once we are allied, the other kingdoms will be too afraid to respond against us."

"Are you certain it is wise for me to travel all that way?" the queen questioned.

"Yes, especially in her condition," Travyn interjected as he sat back down.

"What condition is this?" Ut questioned sharply with the faintest trace of a scowl on his exquisite face.

"She has been too ill to—"

"It is nothing to be concerned about," Ellaniya interrupted. "I will be able to do what is required of me."

"Good. You are the only one I trust to undertake this vital mission." For some reason, Ut glanced at Travyn before turning back to Ellaniya.

"Will you be joining me?"

"Unfortunately not. I have other matters requiring my attention. I must continue the process of gathering all the mercenaries and slowly bringing them here. I do not want them to arrive all at once as spies might decipher our plans and prepare against us." Ut paused for a moment and offered Ellaniya a warm, reassuring smile. "But do not fret, my dear. I have the utmost confidence in you and your devotion to the gods. You will do what needs to be done, and you may trust that I will most ably provide for your safety."

"And I trust you too!" Travyn interjected as he sprung once again from his seat and grabbed Ut by the shoulders. "This will be glorious!"

Ut's smile reinforced Travyn's pleasure in the moment. Of course, he would miss his wife while she traveled to Amyon; however, he would soon be leading an army into battle. Labyn or Shekul, it made no difference to him. Conquest was at hand, and soon he would be emperor. Orrin would be quaking on his pitiful throne.

And yes, the strawberries tasted even sweeter.

# chapter 28

ELLANIYA WAS NOT SURE WHY, but her library seemed smaller with Ut sitting across from her. While she remained drawn to the man, she did not view him in the same way since killing her brother. Most nights remained plagued with her horrific recollections, and there was nobody in the kingdom with whom she could share her angst. The one attempt to confide in her husband had been pointless. He was completely unmoved by the event, and she wondered why she had tried to talk to him. There also seemed little reason to bring it up with Ut, since the plan had been his idea. Vor provided some diversion from her thoughts, but his visits to her bed did not remove the memory of her hands stained with Pharen's blood.

"I thought you were leaving. Why are we meeting again?" the queen asked. While she had attempted to keep her voice even, she was afraid an accusatory tone had snuck in.

"We need to discuss your mission," Ut replied, seemingly oblivious to her question.

"What is there to discuss? You've been very clear."

Ut ran his fingers along the spine of one the books resting on her table. He picked it up and began to leaf through the pages. "I see that you are continuing your religious studies, my dear." She nodded, confused by his change in subject. "The gods are a glorious group, are they not? But from where did they originate? A few predate the formation of our world, but not all—as you know. Most of the texts are unclear regarding this matter. One needs to search deeply to uncover the truth.

"Many of the gods began their existence as humans, just like you. A precious few of the truly devout servants are granted divinity and join the gods after completion of a great and sacrificial task. And you, my dear, are one so blessed to be afforded that opportunity."

Ellaniya felt a giddy excitement brewing within her that nearly pushed away the ever-present image of her blood-stained hands, but then a thought came to mind. "What about Travyn? You previously mentioned his assent too."

Ut inexplicably laughed at her question. When he had previously mentioned the opportunity to join the gods, Travyn had been included in his promise; now he only spoke of her. But instead of responding to her question, Ut asked, "Do you love your husband?"

Ellaniya was taken aback and did not know how to answer. She certainly did not love Travyn, but while he might be an ignorant, prideful fool, she did not hate him, and he was obviously devoted to her. While the lack of intimacy was far from ideal, their marriage bed had been pleasant enough, when she decided to join him. "No," she decided to blurt out. She figured there was no reason to lie as Ut clearly knew the answer.

"Your husband has a role to play, but it is not likely that he will survive to the end." He then gently returned the book back to the table. His eyes locked on hers, and it felt like he was peering into her soul. "I hope you do not have a problem with that."

The queen had no idea how to answer. What did this mean? Would Ut require her to kill her husband too? "I may not love him, but I don't want him to die."

"Of course not, my dear." The words flowed from Ut's mouth like a sweet wine filling a chilled flask. "I don't want him to die either, but, unfortunately, it is likely to happen. I ask again, is this a problem?"

She looked down at the book that Ut had been holding then back to him. "My loyalty is to the gods; I will do as they ask."

"The gods are pleased with your response, and you may rest assured that Travyn's life will not be placed in your hands."

"I'm glad to hear that, but what does any of this have to do with my mission to Amyon?"

"It has everything to do with it, my dear. As I mentioned in the royal hall, the king's son would be a strong ally. Though ambitious, he does not have our piety. Fortunately, his lack of faith will not be an issue. If our plans mesh with his, he will do what we ask of him."

"I still don't understand."

"Your marriage with Travyn may not be what is best for Mephosh in the future. A joining between you and prince Mennum of Amyon will do much to strengthen our position. This will help secure the divine empire, and Mennum will have no qualms with our objective of further establishing the gods back to their rightful place."

Ellaniya was astonished at Ut's words. She had manipulated Travyn into their marriage to further her own ends, but now she would be forced to marry someone else?

"Divinity awaits my dear."

She thought again of her father and brother. Looking down at her hands, fingers began to absently rub at her palm in a feeble effort to scrape away the phantom blood. She then thought of Lynna and Sul. The once mighty Mephosh had suffered so much due to the vile religion, and so had she. It was time to finally eliminate any trace of the heretics. If Travyn needed to be sacrificed, and she would be required to take a new husband, so be it. It was not the outcome she would prefer, but if her obedience helped reestablish the worship of the gods throughout the land, she would do what was needed. Her fingers stopped rubbing as she gazed at the white skin of her palms. Her hands were clean.

Her eyes rose to Ut's welcoming face. "When do I leave?"

"Soon," Ut replied, placing his hands on hers. "Very soon."

After Ut had left, Ellaniya remained alone in her library. Religious texts sat haphazardly about the half-empty shelves. She found that a sad illustration on the state of the faith in her kingdom. The queen was certain that in days past the shelves would have been overflowing with tomes detailing the gods and all their mighty deeds. But despite all she had done—and sacrificed—there was still so much more work to do.

As she stood to leave her private sanctuary, she noticed the bowl resting on the table. Half a dozen strawberries glistened from the candlelight. A slight smile crossed her face as she thought of her husband. Would he really have to die? Would she be forced to marry another man that she did not even know? But those sparse shelves seemed to be calling to her; they needed to be filled. If that meant she would have to marry this prince from Amyon, at least she still had Vor. He was the man she desired, and none of Ut's plans threatened that relationship.

Another glance at the bowl made her wonder if she should join Travyn for the night. It might be a wise choice to keep him satisfied since she would be leaving Mephosh soon. But that thought made her feel like she would be betraying Vor. The irony made her laugh.

She grabbed a berry from the basket and slowly bit into it. The tasty juice burst forth, and she enjoyed the sweet flavor. However, she still had to wonder at Travyn's inexplicable elation for the red fruit.

Following a pause, she popped another strawberry in her mouth then made way to Travyn's chambers.

# chapter 29

DELLEA STOOD FEARFULLY BEFORE HER BED. The hour was late, and she heard no sounds from the dark street beneath her window. She had spent a pleasant day with Hellet and the wolves, but Dellea now felt completely alone. She was tired, but the thought of sleep was terrifying, and the soft bed looked menacing. Her nightmares were coming more frequently, always one of the same two she had previously experienced. Would she ever find peace? Even in the welcoming hearth of Su'Meeryn, suffering followed her.

With a sigh she dropped onto the corner of the bed, her eyes still locked on the blackness outside her window. She wrapped her arms around herself as she turned her thoughts to Hellet, hoping to carry a vision of him into her sleep. She thought of how his youthful body was filling out and that he was growing more attractive with each passing day, but that is not what mattered to her. The bond between them had nothing to do with his appearance, but she could not lie to herself, it was a fortunate bonus.

A deep yawn escaped her mouth, and she knew she would not be able to fight off sleep much longer. With a sigh of resignation, she wormed her way under the blankets, trying to maintain the memory of Hellet's face and the pleasant day they had spent together, praying those thoughts might influence her dreams. But she was fast asleep before she could think on him further.

***

The rocky crags of a small hill plummeted to green grass below. The sky above was a brilliant cobalt with a few billowing clouds like islands in a tranquil sea. A warm breeze enveloped her body when suddenly the hill morphed into a mountain with Dellea atop the summit. She turned and Hellet was standing beside her, gazing over the landscape. Dellea's eyes followed his, and they saw castles of various sizes, but one building dwarfed them all. A variety of shades of golds and silvers sparkled from its massive walls, reflecting the light of the sun. She glanced down, and the mountain was now covered by snow, though the air was still warm.

Hellet turned to her and smiled. He reached out his hand, and she wrapped her fingers around his. His head turned back to the valley below while Dellea's eyes remained on him for a moment longer before she too looked down. The wind was picking up speed and Dellea felt a drop in temperature.

Below, the stones of all the castles began to crumble away. The rocky debris melted into the earth as blood began to flow in every direction, seeping through crevices in the uneven ground. As the blood slowly disappear, Dellea realized that the foundations on which the castles had been built was not earth. They had stood upon mounds of corpses.

The mountain then transmuted back into a knoll, and the only things she could see were the mangled and mutilated bodies of the dead. She tried to look away, but her head would not turn. No matter how hard she tried, her neck refused to move, and her eyes would not close.

Her body began to tremble until she felt fingers gently grasp her chin. Slowly the hand turned her face away from the carnage and death. She was then staring into the eyes of her love, but he was no longer the Hellet she knew. His hair was thin and gray, and wrinkles covered his face. Hellet offered her a grin, but she remained unsettled. Above the smile, she saw an unimaginable sorrow in the depths of those beautiful blue eyes. He pulled her to him and wrapped his arms about her. As she melted into his embrace, her trembling ceased.

**\*\*\***

Her eyes opened, and she squinted into a golden-orange light pouring over her bed. She sat up, the nightmare remaining vivid in her mind, just like the other two. Though this dream had not been as terrifying as the others, the vision of the mangled dead left her trembling. She slowly stood and grabbed her chamber pot, thankful that—while still terrifying—this nightmare was not as torturous as the others. But she remained unsettled. She could not shake the feeling of being surrounded by so much death, but at least Hellet had been with her, though he was an ancient version of himself. And what of that sorrow she saw in his eyes?

Dellea tried to shake the visions away as she dressed. Her anxiety was slowly dissipating as she headed down for a quick breakfast. Once finished, she was to meet Wairren before he had to arrive at the stables.

It still seemed odd that the only remaining cleric in Su'Meeryn had to continue his hard labor, but Hellet often told her that they were fortunate Orrin still allowed Wairren to practice his religion at all.

While spring had arrived, Dellea chastised herself for forgetting to grab her cloak in her haste to leave for Wairren's home, still shaken by her dream. A chill remained in the early morning air as she trotted down the street.

Though she was pleased to have an appointment to divert her thoughts from the nightmare, Dellea was growing weary of these meetings. Wairren's ramblings were exhausting, but perhaps he could give her some insight into her dream, though she doubted it.

While she had no strong desire to meet with the cleric, those times at least provided her with a distraction. Until the date of her marriage the following year, she remained seen as a visitor in Su'Meeryn with no official responsibilities. When Hellet was busy with his training and schooling, she would spend time in the stables with the wolves: feeding them and repairing the damage they constantly made to their stall. When those tasks were done, she would take them out for hikes around the castle and secure their food. But these chores did not take up a full day, so any additional activities were welcome.

She was also starting to spend more time with Perrin. With each passing day, she was becoming more comfortable with Darus's wife. They would chat in Perrin's home or stroll about the markets. They would occasionally visit Darus's family, which was dreadful. As much as she disliked Darus, his brother Rance was even worse. Somehow Rance was more obnoxious and condescending than his older brother.

As she approached Wairren's home, Dellea's thoughts drifted away from Perrin and back to her dream. Her nightmares were the one thing in her life she found even more revolting than Rance, so she hoped this meeting with Wairren would finally provide some insight. If she did not receive some respite soon, Dellea had no idea what she might do to get relief.

After taking a deep breath, Dellea knocked on the door. "Come in, come in!" Wairren bellowed in a joyful tone she had not heard before.

Entering the home, Dellea was shocked at what she saw. In the past, she had always been greeted by disorder, but now the entire room was organized. All the scrolls and books had been stored away, and it appeared that Wairren might have actually cleaned the room. The air smelled fresher than normal, which was an unexpected treat.

"What happened here?" she asked as she sat down at the rickety table.

"Happened? What? Oh," he chuckled. "I guess you're not used to seeing order in here. I'm not either. Ha! I couldn't sleep, and I decided to make use of my time." He smiled broadly as he sat down next to her.

"I had another dream last night. It was different than the other two. While unsettling, it wasn't as terrifying as the others."

"Tell me."

Dellea recounted the dream which remained completely clear in her mind. As she spoke, Wairren nodded his head, and she thought she saw an expression of satisfaction on his dark face.

"Good, good, that's very good," he said when she had finished.

"Good? What do you mean by that? What's so good about it?"

"It seems to mesh with the epiphany I had last night. Yes, it's all starting to make sense."

"An epiphany, huh? I assume you'll enlighten me."

"Yes, of course I will." His countenance beamed in gratification at his own accomplishment, but then the smile faded, and a shadow crossed his face. "As I've told you countless times, there is an evil brewing, and I'm afraid it will surface soon. And I am convinced it will erupt from Mephosh with your former fiancé."

"Travyn?" she replied, shaking her head. "I realize he's the new king there, but he's not smart enough to carry out some grand, evil plot," Dellea pointed out.

"Perhaps, but there is more involved than just him and Ellaniya."

"And what might that be?" she asked.

"I don't know yet, but your dreams are intertwining with my vision. This is not coincidence."

"But what's this epiphany you had? You've been talking about a threat for months now. And what does this have to do with my dreams?"

"I was getting to that before you interrupted me." He took a drink of water then continued. "As you well know, I have long said that Hellet and you would face suffering, but now I understand why. During my mediations last night I received a revelation. Your future husband will have a vital role to play in the fight against the evil, but it is you, Dellea, who is the key. You are the cornerstone of the forthcoming conflict. Everything hinges on you. Don't you see?"

"Me! That's ludicrous. What could I possibly do?"

Wairren stood from the table and walked to the shelf. He pulled out a book then handed it to Dellea. "Do you know what this is?"

Dellea glanced at the bare cover as she took it from his hands. "No."

"This is The Book of Sul. I assume you've heard of it." She nodded. "Have you ever read it?"

"No," she repeated.

"Well, I want you to read it. And not just read it, but study it."

"Why? What good will a book do?"

"The answer is in there, and before you ask me, I don't yet know what that answer is. I will continue to study as well. That's all I'm aware of right now: that the book is crucial. Your dreams are pointing us in a direction, and you will be the key that unlocks the door to victory. However, what you are to unlock, I'm uncertain."

Dellea shook her head in disbelief. While she was willing enough to visit Wairren, she was exhausted with his ramblings about evil and suffering. But was it because she did not want to believe the old cleric since she had finally found some joy and peace in her life? And now this? It all sounded ridiculous; however, she could not shake off those terrifying visions from her nightmares.

"You've grown tired of these visits, yes?" Wairren asked, seeming to sense her thoughts. "I know you question if it's all been a waste of time."

His eyes softened with sympathy as she opened the book. "I wish it was just a waste of time and that you were nothing but a foolish old man," she replied, "but I fear that's not the case."

"If only that were so my young friend." Wairren's hand then grasped her shoulder before he sat back down. "Unfortunately, I have nothing more to offer today; I can't force revelation. Read the book, study it. Then we will talk further."

# chapter 30

THE DINING HALL WAS FULL, BUT HELLET SAT AT THE HEAD TABLE alone with Neffy and Darus. It was not that he wanted to avoid the others in the chamber, but he was aggravated. The three friends had just completed their sword training, and, as usual, it had not gone well. The fact that Hellet excelled at any endeavor he tried—except combat—was supremely frustrating. Why did he struggle so with a blade? The relentless teasing he received from his friends did not help matters, nor did the realization that both seemed to have mastered the sword at early ages. And Neffy's prowess was so well known, discussions had already started as to when he would be appointed the leader of Su'Meeryn's military. Hellet did not begrudge his friends their mirth at his expense, but still, he would like to become at least competent with a weapon.

"Well, a king isn't required to fight his own battles," Darus quipped between bites of his roasted chicken. "So you're fortunate there!"

"Leave him alone," Neffy retorted with a soft punch to Darus's shoulder. Darus shot the large boy a sneer but then just laughed before taking a last huge bite of his chicken.

Hellet gave the two a bemused look. The banter of the three had become redundant of late, but somehow he found that comforting. With the memory of Wairren's dire predictions, he told himself to enjoy these light-hearted moments, but he was still annoyed.

"I just don't know why it's so difficult for me. I…" As Hellet's voice trailed off, he looked down at his own meal, which he had barely touched.

"What, the wonder boy is frustrated that he has to struggle with something?" Darus asked.

Neffy tried to camouflage a giggle as he stuffed a roll into his mouth. Hellet could not chastise his friends at the ribbing, even if it was growing tiresome. He knew they had heard all their lives what a special child he was, and that certainly took a toll.

"I'm glad I can give you two such enjoyment," Hellet replied dryly.

As he did not want to rebuke his friends, Hellet was grateful when the conversation changed to when his marriage to Dellea would take place, along with the typical badgering of Neffy to find a wife of his own. Darus mentioned how much joy he was experiencing with Perrin and admonished Neffy to not wait too long to find a bride.

After servants removed their plates, the large form of Darus's brother emerged from the kitchens. Despite his youth, Rance towered over his older brother. He was about the same age as Hellet, but already rows of fat were visible across his gut. "I've brought you dessert," he mumbled from the thin lips which were surrounded by his pox-scarred face.

"Thank you Rance," Hellet replied as a delicious appearing pastry was placed before him.

"I guess we'll never find you on the training field, eh Rance," Neffy said as he snatched his plate from Rance's hand. "The kitchens seem to be the only appropriate place for you."

"Leave him alone," retorted Darus, with no trace of playfulness in his tone.

"What's the matter, Rance, can't stand up for yourself?" Neffy replied. "Need your brother to fight your battles?"

Rance's mouth hung open as his head swiveled between his brother and Neffy. "I said to leave him alone," Darus repeated. "The kingdom needs chefs as well as warriors."

"And the kitchens are perfect for Rance," Neffy mocked as he reached out and patted Rance's ample belly. "The ladies need company."

Darus shot up from his chair, shoved Neffy's hand away from his brother and glared down at him. Before Neffy could stand, Hellet grabbed his arm to keep him seated. This scene was also growing tiresome. Everyone in the castle knew that Rance was supremely annoying, but Neffy seemed to have a stronger dislike for Darus' brother than anyone else, even more so than he did for Travyn. Hellet did not particularly like the boy either as Rance was even more obnoxious than his brother, and Rance was often belligerent. But Hellet tolerated Rance as best he could. Darus was well aware of his brother's reputation, so he made sure to defend Rance at every opportunity. It had only been through the friendship between Orrin and Rance's parents that he had been permitted to train in the kitchens. If not for that grace provided by the king, Hellet had no idea where Rance would have wound up. Perhaps he would have been assigned to the stables with Wairren to haul away manure.

"Enough of this," the prince ordered. "Thank you for the dessert, Rance," he said as sincerely as possible.

Rance glanced at Hellet, but as he turned back to Neffy he threw the last pastry in Neffy's face before storming off.

With his skin turning red from around the cream, Neffy wiped himself clean, avoiding the stare from Darus.

"You deserved that," Darus said with a humorless chuckle.

"He's lucky you're his protector," Neffy responded, "otherwise I'd give him a solid thrashing."

"I said enough!" Hellet commanded. "We all know of your dislike for Rance, but you need to act differently. He is the brother of our friend, and I expect you to offer him some respect."

"I will give him respect once he deserves it," Neffy replied.

Hellet's eyes closed tightly as his fingers attempted to rub the frustration from his temples. He turned to Darus who remained silent. Darus was no fool; he knew how Rance was viewed, but that just made him more protective of his brother.

The three sat quietly for a moment, and Hellet realized that the entire hall was silent; all eyes were turned to the trio. Darus then reached out a hand, wiped off some cream which remained on Neffy's cheek then shoved it into his own mouth with a laugh. Neffy scooped up the mangled portion of pastry from the table and flicked the gooey substance at Hellet. As they all began to laugh, the tension in the room lifted, and Hellet heard the murmuring of conversations resume.

With his mood improving, Hellet offered his pastry to Neffy which was graciously accepted. After the desserts had been consumed, the three left the table and began once again to chat about Hellet's future marriage. Hellet hoped this would be the last incident with Rance, but he knew that was unlikely. However, he took solace in the fact that the three always got past their discord. If a face full of pastry and the annoyance of Darus' brother was the worst strife he would need to deal with, he would be pleased. However, with Wairren's words hanging over his head, and Dellea's recurring dreams, Hellet doubted it.

***

"How did the training go?"

"Like all the other times. I don't know why, but I just can't improve with the sword, or any other weapon. It's very frustrating."

Orrin's ruby eyes seemed to glisten in the flickering flames of the candles in his private sitting room. Hellet knew how his father's appearance put many people ill-at-ease, but Hellet could see the sympathy in the king's face. "Keep at it."

Hellet slouched into his chair and looked up at the portrait of Kieran, hanging on the wall next to the king. He then thought of the time years ago when Jaleph had called him into this very room. Hellet had been much younger then, and he recalled how Jaleph's advanced age made him uncomfortable. He now wished he had been able to get past his unease and spent more time with his great-grandfather. But he had just been a child, and he refused to blame himself for his childish reactions; however, he still felt a pang of guilt.

"I remember meeting with Jaleph in this room," Hellet stated as he turned to his father. "He wanted me to know what it would take to be a good king, but he never said anything about sword play."

"Jaleph was renowned for his skill, but I hope it's the case that you never have to use a sword. However, you should be prepared nonetheless." The shade of the red eyes seemed to brighten as Hellet saw the look of concern on his father's face. After all the death their family had experienced, he knew Orrin wanted only the best for his son.

"I have been preparing. I've been preparing my whole life. But it seems my time could be better used in other areas. I should be meeting Wairren along with Dellea."

Orrin's eyes again seemed to darken, which is exactly the reaction Hellet expected, but he did not care. He felt compelled to broach the subject again with his father—even though he knew what the response would be.

"We will not discuss this topic further," and Hellet heard the aggravation in Orrin's voice. "I will not have you wasting your time with that old fool. If Dellea wants to study with him, that's her choice. As long as I'm around, you will keep to what is actually necessary."

"But father, Wairren's warnings, and Dellea's dreams. And we can't forget what happened in Mephosh."

"My brother is an idiot. He's no threat to anyone, except himself."

"You do know he hates you, right?"

Orrin took a deep breath, and his head dropped as his shoulders slumped. "I don't know what else I could have done; I tried my best with him." The king looked up and Hellet saw a sadness in his father's face that he had never witnessed before. "I tried to protect him from others, and himself, but you know how he is. Despite everything, he's a proud man. Maybe his pride is so pronounced because of his short comings, but what do I know?" Orrin paused as his gaze began to scan the ceiling. "He's always been difficult to deal with, and I'll admit that I lost my temper with him too many times. He is my brother after all. You two are the only family I have left. I…" As the king searched for his next words, the look of melancholy intensified. "I thought it would be best to send him away, that way he'd be someone else's problem. Perhaps it was cowardice on my part, and I should have ordered him to remain here with Ellaniya, but I just wanted a break from him, especially since I had to establish myself as king. It seemed like a wise decision; maybe it was a mistake."

Hellet sat silently, amazed at the lengthy confession Orrin had just offered. While Hellet loved his father, and appreciated how Orrin always treated him, he had never known the king to be this vulnerable. "I thank you for telling me all this, but isn't that all the more reason for me to be studying with Wairren? If he's correct in his concerns, we need to—"

"Enough!" Orrin bellowed, and the sudden vitriol startled Hellet. "You are not to speak of this again!"

The door then flung open, and an angry Jenna glared in. "What's going on in here?"

Orrin's angry face had taken on the hue of his eyes, but the skin quickly reverted back to its original color after being confronted by his wife. No matter how angry Orrin became, that ire could not remain in Jenna's presence. And Hellet knew it was not solely due to the affection between his parents. After all the death they had experienced as a couple, Orrin had sworn he would never do anything to add to his wife's grief. It was a promise that he always kept.

"Your son and I were having a discussion," the king replied calmly.

"It sounded like more than a *discussion*." Jenna's knowing scrutiny passed between the two before coming to rest on Hellet, making him extremely uncomfortable. She was clearly demanding a response from him, but what was he to say?

"A small disagreement regarding my training schedule," answered Hellet.

"Hmm," was the only reply as Jenna eventually turned her stare back to Orrin.

The king stood from his chair then offered his hand to his son. Hellet grasped it and Orrin helped him up. "Come, let's have a meal as a family," his father stated.

The trio left the room, and though Hellet was pleased that his father's anger had dissipated, he was also concerned that nothing had been accomplished. He remained convinced that peril loomed over Su'Meeryn, and they were doing nothing to prepare for it. While Travyn certainly could not pose a threat to their kingdom on his own, Hellet could not dismiss what had occurred in Mephosh. They still did not know what exactly had happened to the king and Pharen, but Hellet was certain it had been something nefarious. Could Ellaniya have had something to do with the death of her family? He felt certain they should not remain idle because of his uncle's shortcomings and Orrin's hardened heart.

As the door closed behind them, Hellet thought he could feel the portrait of Keiran peer at him through the stone wall. It made him wonder if Jaleph and she would have responded differently.

# chapter 31

TENSION IN THE PRECEDING MONTHS HAD GROWN as reports continued to surface of pagans attempting to establish worship within Labyn. Whenever they were discovered, Gorhum had immediately put a stop to their practices. The restrictions troubled the king greatly as he did not like limiting the freedom of any of his citizens, but he was adamant that he would not give the pagans a foothold in his kingdom. Being aware of the tragic history between Su'Meeryn and Mephosh, Gorhum did not want religious conflict festering in Labyn. Plus, Gorhum had become a staunch convert of the true faith after the arrival of the great prophet years ago.

Tollan sat in his bath after finishing his latest training session with Max, pondering these developments, and feeling even more inadequate than ever. He had seen the difficulty Gorhum was facing, and if his father was struggling, how could he expect to measure up when he became king?

"What's troubling you, my heart?" He heard the sweet voice behind him, but Tollan did not turn. "I can see the tension in your shoulders from here."

"The same as always," he replied as he tried to relax his muscles in the warm water.

He heard his wife's soft steps approaching, then Adria dropped down behind him and began to rub his shoulders. "Did the sparring go well?"

"Well enough," he replied as he leaned back, enjoying the massage. "I'll never be as good as Max, but my skill is improving. I suppose I'm the equal of many of my father's soldiers."

"That's good," Adira replied as she stopped the massage, grabbed a rag and proceeded to wash her husband's back.

"If my father is still struggling dealing with these pagans, how will I ever manage?" Tollan asked as he turned towards Adira.

Her dark green eyes probed his as she dropped the rag into the water. "I've told you countless times, my heart, that you don't give yourself nearly enough credit. You are a wonderful man and husband. You're smart and kind, and all Labyn loves you. You'll be a fine king. I know it. Max knows it—"

"What have you said to Max?" Tollan angrily asked.

Adira reached over and began to stroke his chin. "You need a shave," she commented with a smile. "I've said nothing to Max, but we do talk. He is a good and loyal friend. And he knows the kind of man you are."

Tollan could feel the conflict in his face soften and he regretted his harsh words. "Forgive me Adira. You know how much this all troubles me, but that's no excuse to be short with you."

"I know, my heart. And I know you worry it's your fault that we remain childless. But we are still young. I've heard of many couples that took an even longer time to conceive."

Adira's soft, caring face caused his affection for her to amplify, and he almost forgot his worries. "Perhaps we should try now," he said, preparing to rise from the tub. However, at that moment, a wince crossed her face, and her hand went to her stomach.

"I'm sorry, but not now. I was feeling a little queasy this morning, and it seems to have returned."

Tollan rose, wrapped a towel around himself and helped Adira to the bed. "What is it?"

"Don't worry," she said through a smile as she stretched herself out. "My stomach has been turning a little. I think I just need to rest."

"I was supposed to meet with my father; do you want me to stay with you?"

"No, I'm sure I'll be fine. Do what you need to do. I'll be here when you're finished."

Tollan bent down and kissed Adira on the forehead. She did not seem warm, so he felt it would be safe leaving her alone to rest. He took a moment to look at his wife as she closed her eyes, and he—not for the first time—marveled at her beauty. After dressing himself, he kissed Adira again and made his way to his father's chamber.

Upon entering the room, Tollan found Gorhum sitting alone, his head resting on the table. At the sound of the door opening, the king looked up, and Tollan was stopped short. In the low light of the chamber, it appeared the stress of the pagan situation was taking its toll. His father looked haggard and frail, as if he had aged a decade since Tollan had last seen him.

"Ah, there you are," Gorhum said as Tollan approached. When he sat down, Gorhum's appearance returned to normal, but Tollan was left with the realization that his father was aging. He tried to push the thought aside as the king asked, "Are you okay? You looked troubled."

"Adira is feeling a little sick, but she said she'll be fine after some rest."

"That's good, but keep a watch on her. I don't want anything to happen to my beautiful daughter."

"Of course."

"Now, I have a task for you—well, you and Max. There's been another report of a large group of pagans trying to set up a temple in the village. Take some men out there and deal with it."

"Me?"

Gorhum regarded his son a moment before responding. "Tollan, I know that you've done your best to not burden me with your concerns, but I'm your father, and I've seen it in your face. You doubt yourself; however, rest assured, I have nothing but confidence in you." Before Tollan could respond, Gorhum raised his hand to stop the prince. "We need not speak of it. Take care of this matter, and you will see that you are more than capable.

"Now, go get Max and take enough soldiers so that you don't have any problems." Gorhum then rose from his chair and waited a moment for Tollan to stand as well. "I have some traders to meet with, and I will have your mother check in on Adira."

"Thank you father. I shall handle it."

"I know you will."

***

A dozen soldiers trailed Tollan and Max as they marched under the castle gate and towards the village. "I'm glad you're at my side," Tollan said quietly to his friend as his hand went unconsciously to the hilt of his sword. The prince had swung the weapon in countless training sessions but never once to inflict harm. He prayed it would not happen this day.

Max grasped his friend's shoulder. "We'll deal with them."

Passersby and merchants stared at the group as they made their way down the street, past a few taverns and tradesmen's buildings until they reached their destination on the outskirts of the village: a large barn adjacent to the first field of farmland. Aside from a few animals milling about, they saw no movement.

As they started to work their way around the building, Tollan motioned for the guards to draw their weapons. When they reached the large door, Max also unsheathed his blade; however, Tollan kept his own sword resting in its scabbard.

Before reaching for the door handle, Max turned to Tollan. The prince stood motionless for a nervous moment. This is it, he thought. While he had spent many hours with his father dealing with merchants and guildsmen, this would be the first true test of his royal heredity. Would he make his father proud? He was about to find out.

At a slight nod of Tollan's head, Max took a step, grasped the handle and pushed the large double door inwards. He then rushed in followed by half the soldiers. The other half remained behind Tollan as he too entered.

The inside of the barn was well lit by large windows as well as gaps in the rotting wood. A handful of unknown men and women were within the ancient structure. One older woman wearing a black robe was in the center of the group. She stood before a large basin, emptying a dark liquid into a jewel-covered container; was it blood? Towards the back of the barn, a few men were moving a large idol of a dove while another woman—who wore a white cloak—was sitting on her knees before a huge tome. They all turned towards Tollan and his men with looks of indignation on their faces.

"What are you doing in this holy place?" the white-cloaked woman asked as she stood and stepped away from the immense book.

"I am Tollan, prince of Labyn," he replied, hoping he managed to camouflage his nervousness. "And you know why we're here. Practice of the pagan religion is outlawed in Labyn." He stood as tall as possible and placed his hands on his hips. He made sure to not grasp his sword hilt as he did not want to make the confrontation appear more adversarial than it already was. The last thing he desired was for it to end in violence.

"We are not pagan," the woman replied with an air of haughty arrogance. "We are worshippers of the true religion, the true gods, not like you heretics."

Tollan and Max exchanged a look while Tollan contemplated how to best manage the tense situation. Gorhum had given him no instructions other than to resolve the problem. While he had spent the entire time marching to their destination thinking through the possible scenarios he might face, he now had to put something into motion. He hoped his father would approve.

"I'm not here to debate religion with you. We both think we're correct. Whether it is you are me is irrelevant. My father's orders are clear."

"Truth is the only relevance that matters."

Tollan noticed Max fidgeting next to him, and he raised his hand towards his friend before addressing the woman again. "As I said, I'm not going to debate you." The prince then turned to his soldiers. "Take care of these *items*."

The warriors moved forward and began to smash the idol and the altar with their swords. One man grabbed the book, ripped out the pages and shredded them.

The woman glared at Tollan, appearing like a snake preparing to strike. "You have no right," she hissed.

"I have every right," Tollan replied, letting the volume in his voice increase slightly. "I am the prince of Labyn."

"We will remember this," she stated as the remaining guards forced the pagans from the building.

"And I will learn who owns barn. We will be watching. Now, begone!"

The woman and the others made their way through the field, heads glaring back to Tollan and his men.

When all the artifacts of the pagans were destroyed, Tollan and most of the guards started back towards the castle while a few of the others remained behind to identify the owner of the barn. "You did well," Max told his friend, slapping him on the back.

I suppose I did, Tollan thought, and for the first time in his life a small portion of his fear and uncertainty faded away.

# chapter 32

IT SEEMED THAT ALL PERRIN EVER WANTED TO DO was go to the market, but that was the last activity in which Dellea desired to participate, especially in the cool rain that had lasted for the past few days. Perrin would often chide Dellea about not presenting herself properly as a princess from Pathum and future queen of Su'Meeryn, and Dellea would wonder about the comment; why did she not care about having the finest clothes and jewelry? She was not opposed to pretty things. Maybe it was a backlash at growing up with her father. If she started to dress as a princess, would that, in a way, be a subtle approval of her family? She did not know the answer to her own question, and she did not care. She was happy with her clothes and her appearance, and Hellet was too. She saw no reason to change.

As an alternative, Dellea proposed that they head to the stables to visit the wolves, but Perrin just laughed. While Dellea knew her new friend was not rebuking her, she still regretted making the suggestion. Of course, Perrin would not want to sit in a smelly stall and allow wolves to climb over her. Why had she even mentioned it? Perrin also had no interest to watch the boys in their training; that would be smelly as well. As a compromise they headed to the common area in the palace to work on their needlepoint.

The room was empty when they arrived. They dried themselves off from the rain and then retrieved their fabrics from a shelf. They sat at a table and began to work as Perrin recounted a story of Darus besting Neffy in their training. When she was done, she peered over at Dellea's stitching. "What are you working on, dear?" Perrin asked as she removed the orange and silver scarf from around her neck and wiped her brow. Dellea still found the term *dear* condescending, as it seemed that Perrin acted like she was higher born than Dellea when it was the other way around. Dellea always wanted to say something when Perrin called her that, but she was afraid how Perrin might react. It was nice to have another friend other than Hellet, and she did not want to risk jeopardizing the relationship due to an inappropriate word.

"I'm trying to make a portrait of a wolf," she replied as she tilted the fabric towards Perrin when a few other ladies entered.

A chuckle escaped from Perrin's lips before she could place a hand over her mouth. "I'm sorry, Dellea. I didn't mean to laugh at you."

Dellea's face fell as she looked down at her artwork, but then she laughed as well. "It is pretty terrible, isn't it?"

Perrin sat up straight and looked directly into Dellea's eyes. "Yes. Yes it is." She grinned as she reached out across the table and grasped her friend's hand. "But who cares?" She then took her own fabric and tried to throw it across the room, but it fluttered in the air and landed on the floor next to her.

They both laughed some more, but then Dellea dropped her head into her hands, resting on the table. "How will I ever be a lady, let alone a queen?"

"You didn't learn any of this back home?"

Dellea raised her head and looked at Perrin. How could she respond? Did Perrin know anything of her past life? Had Hellet shared her stories with Darus? Dellea doubted it. Perrin clearly thought it was an innocent question, but that did not relieve the perplexity of how to answer. While she now considered Perrin a friend, Dellea was not willing to make herself vulnerable to anybody but Hellet. "No," was all she could say as she tried to hide the pain from her face.

"Come," Perrin replied as she stood. "Let's do some shopping. I want to buy you something nice."

"Thank you, but I really would rather not." She wanted to tell Perrin how much she appreciated her efforts, how pleasing it was to have another person concerned with her wellbeing, but she could not force the words out. It had been hard enough to open herself up to Hellet, and she was unable to do so with another. "You go without me. I'm going to the stables," she continued as she shoved the stitching into a pocket.

Perrin's mouth curved into a slight smile. "I understand." She then reached down and grabbed the scarf from the table. "Here, I want you to have this. And I will be personally offended if you refuse."

Dellea looked at the scarf. The silver etching twinkled amid the bright orange fabric as Perrin handed it over. While it was pretty enough, she did not want to accept it. She did not need Perrin's charity, and besides, what use did she have for it? She knew Perrin would not really be offended if she refused, but she also wanted to be gracious, so Dellea took the wrap and thanked her as she stood from the table.

Before Dellea could leave, she heard a stern voice from behind, "Where do you think you're going?"

"To the stables," Dellea replied hesitantly as she turned and saw the queen approaching.

"Sit back down," Jenna ordered, while taking the chair next to Dellea. Perrin remained standing, at a loss regarding what to do. "You may go, Perrin," Jenna continued in an authoritative tone. "I want to talk to my future daughter."

"Of course, my queen," replied Perrin. "I'll see you later, Dellea."

As Perrin exited the chamber, Dellea noticed that the other women were staring at her. But after a moment their attention returned to their own matters, and she heard them begin to whisper. Dellea then returned to her seat, her nerves rising like a loaf of bread.

"You have nothing to worry about, Dellea. I just want to talk. Now, show me what you're working on."

Dellea reluctantly pulled the cloth back out and presented it to Jenna. "It's a wolf."

The queen remained silent as she examined the fabric. "Is that so?" she finally asked.

"Well… it's supposed to be, but I guess it's not very good."

"No, it isn't."

Dellea sighed at the critique. It was uncomfortable enough being alone with Jenna, but she certainly did not need to be criticized as well. "I guess it isn't."

"Did my comment bother you?"

The queen's question took Dellea off guard; how was she to respond? Yes, it did bother her, but Jenna's voice had not been harsh, and her face looked sympathetic. Should she respond truthfully? If she lied, would Jenna know? What if she offended the queen? She would not be married to Hellet until the following spring. What if Jenna decided the pairing was a bad idea? Would she be forced to return to Pathum? Dellea looked at Jenna with her mouth agape; she had no idea how to respond.

She felt the queen's hand cover hers as Jenna peered into her eyes. "I know how difficult it is for you to interact with others. I've seen it in you, and I've talked to my son. But someday, hopefully in the distant future, you will be queen of Su'Meeryn. As such, you will need to manage difficult situations.

"Now, we both know your stitching is not very good, correct?"

"Yes."

"I could have been more tactful, but I wanted to see how you reacted. As my son can attest, I am a firm believer in honesty and the power of words. I could have selected different words—and not been so blunt—but still have been honest. However, when you are queen, you will have to deal with all sorts of people." The queen paused and Dellea saw a sly grin form on Jenna's face. "Not all will be as tactful as me.

"Fortunately, you will have Hellet at your side. He is extremely wise already, and very mature." The queen hesitated again, and her eyes—that had drifted away to the stitching—turned back to Dellea, "unlike his father."

Dellea was shocked at Jenna's statement. While she had not spent much time with Orrin, she found him to be almost the exact opposite her own father. Without taking the time to think, she replied, "What do you mean?"

"Don't get me wrong, my husband is a good man and will become a good king—though I disagree with some of his decisions. However, as you know, our family has experienced much sorrow. All the death we have seen has impacted him greatly. Perhaps it is unfair to compare them, but Hellet has dealt with our family's tragedies better than Orrin. Of course, I realize Hellet was very young for much of it, but the way he has responded surprises me.

"And there is the issue of Travyn. Orrin did his best to try to manage his brother, but it was extremely difficult. Hellet is closer in age to his uncle, so they spent much time together, and yet I don't think Hellet ever lost his temper with Travyn. Orrin saw that, and it bothered him that his young son could handle his brother better than he did. Then there was the raid that killed his other brothers. I know that—at least secretly—Orrin wished Travyn had been one of them. Life would have been much easier if Travyn's life had been substituted for another—I can't disagree with that. However, it is a terrible thing to think, and I know the thought has weighed heavily on my husband. Dealing with his brother and the guilt he felt, it was a tremendous burden.

"Hellet is remarkable boy, and though Orrin loves him more than anything, my husband is also somewhat jealous of him, which is an extremely difficult situation to manage."

Jenna reached over and gingerly took the stitching from Dellea's hand. "No, this is not very good. In fact, it's terrible, but what difference does it make? As queen, you will need to handle situations far more difficult than poor needlework.

"There are those who think the queen's role is ceremonial only, but I tell you, this is utter nonsense. In many ways, the queen's job is far more difficult than the king's. The queen must manage her husband when he doesn't know he needs managing. Granted, you will most likely have it far easier with Hellet, but even he is not perfect."

Jenna regarded the stitching for another moment before handing it back to Dellea. "I want you to keep this; don't try to make any improvements. Just keep it as a reminder of our talk."

The queen stood and gently placed her hand under Dellea's chin, turning the girl's face up to hers. "This conversation was just between us; it does not need to be shared with others. Am I understood?"

Dellea nodded as Jenna left the hall. She then looked down at the stitching, her mind racing with thoughts. How would she ever be able to handle these future responsibilities? Could she ever be as wise as Jenna? It was daunting to consider, but the fact that Hellet would be at her side when she would be navigating those uncharted waters brought her comfort.

***

After the stressful conversation with Jenna, the solitude of the stable refreshed Dellea. As usual, the wolves sensed her agitation, and their affectionate licks and head rubs immediately improved her mood. She happily cleaned up after them and inspected the wood for freshly formed damage, but a new thought did dampen her improving disposition. Though it had been several weeks since her last meeting with Wairren, she still found his last words to her troubling. How could she be the key to victory in this unknown conflict? And if she indeed was, what was she supposed to do? It would certainly be difficult to be some kind of savior when she had no idea what was required of her.

She had read through Sul's book countless times. She figured she knew every page and every paragraph by now, but what did it any of it mean for her future? Yes, Sul's journey was fascinating—and tragic— but how did it apply to her? Hellet had read the book in the past, and had reread it at her request, but he too could find no connection.

With this new sense of frustration, the wolves nestled up closer to her. She spent time stroking each, surveying the claw marks in the wall of their pen. "I'm sorry," she whispered. "As soon as this rain stops, I'll take you on a long trek around the castle."

Her soft words seemed to soothe the animals even more. Two closed their eyes at her feet while the third started to gently lick her face. It was about as pleasant of a scene as she could envision. While she did not look forward to having to make another repair to their stall, she could not blame them. Due to the steady rain, she had not gotten them outside in several days. "Soon," she said as her hands continued to stroke fur. The only thing that could have improved the moment would have been if

Hellet had been at her side. The contentment she felt in that moment was so palpable that she could not bring herself to leave. She stretched out in the straw, with the animals next to her, listening to the rain until late in the evening.

✳✳✳

When she awoke in her bed the following morning, any feeling of contentment had vanished. Her head was again full of the horrific visions of her nightmares. But they were different now. Lately they were just a grotesque jumble of images from all three dreams, and she wondered if her torment would ever end.

As she sat up in her bed, she was greeted by the now all too familiar sound of rain pelting the castle walls. Another day that her wolves would be stuck in the stables.

After her morning routine, she asked a servant if there had been any word from Wairren. When she was told no, she sucked in any angry breath and stormed down to the hall for breakfast with Hellet.

"What's wrong with you?" her fiancé asked as she dropped into the chair across from him.

"More dreams. And I read through the book again last night, but I still get no sense of what Wairren expects of me." She took a bite of bread that was on the plate before her, but as her mind remained fixated on her annoyance with the cleric, she did not taste it. Her shoulders slumped as she leaned back in the chair.

"Still no word from him?"

"No," she replied. Her eyes turned from Hellet to the tray before her. The eggs and bread looked savory, but she had no appetite. She pushed the food away as she thought about Jenna's words and her stitching. Apparently she would need to put the queen's wisdom to the test immediately with Wairren.

"I worked hard on this meal," she heard in a high-pitched tone from beside her. "What's wrong with it?"

She looked up and saw the hulking frame of the chef-in-training standing over their table. "Nothing Rance, I'm just not hungry."

"Then why did I prepare your meal? You should have sent word."

"I'm sorry Rance, but I didn't know I was going to lose my appetite. If I had I would've—"

His burly hands snatched the plate away before she could finish. "Courtesy would say that—"

"Enough Rance," this time it was Hellet who interrupted. "Your task is to the prepare the meals. If Dellea doesn't feel like eating, that's her choice. It would be best to keep in mind that you are talking to the future queen of Su'Meeryn."

Rance glared silently at Hellet, his face growing a dark shade of pink. He then stormed off, mumbling under his breath.

"I try to tolerate him," Dellea said, "but he's even worse than his brother. Until meeting Rance, I would have thought that to be an impossible task."

Hellet gave a short laugh. Her opinions of Darus and Rance were well known to him, so there was no reason for him to comment any further. "Well, if Wairren hasn't sent for you, you should go pay him a visit."

"But he's always said that I should wait for him to send for me."

"Haven't you seen him in the stables?"

"No. I guess he's only coming during the night. I'm told he wants to use the day hours to study."

"You are the princess of Pathum, and soon to be the princess of Su'Meeryn. If you wish to visit a subject of this kingdom, you should do so."

She looked into his eyes, and his words of wisdom once again reaffirmed her affection for him. "You're right; I'll do that, but now I'm starting to feel hungry. I wonder how Rance will react when I ask for my food to be returned."

Hellet's laugh was one of pure delight. "Let me," he stated, standing from his chair. And she could hear him laughing all the way to the kitchens.

After finishing her meal, Dellea decided she would first head over to the stables to feed the wolves. Then she would march over to Wairren's home and demand an audience.

***

It took multiple knocks before Wairren finally opened the door to find an angry, rain-soaked Dellea glaring at him. "What, what, what?" he barked. "What are you doing here? I didn't send for you."

"I know, but I don't care. I've been studying your book for weeks with no word from you. I know every line of it, but I don't understand what you're asking of me or how I'm supposed to use it. What do you expect me to do?"

Wairren looked over her shoulder and down the street. He then grabbed her hand and pulled her inside. "I guess it's good that you came." After she was in, he looked down the street again before closing the door.

He guided her dripping body to his table and took a deep breath as they sat. "I am asking a lot of you; I know that," he began. "I haven't summoned you, as I've had no other visions. I've been reading Sul's book too. I know it's all connected, but I still do not know how. We must keep reading.

"But I did receive a new revelation this morning. Within my other studies—reading Naar's words—and my mediations, I am now convinced. The evil I have been foreseeing is on the move. It has begun."

Dellea shivered, but she did not know if it was due to her wet clothes or Wairren's proclamation. "What do you mean, and what does any of this have to do with me?"

"It has nothing to do with you, but also everything. You and Hellet need to prepare yourselves. Your trials are about to begin."

Dellea had no idea how to react. For months Wairren had been issuing his vague, dire warnings while nothing happened, but his tone was now different. Dellea heard an urgency that had not previously been present. It was troubling, but he still told her nothing specific. "What does that mean?" she asked again.

Wairren shook his head. "I wish I knew more, but I don't. All I can say right now is that we need to be wary."

"That's always good advice," she said flatly.

"Are you mocking me, girl?"

"No," Dellea replied, taken aback by Wairren's rebuke. She had no desire to mock anyone, but she remained confused as she thought of the lesson from Jenna. She still had so much to learn regarding how to manage others. However, her current predicament was not solely dealing with Wairren and his undefined warnings. Would Hellet and she be facing some evil? The jumble of her thoughts terrified her. "I just don't know what you think I can do."

"I don't either. Keep studying, and I will do the same. And be watchful."

***

Dellea trekked back to her room through the cold rain. As the water trailed down her body, tears joined in the flow. Frustration was overwhelming her. She had no reason to believe Wairren was correct, but something within told her he was. She remained certain there was a connection between Wairren's warnings and her nightmares, but she could not figure it out. Why did happiness always have to elude her? All she wanted was to be joined with Hellet, to spend her time with him as his wife and be with the wolves. She cared not about being a princess or a queen. Was her simple desire to be with Hellet too much to ask?

The tears continued as she slowly made her way to the palace.

# chapter 33

THE SIGHT OF THE ASSEMBLED FORCES was far less impressive than Travyn had hoped. Ut had told him that this was necessary as a good portion of their still small army would have to remain in Mephosh as a defensive force. The mercenaries which had previously arrived had already left the city since Ut did not want such a large force traveling together as spies might discern their objective. So the various groups would take different routes to meet up in Shekul at the appropriate time. The small kingdom would be surrounded and easily conquered, according to Ut.

At least Travyn had that to look forward to.

The new king was excited to be leading the army, but with Ellaniya recently departed on her own mission to Amyon, Travyn was worried over leaving Mephosh without a ruler. But since Ut had assured him that everything would be fine, Travyn figured he had nothing to worry about—Ut had the king's best desires in mind, after all.

While Travyn was anxious for the coming battle, he was also a little nervous. Though he was a very skilled wrestler, he had never become competent with a sword, and he had given up training years before. However, following the overthrow of Naren, he had started combat training again, but the blade remained a struggle. After discussing his frustrations with Ellaniya, she had recommended that he switch to a hammer, which seemed to suit his strengths. While he had still not mastered the weapon, he felt his strength would compensate for any lack of skill.

The hoof of Travyn's horse combed eagerly against the dirt as his army prepared to depart. Finally, the blaring of trumpets sounded, and he kicked his horse in the flanks. With his head held high and proud, Travyn led the warriors under the castle gate, towards glory.

It was gratifying to finally be moving forward with this next step in his plan to build their empire. Soon Orrin would shiver in fear at the sound of his brother's name. That is until Travyn's hammer crashed down on his brother's skull; Travyn smiled at the thought. The years of bullying and humiliation would finally be avenged. But that brought another thought to his mind: maybe he should not kill his brother. Perhaps it would be more enjoyable to keep Orrin alive for a time so that he might see the emerging greatness of his younger and superior brother. According to Ut, Orrin would need to die for Travyn to ascend to godhood, but there was no rush. Let Orrin witness the fall of each neighboring kingdom into Travyn's hands. Once final victory was achieved, then he would gladly crush his brother's skull. What a wonderful thought, and a childlike giggle escaped his lips as he pushed his horse forward.

**✱✱✱**

Despite the late fall day, the heat of the sun forced a couple extra stops to rest and water the horses. While he knew the delays were necessary, they did little to ease Travyn's anxiousness. At the third stop of the day, he glanced around the group. Although the faces of the soldiers were familiar, Travyn did not know any of their names. With both Ellaniya and Ut elsewhere, Travyn realized that he had nobody to talk to, so he sat alone in the shade of a tree and took a few swallows of water from his wineskin. He felt the pangs of loneliness without his wife, but knowing she missed him too gave him solace. Travyn retained the pleasant memory of Ellaniya finally getting well and returning to his bed; however, that thought just made him miss her more. He tried to push those considerations aside as he pondered the forthcoming battle. He pulled out his hammer and spun it around in his hands, examining its edges. Soon those edges would be covered in blood: the next step on the road to becoming emperor and then divinity. He could not wait to begin.

After his group started moving again, they travelled for a couple more hours before stopping for the night. As the company made camp, Travyn was advised that two of the mercenary parties had just arrived. Before they left, Ut had told Travyn that a third group was moving south from Unimeth and should reach the castle at the same time as the main army.

As Travyn sat next to a fire, warming his limbs from the evening chill, a man approached. Upon acknowledging the king, he identified himself as Aniass, the leader of the mercenaries. He was tall and lean with a sinewy face. Thin strands of muddy brown hair hung down his head like branches while a think, graying beard camouflaged the host of scars on his face. His charcoal eyes regarded Travyn as he knelt onto the ground, raising his hands towards the flames.

"I am told that you are Travyn, the king of Mephosh," Aniass said in a husky voice.

"That is correct," Travyn responded, straightening his body and raising his chin.

The flickering of the fire danced about Aniass' face, reflecting off his skin, making it seem that his eyes were even darker. "Well met," he replied.

Of course, Travyn thought, who wouldn't be pleased to meet a great king. "And you."

"I believe you have our payment with you. I need to confirm our compensation before we continue to Shekul."

"Yes, the servants have the chests with your gold. You will all be paid after Shekul is in my hands."

"Very good. We will arrive in the morning. When we reach the castle I will have my men—"

"You will?" interrupted Travyn. "I am the king; you work for me. I am paying you. I lead this mission. You take your orders from me."

"Excuse me, sire, but I was instructed by Ut that I would command the assault."

Travyn sneered at Aniass. Who did this man think he was? Was he aware to whom he was speaking? How dare a mere mercenary presume to command such a mighty king? "I am the king of Mephosh, and I know Ut well. I lead. If you want to be paid, you will follow my orders."

Aniass' now-appearing jet-black eyes stared at Travyn through the dancing flames of the fire. His head did not move for a long moment until his mouth slowly opened, displaying crooked and rotting teeth. "Ut will not be pleased," he remarked.

"Ut is not here, and I command. I am king. Do you want your gold?" Travyn nearly spat. Why must he always be surrounded by idiots?

Aniass' long, thin hands braced against the ground, and he pushed himself up. "As you say, Travyn," he stated sharply. Aniass glared at the king for another moment before spinning away.

Travyn's lips curled in a sneer as he watched Aniass depart. How dare this servant address him by name? But no matter. Travyn was satisfied that he had corrected the problem of the mercenary's pride before they engaged in battle. They could not afford any confusion during the conflict.

He took another long drink of water before stretching out on the ground. Tomorrow would be glorious.

**\*\*\***

After a short breakfast, the army was quickly back on the move. Reports had reached the king that the mercenaries had captured and killed some scouts from Shekul. Travyn had to acknowledge the skill of the mercenaries, as it was likely that his army would reach the castle undetected. Not that it mattered since the force assembled to begin the empire was now quite impressive.

They passed through the outlying farms without incident. The scurrying away of the field workers made Travyn grin; he reveled in his ability to instill fear in others. When they reached the villages on the outskirts of the castle, the army easily slaughtered the few troops they encounter. However, Travyn was quite upset that he had yet to swing his hammer, but he knew the time would come soon enough.

As they approached the castle walls, Travyn heard trumpets blaring forth from the ramparts. Aniass signaled a halt as the king came up beside him. "Why are we stopping?" Travyn asked.

"We have not heard word from the other group traveling from the north. We must await their arrival before proceeding."

Travyn looked up at the parapets then to the soldiers spread out around him. "We have more than enough men to take the castle. Proceed."

"I was instructed by Ut to await the last group," Aniass replied.

"As I told you before, I am the king and I lead this army. Start the attack."

Aniass took a deep breath as he repositioned himself on his horse. "It's not just the numbers, they are bringing the siege engines. We will wait."

Travyn reached over, grabbed the reins of Aniass' horse and pulled the mercenary closer. "We have ropes and hooks, do we not? We attack."

"We will wait for the others to arrive."

"I am king!" Travyn screamed, spittle shooting from his mouth. "I am paying you, and you will do as you are ordered! We don't know what has caused their delay and even if they will arrive. Attack! Now!"

Aniass' face was turning its own shade of red as Travyn pulled out his hammer. The two men stared at each other for a long moment and Travyn wondered if the first skull his hammer would crush would be Aniass'. But before the king could raise his arm, the mercenary leader turned back to the assembled warriors and gave the order for the assault to proceed.

Dust kicked up and filled the sky as scores of boots thundered past Travyn, rushing towards the castle wall. Through the dust, arrows cascaded down from the parapets like a deadly rain. For as many soldiers that reached the castle, an equal number fell to the ground, impaled by the missiles from the aerial assault.

Ropes were spun over heads as the first group to reach the castle threw their hooks towards the parapets. Many of the hooks missed their targets and the ropes fell harmlessly to the ground. The first few that did catch were quickly dislodged and plummeted down along the wall.

The attackers continued to stream forward amidst the shower of arrows which left a trail of dead and wounded when the second group reached the wall. More grappling hooks sought purchase in the parapets as the attackers unleashed their own archers. Travyn laughed as he spotted a few of the defenders plunging to their deaths.

With Travyn's archers able to keep some of the defenders at bay, the attackers finally managed to begin scaling the wall. Arrows continued to fly towards the parapets, but some of the hooks were freed and scores of the attacking soldiers and mercenaries plummeted to the ground.

Screams from the wounded pierced his ears, and then a pungent smell reached his nostrils. Streams of liquid flowed down the walls, drenching a good number of his men. Travyn wondered what service this liquid would perform until he saw a few flickers of light racing towards it. Then with a roar the liquid ignited, engulfing countless of his soldiers in a flaming waterfall. Their screams were sickening, but Travyn refused to turn away. Soldiers die in combat, he told himself; Ut promised me an empire, and this is required.

Finally he heard the ringing of steel as a number of the attackers had gained access to the ramparts. More bodies fell as arrows continued to fly. Now that some of his men had reached the top of the wall, the number of attacking arrows dwindled considerably.

Additional hooks were hurled up, and more men began their ascent. Travyn dropped from his horse and anxiously twirled his hammer, readying himself to rush to the gate. But then another cascade of oil soaked wall and attacker alike. A renewed stench of burning flesh reached Travyn's nose after the second oily stream was ignited.

He watched as more men fell to their deaths. Burning legs and arms flailed helplessly until they mercifully hit the ground.

As more of his men continued to die at the hands of the defenders, Travyn fidgeted nervously on the ground. "What's happening?" he mumbled. "We're supposed to succeed."

"I told you to wait!" Aniass hollered at him.

The response shook Travyn as he had not meant for his words to reach anyone's ears. He wanted to respond, but what could he say? They were losing. He had been deceived by Ut. Why would the gods snatch victory away from him? He anxiously twirled his hammer as he stammered. He was searching for words, but what could he say? The attack was a disaster. What should I do? he thought. Then his confusion slowly turned into anger. This was all Ut's fault. The messenger of the gods had been supremely confident in the plan, but obviously he had been wrong. He would smash his hammer into Ut's smug face the next time they met.

Just as Travyn was about to order a retreat, he heard his own troops trumpeting back from atop the castle. They had secured the ramparts. He looked about at the bodies littering the ground like a freshly tilled field of limbs and blood. But many more soldiers waited in reserve. While his losses were great, victory might still be at hand.

His warriors continued to scale the walls, and now they did so unmolested. He heard the growing cacophony of combat from behind the walls. Weapon struck weapon and cries of the wounded filled the air.

Eventually he saw the castle gate quiver, then it was thrown open. The remaining invaders rushed forward like water from a burst dam. Travyn hefted his hammer and gleefully followed them in.

With a cry of elation, Travyn swung his massive weapon at the first defender he saw. The man raised his sword, but Travyn's hammer smashed through his defense. The hammer knocked the sword from his adversary's hand then glanced off his shoulder. The Shekul soldier groaned in pain as he tried to retrieve his weapon. That was a mistake. Travyn twirled his hammer back up and crashed it down onto the soldier's head. The weapon smashed against his adversary's helmet, and Travyn heard the metal splinter while blood flowed through the cracks. The man's body slumped as he fell to the ground.

Everywhere Travyn turned, he saw his men engaged in combat. Though the defenders were outnumbered, they foolishly continued their defense. Blood pooled around the bodies of the casualties; some quivered while others remained still. Travyn reveled in the gruesome scene as it was a righteous release from all the torment and anguish he had endured in his young life.

Travyn then noticed some movement approaching from his right; one of the defenders was being pushed back towards him by a few of his warriors. When the defender stumbled by, Travyn's hammer smacked against the man's arm. The king heard bones crack as the soldier fell to the ground. Before the other attackers could strike further, the huge hammer crushed the man's face. Blood erupted from his victim's head like a geyser and showered Travyn. The king rejoiced in the warm liquid dripping down his body. He slowly wiped it from his face, basking in his supreme combat skills.

How could I have doubted Ut? the king thought. He stood transfixed by the combat until he felt a sword brush against his leg. He turned to see a sole defenders engaged with two of the mercenaries. It was a magnificent sight; the defender was fighting them off, and it seemed that he might even have the advantage. Very impressive, Travyn thought as he raised his hammer. With a cry, he swung and struck the back of the soldier's neck. The man lurched forward, and the sword of one of the mercenaries pierced his gut.

Travyn took a moment to admire his weapon as he turned back around. He felt a wave of disappointment when he saw that the remaining soldiers of Shekul had thrown down their swords in surrender.

As his troops gathered up the discarded blades, Travyn strolled amongst the dead, searching for one man. When he finally found Aniass, the mercenary leader was almost unrecognizable. He was blanketed in gore and clumps of flesh hung from his head like a vile sleeping cap. Aniass was sucking in deep gulps of air as he tended to a cut along his left arm. The king was pleased that the mercenary leader had survived the battle, and he savored the words he was about to speak. "And you doubted me," he stated with a sneer.

# chapter 35

THE PRINCE WAS STARTING TO GROW CONCERNED. It had been a couple weeks, and Adira's health was not improving; however, at least it was not getting any worse. She had been spending all her time in bed with Wynyth at her side, and Tollan was thankful for his mother's willingness to attend to his wife while he was away serving Gorhum and the kingdom. A few more groups of pagans had been found attempting to gain a foothold in Labyn, but Tollan and Max had managed to chase them all off without violence. The owners of the buildings in which they had been meeting were found, and Tollan had them thrown into jail. With each passing day, Tollan's confidence grew like a slow budding plant. Unfortunately, any pleasure he might take from his emerging princely skills was tempered by Adira's condition.

After finishing lunch with Max, the two friends left the dining hall and made their way to the audience chamber to meet with the king. As he entered the large room, Tollan strode up to his father who was flanked by his now ever-present guards. "Ah, my two favorite people in all the kingdom!" Gorhum proclaimed as he rose from the throne. The king nodded to Max and grasped his son's arm. "Come," he said as he led the pair into his small private room behind the royal chamber.

"You've done well, my son," Gorhum stated as all three sat at his table. "Both of you."

"Thank you, father."

"We're keeping the pagans at bay, and no blood has been spilled. I'm very pleased. I'm going to release the barn owner from jail in a couple days, and the others will soon follow. They will all be advised that I will be far more strict if they welcome the pagans back on their lands again."

"Very wise," Max responded.

"Is there something else?" asked Tollan.

"Yes, I have a mission for both of you," Gorhum proclaimed. "We have been isolated for far too long. Troubling news continues to be reported from our spies in Mephosh. I want you two to assemble a large company of men and travel there as a diplomatic entourage. You will advise Travyn and Ellaniya that you come with my apologies for not congratulating them sooner regarding their monarchy, and that my desire is to enhance the relationship between our two kingdoms. But while you're there, I want you to get a first-hand look at what is really occurring in Mephosh. Spies can only tell us so much."

Tollan looked hesitantly at his father. "But what of Adira? With all respect father, due to her condition, should I really be leaving?"

The king's face softened as the regarded his son. "I know, my boy. I'm not taking this request lightly. Your mother tells me that Adira doesn't appear to be in any danger. While I have full confidence in Max, I worry that the mission would draw suspicion if you were not there. But take a few days to prepare, and I promise you, if Adira's condition worsens, I will not send you away."

"I appreciate that, father. And I am gratified by your confidence in me."

***

The scene which greeted Tollan as he entered his chamber was not at all what he was anticipating. Adira was sitting up, and a wide smile burst from her lovely face when she saw her husband. Despite the days she had spent in bed, Tollan remained stunned by her beauty, which—even through her illness—seemed to be increasing by the day. Wynyth grinned broadly as well as she regarded her son.

"What's going on?" Tollan asked with a mixture of relief and trepidation, his eyes shifting between the two women. "Has the sickness passed?"

Adira and Wynyth exchanged a glance as they grasped hands. "We've been blessed, my heart," the words almost sang from Adira's full lips. "There was no sickness. I'm with child!"

Tollan stood motionless as the words washed over him, overwhelmed by the emotions which filled his mind, and he wondered at his foolishness for the years of doubt. He had managed the problems of the pagans with skill and grace, and now Adira was pregnant. Had he been so petty to question the providence in his life? Rather than being an untested and unproven prince and future king, he now saw how blessed he truly was. Perhaps the most blessed person in all of Labyn—or the entire land.

"Is this how you celebrate such wonderful news?" Wynyth asked.

Tollan was snapped from his thoughts, and he noticed that Adira's smile had faded a bit. "Of course not!" he exclaimed as he raced forward to embrace his wife.

# chapter 36

THE JOURNEY NORTH HAD BEEN LONG AND DIFFICULT. Ellaniya was not very skilled on a horse and had never traveled so far, and it seemed every inch of her body was sore. It was with much delight and relief that they finally spotted the outskirts of Amyon, but she needed a break and ordered a brief stop for a rest before completing the journey.

The queen dropped from her horse and lamented the state of her garb. A brief rainstorm the previous day had turned the dust to mud, and when the mud dried, it left quite a mess. Of course she had brought other clothes with her, but they had been packed away for the long journey. While she would not be able to present a royal appearance, she decided that really did not matter. What did matter would be her conversation with the prince.

Ellaniya pulled some nuts from her saddle bag and popped them into her mouth. As she began to chew, the queen felt pangs of loneliness as Vor remained in Mephosh and Travyn had marched off to war. While she deeply wanted Vor with her, it had been decided he was the best person to run the kingdom with the king and queen away. It had been a strange time for her prior to embarking on this trek. Vor was the man she longed for, but she had found herself enjoying the nights she spent with Travyn. He was a skilled lover, and it certainly helped that he did not talk during their love making. She often told herself that many kings had concubines, so why shouldn't she? But no matter how she attempted to justify her thoughts, it still felt wrong lying with two men. And now she was to meet a new man who was to be her second husband. Her life had taken some bizarre turns; however, the gods were being worshipped again in Mephosh. Her true desires were finally coming to fruition, but that fact did not dispel her distraught.

After taking a moment to relieve herself behind a tree, Ellaniya gazed at the warrior Ut had assigned to help protect her. He was of immense size; she guessed seven feet in height. He wore a full suit of plate armor and a helmet that covered his entire face and head. He donned thick boots, and gauntlets covered his hands, leaving no trace of flesh visible. But the most remarkable aspect of his appearance was that his complete attire was bright red, including the huge scabbard and sword hilt that dangled from his side.

Ut had not advised her of his name, and the red warrior never uttered a word or removed his helmet. What was even stranger was that Ellaniya never once saw him eat or relieve himself during the journey. The couple times she asked if he was hungry, she had received no response; the head did not even tilt in her direction. She felt uncomfortable around this strange hulking red warrior, but she took solace in the knowledge that he was there for her benefit. She would certainly not want to be viewed as his adversary, and she assumed he would be very formidable in battle, if they encountered any trouble.

After emptying a skin of water, Ellaniya felt refreshed enough to finish the journey. On her order, the soldiers mounted up and they were back on their way to Amyon. Before reaching the castle gate, the red warrior veered his horse to the left and galloped off into the distance. Ellaniya was somewhat surprised but also relieved. She assumed that the huge man had decided she no longer needed protection and headed had off for another task. She could not even guess what that might be, but it was no concern of hers. Ellaniya figured she would see him again when the time came for her to return home, though she had no idea how he would ascertain when that might be.

At the gate, her soldiers displayed the royal insignia of Mephosh, and they were ushered into the castle. When Ellaniya advised the castle guards of her identity, and that she had come to meet with the king and prince, her troops were guided away, and she was taken down a long hallway. She was brought to a small, bare room that contained a few chairs and nothing else. She was advised to wait, and the door was closed behind her.

The queen glanced about the room, but there was nothing to occupy her attention. No decorations adorned the bare gray walls, and there was no rug to soften the cold floor. It was a very odd room to be found in a castle, and she wondered why she had been brought there as she sat down. Not a fitting greeting for visiting royalty, she thought.

As the minutes passed by, Ellaniya became more and more annoyed. Finally she angrily rose from her chair and threw open the door to find two guards standing on the other side of the wall. "What's going on?" she demanded.

One of the men turned to her. "We were told to stand guard until your host arrived."

"And who might that be?"

"I'm sorry, your highness, but I have no additional information."

With a huff, Ellaniya spun around and slammed the door on the guard. She dropped down on the same chair as her anger grew.

After a few more minutes the door opened again, and a slight man entered. "My apologies for this," he said as he sat next to her. "I hope you haven't been waiting long."

"Why am I here? Why haven't I been brought to the royal hall?"

The man stood back up, walked to the corner of the room and leaned against the wall, regarding his guest. He ran his ring covered fingers through his short, flaxen hair, then his hand dropped back to the side of his green tunic and his deep brown eyes perused her face. "I am well aware of you, Ellaniya of Mephosh. I have spies throughout the land, and I have heard of your deeds."

"You have me at a disadvantage."

"Oh, you are right, of course." He pushed himself away from the wall and sat down next to her again. "I am prince Mennum, and I thought it best if you and I meet alone before heading to the royal hall. I again apologize for the setting. Very few people know of this room. I keep it sparse to avoid drawing attention to it. It suits me well to conduct my own private business."

Ellaniya was not sure how to respond; why would the prince of Amyon have the need for such secrecy? She wanted to ask the question, but decided it was not her place, at least not at this time. "It is a pleasure to meet you," she said instead.

"Let us dispense with any awkward pleasantries," Mennum continued. "I know why you are here, and to ease any anxiety you may have, let me assure you that I am in full agreement. We have a mutual acquaintance in Ut. He has explained your situation to me, as I am sure he did likewise for you.

"I am aware of our history, and the role Amyon played in the battles between Su'Meeryn and Mephosh. But I care for none of that. It is true that Amyon was a religious leader amongst the northern lands and aided in the defeat of Lynna and Mephosh, but things are changing. Over the last decades, most of the people here have lost interest in religion. And, as far as I'm concerned, that is for the better. We sacrificed many men in those battles, and, as such, Amyon has never fully recovered and been brought back to its rightful place. My father is a weak man, and he shows no concern for the returning of our kingdom to dominance.

"I was told that you are a true believer in the gods, but to be honest with you, I don't care. Religion means nothing to me. My objective is to re-establish the might of Amyon. If that requires restoring the worship of the gods, so be it.

"Our interests can be aligned. Once your husband is dead, I will agree to marry you. When Amyon and Mephosh are joined together, we will conquer the entire land. You may establish any temples and worship as you see fit, so long as I have the power to rule. That is what Ut promised me. Do we have an understanding?"

Thoughts raced through Ellaniya's head. Ut had told her that Mennum would be a fine ally, but the prince's blunt comments had caught her off guard. Fortunately, it was a pleasant surprise. Any apprehension she had been feeling dissolved away. While Ut's plans for her mission to Amyon had been clear, Ellaniya had wondered how she was going to broach this subject with Mennum. She had rehearsed many different scenarios during her long journey, and she could have never hoped it would resolve so easily. The fact that Mennum had addressed every topic without her having to bring them up was a relief. While the thought remained that Ut was using her as a pawn atop some grand chessboard was disconcerting, at least the goal of that game was synchronized with her own desires. Besides, she had used Travyn as a pawn of her own; however, she told herself this was different. She knew full well the game that was being played, and she was a willing participant.

The fact that Travyn would need to be eliminated was troubling, but she then considered the deaths of her father and brother. Mephosh had suffered much because of the heretics. She was resolute to the plan to build this new empire and finally bring order to the land. Yes, Travyn was a pawn, and when playing chess, pawns needed to be sacrificed to bring about victory. Besides, Mennum was a decent enough looking fellow, and clearly not an idiot like her current husband.

If Mennum was not a believer in the gods, that was disconcerting, but it ultimately did not matter. All that did matter was his willingness to return them to their proper place of reverence. Conviction was irrelevant, all that was required was obedience. As long as Mennum remained obedient to her endeavors, they would get along fine.

"Yes, we are in agreement," she responded.

"That is good. Unfortunately, we should now probably go see my father."

"Very well, but, if you don't mind, I'd like to change first."

"Of course."

# chapter 37

THE ROYAL HALL WAS FULL OF PEOPLE, but only Darus and Perrin joined Dellea at her table, as Neffy had been assigned duties that evening. The celebration of the fall harvest, along with the feast, had concluded. Barrels of wine were being brought into the chamber along with jugs of ale. Though the meal was over, people were still entering the hall as the evening progressed. The room grew louder as drinks flowed, and Dellea was happy she was able to sit quietly and out of the way.

Orrin and Jenna sat at the head table with Hellet, whose eyes routinely checked in on his fiancé. Jenna had offered to have her sit next to Hellet, but he had told the queen that Dellea would be more comfortable remaining on the floor with Perrin while he performed his duties for the festival. When Dellea had asked him what those duties might be, he told her that she would have to wait and see. While the thought of sitting with Darus had been unpleasant, at least she had Perrin with her.

As the clamor in the hall continued to increase, Orrin stood and raised his hand for quiet. It took some time for the room to respond, but when it did, he stated, "I now present for your enjoyment, my son, Prince Hellet."

Dellea watched as Hellet rose and grabbed a lute that was resting behind the dais. He then took a stool and situated it in front of the royal table. Hellet sat on the stool, tested the instruments strings then turned his attention to the crowd. Dellea sat transfixed in anticipation for what would happen next.

As Hellet plucked the strings, his music filled the chamber like a thick fog rolling in across a tranquil lake in springtime. The melody seemed to reach every crevice of the hall and she could almost feel the notes and chords filling her ears. She had never heard anything so beautiful—that is until he started to sing.

Her mouth dropped open in shocked surprise. How did I not know this? she thought. Dellea sat unmoving, captivated as Hellet sang about the land and their blessings, but she soon lost track of his words, so engrossed was she with the magnificence of the performance. When the song turned melancholic, tears began flowing down her cheeks. Though she barely noticed, the entire chamber had become completely still.

Suddenly there was a crescendo in his voice as the tempo of the music increased. The room began to stir as hands started clapping. When the song reached its rousing conclusion, the entire audience sprang to their feet in a round of thunderous applause. Hellet smiled and offered a gracious wave to the crowd as he returned to his parents.

"How… when…" Dellea stammered, unable to form words. She reached into a pocket in her gown, pulled out the orange and silver scarf and dabbed at the tears that still filled her eyes. And though she rarely indulged, she took a drink of wine before continuing. "He's better than any of the traveling minstrels I've ever heard. He's remarkable."

"He's the best there is," Darus stated, pride evident in his voice. "It's pretty annoying."

"Why haven't we ever experienced this before?" Perrin asked.

"He doesn't like to perform, but he said this was special as it's the last fall harvest before his marriage."

Perrin just shook her head. "What isn't he good at?"

"He's terrible with the sword, but that's all I kind think of. He's unmatched on a horse, and he's the best chess player in the kingdom. I can't remember him ever losing."

"I was trained in chess back in Pathum," Dellea remarked. It was one of her only fond memories of home, but she did not share that. "I always thought of myself as very skilled, but I'm no competition for him."

"Like I said, it's very annoying," Darus said with a smirk.

Dellea wanted to be annoyed with Darus, but she knew he did not really mean it. Well, maybe a little. She could tell Darus was proud of his friend, but it was difficult to be surpassed in almost every endeavor. She took another sip of wine and watched as Darus finished off his mug of ale. The nervousness Dellea had initially experienced sitting with the couple had dissipated and she was surprised that she was actually having such a pleasant time.

She glanced over to the head table and saw that Hellet was looking at her with a quizzical expression. Dellea shrugged her shoulders and gave him a smile, and then she saw him relax as a bunch of nobles approached to congratulate him. She lounged back in her chair with a feeling of warmth overcoming her. How fortunate she was that, no matter what he was experiencing, Hellet's primary focus was on her and her wellbeing.

"It seems the festivities are over," Darus said as he stood. "We're heading home. Would you like us to walk you to your room?"

"No thank you. I'll wait for Hellet."

"It was a wonderful evening, my dear," Perrin said as she squeezed Dellea's hand. "Perhaps I'll see you tomorrow."

"Thank you for the company," Dellea replied as she leaned back into her chair and watched as the chamber slowly emptied. Hellet remained at the table chatting with the king and queen, and she delighted in her solitude with the memory of what she had just experienced. But then the door to the hall burst open, and Neffy rushed in directly to the king. Neffy's skin was red, and his body fidgeted in agitation as he spoke into the king's ear. When Neffy was finished, a look of shock and outrage emerge on Orrin's face. Dellea did not know what Neffy had said, but it was certainly not good.

***

"It is concerning, but I can't imagine that Travyn would attack his homeland," Orrin stated. "He may be a fool, but we are his family."

The tension in the king's private chamber was palpable, especially following the joyous festival they had all just experienced.

"He is a fool, but we can't rule anything out," Neffy countered. Orrin glared at Hellet's friend, and Neffy shrunk back a bit. "My apologies, Majesty, but I feel it must be stated."

Dellea saw Orrin's jaw clench; however, the king did not reply further.

"But why would Mephosh attack Shekul?" Jenna asked the room. "We have had peace in the land for generations."

"With whatever has prompted this aggression, we can no longer sit idle," Hellet stated.

"History tells us that peace never lasts." Orrin banged his hand on the arm of his chair, and his ruby eyes seemed to flare in the flickering torch light. He stood up and paced about the royal hall. "You are correct my son: we need to do something."

"Dellea and I should travel to Pathum," Hellet continued. He turned to Dellea, "I'm aware of your issues with your family, but we need clarify our alliance with your father since we're not yet married—in case my uncle causes further problems."

"Very good, Hellet," Orrin replied. "Prepare to leave immediately."

"I will, and I'll take Neffy and Darus with me, in case we run into any trouble."

Orrin walked up to his son and placed both hands on the boy's shoulders. "You will do well. You are a wise young man, and someday you will make a fine king."

Hellet wrapped his arms around this father, and the pair embraced for a moment before Hellet exited the room with Neffy and Dellea following behind.

***

A strong wind from the north brought a chill that caused Dellea to shiver and draw her cloak tighter around her shoulders. She peered at the trees in the palace courtyard and noticed that the leaves were already turning into myriad shades of orange and brown. On a normal day, she might have paused to admire the beauty, but nothing felt normal of late. The omen she had received during her last visit to the cleric had taken a dire turn. Wairren had been pleased to hear that they were leaving the castle, but he told them to take as many provisions as possible. *The time I've been warning you two about has come,* he had said. *You are about to enter into your long struggle. I know not whether you will return to Su'Meeryn. You will need to fight to survive, but there are allies for our cause. Find them. Our hope for victory rests in your hands. Persevere.*

Dellea drew close to Hellet as they walked to the stables, but she did not know if it was out of apprehension over Wairren's warning and having to return home or the crisp autumn air. Perhaps it was both, but either way, Dellea enjoyed the nearness of the prince. If Wairren was to be believed, they would be facing suffering very soon. She leaned in closer to Hellet and the feel of her shoulder against his arm gave her some relief.

Hellet had told her that he felt a pang of guilt bringing Neffy and Darus along as he did not want to subject his friends to their coming trials. However, he felt certain that they would need the assistance of his friends. Besides, would the pair be safer if they were to remain in Su'Meeryn?

As the couple approached the stables, Dellea's pace quickened. With all the turmoil, it would be good to be with her wolves. When the gate opened, Wairren quickly walked up and greeted them. "I wanted to make sure I saw you two before you left," he said. "I wish I could join you, but I'm an old man." He grasped Hellet by the shoulders and peered into his blue eyes. "I have every confidence in you." Turning to Dellea, he continued. "I wish I had more knowledge to provide. Keep studying

Sul's book. I'm certain the answer is there. Hopefully we shall meet again, but I'm not certain."

Wairren then retreated into the stables, and when he re-emerged, the three wolves trailed after. Upon spotting Dellea and Hellet, the animals rushed over with whines and soft barks.

"Be careful, my prince," Wairren said, "and my lady. My prayers are with you."

As the wolves happily circled the young couple, Dellea gazed at the old cleric. While their brief relationship had often been exasperating, she saw a deep look of concern on his face, and she knew that everything he had tried to do was for her benefit—and that of Su'Meeryn. It was not his fault that he did not have any answers, but it was certainly not due to a lack of effort. And despite his grumblings, he had taken good care of her wolves. While she felt apprehension at showing affection to anyone other than Hellet, she took a step forward and hugged the old man. "Thank you for everything."

"Yes, thank you Wairren," Hellet added. "Take care of yourself as well. We will be vigilant." Hellet then spun about and headed towards the castle gate with Dellea and the wolves trailing behind.

# chapter 38

THE NEWS OF ADIRA'S PREGNANCY was met with much jubilation throughout Labyn, but none rejoiced more than the king. With his advancing age and Adira's difficulties with conceiving, Gorhum had wondered if he would ever see a grandchild and if his line would continue after Tollan. If ever there was cause for a celebration, this was it. So the king had delayed the mission to Mephosh as the news of the princess' condition required a lavish party.

Tollan and Max sat with the king and queen on the platform observing the courtyard filled with the happy citizens of Labyn. Though she was feeling better, Adria remained in her room with servants attending to her needs. Wynyth had cautioned that it would be best for the princess to not exert herself so as not to risk the health of the baby.

The autumn sun bathed the courtyard as music from the minstrels filled the air. Scores of people danced, and Tollan noticed that even Max seemed to be enjoying the spectacle.

Slaughtered pigs were roasting over open fires and bales of ale were available for all. The scene was joyous; the only thing that could have improved the atmosphere for Tollan would have been having Adira at his side.

A server brought mugs of ale, and Max and Gorhum each gladly snatched one from the tray. Tollan glanced at the servant but shook his head. He had already downed a few mugs, and he did not want his senses dulled to what he was experiencing.

After finishing off his mug—some ale still in his beard and dripping down his shirt—Max shot up from his seat, slapped Tollan's back much harder than was appropriate and jumped from the platform. He rushed in amongst the dancers and pushed a befuddled young man away from a beautiful girl. He then took the girl in his arms and began to twirl her around.

Tollan heard a chuckle from his father as he grinned at the sight of Max. Yes, his friend's behavior was not proper, but Tollan appreciated that at least Max was enjoying the celebration.

A cool breeze swirled through the courtyard, and Tollan looked up at the castle ramparts. The black and gold flags flapped in the wind, causing Tollan to wonder about legacy and his heritage. Why were the colors of Labyn black and gold? Tollan had no idea, and he wondered why he had never considered that question before. He would have to ask his father about that as, after all, how could he truly pass down the legacy of Labyn to his unborn child if he could not even answer such a simple question? But if that was his biggest concern, did he really have anything to worry about?

Turing his attention back to the courtyard, he saw that Max was still dancing with the same girl. She was smiling while they danced, clearly having forgotten about her previous dance partner. Tollan assumed she was pleased with the attention she was receiving from a person of such importance to the kingdom.

The volume of the music increased as another server climbed onto the platform. Pushing aside his prior concerns, Tollan decided to take one last mug of ale. After a sip, he turned back to watch the revelry when he noticed that some of the dancers were getting rough and a few began to shove each other. Tollan wondered at the cause of the scuffle but figured it was probably due to the amount of alcohol.

"Maybe we put out too much ale," Wynyth commented as Tollan saw that a handful of the dancers were now trading blows. He glanced to his father who motioned for some of his guards to go break up the skirmish.

As Gorhum's guards jumped into the crowd, Tollan returned to his seat and took another drink. Soon the commotion would be quelled, and the festivities could continue.

While the soldiers were pulling the combatants apart, Tollan heard a cry from the crowd, "We don't forget!" and perhaps a half dozen men jumped onto the platform, rushing towards Tollan and his parents with daggers drawn.

"To the king!" a guard called as the remainder on the platform moved to intercept the attackers.

Tollan bolted up from his chair, but he had no weapon with him. He watched as an outstretched arm lunged towards his face. Before the dagger could reach him, a sword crashed down on his attacker's elbow. With a yelp, the man stumbled as blood poured from his wound. Before the attacker managed another step, the royal guard's blade pierced his heart.

Chaos swirled about the platform as more assailants jumped up. The guards tried to keep them at bay, but they were being overwhelmed. Tollan stood confused for a moment, unsure what to do. He then gathered his senses and grabbed the dagger of his fallen attacker.

He sprang at a man who was trying to reach Wynyth and drove the dagger into the attacker's back. The man collapsed as Tollan pulled the blade out. He turned to look for another opponent, but his foot slipped on the blood-covered wooden planks. As he crashed to the ground, he saw Max jump up and join the other guards on the platform. Max grabbed one of the attackers, but Tollan's friend had no weapon and had partaken in a large amount of ale. Max tried to wrestle a foe away from the queen, but the man spun about, and his blade sliced through Max's stomach.

Tollan was back on his feet as his friend collapsed. More guards joined him on the platform while the prince moved towards Max, but the attacker had spun around and was now facing the queen. Tollan darted forward, but he was unable to reach Wynyth in time. Three quick thrusts of the weapon impaled the queen's chest. As Wynyth slumped over, a guard's sword crashed down on the assailant's head while a second blade was buried into his side.

Sucking in deep breaths of air, Tollan looked around the scene. Blood was splattered everywhere. It seemed that all the attackers had been killed, but still the guards moved to surround him. Tears filled his eyes as he saw the body of his mother crumpled in her chair. Blood continued to flow from her wounds, but her eyes remained open, staring lifelessly into the sky.

He turned to the king's seat, searching for his father, but Gorhum was not there. Tollan frantically looked about until he spotted the king's still form on the ground, surrounded by blood and bodies of their foes.

With both his parents dead, Tollan dropped to his knees in anguish. All he could think of now was to find Max. His friend was nearby with two of the guards trying to stop the flow of blood from the gaping wound in his stomach. The prince forced himself back to his feet as he made his way over. When he reached Max, he glanced at the wound and saw the blood continuing to pour out. Tollan's head dropped in despair as he knew his friend would not survive either.

Max turned a tortured, painful look to his friend. "I'm sorry," he managed to say as trickles of blood rolled from the corner of his mouth. "I failed you."

Tollan stooped down and clutched his friend's hand, but it was too late. Max was gone.

Standing back up, Tollan remained in a daze. Bodies and blood surrounded him, including those of his parents and closest friend. The surviving guards started to mill about as they looked towards the prince, awaiting his orders.

"Clean up the area," he finally managed to say, "but take special care of the king and queen, as well as Max."

As the guards began to lift the bodies, Tollan commanded that others search the area for any remaining attackers. He then stumbled away from the platform with a lone guard following. All he could think of now was that he needed to be with Adira and make sure that she was safe.

He was still in shock as he made his way into the castle. Tollan could not push the visions of death away as a new thought emerged: regardless of his readiness, he was now king.

# chapter 39

"YOU FOOL!" UT SCREAMED AT TRAVYN, and the harsh tone jarred the king as he pushed himself as far back as he could into the throne of Shekul. It was not just Ut's words that shocked Travyn but also the man's appearance. Whenever he had seen the messenger of the gods, Ut always looked the same. His shoulder-length, silvery hair hung around his handsome, chiseled face. The same sparkling silver belt circled the white tunic that seemed to repel dirt. But at this moment, his delicate features had melted away. His bright and hairless face looked ashen and sunken, and his eyes had turned black and seemed to have burrowed into his skull. Even his clothes looked different. The white and silver now seemed gray and tattered. Travyn felt like he was staring at a living corpse, and it frightened him.

"I told you to wait for the last mercenary group!" Ut continued to scream. "What have you done?"

"I... I..." Travyn stammered. Instinctively he knew he was the king of two cities now, and he should not be a afraid of a mere messenger. But that thought did nothing to alleviate the fear of staring at an enraged Ut. "But... we won," he finally managed to say. "I thought I did good."

"You lost so many men!" Ut continued to scream, and with each word his face seemed to dissolve a bit more. "Now I must change my plans!"

Ut tilted his head back, and Travyn heard him suck in a long breath of air. When Ut's face came back down—to again stare at the king—he had regained his normal appearance. Travyn was deeply relieved, and he wondered if he had merely imagined the sinister manifestation he had so recently seen.

"I did not want to do this, but I will need to summon a different ally for our next step," Ut continued, his voice now perfectly calm. His menacing eyes remained transfixed on Travyn, and the king thought he saw some kind of battle occurring within the man's countenance. It seemed as if he could transform back into the corpse-like appearance at any moment, but then, as if a veil had dropped, the conflict disappeared, leaving Travyn to again doubt his own senses.

"And you will come with me when I summon my allies. I want you to see what you cost us," Ut continued harshly. "I want you to see the price of further disobedience."

"I don't understand," Travyn replied meekly. "How is summoning an ally a problem?"

Ut stood perfectly still, glaring at the king, and Travyn wondered if his companion was even breathing. For long moments Ut did not move; he did not even blink. Finally he said, "From now on, you will do exactly what I say, when I say it. Do you understand? You have been offered this opportunity for glory and divinity. Do not squander it. But, understand this, you can be replaced." With that, Ut spun around and marched toward the throne room door.

With Ut's terrifying presence no longer before him, Travyn's shock and dismay from the verbal lashing began to diminish. Who does he think he is? Travyn thought; I am the king. I am in control.

He glared at the retreating figure, and he wanted to call to his guards to apprehend this messenger of the gods. However, just before his mouth opened, Travyn thought he saw a dark aura surrounding Ut. It seemed almost like black light coming off the man's body. When Ut finally exited the room, the aura lingered for a moment, crawling up and down the wall. When the door closed, the aura seeped down the portal and slithered through the crack on the floor, as if it needed to catch up to its master.

"I guess I better do what he says," mumbled Travyn.

***

The king looked about the small hill he stood on with Ut, but it was hard to see anything. Clouds covered the night sky, shrouding both moon and stars. And the light from the conquered castle barely illuminated his companion as Travyn tried to look into Ut's face.

"What are we doing here?" Travyn asked. "I thought you were going to show me our new ally."

"That is exactly why we are here."

"But it's night and I—"

"Enough!" Ut interrupted sharply. "You will soon see."

Travyn wanted to question the man further, but the vision of Ut leaving the palace hall still filled his mind. He did not want to witness those traits ever again, so he decided it best to remain silent.

After some long minutes of uncomfortable stillness, Travyn heard what sounded like a rustling in the night. He looked up but saw nothing. The rustling grew louder, and Travyn realized the sound was not a rustling, it was more of a flapping. Off in the distance, he noticed a flicker of light approaching through the black sky. As the flapping grew louder, the light grew, and he saw that it was a flame. The flapping began to circle the pair, and Travyn saw what appeared to be a dark gray mass trailing the flame. He felt a hot wind engulf his body while enormous wings beat against the air. A trail of fire shot through the sky as a large mass crashed to the ground before them. Another flickering of flame shot above Travyn's head, and he realized that the bulky shape was an ivory white, not gray. A few whisps of fire escaped from a huge snout as a long neck lowered. The remaining flame extinguished as Travyn was able to make out a reptilian head scrutinizing the pair.

"Why have you summoned me?" the creature asked.

Its head turned from Ut to Travyn, and the king felt chills all through his body as the beast regarded him. Even though he had never seen one before, Travyn knew he was gazing into the eyes of a dragon. The fact that Ut had previously mentioned that the creatures were not myth did not alleviate Travyn's shock at actually seeing one. And hearing the beast speak was even more astonishing, but the surprise he felt at encountering the creature was chased away by terror when the dragon's eyes refused to turn away from him. The creature's mouth remained open, and a hissing sound escaped from around its huge fangs. Travyn nearly gagged from the stench billowing from the dragon's maw.

"Jokk-al Ystren, my old friend, I want you to meet my new friend, Travyn. He is the king of Shekul and Mephosh," Ut proclaimed.

Finally, mercifully, the dragon turned its attention away from Travyn; however, his horror remained. "I am no man's friend," the creature stated, "and I care not about this insignificant individual and his insignificant kingdoms. Now tell me, why have I been summoned?"

"I have a task for you, and your companions," Ut responded.

"Take care, Ut. Your trivial words are meaningless. You certainly do not propose to command my magnificence."

Travyn felt his hands begin to tremble as the acrid smell of sulfur billowed from around the great beast. "You be careful as well, my friend," Ut continued, distracting Travyn from the stench. "You are aware of whom you are addressing."

"Yes, you are well known to my kind and me. Tread lightly, for we remember your deeds of yore." Then a flicker of flame escaped from a nostril as Travyn thought he saw a smile form on the beast's hideous snout.

"Your thinly veiled threats are of no concern to me," Ut replied carelessly. With a mixture of shock and surprise, Travyn forced his gaze away from the creature and back to Ut. If his companion had no fear of this Jokk-al Ystren, Travyn did not know which of these two he should be more terrified of. "But let us move past this verbal jousting," Ut continued, "and consider the undertaking before us.

"The task I require will be simple for you and your companions. And—as a reward—I offer you this land as your next feeding ground once you are finished in your current territory."

Travyn thought he saw a look of disgust on the dragon's countenance as a few whisps of smoke escaped its nostrils. "Jokk-al Ystren ventures where he pleases," the beast responded.

"Remember, Jokk-al, I have authority over this land, and you are only permitted here if I allow it." Ut replied confidently. When the dragon's head inched menacingly closer to the messenger of the gods, Ut did not blink and actually moved slightly forward himself.

Following a deathly silent pause, it seemed that a sneer formed upon Jokk-al Ystren's muzzle. "Out of reverence to your master, I will agree, but you will be held to your promise, Ut. I shall return here when I need to feed." The dragon turned his attention back to Travyn. A bellow escaped from its fang-infested mouth, which Travyn thought might be a laugh. But what was even more vile was the aroma of sulfur which engulfed him.

"Your pitiful companion amuses me, Ut," the dragon remarked, "but make certain this is what you desire. For as per our prior agreement, there is a limit to the number of times you may call upon us."

"I am well aware of our arrangement," Ut responded coolly. "Now, prepare yourself. The summoning is complete. Take me to Pathum."

With that, Jokk-al Ystren lowered his head to the ground, and Ut climbed up its neck. Travyn had no time to process this unbelievable encounter—or wonder what Ut meant by the summoning being complete—when Ut motioned for the king to join him atop the dreadful beast.

Travyn could not decide what was worse, facing the dragon, or climbing upon its back. He wedged himself against Jokk-al Ystren's spikes, and he tried to dig his feet into the thick flesh of the beast, but that accomplished nothing. So, he grasped the dragon's spikes as tightly as possible, hoping he was secure. Ut sat in front of him, appearing to be utterly at ease.

Travyn was beginning to despise his advisor.

With a couple thunderous beats of its wings, Jokk-al Ystren lurched into the air. Travyn was nearly thrown from the creature, and he released his grip on the spikes and desperately wrapped his arms around Ut's waist as they sped off through the night sky. Travyn regretted not having a cloak or jacket, as the cold wind battered his body, and the speed of the dragon did not help.

The deafening noise from the wings above his head roared in his ears, and as the torturous flight continued, the emperor wondered if he would be able to hear once they eventually landed. And then there was the revolting stench of the beast. It seemed to be a mixture of sulfur and death. The one positive of the frigid wind was that it dissipated the stomach-turning smell somewhat. Hopefully this will be over soon, he thought. Ut had told the dragon to take them to Pathum. Travyn had no idea how long the journey would take, and he also did not know what would happen once they arrived. But he could not ponder those thoughts. He needed to maintain his focus so he would not fall off the dragon's back.

Travyn felt his fingers going numb, and he wondered if the journey would ever end when the noise of those flapping leathery wings seemed to increase. The deafening sound continued to build, but he dare not cover his ears for fear of losing his grip and hurling to the dark ground below. Then he noticed a few dark shadows joining on each side of Jokk-al Ystren. The shapes were immense, leaving Travyn bewildered as to what was occurring. Having come face-to-face with a creature out of mythology was almost more than his stunted mind could process. But this multiplication to his senses threatened to overwhelm him.

As another shadow appeared overhead, the nighttime lights of a city distracted Travyn and brought his mind back to some semblance of normality. That must be Pathum, Travyn thought as the torchlights illuminating their destination grew in size.

When Travyn was finally able to make out the castle walls, Jokk-al Ystren's neck stretched forward. The beast angled down and plunged at the city with a burst of speed that threatened to fling Travyn from its back. As the sight of Pathum grew larger, Travyn smelled an increase in sulfur. Bile rose in his throat as he gagged. He tried to restrain himself, but the bile exploded from his mouth, onto Ut's back. At that same moment, a burst of fire erupted from the dragon's snout. It flew towards the city and struck the castle wall.

More of the dark forms hurled towards the castle as flames shot out from all around him, and Travyn finally understood the meaning of those new shadows that had joined their flight. Pathum was being overrun by a fleet of dragons.

The retched aroma continued to increase as did the exploding sounds of the onslaught. Travyn still could not cover his ears as the beating of the wings and the fiery attack bore into his head like an ax cutting wood. He heaved again as the assault roared on.

With an immense jerk, Jokk-al Ystren rose up from the castle, circled and plummeted back towards Pathum, unleashing another stream of deadly flame. All around the city, the scene repeated. Countless rays of fire assailed the castle from every direction. Travyn wondered how many dragons participated in the attack, but there was no way to know.

Fire continued to strike the walls, and it became easier to see what was occurring. It was a revolting scene as the dragons continued their onslaught against the walls of the castle and the outlying buildings. Dwellings became engulfed in flames, and he saw shapes of the inhabitants scurrying for safety. They found none. Jokk-al Ystren dove again, and a screech emanated from its elongated neck. Could it be laughter? Travyn did not know, but seconds later he watched as perhaps a dozen people were incinerated as they hopelessly ran for cover.

If there were cries from the dying, there was no way for Travyn to tell. His senses were overwhelmed.

As the relentless streams of fire continued to pound the castle, the southern wall began to crumble. It eventually collapsed, followed shortly by the eastern wall. Travyn wondered how many people were crushed in the blazing rubble.

With half of the walls razed, the menacing, airborne fleet now concentrated their attack against the final two which quickly imploded. With the castle turned to rubble, the fire now sought any remaining buildings that still stood.

The stench of the dragons now mixed with the fumes of the inferno below, caused Travyn to retch yet again. He inwardly pleaded for the attack to conclude, but still the dragons released their deadly flames. Fire blanketed the ground, and the assault raged on until the remaining buildings collapsed.

And then it was over. In the light of the blazing fires, Travyn could see the horde of dragons rise high into the air and fly away. With a final snort, Jokk-al Ystren landed amidst the fiery rubble.

The dragon lowered its head as Ut stood up and dismounted the beast. Still in a state of shock, Travyn could not move. The dragon seemingly sensed his presence and shook its body. For fear of what might happen next, Travyn forced himself to stand and warily climbed down the beast's neck. When he joined his companion on the ground, his arms and legs still trembled as he absently surveyed the destruction.

With its riders dismounted, Jokk-al Ystren lifted its head and glared at Ut. "Our task is accomplished." The dragon slowly turned to Travyn, and he thought he saw malice in its huge, dark eyes. "I shall return," the beast warned as its attention returned to Ut. With that, a mighty beat of its wings brought it into the air, and Jokk-al Ystren flew away.

Travyn's eyes followed the beast until Ut grabbed him by the neck and forcefully turned him to the direction of what had once been the kingdom of Pathum. "You see this, Travyn?" Ut hissed. "This will be what becomes of you if you defy me again. Do you understand?"

Travyn remained transfixed by his vision. It was impossible for him to process what he had witnessed. He could form no words.

"I asked you a question," Ut barked. "You will respond to me."

"Yes, I understand," the king finally managed to whisper.

"Perhaps a horse or two have survived. I suggest you find one, otherwise it is a long walk back to Shekul."

Ut then turned and disappeared into the darkness, leaving Travyn alone, staring at the burning remains of the kingdom of Pathum. He was numb from what he had just witnessed. His mind could not process returning to Shekul, and he did not wonder how Ut would travel away.

His eyes remained transfixed on the smoldering ruins. The vile smell still engulfed him, and his stomach heaved again, but there was no substance left in his body to expel.

Eventually he managed to turn his gaze away, and the numbness of his mind began to dissipate. He felt the chill of the night air along his back, but his face was hot from the fires. He shuddered as he finally wondered how he would return to his new home.

# chapter 40

DELLEA WAS SURPRISED TO SEE PERRIN riding alongside Darus. Although Hellet had not requested that Darus bring his wife, Dellea was happy to have the company of another female on their journey. Of course, if Wairren was to be believed, Perrin would be facing whatever struggles that might come their way, but Dellea still wondered if remaining in Su'Meeryn would be any safer.

"Since she's never left Su'Meeryn, I thought Perrin might enjoy the trip," Darus explained to Hellet, as he eyed the wolves with suspicion.

"If you think so," Hellet replied vaguely. It had been a point of discussion between Hellet and Dellea about what they would reveal to their friends regarding Wairren's predictions. After much debate, they had decided to not say anything. What use would it serve to worry the others if Wairren was mistaken? But if he was correct, they would learn soon enough, and it would change nothing of their plans.

"That's a lot of provisions," Neffy pointed out, looking at the additional pack horse. "I thought we're just going to Pathum."

"It's good to be prepared," Hellet responded and waved for them to start, not allowing further discussion.

***

Dellea felt a swirl of emotions as they traveled north, away from Su'Meeryn. She had come to appreciate her time in the kingdom with Hellet; however, she never felt totally comfortable there. But did she ever truly feel comfortable anywhere? It was good to be getting away with her fiancé and the wolves—and Perrin to a degree, but she was certainly not looking forward to returning home. So, she felt some semblance of relief but also anxiety. It was a difficult position to be in, though she was fortunate to have Hellet with her. The visit will be short, she told herself. Then they would head back to her new home. While she still felt some discomfort living in Su'Meeryn, at least she had been welcomed. And she knew that she was slowly acclimating with each passing day.

While it was pleasurable to be out in the open, with the only ones she cared about, the thought of seeing her family caused as much trepidation as the warnings from Wairren. How would her father react to seeing her? What condition would her mother be in, and what would she have to say to her brother? The questions only increase her apprehension. She wanted nothing more than to finally put aside all the trauma of her former life, to have a start fresh with Hellet and not return to the memories of the past.

At midday they stopped for lunch. After they all dismounted, Neffy began rummaging through their packs of provisions, while Dellea and Hellet walked a short distance away from the others. They sat quietly under a tree with the wolves, until the creatures' ears went up as they whined softly. With a wave of her hand, the wolves sprung up and dashed away.

"I wonder what they noticed?" Hellet's question broke the pleasant silence.

Dellea shrugged her shoulders.

"If they are gone for a while, we won't be able to wait for them to return. We'll need to be on our way soon."

"They'll be able to find me," Dellea replied. "I doubt it will be long. When they act this way, prey is nearby. We might be able to have a nice meal before we start off again."

Hellet nodded in understanding, but then his head tilted to the side. "Why don't they kill our horses? They would be an easy meal for them."

Dellea leaned over and rested her head on his shoulder. "I'm not an expert on wolves," she replied. "I guess they realize they are part of our pack, so they don't attack them."

"I suppose that makes sense." He placed his arm around her shoulder, and she nuzzled in closer, enjoying the feel of his warm body next to hers in the crisp autumn air.

Dellea looked up towards the sky at the dark, low hanging clouds. "It seems colder than normal," she said quietly with a slight shiver.

Hellet nodded as he pulled Dellea closer to himself. "I'm sorry, we've talked so much about Wairren's warnings, I haven't asked you how you feel about returning home."

"It's concerning, but it's necessary. I'll deal with it when we arrive," she replied as she nestled further into him. "At least we're together."

He squeezed her a bit more, and she turned to him, but he was looking up at the sky. The breeze had picked up, causing the chill to increase. She followed his gaze to the clouds rolling above. His warmth was nice, and she again longed for their wedding. Soon enough, she told herself.

"Well, we better join them for lunch," Hellet said. As they both stood, they heard a crash through the trees and the wolves emerged, dragging the stiff body of a deer. They brought it to Dellea and dropped it at her feet. Their blood covered snouts then proceeded to lick the pair.

"You see?" Dellea remarked with a broad smile of pride.

"Yes, Neffy and Darus will be happy."

***

The group delayed their departure as they had cooked a portion of the deer for themselves, leaving the remainder for the wolves. Hellet had said a minor delay would not be a problem, so they enjoyed the meal, everyone except Perrin. Watching the wolves devour the rest of the deer had turned her stomach, and she lost her appetite. Neffy and Darus had found the spectacle quite amusing, but Hellet just glared at them while Dellea tried to console her queasy friend.

The rest of the day passed by uneventfully. With the gloom of twilight deepening, they stopped for the night, estimating they would reach Pathum around midday. With the wolves in their camp, Hellet decided they would not need to set a watch. So, they all managed to get a good night sleep, except for Perrin, whose face still looked green.

***

Visions of death filled her sleep. Corpses littered the ground with a strong wind rippling their torn flesh and battered clothes. She was standing on a ridge, the scene appearing like some gruesome, living mural. Then a shape moved through the carnage. The shape turned into a body, and she saw a head glancing about. This lone, living individual attempted to maneuver through the bodies; it stumbled often but did not fall. A howling of the wind pierced her ears as the figure forced its way into the gale, towards the ridge upon which she stood. When the body arrived, the head turned up towards her. A wave of grief filled her when she saw it was Hellet. But it was not the Hellet she knew. He was aged and worn. When he turned to her, tears streamed down from those soft blue eyes, through the wrinkles which etched his face towards a thin, gray beard.

She woke with a start, feeling her heart pounding in her chest. Dellea looked over a few feet away and saw Hellet, his chest rising and falling in peaceful slumber. Would she ever be relieved of these nightmares? She sat up and the wolves that surrounded her stirred. As Dellea rose from her bed roll, she saw that Neffy was already awake, preparing their

188

morning meal. He nodded to her then returned to his chore. Though the morning air was even colder than the previous night, Dellea whisked away the sweat glistening on her forehead, wrapped her cloak tightly around herself and joined him.

"You're up early," Dellea stated.

"As are you," Neffy pointed out.

"Another nightmare."

"Nightmare?"

Dellea realized that Neffy had no idea what she was talking about, and it seemed inappropriate to bring it up now. "I supposed you are trained for this," she said, changing the subject.

"Yes, it's good to be up before first light when we're in the wilderness."

Looking back, Dellea saw Darus and Perrin still asleep on the ground. "I guess Darus missed that lesson."

Neffy chuckled at her comment. "Well, our training didn't include having wives with us."

"I wonder if Perrin is regretting joining. She doesn't seem to be enjoying the trip."

Another laugh came from Neffy. "No, I don't suppose she is, but she seems to be handling it better than I expected."

"Well, I'll let you get back to it," Della said before making her way behind a bush.

Following a quick breakfast, they broke camp and were back on their way. When they had been riding for about an hour, Hellet brought his horse alongside Dellea. "I'm concerned," he whispered. "We haven't run into any scouts or sentries. I would have expected to meet some by now."

"My father never included me in any of his meetings, so I hadn't thought about that. I suppose you're right. It does seem strange."

"I guess we need to continue forward and see what we see."

After they rode a while longer, Neffy brought his horse up to them. "Where are their sentries? We should have found some. This is odd."

"Dellea and I were just discussing the same matter," Hellet replied. "We better be cautious."

"Let's slow our pace so we can keep an eye out," responded Neffy. "I don't like this."

"Agreed. Have Darus and Perrin come up and stay close."

✳✳✳

With their vigilant pace, they did not reach the outskirts of Pathum until just after twilight. Something did not seem right as they came upon the first homes outside the castle. No movement met their eyes. When they passed the first few buildings, the vision before them staggered Dellea. Other than these handful of homes they saw nothing but devastation. Everything was destroyed. Smoke rose from the wreckage, and a warmth penetrated through the cold dusk air from small fires burning in the rubble.

Dellea glanced at Hellet, and she saw a look of shock on his face. What could have done this? None spoke, and the only sound that reached her ears was the crackling of the flames. The wind brought a trail of smoke to her nose, and she almost gagged from the rancid, charred stench.

Hellet ordered a stop as they tried to peer through the gloom. Lights from the castle should have been visible, but they saw nothing. All they could see in the growing darkness was ruins.

Neffy nudged his horse forward, and the rest followed. As they continued on, Dellea flinched in horror. Below them she saw charred corpses interspersed with the debris. Some still smoldered which increased the rank odor. She heard a gasp from Perrin, but Neffy forced them all to continue. Although she knew there was no reason to proceed. If the castle still stood, they would have seen it by now.

Nothing remained of her home. Somehow Pathum had been obliterated. Surely her family had to be dead; none could have survived this destruction. Everyone she knew from her childhood was gone. She then began to cry. Her father and mother had been killed, along with her brother. She felt guilt over her dread to return home. Yes, her childhood had been miserable, but they were still her family. Now they were gone. She would never be able to repair her relationship with her father or forgive her mother. Her brother would never have the chance to mature. Their bodies must be buried in the rubble ahead, and any chance of reconciliation was buried with them.

She could go no further. She stopped her horse and dropped to the ground. The rubble of a ruined building was next to her, and she felt a warmth from within as she leaned against it. The heat brought her comfort from the cold air, but that only intensified her guilt. How could she find any comfort here?

The emotions swelled within until they burst forth. Dellea covered her face as she began to sob. She was vaguely aware that a wolf had come to her and rested its body against her side. But for now, the animals could offer her no solace. She continued to weep. Moments later, she felt arms encircle her. Though she did not look up, she knew it could only be Hellet. However, neither Hellet nor her wolves would be able to console her this day.

Tears pooled around her face like the gushing of a well as her weeping continued.

# chapter 41

"FATHER, MAY I PRESENT ELLANIYA, queen of Mephosh," Mennum proclaimed. "Ellaniya, this is Tellum, king of Amyon, protector of the true faith, and my father." Unsure of what exactly to do as she was a monarch herself, Ellaniya decided to offer a slight bow towards the throne.

The king stood from his throne and walked down the few steps to stand before Ellaniya, taking her hands. "Purple eyes," Tellum observed, "quite rare. You are a very pretty girl; the creator has blessed you. But you should grow your hair longer. The short length is unbecoming."

Ellaniya was rattled by Tellum's comments as the last thing she expected was for Amyon's king to remark on her appearance. She was also surprised that Ut had appeared to be incorrect as Tellum did not look infirmed. His cloak dangled loosely from his tall, thin body while thick, gray hair hung past his gaunt face; however, his brown eyes sparkled as he regarded Ellaniya.

"Is there a problem?" Tellum asked after a silent pause.

"I am sorry your highness. While it is an honor to meet you, the information I had was that you were very ill."

"Yes, yes, I was, but as you can see, I am much better. All praise to the creator." Ellaniya bit her lip, and she saw Mennum's eyes roll behind his father's back.

"I'm gratified to see that," Ellaniya lied.

Tellum released his grip on her hands then returned to his throne. "And I have heard news of you, queen of Mephosh. Troubling news. Now, please tell me why you have travelled all this way to my court."

Ellaniya was stymied by Tellum's request. Her mission had been to meet with Mennum and formulate their plans for conquest; she had not expected to stand before the king, especially a healthy and vibrant Tellum. How was she to respond?

"I am aware of countless rumors that have emanated from my kingdom," she began. "I thought it best to meet with you personally and dispel any falsehoods."

"I have heard many of those rumors, so please enlighten me."

The queen took a deep breath before she continued, as she needed a moment to gather her thoughts. "I don't know how those vile rumors started, but you can rest assured that my husband and I had nothing to do with the deaths of my family. I loved my father and brother. It had been a difficult enough time with the untimely loss of my mother."

Tellum's eyes regarded her with suspicion. "You still have not told me what happened."

Quickly running through the various rumors they had started, Ellaniya finally replied. "My family had taken ill while I was in Su'Meeryn. It had seemed that my father and brother were recovering, but after my wedding, they both began to deteriorate, similar as my mother. It was a very sad time for all of Mephosh as our healers were unable to save them." Ellaniya attempted to summon tears, but she was unable. Still, her hand wiped at her dry eyes.

"Very sad indeed," Tellum agreed. "Blessings of the creator to you and your husband. Now, please tell me why you are here, and why the king is not."

Ellaniya was taken aback that Tellum had so easily accepted her explanation, but now she had to formulate another lie, and quickly. Why had she not prepared herself better?

"First, let me offer my apologies that my husband was not able to accompany me," she began, trying to buy herself some more time. "He offers his greetings and regrets for remaining behind. Someone needs to run the kingdom after all."

"Of course, of course," said Tellum.

"These rumors are the primary reason for my visit. We are well aware that Amyon is the most powerful kingdom in the north, and we did not want you to be deceived by any lies. With the marriage of Travyn and myself, the bond between Mephosh and Su'Meeryn is clearly strengthened. We wanted to make sure that Amyon is aware it has nothing to fear from us. All we want is to build stronger ties with our friends in the north."

"Very well said! This is excellent news, and I am pleased you have traveled all this way to meet with my son and me. You are truly blessed by the creator. Now, let's feast!"

Ellaniya was shocked at the abruptness of Tellum's proclamation. She turned to Mennum who once again rolled his eyes. As the king gingerly rose from the throne, Mennum shrugged as he followed the king towards the large portal. Surprised by the discourse, the queen was pleased with how she had managed the conversation and the outcome.

The meal following the awkward meeting with the king had been extremely trying. While she was used to dealing with fanatical heretics after all the years with Pharen and their parents, she had been unprepared for what awaited her at the dinner table. The king's misguided piety was far worse than Pharen had ever been. The evening had been filled with his heretical babblings, and he even questioned Ellaniya regarding her theology. She had spoken enough with Pharen that she managed to muddle her way through some rudimentary answers, and it certainly helped that Tellum was a dullard. Though he was in no way as bad as Travyn, Ellaniya realized she could easily deceive him and redirect the conversation.

As the evening droned on, and drinks flowed, the queen found being surrounded by the last vestiges of the heretic religion increasingly revolting. Ellaniya knew that the bargain she had struck with Mennum would solidify the alliance between that land and her new empire, but that day was yet to come. For the moment, she lamented being subjected to such boisterous heresy.

Fortunately, when the king had finally excused himself to head to his room for the night, she was able to spend some time alone with Mennum.

"I was not prepared for your father's questions," she began. "Ut told me he was very ill, and I was unsure how to respond."

Mennum chuckled at her comment. "You need not worry. He's not very smart. You did well."

"But will his health alter our plans?"

More laughter escaped from the prince. "It changes nothing. You are a captivating woman Ellaniya. I will enjoy marrying you when the time is right. My father is starting to question me about marriage now that he's better, but I can easily keep him distracted until your marriage is over. And, while he might be better now, his health remains precarious. I foresee no obstacles. Everything can proceed as planned."

***

Ellaniya remained in Amyon only one more day, but she still could not leave the kingdom fast enough. Her discussions with Mennum had gone better than she could have anticipated, but she had been forced to spend a great deal of time with Tellum and his idiotic ramblings. While she was thankful to be leaving, she found the return of the red warrior to her traveling group unnerving. She had to admit that she felt safer having his immense form next to her, but his silent, stoic bearing made her supremely uncomfortable.

At least this leg of her journey would be shorter. Rather than returning to Mephosh, she was heading to Shekul to meet up with her husband. It was a relief that she would spend less time on horseback, but Ellaniya was displeased that it would be even longer before she was reunited with Vor.

A brisk breeze from the north brought a harsh chill on the late fall day. Ellaniya pulled out a thick, wool hat, but it did not seem to help much. She glanced about at her guards, hoping their presence would bring her some comfort, but her eyes continued to turn towards the strange red warrior riding alongside, and her chill increased.

Ellaniya then envisioned Vor's strong arms wrapping around her body, hoping that would bring her some warmth. Unfortunately, the thought of her lover did nothing to keep out the cold. What has become of me? she thought, I'm riding away from my future husband to meet my current one, but Vor is the only person on my mind. Ellaniya then thought again of her father and brother. She had conspired to kill her family and now might be complicit with the death of her husband. As she continued to ride in silence, she pondered the decisions that brought her to this point. Had she made mistakes? If left unchecked, doubt can be crippling, but regret is even worse. Did she regret her decisions? She searched her mind and once again saw the bloody corpses of her father and brother. But did she regret her actions? She would have preferred if they had lived; however, that only could have been possible if they had been true believers. They were not. How could she second guess any decision that would help bring the gods back to their rightful place? No, there could be no regrets: she was not responsible for the faulty choices of others. The excruciating time she had been forced to spend with Tellum reinforced her resolve. She could not allow idiots like him to remain, especially as rulers of powerful kingdoms. If there was any trace of doubt left, she buried it deep in the ground, like the refuse from her castle.

***

Rather than the passing of the day bringing warmth, it seemed that each southward step of the horses brought an increase to the biting cold. Winter was arriving sooner than normal in the land, and that only intensified the frost in her soul.

The red warrior rode in his customary position next to her, and she wondered again how he had known when she would be departing Amyon. The few attempts she had made to engage him in conversation had been met with silence, so she decided it was not worth attempting again.

A fresh swirling blast of wind brought a shiver up her spine and a few tears to her eyes. She wiped them away, but to her shock, more tears took their place.

She glanced about the group of soldiers traveling with her. While the warrior in red refused to speak, her soldiers did respond the few times she spoke to them. Despite their allegiance to her, she could see the fear in their eyes. They tried to mask it, but they could never fully succeed. Her warriors knew of her and her husband's deeds that day at the festival, and nobody wanted to join her family as sacrifices to the gods. The soldiers were always cordial to her, but they were not her friends. As she pondered that fact, she realized that she had no friends. Vor was the only one she cared for, but she sometimes found herself wondering if his affection towards her was simply a duty. Travyn loved her in his way, but he was not someone she could talk to. Perhaps Ut made a show of fondness for her, but she was not fool enough to believe she was anything more than his tool. Yes, a willing tool, but a tool nonetheless.

Ellaniya was surrounded by her soldiers, but while they made their way through the frigid air, she felt completely alone. And her tears continued to flow.

"Majesty," one of her soldiers said, breaking her out from her brooding, "movement from the south, and it's coming towards us."

"What kind of movement?" she asked.

The man peered forward. "It looks like riders." He paused as he continued to stare ahead. "Yes, definitely riders, six horses, and something else smaller with the group."

"Well, we clearly outnumber them, and we have him," she responded, gesturing to the red warrior. "Continue on. Let's see who they are, and what they're doing."

# chapter 42

"I COULD FIND NO SIEGE ENGINES in the debris, or any sign of how this destruction was accomplished," Neffy said as he approached Hellet.

The prince shook his head in bewilderment. None of Wairren's warnings had prepared him for what they saw. How had such destruction been accomplished? The utter obliteration of Pathum demonstrated a power of which he could not fathom. How could he be expected to fight against this? While he felt supremely inadequate to confront the force behind such an unimaginable foe, the sound of Dellea's sobs brought a level of resolution. "We must continue on," he stated.

"What do you mean!" Neffy shot back. "We need to return home and tell your father!"

Hellet forced his eyes away from Dellea and addressed his friend. "Wairren warned us that we might run into trouble. That's why we packed the extra supplies." As he turned back to the still smoldering rubble, he continued quietly, "though we could never have expected this."

"Why didn't you mention this before we left?" Darus asked angrily.

"Dellea and I talked about it. I didn't want to worry anyone in case Wairren was wrong, but if he was correct, it would not have changed anything. We still would have left on this journey."

"So, you just made this decision for us?" Darus continued as his ire grew. "I brought my wife with me!"

Anger and frustration began to grow in Hellet, and he had to take a moment to calm himself before responding. "Remember your place. We might be friends, but I am still your prince. Rightly or wrongly, I made the decision. I had no idea that Pathum was at risk, so I expect you to accept that and move on. Both of you."

Neffy lowered his head, and he nodded to himself. "You're right, of course. I apologize. It's not an excuse, but I guess sometimes we forget your position."

From the corner of his eye, Hellet saw Dellea slowly rise and approach him from the rubble-covered ground. She wrapped her arms around him, and her body heaved as sobs continued to flow. "We need to decide what to do next," Hellet replied as he reached over and grasped her hand.

"Perhaps we should head to Gorthon," replied Darus as Perrin joined him with a look of shock on her face. "We could seek refuge there."

"We could, and they might take us in. But it is doubtful they would help us against Travyn."

"How do you know this is Travyn's doing?"

"Who else could it be? Mephosh already attacked Shekul," Hellet replied. "It has to be them."

"And what do you think we can do against him?" asked Neffy. "He commands the forces of Mephosh and Shekul now. With Pathum destroyed, Su'Meeryn will obviously be his next target. We need to warn them."

"We won't be able to tell my father anything more than his spies and scouts will," Hellet pointed out.

"But what can the five of us do?" Darus asked. "We all see what happened here. How your idiot uncle was able to accomplish such destruction is a mystery. He clearly has a power under his control unlike anything we've ever seen."

"We will travel to Amyon," said Hellet. "They were one of the strongest kingdoms that helped Su'Meeryn during the time of Jaleph. Perhaps they will again."

"Let's mount up," Dellea stated as she removed her arms from around Hellet and moved back towards her horse. "I need to get away from here."

"We'll need to decide how to approach the king once we arrive in Amyon," Hellet continued. "From what we've been told, he is true follower of the faith, but I've heard that his son isn't a believer."

"What difference does that make?" asked Neffy. "The threat from Travyn is real, as we have clearly seen. Religion isn't an issue here."

"Perhaps you're right," Hellet conceded "but I would think we will have a better chance dealing with someone who is a follower of the faith."

"That didn't help Ellaniya's family," Darus pointed out.

Hellet had no response to his friend's comment. What could he say? Darus was correct, after all. Mephosh had fallen to Travyn and Ellaniya despite the king's and the prince's faith, though he was still unclear as to what had caused their demise and how his uncle had acquired the necessary forces to conquer Shekul. And that was not even considering by what means Pathum had been destroyed. He could not conceive of what force might had been required to achieve such devastation, and he was forced to wonder if Orrin was correct. Was all this talk of faith just a waste of time? What had it done for anyone?

But then he considered Wairren's words. While the cleric had warned Dellea and him of forthcoming trials and struggles, those words had not caused him to question his faith. However, Wairren had not prepared them for what they had just witnessed. Faith is easy when suffering is esoteric, but experiencing trauma is a whole different matter. And was this just the beginning of their trials? How would he react if their circumstance deteriorated?

He watched as Dellea mounted her horse, and he felt a mingled combination of both pity and pride for her. The devastation of her homeland would remain with her for a long time, if not her entire life, but she was forcing herself to carry on. If she could push forward, he would have to move on as well. This was not the time for an epistemological debate. He had a task to undertake; he would worry about theology at a later time.

***

The air grew cold as they turned their backs to the devastation of Pathum. Hellet was glad to be getting away, not just for himself, but mostly for Dellea. She had said nothing since they started riding. He wanted to try to talk to her, but he felt now was not the time. He kept his horse close to hers and would turn to her from time-to-time. She acknowledged his glances, but her familiar smile remained absent—horror still shrouding her eyes.

"Winter is coming early," Perrin nervously said from behind.

"Yes, perhaps that will be good. Hopefully winter will slow down my uncle."

"Do you really think so?" Darus asked.

"I have no idea, but it certainly won't help him."

"I suppose you're right."

"A group coming from the north," Neffy called out.

"How many?" the prince asked.

"Hard to tell, but the party is larger than ours."

It was a troubling thought that they would run into a large group on the road. While there was no reason to expect conflict, nothing normal was happening in the land. They had only two warriors in their party, and if they did encounter opposition, it would likely not turn out well for them. Dellea's wolves still trailed the group, and Hellet assumed they would be an asset if Dellea was threatened, and perhaps himself too, but he had no way to know for sure. They would have to be wary.

"Be cautious," he stated. "We don't know what we're getting into." He glanced about, getting a sense of the landscape. He saw nothing of distinction, but he knew the foothills of Unimeth were to the east. If they had to flee, that seemed like the logical destination. "If we need to retreat, we head east towards Unimeth. We could probably find places to hide there."

Neffy huffed at his comment. "But why do you—"

"Enough!" Hellet barked. "We don't have time to debate this. Perhaps they mean no harm, but after what we just saw, we need to be cautious. If we need to flee, ride east. Am I understood?"

"Do as your prince commands," Dellea ordered.

# chapter 43

THE SMALL GROUP WAS COMING CLOSER, allowing Ellaniya to make out the riders. The party consisted of three men and two women. It seemed strange that such a small group would be heading north this time of the year, especially since, despite having a pack horse, they certainly were not traders. She was not worried as her group would be able to handle them if there was any trouble, but it was perplexing. Plus, there were the animals that were following one of the women. She wondered what they might be as they were too large to be dogs.

With the small party coming closer, her vision became clearer, and excitement coursed through her body. "Wolves!" she cried. That could mean only one thing: Dellea. And one of the males must certainly be Hellet. She could not believe her good fortune. Without any effort from her, the gods had delivered their adversaries into her hands. This development made her feel shame for her recent sulking; clearly the gods still favored her. "Half of you, after them," she commended. "Capture Hellet and Dellea, and bring them back to Shekul. I don't care about the others."

The soldiers hesitated while they looked at her. "What are you waiting for!" she screamed.

"Which of us?" one of the men asked.

"I don't care," Ellaniya answered with frustration. She hesitated for a moment before continuing. "You to my left, go!"

The men then spurred their horses and raced towards Hellet's group, and to her surprise, the red warrior followed. She smiled to herself at the thought of capturing the heir to the throne of Su'Meeryn and his betrothed. Ut would have to be pleased with her initiative. Soon she would have the prince of that hated kingdom in her hands. It was almost too perfect.

But just as her men spurred their horses, their quarry tore off to the east. No matter, she thought. It might take her soldiers some effort, but Hellet would not be able to evade them for long.

***

Ellaniya's mood had improved dramatically since ordering the capture of Hellet and Dellea. The unseasonable bitter cold continued, but soon she would be warming herself in Pathum—before a blazing fire and a hot meal. It would not be long after that she would enter Shekul and be reunited with her husband. While she would much prefer the company of Vor, Travyn would have to do. She knew she would never love him, but the thought of his dumb face made her smile. He was far from an ideal companion, but she had to admit he was adequate.

Ellaniya's thoughts then returned to Amyon and Mennum. She found the prince compelling in a way. He might not be a follower of the gods, but he was honest in his intentions. They were similar, to a degree: both compelled to see their desires fulfilled. And while they had different motivations, those desires were aligned. Yes, this second marriage would be a beneficial pairing. It seemed clear that she would never marry out of love, but the abundant blessings of the gods were apparent.

Her annoying meeting with the king of Amyon then came to mind; it would be a joyous day once these idiotic heretics were finally eliminated and she had burned every last copy of Sul's book. The ultimate justice of the gods would finally be meted out against the heretics and Su'Meeryn for the harm that had been wrought against Mephosh. They all needed to pay for what had become of her kingdom and her family. She wrung her hands in fury and thought of where she would be at this moment if Lynna's legacy had thrived in Mephosh. She would likely be sitting in her warm library, studying the sacred texts and not married to Travyn, but she had done away with any semblance of regret for her deeds and choices. She was following the plan laid out for her by the gods, and there would be nothing to stop her from having the promised divinity bestowed upon her: a righteous recompense for all her sacrifices.

She did have Vor, and perhaps she loved him; however, she often wondered if the affection was reciprocal. And she had her husband. In a sense she was not lonely, though she did know she was lacking that bond she had seen between some other married couples. But how many people were truly able to experience such love? If a loveless marriage was her greatest cost to achieve divinity, she told herself it was a price worth paying.

"We should be nearing Pathum, but I see nothing," one of her guards said, interrupting her ruminations. Ellaniya should have been concerned by the man's words, but they did not immediately register within her. With her thoughts broken, she noticed the cold. Her body once again felt miserable, and her anger resurfaced.

"Highness!" the same guard called out, his hand pointing ahead.

"What is it?" she replied angrily.

"Pathum!"

Ellaniya pulled her hat down past her ears, trying to keep the cold at bay before looking up. "I don't see anything."

"Exactly! We've reached Pathum, but there is nothing here!"

"What are you talking about?" She glanced about as the scene before came into focus. All she saw was rubble—rock and stone as far as her eyes could see. Destruction was everywhere; Pathum had been obliterated. But how had this occurred? What force could raze the entire kingdom?

She saw some movement off to her right, and one of the guards spurred his horse in that direction. After a few moments he returned, dragging a disheveled woman behind. She was covered in filth and patchy hair jutted out in grimy, crusty strands. Her face displayed a wild expression as she wailed.

"Maybe she can enlighten us," her guard stated.

"What happened here?" Ellaniya demanded.

The woman's head jerked to Ellaniya. Her mouth quivered until a shriek shot out past her soiled lips. The woman then fell to her knees with her hands covering her face. The guard dropped from his horse, pulled her back up and shook the terrified woman, trying to coax out a response. "Answer the queen!"

"Fire!" the woman replied frantically. "Fire from the sky! All directions. Nighttime. Destroyed the castle, our homes! Dead. Killed everyone. Fire from the sky. How?" She wailed as she tried to break free from the soldier's grip.

"Fire from where?" the guard asked, but no further response came. He slapped her face, but her wailing did not stop. A second slap brought no additional reply.

"She's mad," Ellaniya stated.

"What should we do with her?"

Ellaniya glanced about for the red warrior, forgetting for a moment that he was pursuing Hellet. But even if he was with her, he would have provided less information than this raving woman. However, for some reason, she was certain the warrior would know what had occurred to

Pathum. She sensed that Ut must have had something to do with the destruction.

"What is your order?" the soldier asked.

"We can't just leave her here on her own," Ellaniya replied, "and I'm not taking her with us." She then kicked her horse forward as she glanced about at the devastation. Pathum had played a vital role in Su'Meeryn's defeat of Mephosh, and now they had paid the price for their treachery. A smile crossed her face as she almost forgot about the chill. "Put her out of her misery."

# chapter 44

THE LAUGH FROM ANIASS' THIN FACE did nothing to lighten Travyn's mood. His body ached from the torturous ride on Jokk-al Ystren's back, and the chill from the numbing cold remained in his bones. He had found no horses remaining in Pathum following the destruction inflicted by the fleet of dragons, but he had been fortunate enough to find a cloak in some of the debris. it had been a long, cold walk until he came upon a farmstead where he had been able to purchase a horse with some gold coins he had in a pocket. The family had provided him a hearty meal along with a hat and gloves, and while far from a pleasant trip, he had been able to return to Shekul without additional difficulty.

Though Travyn did not appreciate the mirth from the mercenary leader at his expense, he was relieved to finally be back within the walls of his newly conquered castle. He dropped to the floor in the royal hall, next to a fire and enjoyed the pleasing warmth that began to mercifully seep in through his pores.

"What happened to you?" Aniass asked the emperor with an annoying smirk on his face as Travyn angrily snatched a flask of wine from a servant.

Travyn took a long gulp from the container before responding. "Ut took me to Pathum." Following another drink, he wondered if he should say more as the memory of the destruction of the kingdom, and Ut's threatening words, hung around him like a necklace of heavy stones. Travyn did not want to discuss the trip further, and he waved Aniass away.

"What did you do there?" Aniass persisted, apparently oblivious to his dismissal.

Travyn turned away from the fireplace—the flames suddenly bringing back the memory of what he had experienced—as he allowed the heat to massage his back. He glared at the mercenary leader, but

Travyn could find no anger within himself. The only emotion he found was trepidation as Ut's threats remained paramount in his thoughts. Finally, he simply said, "Pathum is destroyed."

"Destroyed? What are you talking about?"

"It is as I said," Travyn continued, the pitch of his voice increasing. "Ut destroyed the entire kingdom!"

Aniass stared at the emperor with a look Travyn could not decipher. "And how did he accomplish such a miraculous deed?"

His companion's tone resembled that of so many others: talking to him like he was a hapless child. The familiar arrogance of this servant caused the emperor's disdain to grow. I am not a child, he told himself; I rule two kingdoms and witnessed the destruction of a third. My enemies fall by my hand, and I should be feared, not patronized. However, before he could lash out, Ut's vile face flashed before him, and his ire faded. "Dragons," he dejectedly replied. A sneer formed on Aniass' ugly face, and his mouth opened, but before the man could speak, Travyn continued. "Yes, you heard me, dragons. I was there. We flew on the back of one to Pathum while others joined; I don't know how many. When we arrived at the city, they all attacked. Fire erupted everywhere, beating down onto the castle until the walls eventually crumbled. The whole kingdom was annihilated. There is nothing left; everyone is dead."

"You flew on a dragon?" Aniass laughed at him, and it was not a laugh of cheer. It was a laugh of mockery. "And you saw others?" He chuckled again.

The disdainful tone was too much for Travyn to take. He sprung from the table and grabbed Aniass by the collar. "I was there!" he bellowed as he felt his face flush. "I saw it all! I experienced it. If you don't believe me, go find Ut and ask him yourself."

Aniass' expression barely changed, which infuriated Travyn even more. How could this minion have no fear of a raving emperor? Was he truly that feeble of a man, just a joke to those all around him? No, he told himself; I am the sovereign, and I will be respected—especially in my own hall. His fear of Ut morphed into frantic ire, and with the back of his hand, Travyn smacked the mocking grin from Aniass' face. He then shoved the mercenary with all his might, and Aniass flew into the wall as the emperor screamed, "Now get out of here and leave me alone!"

✳✳✳

The following days did nothing to improve the emperor's mood. He spent most of his time sulking in the royal chambers, only venturing out for meals. As Aniass was keeping his distance, Travyn had no one to speak to; he knew nobody else in all of Shekul. After returning to his room following his latest midday meal, Travyn dropped dejectedly onto his bed and thought, why can I find no pleasure in my monarchy?

His eyes turned to his window, and he wanted to stand and peer out to survey the lands of his new kingdom, but he could not find the energy. Instead, he propped up his pillows and gazed at the blue sky. With thoughts of melancholy, he drifted off to sleep.

The room was dark when he awoke, but he sensed a presence moving about. "Who's there?" he called out.

"I've returned, husband," the sweet voice of Ellaniya replied.

With all traces of despair immediately dispelled, Travyn shot up from the bed and embraced his wife. "I have missed you so, my love. It's been far too long."

"I'm pleased to see you as well," Ellaniya responded with little emotion, obviously exhausted from her journey.

"How was your trip?"

"The meetings in Amyon went well," she replied. "They will make a strong ally." Ellaniya then told him about spotting Hellet and Dellea on the road and that she had sent half of her guards in pursuit of them. Upon her arrival to Shekul she had immediately dispatched additional parties to search for Travyn's nephew. His wife then said who she had found Pathum totally destroyed.

"Pathum," responded Travyn, "it was horrible."

"What do you mean; do you know what happened there?"

Travyn took a moment to light a few candles so he could see his lovely wife's face. He wanted to lie to her about the ordeal, but he knew Ellaniya was the single person in whom he could completely trust. "As you know, I conquered Shekul, but Ut was mad at me. Why would he be angered regarding victory?" He paused—the memory of an enraged Ut still fully visible in his mind. "He took me to Pathum. I witnessed everything."

"Took you to Pathum? You were there?"

"Dragons, my love. I flew on a dragon—Jokk-al Ystren. And they speak! We went to Pathum, and other dragons came too. They attacked the castle and obliterated it. Dragons. Aniass didn't believe me."

Ellaniya remained silent for a time. "I figured Ut must have had something to do with it. I saw the destruction, but I had no idea how it was achieved. The old woman was raving about fire from the sky. I guess Ut was correct: dragons are not a myth."

"It was horrible—the stench and the destruction… The threats."

"Threats?"

In the dim candlelit room, Travyn stared into her soft, purple eyes. As much as he loved and trusted his wife, he could not bring himself to elaborate any further. Why bother his adoring spouse with his problems? She had just experienced much hardship by being separated from him, after all. "It doesn't matter now; we are finally together again. That is what's important."

Ellaniya wrapped her arms around him, and it was an indescribable joy to be within her embrace. Travyn guided her to the bed, and he relished the opportunity to finally share intimacy with his wife again, although her enthusiasm was lacking. She was just exhausted, he thought. After his desire had been released, Travyn quickly fell asleep with a sense of happiness and contentment he had not felt in a long time—the menace of Ut briefly forgotten.

***

Travyn sat on the throne in the royal hall of Shekul, with Ellaniya beside him, when Aniass entered and strode to the dais. The mercenary leader glared at the emperor, a yellowing bruise still visible under his eye before turning his attention to Ellaniya. "It is good to have you back, my lady," he said with much pleasure.

"Of course it is!" Travyn proclaimed. "My beautiful wife brightens every room she enters."

"I was summoned, how may I be of assistance?" Aniass asked, but he did not turn his head to acknowledge Travyn.

"Who summoned you?" the emperor asked.

"Winter is arriving early," Ellaniya replied, ignoring her husband's question, "but we can't stop the campaign. We now have the full complement of mercenaries along with the siege engines." She turned a disapproving eye to her husband, and he dropped his head in shame. "Pathum is no longer a threat and does not need to be attacked, which will help greatly due to the large number of warriors we lost taking Shekul." She paused, and Travyn wanted to protest her comment, but he decided it would be best to remain silent.

"I don't want to give Orrin any additional time to prepare his defenses," Ellaniya continued. "It will be a hardship, but we need to push on immediately."

"But we have not heard from Ut," Aniass pointed out.

"That's true, but we all know the objective. And the assault will be different this time."

The fact that he was being ignored became too much for Travyn. "How so?" he asked in a tone mixed with annoyance and desperation.

"I will be coming with you, Aniass," his wife continued, still addressing the mercenary. "We will make sure that the mistakes made here in Shekul are not repeated."

"You're going to come with?" Travyn asked. "Are you sure that's wise? It will be a difficult time."

"Yes, I'll be joining Aniass, but you misunderstand," Ellaniya replied, finally turning to her husband. "I am going. You are not."

"What do you mean? Of course I'm going. I can't miss the battle to conquer my home. I need to be there to take the throne away from my brother."

Ellaniya's face hardened, and the glare she gave him chilled his blood like the streams that would soon freeze with the early arrival of winter. Her face turned a bright shade of red and her lips quivered below her flashing violet eyes. She took a few moments to control herself before she replied. "I have an even more important mission for you, my husband."

"A mission for me, but I am emperor," he whimpered.

"Yes, you are, that is why I am appointing you to this vital task." Travyn did not appreciate the tone of his wife, but the vision of Ut returned, so he decided to acquiesce. "I want you to gather up a few more soldiers and join the hunt for Hellet. No word has returned from the searches, so he must still be at large. We need to capture your nephew so that we can fully secure Su'Meeryn. The heir to the throne must not be allowed to live."

"But we've just been reunited, my love. I've missed you."

"And I've missed you, husband; however, sacrifices are required of us to follow the gods' plan." The look upon her sweet face and the tone of her voice confirmed her despair that they would be parted again so quickly.

Travyn pondered her words, and he could find no fault with them; however, he wondered if searching for his nephew in the wintery wilderness was the best use of his many skills. His hammer still bore the stains of his slain foes, and he craved unleashing his might at the gates of Su'Meeryn. But before he could respond, Ellaniya turned back to the mercenary standing before them. "Do you have a problem with anything I've stated, Aniass?"

"Of course not," he replied with a bright smile that greatly aggravated Travyn. "I look forward to having you along on this campaign.

# chapter 45

THE HORSES CHARGED HEADLONG through the thick brush towards the foothills which were barely visible in front of them. It was difficult to read the rough terrain due to the foliage which hampered their speed, and to make matters worse, Dellea could not tell where the wolves were. But she knew they had to be close by.

"They're gaining! We have to go faster!" she heard Neffy call from behind. Dellea grunted in frustration as she leaned into the mane of the horse and kicked its flanks. The beast lurched forward, and Dellea nearly lost her grip on the reins as her fingers were starting to grow numb from the cold wind biting into her flesh.

Arrows flew from their pursuers and Dellea saw bolts strike Perrin's and Hellet's horses. However, before she could tell what happed, she felt another jolt, but this time it was not from an increase in speed. Her steed's leg buckled after catching a root, and the horse collapsed, sending her flying through the air. A scream escaped her throat as she anticipated the imminent collision. Fortunately, her body was horizontal, and she skidded across the grass when she landed. The impact expelled all the air from her lungs, and she felt her right thigh smack against a large rock. She slid for a few feet as she tried to regain her breath. If she suffered any additional injuries, she could not tell. Dellea turned over on her back, still trying to suck in air, and attempting to decipher the jumble of sounds all around her.

When she was finally able to breathe, she sat up, but all she could see was confusion. Horses circled about; however, she was unable to make out the riders. Swords were held high, and with only two warriors in their small group, they stood no chance of fighting off their pursuers. It seemed their fate would be far worse than anything Wairren had predicted. Their doom was sealed.

She heard a thunder of hooves to her left. Dellea looked up to see a horse bearing down on her, and she knew there was nothing she could do to stop it. She remained on the ground, paralyzed and helpless. As the horse approached, a gray shape sprung from her right. Fangs reached out, and a wolf's mouth grasped the beast's throat. With a squeal, the horse collapsed—its rider trapped against its bulk. The man tried to break free, but the wolf's attention turned to him, and within seconds the wolf ripped open the trapped soldier's chest. The wolf turned to Dellea with blood dripping from its snout. It glanced around her before springing back into the melee.

Dellea regained her wits and managed to turn her attention back to her surroundings, and she saw Perrin pinned to the ground by a pair of assailants. As Perrin struggled to break free, the other two wolves sprung at her attackers. Before they could tell what was happening, the assailants were forced to the ground by the beasts. Dellea heard their screams of pain as blood exploded in all directions.

At that moment, Hellet rushed to her side. "Are you okay?" he asked.

"I don't know. I think so." She felt a throbbing emanating from her right leg, but that was not an immediate concern.

"Get to the tree line," Hellet said as he unsheathed his sword. "I better see what help I can offer," he said before dashing into the fray.

As Hellet sprung forward, Dellea tried to stand, but a pain shot through her leg, and she collapsed. She winced in pain and looked up to see three men still on horses, though, strangely, one was not moving. The solitary, immense figure sat motionless on his steed, behind the fighting, watching. What was even more strange was the appearance of the warrior. Full plate armor covered his entire body, and every inch of it was a deep scarlet. Even from this distance, Dellea could tell the warrior dwarfed all the others, so she could not understand why he did not join the combat.

She pulled her eyes away from the strange warrior and saw Darus engaged with two foes. She had often heard the young soldier boasting of his skills with the sword, but he was clearly overmatched by his two opponents. Hellet was racing towards them, but that just increased her angst. While her fiancé had many skills, she knew he was lacking with a blade.

As Hellet just about reached Darus, the first wolf shot in and grabbed the leg of one of Darus' adversaries. The attacker cried out and tried to swing his sword at the wolf, but he was off balance, and the sword flew from his hand. As he fell to the ground, the wolf released his leg then latched on to his right shoulder. The man screamed again and tried to punch the beast with his left hand. A few blows struck the side of the wolf, but it did not seem to notice. The snout of the wolf then turned to his face, and Dellea turned away, not wanting to witness the man's horrific demise.

Hellet and Darus now outnumbered their enemy, and Hellet threw a few clumsy strikes at the man. The blows were easily blocked, but the diverted attention was all Darus needed. His sword struck against the man's hip. The soldier stumbled but remained standing. As he turned to face Darus, Hellet's sword smacked against his elbow. The warrior tried to turn back towards Hellet, which gave Darus his opportunity. Darus lunged and drove his sword into the man's midsection. His body convulsed as blood gushed from his mouth. Shaking hands grasped at the blade protruding through his body. He dropped to his knees and glassy eyes stared ahead. Unfortunately, his blank gaze found Dellea. She stared back as blood continued to pour from the man's wound. His eyes remained transfixed on her, and she watched in horror as the man's life drained away. Somehow his body was perfectly balanced in the squatting position, and his eyes remained trained on her, even though the last traces of life had left him.

The violence around her became too much for her to take. Dellea remained where she sat, numb; thoughts of fleeing did not enter her mind as she began to cry. First Pathum, and now she had been forced to witness these gruesome deaths. The tears continued to flow as she watched Neffy battle with the last surviving foe. They both remained on their horses, trading strikes. Neffy then unleased a dizzying array of blows which left the man off balance in his saddle. Neffy took the opportunity and rode his horse into his adversary's steed. The animal jumped aside and threw the man from the saddle. As he hit the ground, Neffy pulled on his reins and brought the hooves of his horse down onto the man's head. Dellea heard the cracking of the skull as she covered her face.

And then she heard nothing. Dellea looked back up and saw that all their attackers were now dead—all except the red warrior. Neffy turned his attention to the mounted soldier, and Dellea could tell he was wondering if he should charge the immense man. But before he could make a decision, the red warrior calmly trotted away.

Neffy turned a questioning eye to Hellet, and the prince just shrugged his shoulders. "Let him go. We need to figure out what condition we're in," Hellet stated. Neffy nodded and rode back to the group as Darus rushed over to check on Perrin who was on the ground, flanked by two bloody bodies.

Dellea remained where she had fallen, the still erect corpse staring at her. Tears streamed down her cheeks, and she again felt the ache in her thigh. She slowly forced herself to stand, but she could not turn away from the dead eyes which continued to regard her. Finally, the man's head dropped, releasing her from its gaze. Her body heaved in sobs as she collapsed again to the ground, and she felt a large tongue begin to lick her face. She managed to turn away from the corpse as she wrapped her arms around the neck of the blood-soaked wolf. The other two wolves began to howl as the large tongue continued to lap up her tears.

# chapter 46

HELLET STOOD STILL, his sword dangling loosely by his side—gazing about the grisly site. The many bodies of their attackers were strewn about: blood covered the corpses and flowed to the ground like leaking flasks. He saw only one uninjured horse, which Neffy still sat atop. One of the horses was dead and two of the wolves were feasting on the body while the third sat with Dellea. The remaining steeds had either galloped off or were in various states of injury and suffering. Their pack horse was nowhere in sight.

How none of his group had become a casualty was astounding to Hellet, but he knew the only reason they had all survived was due to Dellea's wolves. Clearly they viewed the entire company as part of their pack, and the animals would certainly be of assistance if they ran into additional trouble.

The prince apprehensively approached the two that were devouring the horse. He was unsure how they would react with him interrupting their meal. They both turned their eyes to him as they continued to pull flesh away from the body. He stopped moving and peered at them; both rose and approached him, their heads low. The crimson-stained fur of the faces nuzzled against his sides, and he rested his hands on their heads.

He then turned back to Dellea who remained on the ground with the third wolf. She looked at him with mourn-filled eyes as he approached with the other two wolves trailing behind. When he dropped next to her, the wolves all left and returned to feast on the dead carcass.

Hellet wrapped his arm around her shoulder, and the pair watched as the wolves continued with their meal. "We would be dead, if not for them," Hellet said quietly.

Dellea dropped her head on his shoulder, and he felt her body heaving with sobs. Although he did not want to, Hellet stood and pulled Dellea up with him. "We need to figure out what we're going to do now," he said. Grasping her hand, they moved towards the rest of the group, and Hellet noticed a slight limp in Dellea's steps.

"I guess we owe a huge debt to your wolves," Neffy pointed out as they approached.

"We only have one horse now?" Hellet questioned, though he already knew the answer.

"Yes," Darus answered. "The ones that are still here are either injured or dead."

"And our extra supplies are gone," Neffy pointed out.

Hellet glanced around, trying to figure out what to do. "Is everybody else okay?" he asked.

"We're fine," Perrin responded, and Hellet heard a tremble in her voice. "How is Dellea? That was a scary fall."

"I hurt my thigh, but I seem fine," Dellea answered after a final sob.

"Good to hear. We're lucky we got out of this unscathed," Neffy paused for moment. "Actually, it's amazing."

"But what do we do now?" Perrin asked. "All our supplies are gone." Hellet saw her body shaking as she clutched her husband.

Hellet glanced at the carnage, and he was at a loss for a response. Nothing in all of his training or the sessions with Wairren had prepared him for this. "That red warrior was concerning," he finally said. "I don't know why he didn't participate in the combat, but certainly he's going to report back on our whereabouts. Without our horses we will be moving slowly, and it appears winter is already here. They will know we were heading east, so they probably expect Unimeth was our destination. We need to change our plans. I think we should make our way to Labyn."

"Labyn! Are you crazy!" Neffy blurted as he came towards Hellet and Della. "Unless we can get more horses and provisions, how do you expect us to make that journey?" As he paced by the feasting wolves, two of them stopped eating for a moment as their lips curled above their teeth. Low growls caused Neffy to briefly stop before he hurried back over to Hellet.

"Don't disturb them while they're eating," Dellea advised.

"I didn't; I just walked past them."

"I guess you got a little too close," Hellet said, as Neffy looked back over his shoulder. "I know it's going to be difficult, but what's the alternative?" the prince continued. "They will be expecting us to be heading east, so we can't go to Unimeth, and we probably would receive no assistance in Gorthon. I don't think they'd expect us to double back to the southwest. Plus, Labyn will be concerned that they will be the next target, assuming Su'Meeryn falls.

Neffy scowled at his friend's logic, but he did not comment further. Instead, he spun around and headed back to Darus who was still comforting a trembling Perrin, this time keeping a wide berth from the feasting animals.

"Let's cook up some of the horse meat before we leave," suggested Hellet. "With the temperature dropping, it will hopefully last us a while. Once the meat is ready, Dellea will be the first to ride since she's injured. Unless we can find other horses, we will all take turns, so we stay as rested as possible. Let's try to save as much of the hide as we can. We might need it to keep ourselves warm.

"While we are doing that, Neffy, see if you can find the pack horse. I know it's not likely, but perhaps we'll be fortunate."

***

Neffy returned shortly after they had finished preparing the horse meat, but he had not been able to find their supplies. Once they were packed up, Hellet led the group on foot with Dellea riding next to him. While he was thankful that they had all survived the battle, it did not change how inadequate he felt. Under his leadership, they had lost all but one horse and most of their supplies, and he had been practically useless in protecting his friends and the woman he loved.

What good am I? he thought; the only reason they had survived was due to the wolves. And if Wairren was to be believed, somehow Dellea and he were the keys to stopping this spreading evil. How could that be if he was such an inept fighter? He had always been convinced he was a better strategist than Neffy or Darus, but he now questioned that thought. And, even if he was, how would that help when they were such a small group, alone in the wilderness?

He glanced up at Dellea, and she returned his gaze with a sad smile. While they had all experienced the trauma of the battle, she was the one who had to face it immediately after seeing the absolute destruction of her homeland. Before they started moving again, he had wondered if she would be able to set that distress aside. While he was relieved that she seemed to be coping for the moment, he knew she could not have gotten past it yet. Would she eventually be able to come to grips with her tragedy and loss, or would she have to pay a steep price for burying the pain deep in the recesses of her soul?

I can't worry about that now, he thought; I just need to get her safely to Labyn. She and the rest of the group. One of the wolves trotted up to him and rubbed its head against his side. He reached down and scratched its rough ear. "Thank you, my friend."

# chapter 47

A BITING WIND BLEW through his cloak as Travyn galloped away from the castle with a handful of soldiers. His relegation to searching for his nephew in the blustery conditions still aggravated the emperor, but the fact that he seemed to have no say in the matter was even more concerning. How could the ruler of two kingdoms be nothing more than a servant? He was feeling even more demeaned than he had during the previous years of dealing with his brother and all the others in Su'Meeryn. "I wish I'd never met her," he mumbled. Would he be better off if he had married that homely girl from Pathum?

But I am emperor, he told himself. He just needed to find Hellet, then he could return to the comfort of Shekul, or perhaps to Mephosh. If it took a little hardship to solidify his empire and reach divinity, the suffering would be well worth it. And despite his annoyance with his wife for assigning him to this miserable task, he knew they loved each other. He chastised himself for his momentary thoughts of regret. Once he had secured Hellet, he could return to his beautiful Ellaniya's affectionate arms.

Travyn's group continued away from the castle in the general direction of Unimeth. With all the other scouting parties that had been sent out, the emperor was certain Hellet's group would be captured soon. He still felt unsure about killing his nephew, but the rest of Hellet's party were of no consequence. He did not know the identity of Hellet's companions, but he assumed Darus and Neffy would be with the prince. Travyn recalled all the sneers and mocking jibes he had endured from that pair in the past; their deaths would not bother him in the least. Though he had no desire to see Dellea killed, if that ended up being her fate, he would not mourn. His preference would be to drag Hellet back to Shekul where he would be Ellaniya's or Ut's responsibility. If they killed him, at least Hellet's blood would not be on his hands.

The ride throughout the morning continued without incident. After stopping for a brief lunch, they were back on their way. The journey took them north with the hills of Gorthon to their right. Travyn was cursing the cold as he pulled a scarf from his pack to wrap around his face. While doing so, he almost did not see the horses before him stop. He pulled hard on the reins to keep his own mount from galloping into the others.

"What's going on?" Travyn barked, but then he saw a score of horses before them. The men staring back at him were clearly soldiers, and he was greatly outnumbered.

Despite some apprehension, Travyn pushed his steed in front of the rest of his men. He might have been demeaned with this trivial assignment, but he was still the leader of two kingdoms. Now he would act like one.

"Why have you stopped us?" he asked.

One of the riders before him raised an arm and pushed his own mount up a few lengths. The hand then pulled down a face covering, and Travyn recognized the unmistakable dark skin of an individual from Gorthon.

"Who are you?" the man asked, ignoring Travyn's question.

"I am Travyn, emperor of Mephosh and Shekul. And these are my men," he blurted out. "Now answer my question. Why did you stop us?"

"Emperor, eh?" the man stated with a grin that Travyn found annoying. "Perhaps not the wisest confession to make when you are so outnumbered."

"Why should my identity concern you? Gorthon is no enemy of mine."

"We care little what happens in the land of you colorless folk, but we are aware of certain developments."

Frustration was growing in Travyn. First, being relegated to such an awful mission, now this man and his condescending attitude. "We are not in your land. Part and let me be on my way."

The Gorthon warrior did not move his horse but instead rested his hand on the hilt of his scabbarded sword. "We care not who rules your pitiful kingdoms, but we have been tracking you and other groups leaving Shekul and heading north. This is odd behavior in such cold weather. We desire to know what is happening so close to our homes."

"Nothing that concerns you," Travyn responded defiantly, placing his own hand on the handle of his hammer.

"I would suggest you think wisely, *majesty*. Now, answer my question."

"If you really must know, we are searching for my nephew."

The man laughed in surprise. "And why is that?"

"Because—"

One of Travyn's riders had come up alongside and grasped his arm before Travyn could continue. "He and his group are criminals. They are fugitives we're trying to track down."

The man laughed again. He moved his gaze away from Travyn to the other soldier. "You realize this man is a fool, do you not? How does it feel following an imbecile?"

"Do not speak of me in such terms!" roared Travyn. "I am the emperor!"

"That may be, but you are a fool, nonetheless." The man sighed as he looked at each of Travyn's warriors in turn. "You may go, but I recommend you keep your distance from our mountains. We will be watching you." Before Travyn could respond further, the man pulled the covering back down across his face and raced his horse away.

Inarticulate noises stammered from Travyn's throat as his narrow eyes followed the retreating Gorthon warriors. How dare some menial soldier speak to him that way? Maybe Gorthon should be their next target after Su'Meeryn and Labyn were secured, then they would see who the imbecile was. He would discuss this idea with Ellaniya and Ut once he had the chance. Travyn was tired of being belittled, and he was ready to dole out his mighty vengeance on all those who had wronged him. As the monarch of two kingdoms, he had thought his days of being mocked had passed. While the horses of Gorthon disappeared from view, he realized that was not yet the case.

His anger seethed as he ordered his soldiers to move out. This man of Gorthon had made himself an enemy, and he would pay the same price as all his other foes. He remembered the day when he had smashed Naren's skull. Ellaniya's father and brother had received their justice for their torment of his wonderful wife, and Orrin would soon join them as a sacrifice to the gods. Then he would convince Ut of Gorthon's threat to their new empire, this belligerent soldier would receive his justice from Travyn's hammer as well.

The search party rode away with thoughts of honorable retribution rummaging through Travyn's mind, until he became distracted by the growing cold as the speed of his steed increased. It was miserable, but he knew it was temporary. Soon he would be back with Ellaniya, and he longed for the moment to again melt into her loving embrace.

# chapter 48

TINY, SHARP ICY FLAKES OF SNOW swirled in the driving wind, assaulting the small group. Dellea tried to reposition the hide around herself, but the attempt did little to keep the cold at bay. The snow found entry to every exposed piece of flesh and stung her skin as it struck.

She still limped a little from the bruise on her thigh, but she had refused to take any extra turns on their lone horse. Everyone will get their allotted time, she would say whenever Hellet broached the subject. She started to get annoyed the last time he mentioned it, and so he refrained from bringing it up again. Dellea regretted her harsh tone as she knew Hellet was only trying to help, and the continuing pain caused her to question her decision. But it was not to the level where she felt she needed any special treatment. She knew nobody in the group would think less of her if she did take some extra time atop the beast, but unpleasant memories of childhood kept emerging in her mind. Growing up with no friends and an uncaring family had been extremely difficult for her, and she did not want to alienate this new community that was developing. Rationally, she knew that would not be the case, but she refused to take the risk. A little physical pain was far better than potentially adding to her emotional pain.

As they continued their southward trek, they had spied a few of the search parties they assumed were from Shekul and they were spotted a couple times as well. Fortunately, each time they had managed to elude their pursuers. The only advantage to the relentless snow was it quickly covered their tracks. Though Hellet did not want to, their path away from the search parties kept forcing them to the east and the mountains of Gorthon.

They were not fearful of meeting inhabitants of that mountainous realm, but the people of Gorthon were renowned for their fickle behavior towards their light-skinned neighbors. Hellet felt it would be best to avoid them all together, if possible, but that was appearing less likely as, through the shrouding of the snow-filled sky, the Gorthon mountains were becoming more visible with each passing step. Since they were nearing the realm anyway, Hellet had decided that they might as well make their way to the mountain line and look for shelter for the night. After following along the low-lying hills for about an hour, they found a small cave just as the daylight was fading.

The group entered the cave around the same time as the wolves returned. They had left some time ago to hunt, but they brought back only a small hare. As they still had a good amount of horse meat left, Dellea motioned for the animals to feast on their catch themselves.

The cave was not very big, but there was room enough for all of them and deep enough that a small fire should not be spotted from the outside. Perrin brought the horse in, and it appeared relieved to get away from the wolves. The rest scrounged around and found enough debris to start the fire. Once Neffy had the flames ignited, they searched for more fuel, but they did not find much. The fire would not last long, though it would give them a bit of a reprieve from the biting cold and allow some of their garments to dry. While Dellea tended the flames, the rest searched outside for additional fuel, but in the dim light and now heavy snow, they found nothing. When they reentered the cave, Neffy, Darus and Perrin situated themselves on the far side of the cave with the horse while Dellea and Hellet remained near the opening with the wolves.

"How's your leg?" Hellet asked.

"Still a little sore, but not too bad."

"That's good." Hellet took a bite of his meat and began to stroke one of the wolves. "It seems it's going to take us a while to get to Labyn. Are you sure you're up for it?"

"Yes," she replied in a clipped tone that she immediately lamented. "Sorry," she quickly added.

"That's alright," he responded as he offered her a hunk of the meat. "This is a trying time for all of us."

"Just like Wairren predicted."

"I guess he was correct."

She bit into the meat, which was tough and flavorless, but at least it was proper sustenance. "Do you still think we should avoid the people of Gorthon?"

"Being this close to their land, I assume we will run into them at some point. There is a good chance they already know that we're here. But I still think it best to keep away from them if possible. They are not an evil people; however, they have no affection for their neighbors to the west. I doubt they'd hinder us, but they certainly won't help us against Travyn."

Dellea wondered if Hellet might be a bit mistaken regarding the people of Gorthon. She did not expect much assistance from them either, but she thought they might likely offer weary travelers some supplies. She wanted to discuss it further, but Hellet had been clear since the beginning regarding his position on the matter. Leaving that topic aside she decided to broach another subject.

"You'll be of age in the spring. If Su'Meeryn does fall to your uncle, we should marry in Labyn, assuming we make it there."

Hellet had been taking a drink of water, and he coughed after hearing her comment. "Marriage? Are you sure we should be considering that with all that's happening?"

The light had completely faded from outside the cave opening, and Darus had added the last of the brush to the fire. The flames flickered and rose, bathing Hellet's face in an amber glow. She looked into his eyes, and they seemed to engulf her like a mother bird landing in a nest, covering her young. His wisdom and intelligence belied his age, but there was that ever present softness of spirit, especially when they were alone. After all they had recently faced, she felt a sense of comfort and safety being in his presence. Despite her quirks and plainness of features, she knew he loved her. And every minute they were together increased her love for him. She wanted to say those words to him, but she remained apprehensive of making herself too vulnerable. She knew she should not be as his feelings for her were clear, but the trauma of her past would not allow her to voice those words, at least not yet.

"Yes," she answered. "I have no home to return to, and likely you won't either. We have been waiting all this time, and I see no reason we should wait any longer than necessary. I want to be married, and I want to be married to you." She desired to say more. She longed to tell Hellet how much his unequivocal acceptance and love for her almost made her forget about her past and the destruction of Pathum, but that was all she could utter.

"I yearn to be married to you as well. If that is what you want, we shall be wed at the first opportunity."

Hellet's tender face seemed to take on an angelic hue in the flickering light of the campfire. Despite all they had experienced, his soft smile brought her a level of hope and peace; however, she was fearful to pose the question that had troubled her for so long. Even though their history together told her otherwise, she remained frightened. Her mouth opened, but no sound came forth. She reached over and began to pet one of the other wolves. It raised its head as if sensing her trepidation. "Why me?" she eventually managed to ask, just above a whisper.

She felt his hand grasp hers as his blue eyes seemed to almost consume her. He pulled her hand to his face then gently kissed her fingers. "I don't know, and I can't explain it. That first time we met, something immediately drew me to you. You were the girl with the wolves, but that wasn't it." He paused for a moment. "I had to cast my feelings aside since you were promised to Travyn, but once I saw the opportunity, I knew I needed to pursue it—to pursue you.

"Why or how this bond formed—does it matter? Explanation is unnecessary. We're connected, and that is all that matters to me."

Tears started to roll down her cheeks, but Dellea did not know why. It was not like this was a new revelation from Hellet, as they both knew their feelings for each other. Perhaps it was a release from his pronouncement. After all the dire warnings from Wairren and the trauma she had experienced, this was something in her future she could look forward to. As the daughter of a king, she had never envisioned herself loving her husband; she had seen that all too clearly with her mother. And then she had been promised to that fool Travyn. She had suffered much—and still suffered—but she had been granted the opportunity to marry the man she loved. And that day was coming soon, if they actually reached Labyn. So they were tears of both trauma and relief.

The wolf she was petting dropped its head and stretched itself out on the hard ground. She gazed at all three. She never thought her love for those beasts would be eclipsed, but the arrival of Hellet in her life had dispelled that notion.

Dellea leaned down and rested her head in Hellet's lap. He stroked her hair and thoughts of their marriage permeated her mind. As a princess of Pathum, her marriage would have been a huge celebration, but Pathum no longer existed. Was she even still a princess? None of that mattered now. She did not care if there would be a celebration at all. In fact, she hoped there would not be. The marriage had nothing to do with kingdoms or royalty any longer. It was now just between the two of them, and she decided a private, brief ceremony was all she wanted.

While she knew that they would have to face much to reach that day—if they ever did—the thought increased her motivation to triumph over these hardships. Nothing would stop her from reaching Labyn with Hellet.

Pathum was destroyed, and her family was dead. She still mourned that loss and knew that they would suffer much before they could wed. But the anticipation of marriage pushed away all the torment for the moment. As Hellet continued to stroke her hair, she drifted off into a pleasant sleep.

**\*\*\***

Dellea awoke the next morning with Hellet beside her. She looked over at him, and his face displayed a peaceful grace in his slumber. Despite the harsh conditions, she felt refreshed as her nightmares had not returned. A cold wind swept in through the cave entrance, and the horse hide covering her did little to bring warmth. A glance around revealed that the wolves had already left, presumably to hunt. She heard a rattling at the far end of cave and turned to see Perrin gathering up the supplies. Dellea rose from the hard ground, stretched out her still-sore leg and carefully stepped over the sleeping men to join Perrin. "Let me help," she said quietly as she bent down to Perrin's bed roll.

"I fear today is going to be even colder," Perrin stated. She reached into a bag, pulled out an apple and gave it to the horse. "We're going to run out of food for him if we don't find something soon."

"We can deal with that when we have to," Dellea replied.

"I wish I never joined this journey." Perrin said bitterly, her tone displaying none of her customary joviality as she angrily shoved her blanket into a sack.

"You might not have been better off at home. With Travyn's forces searching so hard for us, they certainly have Su'Meeryn in their sights."

"I'm so cold," Perrin said, as if she had not heard Dellea's reply. Dellea noticed that her eyes had widened, and she was rushing her words. Perrin's hands continued to shake as she fought with the blanket.

"At least you're with your husband," Dellea replied in a soft voice, trying to soothe her friend's anxiety. "We also have Neffy and the wolves. We'll get through this and reach Labyn. I told Hellet that I want us to marry once we reach that kingdom. I'm not going to let some snow stop us!"

Perrin's thumb went to her mouth, and she began to bite at her nail. It was hard to see in the low light of the cave, but—looking at her hand—Dellea noticed that Perrin's other nails had been gnawed down to the skin. Her eyes darted about the cave and Dellea wondered if Perrin had even heard her words.

"Do you think it's going to be colder today?" Perrin asked.

Dellea remained silent for a moment, unsure how to respond. Her companion's eyes displayed a look of terror, and Dellea was afraid for her friend. She grasped Perrin's shoulders and said, "We're going to need you to get through this. Darus will need you." Perrin's face flushed as she raised her fingers to her quivering lips. Her eyes darted about, and she began to sob. Dellea then heard a stirring behind her as the commotion roused the men from their slumber.

Dellea wrapped her arms around Perrin, and Darus had sprung to their side. He looked from Perrin to Dellea with an expression of confusion. Dellea guided Perrin's shaking body to her husband, and he wrapped his burly arms around his wife as she buried her face in his chest. Dellea then turned and walked past a bewildered Neffy and came up to Hellet. "This is trouble," she murmured in his ear.

# chapter 49

"HE TOLD YOU THE SAME TALE, EH?" Aniass asked as he sharpened his sword. Ellaniya rarely entered an armory, but she figured it would probably be a good idea to have a weapon for the next stage of the campaign, though she could not envision using one.

"Dragons were referred to in some of the texts I studied, and Ut once mentioned that they are not myth."

"I've travelled all over this land and fought in many battles; I've met countless people. Never have a I encountered a dragon or heard anyone mention seeing one."

"Why would he lie?" asked Ellaniya.

"Maybe he was confused. That wouldn't be so difficult to imagine."

The smirk on the mercenary's face irritated Ellaniya. While she respected Aniass, as simple as Travyn might be, she did not appreciate her servant poking fun at him. "Careful Aniass, he is my husband and your king."

"He is not my king. I am a mercenary," Aniass replied without hesitation, still working on his sword.

Ellaniya's aggravation grew, but she pushed it aside. Now was not the time to cause strife with her most important ally. "You forget, I was at Pathum. I saw the destruction myself. It could not have been caused by ordinary means."

After finishing with the stone, Aniass tested his blade with his fingertip. Satisfied with his handiwork, he sheathed the weapon before turning back to Ellaniya. "Maybe he's right. If Ut had something to do with the attack, I suppose it's possible. However, unless these *dragons* attack with us—or are defending Su'Meeryn—it makes little difference to me. All I care about is surviving and receiving my payment."

"Fine, fine." Ellaniya waved him away, and when she was alone, she searched about for an appropriate weapon for herself. She considered a few short swords, but they seemed too bulky for her. Then on a shelf in the far corner, she came across a dagger in a bone-encrusted sheath with sparkling jewels. It seemed strange finding such an ornate weapon in the armory, but she was pleased with her discovery. This fine weapon would suit an empress.

Ellaniya was greeted by cold air and large flakes of snow as she made her way from the armory with her guards trailing close behind. She thought of Travyn out in the wilderness, and her ire rose again at Aniass' derogatory comment. But could she blame him? With a shiver, she wondered how her husband was faring in his task. There was no reason that Travyn needed to be in one of the search parties except to keep him away from the coming attack, but since she was joining the army, Ellaniya would have been able to manage him if he started to cause a problem. Was it guilt she was feeling for how she was treating him? But guilt was not something she had time to entertain. She could revisit these considerations once Hellet was captured and Su'Meeryn was in her hands. For now, nothing would distract her from her service to the gods.

***

Moving the army was a slow process in the bitter cold and unrelenting snow, and Ellaniya questioned her decision to attack Su'Meeryn in the winter. It was still early in the season, and nobody had expected this type of weather, so she told herself that the strategy was still sound. But even correct decisions can be undone by unforeseen circumstances and turn into a mistake; she was starting to think that this might be one of those unfortunate times.

Despite her furs, the cold still found ways to penetrate her defenses and attack her skin. No matter how she situated herself on her horse, or rearranged her many garments, the struggle to stay warm was a losing battle.

She was miserable.

The sight of the massive army surrounding her brought some level of pleasure, but it was not enough to improve her foul mood. Aniass rode beside her, and she wanted to bark at him for agreeing to this foolish plan, but she knew it was not his fault. He was a mercenary, and he did as he was ordered. If she wanted to pay him for journeying through the snow, that was what he would do. It was against his code to complain to his employer, so she knew she would hear no grumblings from him. That just increased her frustration. She would prefer to have someone to lament her situation with, but she would have to remain alone with her complaints.

In this brutal weather, the trek to Su'Meeryn would take far longer than normal. They did not possess enough horses for all the soldiers to ride, but that was not relevant as they were dragging the siege engines. And the snow was slowing them down even more.

She was grateful once evening finally arrived. While most of the men would have to make do with sleeping in the open with only a bedroll, she was one of the few who had a tent. After much work, a guard established a fire outside her enclosure then added stones which would be used to provide her heat. When Ellaniya was alone inside, she stripped out of her sodden clothes and pulled out a fresh set from her bag. Unfortunately, much of the driving snow had seeped into the sack, and those clothes were only slightly dryer. Angrily, she wrapped a blanket around herself and stretched out on her roll.

Being surrounded by all these soldiers—yet alone—she missed having Vor with her. Not for the first time she regretted the decision of leaving him back in Mephosh, but what other choice was there? She needed someone trustworthy to run the kingdom, and that certainly was not her husband.

While impatiently awaiting the warming stones, she began to wonder how Travyn was faring. Likely he was even more miserable than she, alone on the cold ground. She surprised herself that she actually missed him somewhat. If Vor could not be with her, it would be nice to at least have the warmth of Travyn's body next to hers. Though he had his many flaws, he was a capable lover, and his absence increased her sense of isolation.

The fact that she was the only woman in this camp of soldiers did not help either. All the warriors possessed some level of allegiance to her—either as a subject or paid mercenary; however, none of these men were anybody she could talk to. Not that Travyn was a quality conversationalist, but he would be better than nothing, and—being honest with herself—Vor was not much better with the art of speech. While dialogue might not be his strong suit, he made up for that in so many other ways.

She tried to put her loneliness aside while squirming in her bedroll. Though thick, it did not eliminate all the lumps from the ground beneath her, and she struggled to find a comfortable position on the cold, hard ground. The warm stones servants brought in eased her chill; however, she knew the heat would not last. It all just made her miss having Vor with her, or even Travyn.

With a sigh, Ellaniya turned her eyes to the top of the tent, trying to peer into the heavens and see the gods. She was certain they found favor with her many sacrifices and would offer their blessings, eventually making all the misery worthwhile.

Sleep did not come easily. She could not make herself comfortable, and the stones eventually lost their heat. She called out for more to be brought in, but apparently nobody heard her. The thought of rising out of her bedding was not appealing, so she remained huddled on the ground as her thoughts turned to Ut. She wondered where he was and what he might be doing. It had been a long time since he had presented himself to her, but she supposed his presence was not currently necessary. He had provided the mercenaries to her army, and she was progressing with their plan.

Would Ut have approved of her strategy to continue the campaign during this early, harsh winter? Ellaniya was confident that he would have. Despite the difficulty of moving her troops through these miserable conditions, she was certain Ut would be unconcerned regarding the hardships she and the soldiers faced. Success was all that mattered.

Ellaniya thought back to the first time she had met the messenger of the gods. Why had she trusted him so easily? She was not regretting that decision as Ut had fulfilled all of his promises to her. She now ruled her homeland as well as Shekul, and soon Su'Meeryn would be added to her empire. It would be the dawn of a new age, and she wondered if she should take on a new name once Labyn was also conquered. Empress Lynna, she thought. Yes, that would be appropriate, a fitting tribute to the last great monarch of Mephosh.

As she unsuccessfully tried again to find a comfortable position, her mind drifted to Pathum. If Travyn was to be believed, Ut had orchestrated the destruction of that kingdom with scores of dragons. It still seemed unbelievable, but she had no reason to doubt her husband. Surely Travyn would not lie to her. He was not savvy enough to fabricate such an intricate story, and Ut did seem to possess some level of divine powers. Plus, she had seen the aftermath, and the raving woman had mentioned fire from the sky. What other explanation could there be?

Oh, how glorious it would've been to witness the destruction myself, she thought. What joy it would have brought to watch dragons sweep down from the sky and bring down fiery justice to that despicable kingdom which had played such a pivotal role in Lynna's defeat. However, it was a shame that it had been obliterated as there was now one less kingdom in which the true gods would be worshipped.

Empress Lynna, yes, that sounded perfect, and her empire would expand even more once she was wedded to Mennum. Despite her current misery, everything was coming together as Ut had promised.

She offered a prayer of thanks to the gods for their many blessings and reiterated her promise to faithfully serve them the rest of her days. With a feeling of pious satisfaction, she finally drifted off to sleep.

***

The following morning brought no relief from the bone-chilling temperature and torrential snow. With the abysmal cold, the snowflakes were small and hard as they whipped through the camp. Following a less-than-appealing breakfast, all the supplies were stored away, and Ellaniya mounted her steed. As the army slowly resumed their miserable trek, a wind picked up and drove the biting flakes into her face. Ellaniya felt an urge to offer a curse for her predicament, but the idea of Empress Lynna immediately returned to her mind. She would only have to suffer a short while more—until they reached Su'Meeryn. With the might at her command, the kingdom would fall quickly, and she would soon be warming herself at Orrin's fire. Maybe she would even have him present, in chains, to witness her glory.

Another blast of bitter cold set her body into shivers as she wrapped her scarf tighter around her face, but it did not help. There was nothing she could do but put her head down and continue the journey towards Su'Meeryn. She leaned down, closer into her steed's neck and plowed through the torment like a sword slicing through the flesh of Su'Meeryn soldiers.

# chapter 50

"WHY DO I HAVE TO BE DOING THIS?" the emperor whined as he tried to rip apart a piece of frozen, salted meat. "This is a waste of my skills. I should be leading the attack on Su'Meeryn." He glanced around at the men as they milled about during their mid-day break, but none responded. Their silence only increased his aggravation at his current situation, but what could he do? He could not punish them as he needed every man for the search for his nephew. "How are we ever going to find him in this?" he mumbled, gesturing at the relentless downfall of snow. Once again, he looked around at the soldiers, but still they all ignored him. "Divinity better be worth it," he remarked as he again attempted to rip off a hunk of meat. He felt a popping in his mouth and wondered if he had cracked a tooth before hurling the meat away. It quickly disappeared, shrouded by the falling snow.

A quick check of his mouth revealed no damage, so he rose to take a few steps away to relieve himself, which was an even less pleasant experience than trying to eat the meat. Once finished, Travyn and his men mounted up to continue their quest.

The cold was draining, but what caused him even more distress was his separation from Ellaniya. Travyn thought back to all the bullying he had received from Orrin when he was younger, along with the multitude of harsh, unwarranted comments from so many others. In retrospect, he could not say that he ever had a friend. Hellet was the closest person he might say was friendly to him, but his nephew always had Neffy and Darus with him, and they were worse than Orrin. He felt extremely fortunate to have finally found someone that loved him so deeply, but he was separated from her. And that was far worse than the cold.

He pulled some seeds out from a bag, but they were almost as difficult to eat as the hunk of meat he had hurled away. "What I would give for some strawberries," he muttered.

As his party pushed through the harsh conditions, Travyn watched the back of the warrior in front of him, and his mind seemed to go numb from the frigid weather and the almost hypnotic motion of the rider. Then his mind returned to his ride on the dragon with Ut and the destruction of Pathum. Would he ever experience a more terrifying scene? Perhaps he had when Ut had threatened him. Though it seemed impossible, Travyn wondered if Ut was in fact more terrifying than a fleet of dragons.

But he had survived the dragons and Ut's threats. He was the emperor of two—soon to be three—kingdoms, but he had been humbled to be nothing more than a servant suffering in the cold. He eventually managed to swallow the frozen seeds as he longed for spring and fresh, sweet strawberries. And he missed his love even more.

**✱✱✱**

They were still skirting the foothills of the Gorthon mountains as evening finally approached. Travyn was considering signaling for a stop when one of his men called out that movement had been spotted through the pine trees in the low hills to the south. His men spurred their mounts, but the thick snow did not allow for much additional speed. After a few moments, Travyn saw the movement too. Whatever the small group was, they were traveling slower than his, so they could not be on horseback.

As the horses raced towards their quarry, they were noticed. Travyn heard a cry from the still-unidentified group carrying across the distance. As they grew closer Travyn counted four people on foot and one on horseback. He felt certain it must be Hellet's party.

The figures darted to the east, and Travyn briefly lost sight of them amidst the trees. The rocks of the hills helped camouflage their prey, as did the snow, and the quickly fading light only made matters worse.

"Find them!" he barked as he pushed his steed eastward. When they approached the hills, he saw additional movement. "There!" he called to his men, pointing towards the dark shapes scrambling around the hills.

But then they disappeared from his sight again. Travyn desperately peered about the rocks and boulders; however, everything seemed to flow together as the sky darkened and snow shrouded his gaze. Then from out of the gloom he heard some commotion and saw a large shape heading towards them. He tried to bring it into focus then realized it was the horse. But it was riderless. What happened? he thought; why did they set the horse free?

"What's going on?" he asked as the horse galloped past his group.

He heard a sigh next to him before one of the soldiers replied. "They obviously found somewhere to hide but had no room for the horse. They figured hiding was more important than keeping the animal."

"That wasn't very smart of them."

"That might be so, but now they will be able to move about the foothills with more ease."

Travyn chaffed at being contradicted by a subordinate, but the man made a valid point. The light was fading fast, so they would not be able to search any longer. "I want extra sentries patrolling all night," he commanded. "We resume our search at first light."

# *chapter* 51

SENDING THE HORSE AWAY had been a difficult decision, but Hellet remained convinced it was necessary. What good was a horse if they were caught? Besides, the alcove within the rocky hills they had found could barely hold the five of them. While they should be able to rest safely for the night, he wondered what the morning would bring.

With the horse gone, they would be able to carry fewer supplies, but that would be less of issue as their stores were dwindling. The cold provided some benefit in that the meat they still had was frozen; however, this also made it difficult to eat. And they could not risk starting a fire to thaw it out as their pursuers might spot the flames.

As they situated themselves in the cold, dank alcove, all five of them were on edge, but Perrin's situation was threatening to become dire. The hardship was impacting them all, but she seemed to be struggling more than the others. Darus comforted her as much as he could, but as the daughter of a noble, she'd had no practice in dealing with suffering. While the men had experience with their training, and Dellea was clearly familiar with torment, Perrin had been raised in relative luxury and had never before been separated from her comforts.

Perrin's attempts to rally her courage had been met with varying degrees of success—and failure. As her moods had shifted during their miserable journey, so too had Darus'. His temper had become shorter, which caused Neffy to also become more volatile. Hellet often had to soothe the tension between his two friends, but the strain was trying for him as well. Dellea appeared to be managing better than all of them, but he sensed her agitation as it had been a while since they last saw the wolves.

Wairren's dire warnings of suffering and evil kept coming to his mind. How long would they be able to endure, and how could they ever hope to reach Labyn this way? It seemed an impossibility. He wondered how they would even get through another day. How could they prevail against the prophesied evil if their very survival looked questionable? Maybe we should just enter Gorthon and see what they do with us; it couldn't be worse than this, he thought.

After finishing a difficult meal, the five made themselves as comfortable as possible on the hard, cold ground, huddled together for warmth. It took a long time for sleep to arrive as Hellet's mind raced over his decisions. Had he made any errors? Based on their current circumstance, he figured there must have been opportunities for better choices, but what might they have been? Mistakes are not always the worst things as one can learn and grow from them. Of course, one cannot learn if a mistake leads to death. We're not dead, he told himself, but how long can we last?

Sleep finally overtook him sometime late into the night, but, unfortunately, that sleep was far from restful. His dreams were plagued by horrific visions, and he awoke often. He wanted to rise and stretch his legs, but he did not want to disturb the others. Hellet glanced over to the opening and saw the unmistakable form of Neffy standing guard. His large friend seemed to sense the movement and turned back. In the darkness, Hellet could not see Neffy's face, but that did not matter. What did matter was that they were together, and he could not think of a better person to have with Dellea and him. Hellet offered his friend a slight wave and closed his eyes again. He quickly drifted back to sleep with feelings of gratitude for Neffy's presence.

When dawn finally arrived, Hellet forced his stiff body up from the rocky bed, feeling even more tired than he had the night before. Stretching himself out, he felt a stinging in his left hand. Pulling off his glove he noticed a hole in the fabric and that his index finger was red. He tried to massage it out, but the rubbing only increased his pain. He did not have an extra glove, so he managed to tear off a small piece from the horse hide covering Dellea and shoved it down towards the hole.

As the rest of the company began to stir, Dellea reached out her hand and Hellet helped her to her feet. "No sign of them?" she asked, and Hellet knew she was not referencing their pursuers.

Hellet shook his head. "It is a new day," he pointed out. "I'm sure they're still hunting, but this weather has to be difficult for them as well."

"The snow finally stopped," Neffy reported from the opening to the alcove, "but there was plenty last night to cover our tracks. Unfortunately, it doesn't seem to be any warmer."

"Do you still suppose these parties are from Shekul?" Darus asked, his eyes never leaving his wife. Perrin was standing by the opening, her body shaking, as she peered out into the snowy wilderness.

"They must be," Hellet responded. "I don't know who was in that group coming from the north, but they must have recognized us. Who else would be so adamant to find us in these conditions? If Su'Meeryn is their target now, I'm a threat as the royal heir."

"I'm sure you're right, but it's still so hard to believe this is actually happening," replied Neffy.

"I know, but it is" stated Hellet. "We should get moving. Let's eat what we can then be on our way."

"And which way is that?" asked Darus.

"I pondered that much of last night. I think we should stay in the foothills. We will likely run into scouts from Gorthon, but I guess that's better than meeting our hunters."

"Agreed," Neffy said. "While I'm not anxious to continue this journey, at least moving will generate some heat."

After leaving the alcove, they continued southward amidst the Gorthon foothills. With the snow finally having stopped, they were greeted with a bright blue sky which gave them the opportunity to gaze at the mountains to their left. Hellet had never been this far east before, so his first view of the mountains was an impressive sight. The tall peaks ranged as far as his eyes could see from the north to the south, and the rocky crags high above were shrouded in blankets of bright white with traces of grays, browns and blacks peeking out in various locations. On some other occasion, Hellet would have paused to admire the majesty of the sight, but this was not that day.

They had not traveled far when three shapes raced noiselessly towards them. Dellea squealed with delight as the wolves rejoined their party. They were carrying two small foxes which they dropped at her feet. She greeted them each in turn and then they approached Hellet with soft whines and tails wagging. As Hellet rubbed their heads, Dellea handed one of the foxes to Neffy, who promptly began to skin it. Once Hellet had finished his greetings, the wolves returned their attention to their second kill and promptly devoured it. After Neffy was finished with his chore, they continued their dreadful march.

Despite the piercing blue sky, the temperature was even colder than the previous day. As they trudged through the snow, Hellet continually fidgeted with his glove. Unfortunately, the frigid air kept finding purchase through the make-shift patch to assail his skin. While he was attempting once again to reconfigure the patch, he heard a low growling from the wolves. He looked about but saw nothing. The growling increased in pitch as the fur on the backs of all three wolves rose into the air. Hellet lifted his arm, ordering the others to stop. The wolves positioned themselves around the group with their heads low, fangs on full display. Hellet slowly pulled his sword from his scabbard as Neffy and Darus did the same. He held it before him, but still saw nothing.

As the wolves continued to growl, Hellet noticed flickers of motion all around. Suddenly scores of leather clad warriors emerged from the rocks and hills. Spears and swords were pointed at the group. The wolves' growling grew in volume and Dellea immediately grasped the neck of the wolf nearest her. It was a remarkable sight, seeing that slight girl trying to wrestle the large beast back. But even with their animal protectors, Hellet knew his group stood no chance if they engaged in conflict with these warriors.

Hellet heard a chuckle from one of the men as he lowered his spear and took a few steps forward. The man pulled the scarf down from his face, and Hellet saw his dark skin. Clearly these were warriors from Gorthon, not their pursuers from Shekul.

"An interesting group we have found trespassing in our lands." His dark eyes darted about the group and lingered for a few extra moments on the animals. "I've never seen travelers in the company of wolves before. I'm sure you have a fascinating tale to tell, but first you will need to convince me why I shouldn't kill you all right now."

Hellet took a step forward and lowered his sword while raising his head, giving the man a hard glare. "Are you always this rude to visitors in your land? We are certainly no threat to the people of Gorthon."

Another chuckle escaped from the man's throat as he continued to step forward. "Strong words from a boy."

"I am the leader of this group," Hellet responded, "and you need not concern yourself with us; we don't plan to stay long in your land."

"You must be prince Hellet," the man replied as he handed his spear to the soldier standing next to him.

Hellet was shocked at the words. How could this man possibly know his identity? He wanted to refute the statement, but he decided there would be little point to deny it. "How do you know who I am?"

"Your uncle is an idiot. I ran into him a few days ago. He is searching for you, as I assume you know. He called you criminals."

"We are no such thing. Now, are you going to let us pass?"

"No, I suppose you are not." He paused, looking at the other four before returning his attention to the wolves. Low growls still rumbled from their throats, and the animals appeared poised to strike at any moment. "We are aware that many groups are searching for you near our border. We know of the fall of Shekul, and that an army is marching on Su'Meeryn. My guess is your fool of an uncle wants to capture you to execute you, as I believe you are the heir to the throne of Su'Meeryn."

Hellet did not know how to respond to this warrior. He had accurately discerned their situation, but Hellet could not decide if this was a benefit for them. Would these men take them prisoner to deliver to Travyn in hopes of gaining his favor? They were experiencing the exact issue he had been fearful of by entering Gorthon lands. Had he made a grave mistake?

"Will you allow us to pass?" was all he could think to respond.

"We do not relish the thought of conflict near our realm."

"How is any of this a threat to you or your people?" Dellea spoke up. "Aren't you safe in your mountains?"

"Ah, the girl speaks!" the man replied with more joviality than Hellet thought appropriate. "Of course you and that clown *emperor* are no threat to Gorthon, but we want stability near our border."

"Well, it doesn't appear you have that," Hellet pointed out.

"Yes, Shekul is in your uncle's hands. While that might not be ideal, we care not who rules in your kingdoms. We just don't want to see disruption to our trade routes."

"As you can see, we are no threat to your traders," Hellet countered.

"No, I suppose you are not." His eyes turned back to the wolves that had sat next to Dellea and Hellet but remained alert. "I would be interested to know how you came to have these creatures as part of your group."

"It's a long story, and it is a bit cold to stand around and chat further," responded Hellet.

"You are correct there, my colorless friend. I will allow you to pass if you desire; however, Gorthon is a vast land. Since I like you, I would be willing to offer you and your group refuge. We have plenty of room for you all. Well, the five of you, the wolves are not welcome."

"I thank you for your offer," Hellet replied before anyone else could speak up. "Shelter would certainly be welcomed, but the wolves are members of our group. Plus, we have more pressing concerns. Unless you and your people are willing to ally with me against Travyn—which I am certain you are not—we need to be on our way."

"Well then, I will bid you farewell, and I suggest you leave our land immediately. It would be best for you if you do not reenter Gorthon lands since you have rejected my hospitality."

"We appreciate your graciousness," Hellet responded, attempting to sound sincere, "but, before we depart, might I implore you for some supplies? We are running low."

"Unfortunately, we only take enough for the length of our missions, so I have nothing to offer; however, I will give you this." He reached into a pocket and pulled out a small bottle. "This is a salve we recently developed. It does much to alleviate pain. I suppose you might experience some since you will continue your travels in this inhospitable weather. Perhaps it will be of some use to you."

The man tossed it to Hellet. He caught it and winced when it struck his finger. It might be of use soon, Hellet thought.

"Now, be on your way," the man stated, and he and his group stood motionless while Hellet's group made their way out of the foothills.

"That could have been worse," Hellet whispered to Dellea as they resumed their trudge through the snow. He then looked at each of his friends, wondering what they thought of his decision to depart from Gorthon. Darus and Neffy would not leave his side, but he remained concerned about Perrin. He was thankful that she had been quiet during the confrontation, and he wondered if he should have offered for her to stay. But she clung to Darus as they turned their back to the mountains. She probably would have been better off remaining, but being separated from her husband might have broken her completely, and he could not offer Darus to stay; he needed the two soldiers with him. Hellet could not be certain, but he hoped he had made the correct decision. Though he wondered if he would ever be able to tell what decisions were correct and which were in error.

The wolves loped ahead, happy to be away from the tension of the encounter; they then darted off, looking for more prey. Hellet wrapped his arm around Dellea and felt another sting of pain in his finger. He would have to give the salve a try if the pain became any worse.

# chapter 52

ELLANIYA'S PULSE QUICKENED, and she felt her heart pounding in her chest when the walls of Su'Meeryn first appeared in the distance. The trek to reach the kingdom had been long and miserable, and she was excited and nervous to finally reach their destination. Ellaniya's bones ached, and her skin, hands and feet were numb. Her back and hips, already sore from the long ride to and from Amyon, were now throbbing after the hard trek through the thick snow. She knew her body needed a break, and she would gladly take that once Su'Meeryn was subdued. But, while she fully expected that the assault on the castle would be successful, victory was not assured.

Horns blared from the parapets, announcing the arrival of Ellaniya's army. Aniass trotted his horse up alongside the queen. "We have them vastly outnumbered," he began, "so I anticipate victory. However, we need to be ready for unforeseen contingencies as I've never mounted an assault in these conditions before."

"Why are you telling me this?" Ellaniya barked. "You are the expert, and I expect you to do what is necessary. Get on with it."

"Of course, your majesty," the mercenary leader replied. "I recommend you remain here; there is no reason to put yourself at risk." Ellaniya's hand went to the hilt of her dagger, and she nodded her agreement to the ridiculously obvious suggestion. "I will take my leave and see to the attack." Aniass continued.

With a wave of her hand, Ellaniya sent him away. A cloud of white kicked up behind his horse as Aniass sped off. Finally I will have my revenge, she thought.

Ellaniya remembered back to her visit as the emissary from Mephosh to attend the marriage of Travyn and Dellea. How fortunes change. She had been delighted with Jaleph's death, but it was a hollow joy. While she celebrated the demise of one of the men who had brought so much harm to her home, at his advanced age, his death was inconsequential. But her attendance at the funeral and the delay of the wedding had allowed her the opportunity to maneuver and marry Travyn. At the time, she thought the union might provide her a way to harm Su'Meeryn from the inside, but that had not occurred. However, this outcome was even more savory: leading an attack against the loathsome kingdom.

And what of her husband? Had there been any actual benefit to the marriage? All her accomplishments had nothing to do with Travyn. Everything had been orchestrated by Ut. Now her husband was nothing more than a pawn on her grand chessboard. Soon he would either be dead or discarded. She smiled a little at the thought of his dumb face and his mouth filled with strawberries. She again hoped that he did not have to die, but she would have no qualms with casting him aside. She would soon be married to Mennum and still have Vor. All was well.

Her mind returned to the battle that was about to begin, and she watched Aniass conferring with his division leaders. All the troops halted as the catapults were brought forward. Cries from Su'Meeryn reached her ears as arrows flew from the walls. The missiles landed uselessly about since their foe was not yet in range.

Following a few more minutes of pushing forward through the snow, a blue flag was raised, and the catapults stopped. Ellaniya watched while the arm of one of the mighty machines was pulled down. A small boulder was lifted from a cart and loaded into the basket. Once the missile was situated, the catapult fired. The boulder flew through the air—a dark shape against the brilliant blue sky—and plopped into the snow, a number of yards from the castle wall. A red flag was raised, and the catapults were hauled forward once again.

More arrows flew from the walls, but the attackers below still remained out of range. The blue flag was raised a second time and the catapults halted again. Boulders now found their way from the trailing carts to all the massive weapons. As they were being loaded, Ellaniya saw some movement before the siege engines. Planks that had been covered by snow appeared as they were raised from the ground. Soldiers streamed out from tunnels with swords held high. Light from the winter sun reflected off steel as blades fell amidst the operators of the catapults. A stain of crimson began to flow out and disrupted the pristine visage of the sparkling white landscape.

With their purpose accomplished, the first wave of defenders darted back towards the castle as a second group emerged. They too dashed towards the machines and hurled what Ellaniya assumed were buckets.

The empress could not hear what was happening amidst the chaotic jumble of orders which were being called out from the warriors. Her attacking troops began to move forward as their own archers let loose volleys at the Su'Meeryn warriors. She noticed that the first group of defenders had disappeared apparently back through the tunnels in the snow. As the second group also fled, she spotted off to her right a row of archers emerging from the snow-covered gardens. Arrows engulfed in flames flew at the catapults. Those which impacted the wood of the deadly machines ignited what had obviously been oil and soon all the catapults were ablaze. But before the Su'Meeryn archers could retreat, scores of arrows flew in their midst. There were so many arrows, that Ellaniya doubted any of those men could have survived.

"Orrin is smarter than I've given him credit for," Ellaniya hissed to herself as her soldiers regrouped around Aniass. "This assault is going to be harder than we expected."

# chapter 53

THE DAY REMAINED BITTERLY COLD, but the absence of falling snow was a pleasant change. The azure sky presented a stark contrast to the glistening sea of white blanketing everything on the ground. A part of Dellea wanted to appreciate the beauty of the tranquil scene, but all her fingers and toes were numb. And she remained haunted by the battle she had witnessed, along with the sight of Pathum completely razed. How Travyn and Ellaniya had accomplished the destruction of her home remained a mystery she did not have the luxury to ponder. Their small party was still being hunted, so all she could think on was remaining alive.

The pain from her leg had finally subsided but plodding through the heavy snow remained difficult. The white powder often found ways to enter her boots, but, fortunately, it was never enough where she thought it necessary to stop and remove her footwear. Hellet was still struggling with his glove and keeping his finger warm. He tried switching hands, but the gloves were then uncomfortable, and he worried about causing an issue with another finger. Dellea offered to swap with him, but he refused. And he refused to say anything to the others. "If this is the worst I have to suffer, I will deal with it," he said.

Neffy divided his time between the two couples and Dellea could tell by his demeanor that he did not agree with Hellet's decision to move away from Gorthon. But their large friend had resolved to abide by his prince's decision and would not complain. What little conversation they had was regarding Perrin, whose emotional deterioration was a deepening concern. Darus remained constantly at his wife's side, behind Dellea and Hellet, and Neffy would report to Hellet that Perrin seemed to be getting worse. She would mumble endlessly and then remain silent for long periods, but her eyes were always frantically searching the horizon. Neffy wondered how much longer she would be able to continue. Dellea saw Hellet's face fall with worry following each update from Neffy. It was as if the weight of his decisions were a heavy sled he was dragging through the tundra.

As they continued their plodding march the wolves would come and go, checking in with the group before racing off to continue their hunts. It was as if the encounter with the soldiers from Gorthon had put them on alert, and they seemed to be acting as sentries for Dellea and the others. She was pleased to see them when they returned, but she was also relieved when they headed off. They would need food soon, and hopefully the wolves would return with a kill.

"It doesn't look good," Neffy said as he approached. He then pointed back towards Darus and Perrin. Dellea looked over and she saw Perrin's fingers at her mouth, trying to bite her nails through her gloves.

"If she keeps this up, she will bite holes in them, and that will make things even worse," Dellea said.

Midday found them walking along the bed of a frozen creek. Pine trees lined the bank, jutting up from the snow, and white clumps clung to the branches. It was as if the snow was trying to camouflage the trees from the eyes of the group; much like Dellea and the others were trying to stay hidden from their pursuers.

"Let's stop and try to eat something," Hellet said, glancing back at Perrin and Darus. But as he spoke, his foot slipped, and he tumbled down the small embankment. He landed on his face, and Dellea heard a cracking sound. As Hellet tried to scramble back up, Dellea saw his left arm crash through the ice. He quickly yanked it out and managed to climb back up the embankment. His arm was soaked, and icy water dripped off his jacket and his now fully exposed hand.

As Hellet yanked off his wet coat, Neffy ran to pull out one of the horse hides from a pack while Dellea ran her hands up and down his shaking body. "Are you alright?" she asked.

"I don't think I'm injured," he replied as he glanced over himself, his eyes coming to rest on his hand.

"We'll have to share gloves now," Neffy ordered as he wrapped the hide around the prince. He then ripped his off and shoved it towards Hellet before the prince could object. "You won't be able to continue on without one."

Dellea could tell Hellet wanted to contradict his friend, but he knew that that was no longer an option. Hellet shook his hand then wiped off the remaining moisture on the hide. Before donning Neffy's glove, he pulled out the vial of salve he had been given by the Gorthon warrior and rubbed some of the ointment on his hand with most going on his finger.

"How does it feel?" Darus asked.

"It tingles a bit. I guess ask me later. Now let's try to eat something."

Neffy and Darus brushed away snow from around the trees then pulled out some of the frozen meat. As they sat, Perrin slid down the side of a tree and began to giggle softly. All heads turned to her as her laughter continued to increase in volume. "This is perfect!" she bellowed between laughs.

Dellea could not take her eyes off the girl. She wanted to go to Perrin, but she was frozen in place. The hysterical cackling sent a chill down her spine and goosebumps up each arm. Darus grabbed his wife, wrapping his arms around her. Dellea could still see Perrin's face over Darus' shoulder, and her cheeks were turning a bright shade of pink as the laughter continued. After a few more agonizing minutes, Perrin finally stopped. Her glassy eyes peered out from her expressionless face. A moment later, Dellea saw tears form in the corner of her eyes. Perrin's head began to shake as more tears streamed down her cheeks. A loud wail suddenly escaped through her quivering lips followed by uncontrollable sobs. Her wails echoed through the wilderness, and Dellea began to fear that their pursuers might hear her. Darus gently placed his hand over her mouth to muffle the sound, but with his one arm released, Perrin wiggled out of his grasp. She then pushed him away with a force Dellea did not think possible. Darus was sprawled out in the snow while Neffy shot up, standing before the two. Dellea had no idea what Neffy might do, but before he could make a decision, all sound from Perrin abruptly ceased. She again leaned back against the tree staring into the sky.

Hellet and Dellea looked at each other in stunned bewilderment. What should they do? Dellea had no idea, but at least for the moment, Perrin was silent.

Darus rose from the wet ground and cautiously made his way back to his wife. She did not seem to notice as he settled down next to her. He gazed at her, but Perrin's vision remained focused on the deep blue sky above. He gently placed his hand on her knee, but she did not acknowledge his touch.

Dellea reached under her cloak and pulled out the orange and silver scarf that Perrin had given her not so many months ago, though now it felt like ages. She thought of offering it back to her friend. Perhaps a pleasant memory of the past might help Perrin fight through their current sufferings. But then she thought that—in Perrin's current state—memories of the past would likely just compound the problem. As her eyes moved from the scarf, back to Perrin, Dellea thought of the times the two had spent shopping. While Perrin had shown kindness by making an effort to befriend the awkward girl from Pathum, Dellea had to admit that she had viewed Perrin as spoiled, but now she just wondered how Perrin would survive. Would any of them survive?

"I don't know what we're going to do," Neffy said as he approached.

"What can we do?" Dellea replied, shoving the scarf back under her cloak.

"You don't want to hear this Hellet," Neffy continued, "but maybe we should return to Gorthon. How are we ever going to make it to Labyn?"

Hellet's head turned from Neffy, to Perrin, and back again. "I know it seems foolish, but we can't. We all know Gorthon won't aid us against my uncle. We must continue."

"I still don't know what you think the few of us can do. Certainly nothing if we're dead."

"Wairren said that Dellea and I are the key. We will not retreat while we still have a chance."

All three faces turned as Perrin began to sob again. "You're really going to risk her life based on the rantings of a stableman?" asked Neffy. "And Dellea's?"

Dellea saw frustration building in Hellet, but he controlled his anger. "You think I want this? You think I want to risk the life of the woman I love? Of my friends? This is killing me. There is nothing more that I want then to take us back to Gorthon. But I can't surrender. If we go to Gorthon, even for a short time, I'm afraid we'd grow comfortable and never leave. This is a battle we must win."

Resignation crossed Neffy's face as he replied. "Very well. I will not speak of it again." He then rose and made his way back to Darus and Perrin.

"The finger seems to be getting warm," Hellet said as he rubbed his hand.

"That's good."

Hellet turned back to the others as Perrin's crying had stopped, and she glared down at the ground. "Am I making the right decision?" he asked.

Dellea reached out and placed her hand on his shoulder. Her thoughts went back to the stitching she had tried to make. She felt foolish at having been upset over her lack of skill with the needle. It certainly made no difference now, but she remembered Jenna's words: how it was far more important for her to learn to handle difficult situations than worry about poor needlework. And she could not imagine a more difficult situation than the one in which they found themselves.

"I don't know," she finally replied. "I spent more time with Wairren than you did, and he never told me anything specific. If you and I are the key to victory, who's to say that it can't be accomplished in Gorthon?"

"But that's the problem, we don't know. Everything he told us seems to have been correct, but we still don't know what to do. We can only make our decision based on what we do know, and Gorthon won't help us against Travyn and Ellaniya. Labyn will have to. I'll admit that I can't say this with certainty, but it does seem right to me."

Dellea reached her hand up and brushed her fingers against his face. She could see the soft stubble of his adolescent beard but could not feel him through her glove. She wanted to continue to caress him and smooth away all the lines of stress marring his beautiful face, but she stopped herself. "There is nothing more that I want to do but head to Gorthon and start a peaceful life with you, but I too sense it would be a selfish decision." She stopped as Perrin's sobbing returned, and it reminded her off all the trauma she was experiencing and had experienced. All she wanted was relief from the pain and to be with Hellet, but it seemed that was not to be. She had to force the next words from her mouth. "I think you're right. We should continue forward."

# chapter 54

ELLANIYA WATCHED THE ARROWS FLYING from the combined forces of the Mephosh army and the mercenaries towards the parapets of Su'Meeryn, but she did not expect the missiles to find many targets. The hope was the frenzied assault would keep the defenders at bay while the attack regrouped. She then spotted a horse turning from the battle and racing back towards her, with two other riders trailing behind.

"We found no additional tunnels in the snow," Aniass stated as he came up next to her.

"That's good. With the catapults destroyed, we will lose more men than we had anticipated, but we should still take the castle, correct?" the queen asked.

"Yes."

"Very well. Carry on."

Aniass nodded and motioned to the heralds next to him. They lifted horns to their mouths and blew two long blasts. Moments later, Ellaniya heard an answering call, and from the back of the army yellow banners were raised. The archers continued to let loose what seemed to be an endless supply of arrows as the siege towers began their forward trek through the thick snow.

The rest of the army slowly moved behind the towers as Aniass and the heralds spurred their horses, leaving Ellaniya on the slight ridge, watching the battle all alone.

As the towers approached the castle, arrows flew from the top of the walls, mostly striking wood, inflicting no damage. Great shields had been erected on the side of each tower to protect the men pushing them forward. Though Su'Meeryn's counterattack against the catapults had been inspired, the towers were making their way forward, mostly unmolested. However, Ellaniya knew that would not remain the case: the defense would become far more ferocious once they reached the walls. Orrin was not a fool, and he would have further surprises planned.

In what seemed to be only a short moment, the first tower reached the stone structure. Arrows continued to stream down at the attackers, but so too did large rocks and cut sections of tree trunks. These smashed into the towers, and Ellaniya saw a few of her men crushed by the falling debris. She was too far away to hear the impact or tell if the defense was having a substantial effect, but other towers were now reaching the walls. She watched as what she knew must be oil poured down the walls, drenching the siege engines, and then flaming arrows raced towards the towers. When the missiles struck, the engines ignited. Fire and smoke billowed into the sky, and she saw a number of soldiers drop into the snow, trying to extinguish flames before they were burned alive. But Aniass had prepared for this maneuver. After a few moments, it seemed that the fires flowed off the towers to the snow-covered ground. Aniass had ordered two layers of covering be constructed over each tower. Once the towers seemed to be fully engulfed, the first layers were stripped away. Some sections remained aflame, but not enough to stop the attackers from climbing the ladders within the structures.

The first of Ellaniya's forces reached the top of the walls as more men rushed forward with additional ladders. Arrows continued to fly at them, and she saw numerous warriors plummet to the ground. But as more attackers reached the top, the arial defense quickly ceased and her men were now able to scale the walls unmolested.

She faintly heard a confused jumble of rattling and clanging, and she watched while soldiers fought atop the parapets. Sunlight reflected off steel as blades struck. More men fell from atop the walls, and she could not distinguish between her soldiers and defenders. Did it matter? Scores of her warriors continued to reach the ramparts. She thought she might be noticing a crimson stain beginning to form in the snow in front of the wall, but she was not certain. She was thankful that she could not see the blood of the dead and dying, as she glanced down at her hands. The memory of the murder of her father and brother remained with her, and she had no desire to see the blood of others.

The fighting along the top of the wall had now ceased, and though she could not see, she knew it had shifted to the courtyard. The stream of soldiers ascending the wall stopped, and the remainder stood poised outside the gates. Success seemed inevitable. She moved her horse forward; despite her misgivings of watching the battle further, she needed to see what would happen next. While she moved closer, so too did the remaining attackers. They all now stood before the castle; she could sense the anticipation. Blades were raised as finally the castle doors swung open, and her warriors poured in.

She continued to advance, watching the combat swirl about the courtyard. She was now able to clearly see the blood spilling on the ground. Despite the blood, she found herself smiling at the scene, but then the noise of combat drifted away. With the outcome of the battle decided, the surviving warriors of Su'Meeryn threw down their weapons and knelt to the blood-drenched ground in surrender.

Ellaniya kept her horse moving forward, towards the courtyard, her head turning in all direction. The carnage was everywhere. Scarlet stains covered much of the scene. Broken bodies lay strewn on the ground with gaping wounds displaying organs and bones. Some still moved, and cries and moans filled her ears. It seemed that everywhere she looked she saw a vision of her father or brother. Death surrounded her; deaths caused by her command. She glanced down at her hands again as she forced the unwanted thoughts from her mind.

When she looked up again, Ellaniya saw Aniass approaching. He was guiding a man towards her at sword point. When they neared, she saw the unmistakable red eyes drilling into her. Though covered in blood, Orrin appeared to be uninjured.

"May I present to you Orrin," Aniass called out, "the former king of Su'Meeryn."

The queen's smile returned—her father and brother forgotten. She now ruled Su'Meeryn, Shekul and Mephosh. And once it was rebuilt, Pathum would be added to her domain. But she would not stop there; Labyn would be her next target. The path was clear; her empire was being established, and then the final step would be ascending to join the gods on high in her promised divinity. Ellaniya's grin widened at the thought, but then it faded as behind Orrin she saw a wounded soldier being put out of his misery. She watched as more blood flowed to the ground. She was not responsible for this man's demise, she told herself; the citizens of Su'Meeryn had made their choice by rejecting the gods. She had only done what was required of her.

"So, this is what you wanted all along." Orrin said, his red eyes flashing in the winter sun. "What now?"

Aniass' hand smacked the back of Orrin's head. "You need to be more respectful of your monarch."

"His tone is of no matter," Ellaniya replied. "Su'Meeryn is mine. Orrin is inconsequential."

"And where is my brother?"

"My dear husband is out hunting for your son. Rest assured, Hellet will be joining you soon." Orrin's eyes seemed to darken at her comment, and his face turned a crimson hue, matching the blood-splattered scene.

"What do you want done with him?" Aniass asked while Orrin continued to glare at the pair.

"Find his wife and throw them both in a cell."

As Aniass pulled Orrin away, Ellaniya took in a deep breath. Corpses were starting to be dragged away while the wounded were being tended to or dispatched. She was horrified by the carnage around her, but she was also exhilarated. Everything was progressing perfectly.

# chapter 55

THE PAIN IN HIS HAND HAD LESSENED since he started using the salve, but his finger remained extremely worrisome. The skin had turned a darker shade of red, and he was having a difficult time moving it. But the concerns for his discomfort was overshadowed by Perrin. Her mood continually shifted between stoic silence and what seemed to be incoherent ramblings. Hellet did not know which was worse. When she was silent, her expression displayed a seething rage. It seemed that she would explode at any moment. But when she broke her silence, her tone was more of hysteria and confusion than of anger. Hellet continued to wonder if it would have been better to leave her in Gorthon, but the decision had been made for her to stay with Darus. She was here with them, and she kept moving. There was nothing he could do about it now, and he questioned if any of his decisions had been correct since leaving Su'Meeryn. Was he the victim of his own pride? Jenna had warned him regarding his lack of experience, and he wondered if they were all now paying the price for his folly. He glanced about, and seeing the beleaguered condition of Dellea and his friends just increased his doubt.

The wolves had been absent for over a day, and that—along with the constant strain Perrin injected into the group—was taking a toll on Dellea. She said little and would only mumble a bit when someone spoke to her.

A light snow began to fall, which Hellet appreciated. They needed more of it to cover their tracks as Hellet was certain they were still being pursued.

They stopped for a midday break at the outskirts of the thin forest skirting the foothills of Gorthon. Once they were on the move again, the group would be traveling through the open space of the Eusutal Plains for long periods. Hellet was concerned regarding the lack of cover they

251

would find, but there was no way to avoid it if they were going to continue on to Labyn.

Neffy pulled the last of the horse meat form his pack then announced. "This is it. I can't believe I'm saying this, but I hope those wolves return soon. And I hope they were successful."

"They have done much for us so far," Hellet pointed out.

"I know, but I don't like the way they look at me. I'm afraid I'll be their next meal if they don't find something else."

"Well, with each passing day there is less of you for them to feast on," Hellet said, patting his friend's stomach.

Neffy chuckled at the jest as Hellet turned his attention towards Dellea, but before he could take a step, they heard a pounding sound from the north. Both drew weapons as they saw the unmistakable shapes of horses bearing down on them. Hellet considered dashing back into the forest, but he did not think they would have time, and, by doing so, they would likely get separated. Plus, that would put their backs to the enemy. As he braced himself, he hoped he was wrong, that these were not pursuers from Shekul. But he knew those odds were miniscule.

Darus too was now at his side, and the three young men readied themselves.

Before Hellet could consider where Dellea and Perrin were, the first horse reached them. Neffy grabbed Hellet's collar and threw him out of the way. The rider lowered his sword as Darus and Neffy both jumped to either side and swung at the animal. Their swords slashed the horse's chest. Its legs buckled from the impact, and it collapsed in a crash of snow. The rider was thrown forwards landing hard on the ground. Hellet's friends then raced past the soldier—Darus' blade quickly pierced his throat—and back to their group. The riders tried to maneuver their mounts, but the horses had a difficult time turning in the thick snow.

Hellet pulled himself up from the ground and stood beside Neffy with his sword ready. One of the horses was making its way back, and the rider swung at Hellet. He managed to block the blow, but the force of the strike knocked him back down to the wet ground. He turned and saw Neffy's blade slice into the rider's leg. The man roared in pain as he looked to swing the horse around again.

He did not have time to count the number of horses, but they were vastly outnumbered. Soon they would be surrounded, and there would be no way for them to emerge victorious this time.

Hellet sprung forward as he saw two horses approaching Darus, but he did not know what assistance his meager skills would bring. When the horses reached his friend, Hellet expected Darus to jump to the side, but instead he dove to the ground and chopped at the leg of the lead horse.

The animal skidded to its right—somehow missing Darus—and collapsed into the other horse. The impact threw the second horse off balance and both riders flew to the ground. The two men were up quickly, and both pulled out weapons. One readied his sword while the other held a large hammer above his head. Darus had risen and was able to parry the blow from the sword, but the hammer crashed down on his shoulder. He bellowed in pain, falling back into the snow. Hellet had reached the pair and swung wildly at the sword wielding man. The warrior quickly spun around and easily parried the strike. Hellet's momentum pushed him forward, and he was past Darus before he managed to skid around. When he turned back, he saw the face of Travyn smile while he raised his hammer. Time seemed to slow as Hellet heard a giggle from his uncle. Hellet cried out—but it was to no avail—and Travyn's huge weapon came crashing down. Hellet heard the sound of bone cracking and saw blood erupt into Travyn's face as the hammer crushed the skull of his life-long friend.

Blinded, Travyn tried to wipe the blood from his eyes and face. With his uncle momentarily incapacitated, Hellet only needed to face one foe. He had no time to mourn for Darus, or he too would meet the same fate. The man looked at Hellet and gave him an evil grin as he swung his weapon. Hellet barely managed to parry the blow, and he knew he was grossly overmatched. A few more swings were clumsily blocked, and Hellet got the impression that the soldier was toying with him. Hellet tried to remember his lessons with the blade, but it seemed unlikely that we would recall enough to defeat his attacker. The man raised his sword again, preparing to strike, but then his body went stiff. The smile fell from his face as blood trickled from the corner of his mouth. He fell forward with a sword sticking out the back of his neck, and Perrin stood above him. Her face gave Hellet pause. She had the look of one sitting before a banquet table after a long fast. It was the look of anticipation and delight which sent a chill down Hellet's spine. Before he could say anything, Perrin yanked the blade from the body of her victim, her eyes scanning the scene.

Hellet took a moment to get his bearings. He could not see Dellea, and he wondered what had become of Travyn. He then saw the hammer swinging at Neffy who was surrounded by warriors, all of whom were now on foot. Evidently, Travyn wanted to finish off the last remaining warrior before turning his attention back to his nephew. Hellet stood paralyzed. What should he do? He wanted to help his friend, but the two of them would not be able to prevail. He thought about finding Dellea and trying to flee with her. But he cursed himself for his cowardly thought. And what of Perrin? He had no idea what to do.

Neffy's ferocious skills were on display as he fought off the warriors, but it was ultimately a futile effort; they were too outnumbered. But then three shapes came flying in. The wolves raced forward with jaws ripping into the legs of the attackers.

Their assailants were now in disarray. They tried to swing at the beasts, but as they turned their backs to Neffy, his sword sliced the arm of one man then split the skull of another. The arrival of the wolves pulled Hellet from his paralysis; however, before he could rush into the melee, Perrin bolted past him. She reached a man who was attempting to fight off a wolf that had his leg. The warrior tried to swing at the animal, but before his sword reached its target, Perrin drove her blade into the man's face.

The wolves had taken down two other men, but a further pair had turned back to engage Neffy. So far, he had managed to keep them at bay, but he was slowly being overwhelmed. Before a blade could find his friend's flesh, Hellet leapt at one, burying his sword in the man's back. Neffy was then able to disarm the other, and the second man fell to the ground in surrender. Neffy placed his boot on the sword and held his own blade to the man's throat.

With all their foes now dispatched, Hellet looked around for his uncle and saw one lone figure riding away. He did not need to see the face to know it was Travyn. He hoped the wolves would pursue his uncle, but after finishing off the other attackers, they bolted after the surviving horses that had all galloped off.

Hellet wanted to turn his attention to their prisoner, but there was a more pressing matter. Where was Dellea? He looked about then spotted her sitting next to Darus' body. His vision remained on the broken body of his friend for moment, but he would have to put his grief aside. He first needed to get what information he could from their captive.

Neffy's sword remained a hair width from the man's throat as Hellet approached. But before he could ask any questions, Perrin raced over and swung her blade, plunging it into the side of their prisoner's neck. The man gurgled as blood poured forth. His hands went to the wound in a feeble attempt to dam the flow as crimson poured from his mouth. He was unsuccessful. His body went limp, and he collapsed, blood staining the ground at Perrin's feet. She hissed at the man then wiped off her blade in his hair.

Hellet gazed in shock at the widow of his friend. Her sneer remained while she glared at the corpse of her victim. When she finally turned her attention away, she stared at Hellet with a fearsome expression. Her eyes were wide and unblinking as her tongue traced across her upper lip. He saw a slight tremble when her glare returned to the body at their feet. The red-stained snow had reached her boots which seemed to give her pleasure. Should Hellet be concerned for her or afraid of her?

After a vicious kick to the head of the corpse, Perrin walked over to one of the maimed horses that was struggling to lift itself from the ground. She quickly slit its throat. "Let's move," she said flatly. "We have meat to prepare."

# chapter 56

ELLANIYA'S HANDS SLID OVER the polished wood of the arm rests of the throne in the royal hall of Su'Meeryn. Her fingers lovingly caressed every inch of the smooth surface she could reach and traced through the etchings on the sides. Jaleph once sat here, she thought. His right hand had rested on this same wood, but, of course, he had no left hand to place on the other. She relished the turn of fortune that put her on this throne. Jaleph and Su'Meeryn had been directly responsible for the decline of Mephosh and the heresy that had infected her family. Now she ruled—a messenger of the gods to restore the proper order.

The nobles of Su'Meeryn stood nervously before her, flanked by her sword wielding guards. While they were rightfully fearful for their futures, Ellaniya harbored no desire to kill or ruin them. They were not responsible for Jaleph's misdeeds. All the nobles she knew back in Mephosh were primarily worried with one thing: their own self-interests and their position in the court. Piety was not their concern. Ellaniya was certain the Su'Meeryn nobles were the same, so she had no reason to punish them.

Their fear was palpable. It filled the entire hall like water pouring into a large basin. She thought of rising from the throne to address them, but she was enjoying the moment. Ellaniya allowed their agitation to grow as she silently claimed her authority over them. The empress gave herself over to the pleasure of resting in the silence, as if she was sitting in a warm bath. Ellaniya had sacrificed so much to get here, and she wanted to savor her victory.

Her purple eyes travelled amongst the nobles while her thoughts turned to the deposed king. She had been told that Orrin was not a believer in the heresy, but that the queen was. Well, the royal couple would be dealt with shortly, but first she needed to address those assembled before her.

Finally she began. "Nobles of Su'Meeryn, as you know, I am Ellaniya, queen of Mephosh and Shekul, wife of your prince Travyn. I now claim this throne in my name and also the name of my husband. Su'Meeryn is hereby annexed into the greater Mephosh empire. However, you may all remain at ease; I have no qualms with the nobility of Su'Meeryn. None of your positions are at stake. You may all continue to carry out your business as you see fit. In fact, now that we are all one empire, I expect your wealth to grow. There are but two things I ask of you. First, you all must swear allegiance to me," she paused a moment for her words to resonate, "and to Travyn. Your rulers must be assured of your fidelity, after all.

"Second, any of you who are following the heretical religion must renounce it immediately. A temple of the gods will be established forthwith, and you will all be expected to profess and practice the true faith.

"Now I will demonstrate the seriousness of my demand." She waved to her left and Aniass dragged forth a bound and gagged Orrin and Jenna. A quiet murmur and a few gasps came from the nobles as the mercenary leader shoved the pair before the throne. Jenna fell sobbing onto the floor as more soldiers emerged and pulled her up while another pair grasped her husband. Orrin stood defiantly, his red eyes glaring at Ellaniya from above his gag. That was fine with her; his ire would not last much longer.

"Whether you are aware of it or not," Ellaniya continued, "the gods demand sacrifices to appease their anger and as a petition to their good will. In recent times, animal sacrifices were the normal practice, but, in the distant past, human sacrifices were offered in extreme circumstances. The gods have been enraged by Sul's heresy and that we have neglected offering the ultimate tribute for so long. Therefore, I have reinstated the ultimate form of worship." She nodded to Aniass who drew his sword. Orrin's red eyes widened in horror as the mercenary calmly slit the throat of his wife. Unintelligible sounds billowed from behind his gag while Orrin desperately struggled against his bonds, trying to break free from his captors. Aniass allowed Jenna's limp body to drop to the floor as he turned his attention to the former king. The sword still dripped Jenna's blood when it was raised before Orrin's face. As the former ruler continued to struggle, the blade sliced through his throat as well. Blood poured out to intermingle with that of his wife as he dropped beside to her.

"The gods' anger towards the heresy of Su'Meeryn is currently quenched," Ellaniya announced calmly and emphatically. "I am certain that you will all make sure that their anger does not resurface and create the need for additional sacrifices."

The nobles stood transfixed by the sight before them. Eyes darted from the slain couple to Ellaniya and back again. No one spoke, and an eerie silence filled the chamber.

With a wave, the empress excused the nobles from the hall, who all eagerly exited as quickly as possible. Aniass considered the bodies that remained at his feet then ordered servants to take them away. "What is next, your Majesty? Do you have a further task for my men and me, or am I dismissed?"

"You have served me well, Aniass, and you all will be handsomely compensated. But I cannot discharge you yet. I have lost many warriors from these conflicts, and I must rebuild my army. I need you to stay in my employ. May I assume you are wiling?"

"Of course. I know that you are very generous." He paused as he sheathed his still dripping blade. "May I ask, what's next? We are still early in winter. Conditions will likely grow worse."

"That is probably true. We will need time to consolidate my victories and grow my army. Labyn will be our next target. While they will have time to prepare to face us, we must re-strengthen ourselves. The remainder of this winter will be spent resting and spreading the true religion. In the spring, we will resume our campaign, stronger and with additional blessings from the gods." By his expression, Ellaniya could tell Aniass cared not regarding the god's blessings. He was a mercenary, not a pious man, but she would deal with his lack of faith in due course. For now, she needed his sword, and the swords of his men.

"As you command," Aniass replied with a slight bow of his head.

After the leader of the mercenaries exited the hall, Ellaniya sat quietly on the throne. The bodies of the former monarchs had been removed, but the streaks of their blood forced her mind to return to thoughts of her father and brother. She had been surrounded by so much death since her first visit to Su'Meeryn. Had she become so jaded that death no longer affected her? Perhaps. But she was convinced it had all been necessary. As a quality sword is tempered and crafted, she had been as well. A sword cannot be made without being subjected to the fire of the kiln. She had experienced that fire. Any imperfections had been burned away. She had emerged from the fire as a masterly crafted, fearsome weapon; a blade which required battle to fulfill its legacy.

Ellaniya's thoughts then turned to her husband, and she wondered how he was faring. However, in all honesty, she no longer cared; Travyn was inconsequential. And if Hellet was not captured and killed, she wondered if that even mattered. Su'Meeryn was safely in her hands. What threat could the boy be?

# chapter 57

AFTER HARVESTING PLENTY OF HORSE MEAT, and searching the bodies for supplies, Hellet ordered the burial of Darus. However, the frozen ground made the chore impossible. Hellet was then going to search for kindling to burn the body, but Perrin refused. She did not want to send a signal to any other pursuers, if they would even be able to start a fire. Hellet had objected, but Perrin said that Darus had been her husband, and it was her decision. She did not want to risk any more death, and she said that he would remain where he lay. Without further word, she set off to continue the long, cold march. The others could do nothing but follow.

The frigid air seemed to find every seam in Dellea's clothing as the four trudged through the thick snow. Dellea was physically and emotionally exhausted, but she managed to keep her weary feet moving. The wolves followed close to Dellea and Hellet, and she was pleased to have their calming presence. Since they had gorged themselves on one of the other horses, she knew they would not set off to hunt for another day or two.

She wondered how much more of this misery they would be able to take. They had witnessed and caused so much killing. She had been nearby and saw the blow from her former fiancé which crushed Darus' head. While she had not initially cared much for Darus, a bond had grown between the five of them since coming upon her devastated homeland. Though she would not have considered him a friend, he had become something more than a companion, and he was the husband of her only other close friend in the world.

Dellea was thankful that Hellet was at her side, but that could not take away her memories. And those memories were filled with the calamities she had witnessed. As if sensing her mood, one of the wolves came beside her and forced its head under her hand. With a smile she began to stroke the beast.

"I don't know what to make of her," Hellet said, interrupting Dellea's troubled thoughts. "I feared for her sanity, but now this?" He gestured ahead to Darus' widow who plodded along as if she was one magnet being drawn to another, leading the small group to their unseen destination.

Dellea chastised herself for her self-pity. Yes, she had suffered. There were all those terrible nightmares she had endured, and they had all seen the aftermath of the destruction of her home. But Perrin had lost her husband; her anguish must certainly be greater than any of theirs. And now Perrin had displayed a viciousness to their enemy that Dellea could never have expected, but at least she did not appear to be a liability anymore.

"I can't believe he's gone," Hellet said quietly.

"I know," Dellea replied, reaching for his hand. He winced but would not allow her to release her grip. He had acquired gloves from one of the dead soldiers, but his hand remained painful, and his finger was getting worse. Dellea glanced back at Neffy, who seemed to be purposely keeping his distance. "You were friends a very long time." And she wondered what that felt like. She had not had any friends growing up in Pathum. There were plenty of servants that she had been kind to, but she was certain any affection from them had been a façade. She grieved for Hellet and the others for the loss of Darus, but it was their loss. She was sad that Darus had been killed—especially by that fool Travyn—but she did not feel the grief of the others.

Maybe her father had been right about her all along. Would not a normal person be moved by the death of someone with whom she had spent so much time? She knew that she would have been crushed if it had been one of the wolves that had been killed rather then him. What did that say about her? No, she told herself, I will not put myself on that road again. I am sad that he was killed, but I do not have the grief of the others. He was not my friend; I should not be expected to have the same emotions as them.

The frigid temperature worsened as their miserable trek continued. Perrin remained their stoic guide, seemingly unfazed by the cold. Dellea regarded her friend as her self-doubt resurfaced, but then she thought of Hellet. Certainly this wonderful young man would not love her if she was such a terrible person. She offered a quick, silent prayer for Perrin and gently squeezed Hellet's hand.

**\*\*\***

As if the recent events and their dismal journey were not burden enough, Dellea's horrific dreams had returned. Her sleeping hours were constantly assailed by visions of crimson-stained corpses with mangled and twisted limbs. Each time, the fields of the dead overwhelmed her tear-filled eyes. And, amidst it all, Hellet was always there, bathed in blood—a strong wind threatening to drive his body down into the grisly landscape. But despite the forces pushing at him, his head would not move, his beautiful blue eyes, filled with sorrow, seemingly locked on hers.

Did the return of the dreams have something to do with the death of Darus? It was possible, but the dreams had started before they had left the comforts of Su'Meeryn. She did not know what to make of the return of her nightmares; all she knew was that they added to her misery. In the mornings, she would recount her visions to Hellet, but despite his uncommon wisdom, he was as perplexed as she. Wairren thought there was some connection between her dreams and his visions, but what could it possibly be?

Every morning her frustration grew. If she was not going to receive any answers, what good was it for these visions to plague her sleep? She prayed that the torture would stop, but so far, her prayers had gone unanswered.

Aside from the nightmares, the next few days went by uneventfully. They had caught no sight of any further pursuers and begun to wonder if Travyn had called off the search. Dellea hoped so, but if Travyn had given up, what was the reason? Had Su'Meeryn been conquered? If Travyn no longer viewed Hellet as a threat, was Su'Meeryn firmly in his grip now? It was a terrible thought to consider; however, if they were no longer being sought, at least they should be able to safely reach Labyn, assuming they could survive the frigid wintery conditions.

While it seemed that they were able to move freely through the snow-covered Eusutal Plains, they were still facing a major concern. Hellet's finger was becoming worse. He had run out of the salve that the man from Gorthon had given him, and his skin was no longer red. It was turning purple, and he was having a difficult time moving it. When Neffy tried to talk to him about the issue, Hellet had stopped him short. He knew what he was facing: if the finger did not improve soon, it would have to be removed, or he would risk losing his whole hand.

"We should just cut it off now," Perrin said flatly, during one of their breaks. "It's only going to get worse."

"That might be the case, but I'd like to give it some time to see if it starts to heal first, if you don't mind." replied Hellet. "I'm not very anxious to chop off my finger, especially out here."

"We can do it now, or in a couple days," Perrin replied flatly. "It won't make any difference."

Before Hellet could retort further, Perrin turned her back on him and started off, in her now customary position of leading the group.

"I could never have imagined that this is how she would react to Darus' death," Neffy said while he too stood. Dellea regarded the large man as he stepped behind a snow-covered bush. Hellet and she had been so concerned about Perrin's transformation, she realized they had not put much thought into how Neffy was handling his friend's death. Since the two were a couple years older than Hellet, they had been friends longer. They would argue and jest with each other, but the two had been as close as brothers. She marveled at Neffy's strength through all they had endured, but Dellea had seen the sadness in his eyes. Despite everything, Neffy's behavior had not changed. He clearly missed his friend, but he was putting the grief aside for the time being. He had a job to do, and he could not let his friend's death interfere with protecting Hellet. Perhaps he would grieve if they reached Labyn, but now was not the time. Dellea was thankful that Neffy was with them, and she just shook her head as she recalled the initial dislike she had felt towards him. Now she could not imagine a more loyal friend, and she wondered what they would have done without him.

Dellea then looked back at Hellet, who was rubbing his hand. She knew Perrin was correct. The finger was only getting worse; it would not miraculously begin to improve now, but she understood that Hellet was not prepared for the inevitable outcome. They all knew what would be involved. Cutting it off and cauterizing it in this snowy wilderness would be dangerous and agonizing, and they had nothing to ease Hellet's pain. No, it made more sense to try to get to Labyn first. If the injury progressed further, they would be forced to deal with it, but the discoloration had yet to spread from the finger. They did not need to rush the amputation. Hellet still had time, but that time was running out.

The three began to trudge after Perrin while the wolves loped playfully through the snow. At least they are content, Dellea thought.

After a few minutes, Neffy dropped back to scan the horizon. It seemed unnecessary as the day was clear and they could see for miles. There were no enemies in the vicinity, but if Neffy felt that he was offering them some extra protection, she figured it was good for his mental state. Though she wondered if he might be better off being alongside them. He had not spoken of Darus since his friend's death, and that troubled her. She did not think he should be alone, but she did not want to press the matter.

The cold air was causing her eyes to water, and she reached into a pocket and pulled out the orange scarf to dry them. She felt the softness of the material against her face then peered ahead at Perrin who was marching forward, creating a trail through the snow. Looking at the scarf and Darus' widow brought back a flood of memories. Dellea remembered those days shopping with Perrin and the discomfort she had felt. Now she longed for that time. As she shoved the scarf back into her pocket, the memories caused her tears to return.

# chapter 58

TRAVYN DESPISED HIS FORMER FIANCÉ even more than he thought possible. If not for her and those damned wolves, Hellet would be his prisoner now. At least he had the satisfaction of having killed Darus, and he was thankful that he had managed to escape the violent encounter unscathed. Since the rest of his group had been killed—as far as he knew—and Ellaniya was no longer in Shekul, he decided he would make his way to Su'Meeryn. He did not know if the attack against his former home had been successful, but he would find out soon enough.

The trip back to Su'Meeryn was far from pleasant. The pack on the horse he had taken was low on supplies, and the weather remained brutally cold. The small amount of food he had was frozen, and his horse struggled to keep up a good pace in the high, hard snow.

The sun was low in the sky after two full days of traveling when Travyn finally spied the castle walls. He was in a foul mood due to his hunger as he had consumed the last of his meager rations that morning. And it did not help that he had cracked a tooth on a piece of frozen meat.

He cautiously made his way around the high walls to the front gate. Even in the low light, he could see frozen, crimson stains streaking the stone walls as well as piles of red snow at the bottom. Obviously, the battle had taken place, but he could not determine who had prevailed. He stopped his horse and gazed at his childhood home, befuddled what to do next. Based on the size of his army, he assumed that Ellaniya had prevailed, but how could he be sure?

His stomach growled at him, and he clenched his teeth. Unfortunately, that just set a wave of pain coursing from his mouth and down his spine. A cry escaped past his lips as his hands went to his face. Once the throbbing had subsided, he turned his attention back to the gate, still uncertain what to do next.

It was not much longer before the portal swung open. Two men on horseback emerged and rode towards him as a score of soldiers stood ready in the opening. Travyn remained still as the pair approached. He considered kicking his horse to flee, but where would he go? How much longer would he be able to survive in the winter-battered wilderness on his own? All he could do was pray to the gods that the approaching soldiers were friendly.

"The emperor!" one of them cried out as he got close enough to recognize Travyn. "The emperor has returned!"

Travyn breathed a sigh of relief at that announcement. His fears quashed, Travyn arched his back, sitting up high and proud in the saddle. "Yes, I have returned to my homeland, a skilled and valiant warrior. I have faced the enemy and emerged victorious. And I see that my bride has prevailed as well. Now, escort me into the castle and send word to my beautiful wife. Also, I need food," he commanded in a tone as majestic tone as he could muster, but then another wave of pain shot from his tooth, and he hunched over on his steed as he followed the soldiers through the gate.

***

"It is good to see you, husband," Ellaniya stated placidly as she lounged on a couch in Orrin's private room. "It has been too long."

"Yes, yes, yes, too long!" Travyn agreed noting the look of satisfaction on Ellaniya's face. She must have missed me greatly, he thought; I have never seen her looking so serene and satisfied before.

"Since you have returned, does that mean that Hellet is dead?"

"Darus is!" he blurted out.

"Darus? Who's that?"

"He was one of Hellet's friends. I killed him myself. His blood stains remain on my hammer!"

"So, you found Hellet?" Ellaniya asked as her body straightened. "What happened?"

Travyn took another tentative bite of the bread that had been brought to him. It was the only thing he could manage to eat without increasing the misery in his mouth. "I'll have to have this tooth removed tomorrow."

Ellaniya sucked in a long breath of air. "Hellet? What happened to Hellet?"

Travyn hesitated, considered lying, but then the vision of a raging Ut returned to his mind. What would happen if he fabricated a story regarding Hellet's death and he was later found to be alive? Best to tell the truth he decided. "We found them. They fought well, but we had them surrounded. I would have killed them all, but those wolves came from nowhere. I barely managed to escape, but not before I crushed Darus' head with my hammer. I don't see how they can survive much longer in this winter."

Ellaniya glared at him for a moment, but then her face softened as she settled herself back on the soft cushions. "No matter. We have captured Su'Meeryn; it is fully in our hands now. What can that boy do to us? He is no longer relevant."

"What's next?" Travyn asked, relief coursing through his body. "Have you heard from Ut?"

"No, he has not returned, but that's fine. The winter is getting worse. We will take this time to rest and rebuild our army. Then we continue the campaign in the spring. Labyn will be the next to fall!"

"That is wonderful, my love. Now, let's retire to the bedchambers I have missed being with you."

"Not tonight, husband. You are exhausted and filthy. Bathe and rest. Tomorrow attend to your tooth. Perhaps after that." The concern on her face showed Travyn how difficult it was for her to turn him away, and he again thanked the gods for her. How different it was for him to have someone in his life that cared for him so deeply.

***

Travyn's eyes slowly opened, taking in the light of the bright morning sun. He adjusted his body amongst his blankets and pillows, enjoying the comfort of his own soft bed. While it was a strange feeling being back in his boyhood room, it was a welcome change from his time out in those horrid conditions.

He reached for Ellaniya before remembering that she was not there. She had spent the night in Orrin's and Jenna's chambers as she was concerned that her presence might disturb him while he recovered from his ordeal. His affection for her deepened at how willing she was to make sacrifices for his wellbeing. He briefly wondered if he deserved such a perfect mate, but of course he did. He was emperor—slayer of mighty foes.

After dressing, he left the chamber and instructed his guards to escort him to the healers. Upon entering the large room, he saw many wounded soldiers laying in beds. Some had lost limbs, others were badly burned. Moans greeted his ears as he strode past. One of the healers was changing the dressing on a burn victim, whose hair on half of his head was gone, revealing a charred and blistered skull. The rest of his face remained covered by crimson-stained bandages. Before she could finish changing the dressing, Travyn grabbed her by the arm. "Come with me," he commanded. "I require your assistance."

The woman looked at him, her mouth opened to say something, but she stopped herself. Travyn thought he noticed a look of recognition in her eyes as she carefully set the fresh bandage down. "How may I be of assistance?" she asked.

A straight finger pointed at his mouth. "I need this tooth removed."

The woman's eyes traveled from Travyn to her patient then back to the emperor. "Of course, sire. Please come with me."

***

Travyn sat high on the throne, watching while the royal hall filled with the nobles and ruling class of Su'Meeryn. His mouth still ached, but the discomfort was quickly forgotten as he glanced at Ellaniya beside him, her soft hand resting on his forearm. She was dressed exquisitely in a lavender gown which matched her eyes, and her expression displayed royal confidence as she peered out into the chamber. He smiled at his wife, looking forward to her return to his bed later that night, as he stood to address the crowd.

"People of Su'Meeryn," he began, reciting the words he had spent the day memorizing, "you remember me as Prince Travyn; however, I now stand before you as Emperor Travyn. You should no longer think of yourselves as citizens of Su'Meeryn as Su'Meeryn no longer exists. You are now all part of the great Mephosh empire. But do not... do not..." He paused for a moment, trying to remember the next word.

"Fret," Ellaniya whispered to him.

"Oh yes, do not fret. You will all maintain your positions of honor in our glorious empire. Your taxes will be paid to Ellaniya and myself, and you shall all provide soldiers for our great army. Do as you are asked, and you will find the empress and me to be most generous. But, be warned, any disloyalty will result in you receiving the same fate as Orrin. Now, bow and offer your allegiance to your rulers."

With his task complete, Travyn dropped back onto his throne, congratulating himself on his marvelous speech. He then thought of his brother. While pleased that his life-long tormenter was dead, he wished he had been present to witness the spectacle. Travyn would have gladly been the one to end Orrin's life; he had done such a fine job with the sacrifice of Naren after all. Though he was somewhat sad that Jenna had received the same fate as she had always been reasonably pleasant towards him. But she had never intervened on his behalf, so perhaps her death was for the best too.

The nobles approached the dais in turn to bow before Travyn and Ellaniya. The emperor knew the faces of many of them, and his smile grew as each pledged their allegiance to the empire. I'm finally getting what I deserve, he thought.

✱✱✱

Despite the glory he received from the ceremony of the previous day, the next morning was frustrating for Travyn. Ellaniya had once again avoided their chambers the previous night, but when they met for breakfast, he saw that familiar look of contentment on her beautiful face. Perhaps she had been ill and did not want to risk passing the sickness on to him. His frustration disappeared when he realized that her satisfaction was due to her joy of being in his presence again.

"I hope you are well, my beautiful and stunning empress."

"I am fine," she replied stoically. "Is your mouth healed?"

"It is good."

She smiled at him with an enigmatic look as they began their meal. But before he could ponder the cause of her expression, the door to the dining hall swung open, and the unmistakable figure of Ut entered and marched towards them.

"You have done well, my dear," he said, clapping his hands and joining them at the table. Ellaniya motioned to the servants to bring an extra plate, but Ut waved them away. "I am pleased to see Su'Meeryn has been conquered, and that it did not need to suffer the same fate as Pathum." His expression hardened as he glanced at the emperor, but it immediately softened when his eyes returned to Ellaniya. "The empire of Mephosh is growing. I assume you have begun the purge of the heretic religion?"

"Of course," Ellaniya replied with a beaming smile.

"Very good, my dear."

"I killed Darus!" Travyn cut in triumphantly.

Ut turned back to Travyn. "Yes, I have been made aware; however, Hellet lives."

"Ha, what can my nephew do to us?" Travyn proudly pronounced as his vision travelled about the hall.

"You would be surprised at the power one individual can possess," Ut responded.

"I thought that since Su'Meeryn has been secured, Hellet would no longer be a threat," Ellaniya interjected. "With the deepening of winter, can he even survive being on the run? Therefore, I ordered no further search parties."

Ut remained silent. He turned from Ellaniya and stared at the ceiling. Travyn's eyes darted between the pair while he shoveled eggs into his mouth, happy that his tooth no longer caused him pain. When he finished eating, Ut still had not spoken, and Travyn looked at his wife in confusion. Ellaniya appeared equally perplexed, which made Travyn nervous.

"It would be preferrable had Hellet had been killed," Ut finally stated, "but perhaps you are correct. For now, we need to consolidate our victories. If required, we can deal with Hellet later. We will prepare to move against Labyn once winter breaks."

"That was my order," Ellaniya pointed out.

"As always, you are wise my dear," Ut replied. "The top priority for now is ridding the land of this blasphemous religion."

"When do we get our divinity?" asked Travyn eagerly, thankful that he was not being chastised for letting Hellet escape.

"Soon, my friend. You must be patient. But rest assured, the gods are pleased with all you have done for them and the sacrifices you have made." Ut reached over and took a bite of Ellaniya's eggs before continuing. "Their gratitude will be displayed in time. For now, we must make sure there is no disloyalty brewing in the empire. Ellaniya, I recommend you remain in Su'Meeryn to consolidate our power while Travyn returns to Mephosh. And we should appoint a regent to administer Shekul."

"Ellaniya and I will be separated again?" Travyn blurted out. "She needs me!"

"Your wife will just have to find some way to manage without you," Ut responded dryly. "I have other matters to which I must attend, so I may not be able to check on you, Travyn. We will send Aniass to accompany you, along with ample gold and instructions from me. And I trust that you will do as he says." Ut's words were slow and hard, and for a fearful heartbeat, his face seemed to lose its handsome appearance as a black aura briefly, almost imperceptibly, emanated from his mouth. "I am certain that I am understood."

The memory of the confrontation at Pathum washed over Travyn, and he nodded quickly.

"Now, we need only decide on whom to send to Shekul, and I have an idea."

# Chapter 59

THE ICY WIND WHICH SWIRLED around Hellet was not the only chill he felt. He had killed a man. He did not regret his action since it had been necessary to protect his friends, but this knowledge did not remove his remorse. If they were put in the same situation again, he would act the same way, but the memory remained a struggle for him. After all Dellea had been through—the destruction of Pathum, the brutal deaths she had witnessed and the ongoing nightmares—he did not want to add another burden to her. Instead, he kept his turmoil to himself and trudged on.

As bad as he felt about the killing, his hand was a more immediate concern. The pain in his finger had become unrelenting, and with all the salve gone, there was nothing he could do to soothe it. The color had turned from purple to black, and he was aware of what must be done. However, he struggled to find the courage to move forward with the task. Hellet kept telling himself that there was still time to reach Labyn before the blackness spread further, but he knew that was a lie. While the discoloration had not yet spread from his finger, the pain was beginning to claw its way into the hand. Despite what he knew he would have to deal with, Hellet could wait no longer. As darkness began to set in, and they made camp for the night, he announced his decision to the group.

"You should have listened to me earlier," Perrin stated with no emotion in her voice.

He bristled at the response of Darus' widow, but now was not the time to rebuke her. Would there ever be a time? The transformation in her since Darus' death had been so startling that Dellea and he still did not know how to handle it. She had shifted from being on the verge of madness to a constant rage. What little she said since that day had been focused solely on reaching Labyn. Once they arrived at that kingdom, she would begin formal training with the sword. Then she would join their warriors and fight against the forces of Mephosh. Regardless of the size of the army around her, or that of her foe, she would kill as many of the enemy as she could. If that meant her death, she did not care. Her sole desire was vengeance.

"Get a fire started," she ordered Neffy as she pulled out her sword. Dellea came up beside Hellet and wrapped an arm around his waist. He looked into her eyes, but she said nothing. What could she say? Once the fire was started, the finger would be hacked from his body, and glowing steel would burn his flesh. He hoped in a few days the pain would be gone, but he would be in agony for the night and likely would get no sleep. Neffy looked at him as he placed branches he had pulled off from a nearby tree on the ground after brushing away the snow. Hellet saw the look of concern on Neffy's face, but his friend also said nothing. Despite the freezing temperature, sweat formed on Hellet's brow and his skin began to feel clammy. Dellea's hand trembled as she grasped his.

The wolves began to pace around the campsite with low whimpers escaping from their muzzles. Perrin, seemingly oblivious that anything traumatic was about to happen, absently examined the edge of her sword.

Hellet thought of Wairren's final words to him before they had left their home. He had warned that they would suffer, but Hellet had no idea how true those words would be. First this early and harsh winter, then the death of Darus, and Perrin's subsequent transformation into someone unrecognizable. He had killed a man, and now he was about to have his finger amputated. How much more could his small group withstand?

Neffy struggled to start the fire, but eventually a spark lit a small flame. He added more branches, and the fire slowly grew. Hellet worried that pursuers would see the smoke and flames, but there had been no sign of anyone else since the last battle; they seemed to be the only fools traveling in this brutal weather. Once the fire was large enough, Neffy pulled out his sword and placed it in the flames while Perrin sat—as if in a trance—with her own blade in her hand, staring at Hellet. Though it had not been discussed, Perrin had determined that she would be the one to perform the dreadful act.

As there was not much fuel for the fire, it was not very hot, and it took a long time for the blade of Neffy's sword to begin to glow. When it was finally ready, Hellet drew in a deep breath. It was time.

Hellet tentatively removed his glove. Before he could place his hand on the ground, Dellea drew it to her mouth and gave his palm a soft kiss. He looked at her and could not help but smile. He was grieved that she had been forced into this situation, but he was also thankful to have her with him. Regardless of what they were enduring, he remained beyond grateful that she had been brought into his life. The thought of reaching

Labyn and marrying her gave him the courage he needed. If losing a finger was required for that to occur, he would gladly part with it. "Let's get on with this," he mumbled as he rested his hand on a flat rock with his healthy fingers and thumb carefully tucked away. He could feel the cold of the stone against his hand, but not his finger. "Don't miss."

Perrin raised her sword, and Hellet gazed into her eyes. While he thought he might see pleasure there, he saw nothing. Her glassy eyes were empty, her expression wooden. Hellet then felt a pang of guilt at his brooding as a finger was a far cry from the loss of a husband and one of his closest friends. But that guilt quickly disappeared as her blade swung down. He felt the bones crack and splinter, and he screamed in pain. He shot up from the ground with his right hand clutching the wound. He cried out again as Dellea pried his hand away to expose the bloody mess. Neffy approached with the glowing sword then Hellet heard a sickening hiss and smoke rose from his flesh as a new wave of agony coursed through his entire body. His screaming turned to tears as he collapsed on the wet ground. The misery was so intense he wished he would pass out, but that did not happen. He could smell his burnt flesh as the pain flowed through him like a mighty waterfall in early spring.

His tears mingled with the snow as a hand rubbed his back then he felt two large tongues licking the sides of his head, trying to reach his mouth.

The agony continued to surge through him, and his tears flowed freely to the ground. But they were not solely due to the physical pain. He wept for the transformation of Perrin. He wept for Dellea and all she was being forced to endure. And he wept for Neffy, who had lost someone that was closer to him than a brother.

It was all too much to withstand; he could not stop his sobs. He could still smell his burnt flesh as a glove full of snow was forced onto his maimed hand. Unfortunately, it made little difference to his torment as he kept his head down and eyes closed, trying to will the pain away.

The large tongues continued to caress his face, lapping away his tears, while Dellea's arms wrapped around his shaking body. As Hellet continued to sob, he knew he would get no sleep that night.

# chapter 60

THE DEEPENING COLD seemed to constrict Ellaniya's bones as she stood atop the ramparts of the castle that had been the kingdom of Su'Meeryn. Travyn and his entourage were passing under the gate, and he cast his vision up towards her. Despite the distance, she could see a forlorn expression on his face, and her mind returned to the previous night. Once again feigning an illness, she had refused to join him in bed. Ever since she had concluded that he was useless as a husband, she had lost what little affection she had once felt towards him. She had to admit to herself that their love making had once been pleasurable; however, she now found the thought distasteful. He was nothing more than a pawn—a fairly useless pawn. How could she ever be intimate with him again?

With Travyn leaving, she realized that she felt a little sorry for him. His simple mind was easily manipulated, and she had taken advantage of that to suit her interests. But if those interests had been to reestablish the truth of the gods, had it not also been in Travyn's interests as well? She knew she did not love him, but despite his flaws, Travyn was at least committed to her. Had she wronged him?

As Travyn's horse began to slowly shrink into the distance, Ellaniya wondered if Ut had made the proper decision. Perhaps she should be the one returning home to Mephosh and leave this land that had caused Mephosh so much pain in the hands of her husband. The thought of traveling in these conditions was not pleasant, but it would have reunited her with Vor sooner. However, once Travyn and Aniass arrived in Mephosh, the order would be given for Vor to join her in Su'Meeryn. She just needed to be patient, and he would be with her soon.

"He may be a fool, but he is a useful fool," Ut said as he strolled up next to her. Even in the cold, he was dressed only in his customary white tunic. Ellaniya wanted to ask him about his garb, but she figured there was no real point; what did his resistance to the cold matter?

"How exactly has Travyn been useful? Tell me what he has done."

Ut's head tilted to the side as he looked at her face. Ellaniya could tell he was considering his response, a reaction not normal for the messenger of the gods. "We are both aware of his shortcomings, but his loyalty cannot be questioned." He reached out and grasped her covered hands with his bare fingers. "Your strength and determination are well known to me, my dear. But the empire will require time to see you as I do. For now, we need an emperor, at least until all your power is consolidated."

"Then what? Are you planning to kill him?" she asked, thinking back to their prior discussions. She had previously been lackadaisical regarding the thought of Travyn's future, but would she mourn his demise? As Travyn's horse finally disappeared from her view, all that was left was the endless snow, glistening in the morning sun, and she wondered whether she would ever see him again.

"As you know, I speak for the gods. They can sometimes be fickle. Travyn has been gaining their favor by his loyalty. He obeyed their direction to seek for his nephew. While he did not bring us Hellet, he did kill one of his friends. Perhaps the gods will find a way for him to survive.

"However, we must keep our eyes on the ultimate outcome, not inconsequential emotional entanglements. The empire of Mephosh must grow so we can finally destroy the last vestiges of the heretics, my dear. We still need Mennum for that. He must remain agreeable to marriage with you for us to reach our unified goals. We had previously wondered who should oversee Shekul. I believe Mennum would be a wise choice."

"I don't disagree, but how might his father react to him being gone for so long?"

"The king need not know the full extent of his son's mission."

"But what would be the reason for Mennum's departure?"

"Amyon will soon learn what has happened here. We can invite the prince to visit to show we have no intentions of conflict with the northern kingdoms. Once he arrives, we can offer multiple reasons for his continued stay. Once your marriage to Travyn has ended, you and Mennum can be wed. And I am certain his father will not survive much longer as I hear his illness has returned."

Ut paused, allowing Ellaniya to absorb his words. "This cold is becoming unbearable," she said. "Let's return indoors."

"I do apologize, my dear, for my inconsideration regarding your comfort," replied Ut, motioning towards the stairs.

As they made their way down into the castle, Ellaniya wondered if she should chastise Ut for the familiarity with how he addressed her; she was empress after all. But how would the gods react if she were to chastise their messenger? Would they be insulted? She decided it was not worth the risk of angering them at such a critical junction.

The pair continued on in silence as she headed to her private chambers. While she had not invited Ut to join her, he followed her into her rooms and sat at a small table near the bed. "I see you are making yourself comfortable," she stated, unable to mask the sarcasm in her voice.

"We must finish our conversation," he replied. Ut either had not noticed her tone or had chosen to ignore it. She was certain that there was nothing that Ut did not observe, so it really was not a question. "May I assume that you remain fully committed to the gods?" he asked.

"Of course. All I have done, I've done for them," she replied angrily. How could he doubt her after everything she had accomplished and the sacrifices she had made?

"Yes, my dear, but we can't stop now. Much work remains, and Mennum is a vital component to our plans. He is ambitious and will do what needs to be done to build his power, which will also be your power."

She thought back to her visit to Amyon. Mennum, was a logical ally for her, but she did not think she would ever love him. Her mind turned to Vor, and Ellaniya wondered how she would be able to marry another man she did not love.

"Your union to Mennum need be only political. Marriage does not have to be about love," Ut said, as if he could hear her thoughts. "If Travyn does not die, you will divorce him. You may keep him around, if you desire, though I do not know why you would." Ut paused as he ran his fingers through his fine white hair. "I am well aware of Mennum's many mistresses, and I am certain he has no desire to ever restrain himself. And you will still have your guard that you have become so fond of."

What has become of me that I find comfort in those words? she thought. She would serve the gods no matter what and knew additional sacrifices would likely still need to be made, but, so far, the gods had held up their end of the bargain. She ruled Mephosh and had conquered Su'Meeryn. The heresy that had grown due to that damned Book of Sul was being destroyed. And divinity was still being promised to her.

"There is no reason why you cannot have everything you desire," Ut continued. "The gods are offering you their many blessings. All you must do is reach out and grab them."

"Forgive me if I had brief moment of anger," she said, lounging back into the pillows on her commandeered bed. "I'm pleased to hear that Travyn's demise is not guaranteed, and that Vor will be with me soon. I will, of course, do what is required."

"Very good, my dear."

# chapter 61

THEY WERE PASSING THROUGH FIELDS that would be farmland during the warmer months, and then they reached the edge of the outlying village. Little movement was visible which was understandable due to the still harsh weather. As they walked past the homes, they spotted eyes peering at them from a few doorways and around corners, but they did not stop. They had nearly reached their destination, and they wanted no further delay.

The castle was large, much bigger than Pathum's had been, and Dellea guessed it was larger than Su'Meeryn. The walls were of an imposing height, and black and gold banners flapped in the cold wind. It was an impressive sight. They had finally reached Labyn.

It had taken them many weeks to travel through the frigid landscape after amputating Hellet's finger, and there had been days they had gone without food. If not for her wolves, Dellea was certain they would not have been able to complete the arduous journey. As the cold winter had offered no respite, the wolves had had a difficult time finding prey. The few hares they managed to procure barely satisfied the group's hunger. Fortunately though, it had been enough. The one advantage to the thick snow was that they did not have to worry about thirst, and it added something to their stomachs when they had no food.

None of them had spoken much over the last couple days. Even Perrin seemed to be losing some of her rage, but Dellea felt certain it had more to do with weariness and the cold than a softening of her attitude.

As Dellea and the others trudged up to the castle gate, they all remained silent and the wolves clustered behind them, seemingly knowing they might not be greeted warmly.

"Hold!" a voice called out from atop the wall as they approached. "Who are you? What business have you in Labyn?"

"I am prince Hellet of Su'Meeryn with my betrothed, Dellea of Pathum. And these are our friends. It is most inhospitable out here, and we have traveled a long distance. We would appreciate being offered the welcome of our neighbor."

"Su'Meeryn?" the man laughed. "Su'Meeryn has been conquered and is no more. If you are indeed a prince of Su'Meeryn you would be aware of this."

"We assumed that's what happened to our home, and it is the reason you find us as we are. Now, please open your gates and let us in."

After a pause, the man continued. "Of course, we shall let you pass. I'm certain the king will want to talk with you. I will… wait, are those wolves?"

"Yes, they are our companions. They were raised by Dellea since they were pups. They are no threat to you. We would not have survived our journey without them."

The soldier leaned over the wall, trying to get a better view of the animals, and Dellea could see confusion on his face. "I can't let them into the castle… At least I don't think I can." He hesitated again. "This is quite a unique request. I'm not quite sure what to do."

"You can take them to your stables. They are used to that," Dellea replied. "I can assure you they'll not harm anyone, or any of your animals, as long as they're given food."

The man looked at Dellea then back to the wolves. "It's been a harsh winter, as you well know. We do not have a lot of extra food to give to wild animals."

"As I said, they are not wild animals," Hellet retorted. "Would you refuse this request from visiting royalty?"

The soldier stood perplexed, unsure how to respond. Eventually he shrugged his shoulders and continued. "Very well, I will open the gate and have you escorted to the king while your animals are taken to the stables, but I can't be responsible for their safety if they cause problems."

"Thank you," responded Dellea, "but it would be best if we go to the stables with them before meeting your king. It's been a taxing winter for all of us."

"Yes, that is probably wise," the guard agreed as the gates opened.

**✳✳✳**

The air of the castle felt like a blacksmith's shop as the group was led into a warm chamber. After removing their coats and gloves, servants took the tattered and frozen garments from the group and provided them with soft robes. But despite the relief, Dellea found her apprehension returning as they were escorted from the room and walked the brightly lit hallways of the palace and entered the royal hall. How was it that she had been able to endure their miserable trek, but standing in this room of strangers brought her more distress? The wolves were not with her, and she missed the comfort of their presence. But she knew they were safe as she had overseen their feeding before they left the stables. She felt her anxiety growing as she reached for Hellet's hand. As their fingers clasped, it felt odd with the one missing. This was the first time that they had embraced as such since the amputation as they had not removed their gloves the rest of the journey.

"So, this is prince Hellet of Su'Meeryn," the king said, rising from his throne. He was a handsome, young man, perhaps five to ten years older than Dellea. Straight dark hair hung down from his crownless head in a long tail. He was of medium build, but Dellea saw the outlines of muscle below his silken shirt. The lines of his face were chiseled like a statue, and piercing gray eyes regarded the foursome. "I am Tollan, king of Labyn. My apologies that the queen is not here to greet you. She is not well and is resting in our chambers."

Tollan moved past his guards, approaching them, and regarded Dellea. "And this must be Dellea. I have heard of you: the girl with the wolves. I'm told that they are currently in my stables. I very much look forward to meeting them. And who are these other two?"

"These are our friends, Nefalel and Perrin, comrades from my home. They have endured much with us," answered Hellet. "We are grateful for your hospitality."

"I am always willing to offer kindness to friends; however, I do not know that I can consider anyone from Su'Meeryn to be a friend."

"I'm unsure what exactly has occurred in my home, but we've been told it's been conquered by my uncle Travyn and his wife Ellaniya of Mephosh. It was because of my uncle that we were on the run. We suffered much in the frozen wilderness, and we lost a friend, Perrin's husband during our journey. He was killed by my uncle. We have no loyalty to the current rulers."

"There is nothing more that I want then to kill them all," Perrin interjected, her acid tone dripping from her mouth.

Tollan regarded Perrin for a moment before returning to his seat. "And what of you, princess Dellea? My scouts tell me of the destruction of Pathum, though nobody knows how that was accomplished."

Dellea began to tremble as she squeezed Hellet's hand. "We saw the destruction," Hellet replied on her behalf, "and we too are at a loss as to how it was achieved. We were actually traveling to her homeland when all this began. The destruction of Pathum was a gruesome sight for her, for us all."

"I imagine so. But why have you come here, to my land?"

"It is the logical place. We ran into a score of warriors from Gorthon. They offered us refuge but no assistance. Labyn seems to be our natural ally."

Tollan laughed at Hellet's reply. "Ally? I see only four standing before me, and two of you are women."

"Do you think Travyn is going to stop with Su'Meeryn? He will come after Labyn next. Most likely in the early spring," Neffy stated.

"Neffy is right. I know my uncle. He is not a smart man. He could not have accomplished this on his own. Ellaniya must be influencing him. If they conquered Shekul and Su'Meeryn—and somehow destroyed Pathum—Labyn will be their next target."

"Your uncle may be stupid, but I am not," answered Tollan. "The threat to Labyn is well known. We are already making preparations. But I still don't know what assistance the four of you can offer."

"I will kill many of them," Perrin replied.

Tollan glanced over with a trace of surprise on his handsome face and said, "I don't doubt it."

"Perrin wants to be trained to fight," Hellet continued. "And Neffy is a skilled warrior, probably the greatest fighter in Su'Meeryn. I am not a warrior, but Wairren—a cleric in our home—told Dellea and me that we would have a role to play in all this. We don't know what that role will be, but so far, everything he warned us of is coming to pass."

"Wairren, you say?" Tollan replied with a startled expression. "That is quite interesting." The king's hand rubbed his chin then straightened his long tail of hair. "I have someone here who will want to meet you."

"That's fine,'" Hellet said, "but might we eat first? We have not had a decent meal in a very long time, and we could all use a warm bath."

"Certainly, my apologies for my lack of manners," Tollan responded. "Let me take you to my dining hall."

After finishing their first real meal since leaving Su'Meeryn, they were brought to their own rooms where they found baths prepared and fresh clothing laid out. Once they were all situated and refreshed, Perrin demanded that she be taken to the soldier's barracks without further delay so she could begin formal sword training. Tollan had suggested that she rest for the remainder of the day so he could prepare his men for the sight of the first female warrior that most of them had ever seen. She refused, and even the king of Labyn seemed a bit intimidated by the sinister look on her face. When Neffy agreed to accompany her, Tollan acquiesced and ordered a guard to escort them to the barracks.

"I don't know what to make of your friend," the king said as he and a half dozen guards led Dellea and Hellet away from the palace and into the streets of the town.

"Neither do we," admitted Hellet. "It seemed she was on the brink of losing her mind when we were being chased, but something snapped when Darus was killed. I've never heard of anything like this."

"I haven't either, but if she wants to fight, I'm not going to stop her. I expect we will need all the help we can get against your uncle."

"Yes, agreed. But you haven't said where you're taking us."

"True, but I ask that you indulge me a bit. I was surprised by your arrival, and I'm looking forward to giving you a surprise."

Dellea moved in closer to Hellet at Tollan's last comment. It was bad enough that she was now in a completely unfamiliar city, surrounded by strangers, and now Tollan was promising them a surprise. What possible surprise might they receive when they were not even expected? And a surprise was the last thing she wanted to experience.

Tollan then turned his attention to Dellea. "You've not said much since your arrival, princess."

"No," Dellea agreed, hoping Tollan would probe no further.

"We've been through a lot and are having a difficult time relaxing," Hellet explained. Once again Dellea was thankful for his discernment of knowing when to interject himself on her behalf.

"Of course. I can't imagine all you've been through; please forgive my rudeness." The king turned down a narrow street and they continued in silence as they passed many small homes. Dellea relished the quiet; she often wondered at the need of some people to speak incessantly. Nothing gave her more comfort than being with Hellet without the pressure to talk.

"We've arrived," Tollan announced as they came to a tiny hovel at the end of the street. "I'm certain he will be here as he's not able to get around anymore." After a knock on the door, he called out, "It's the king. I'm coming in, and I have guests."

When Tollan opened the door, Dellea saw a small, one-room home that consisted of nothing more than a bed, a chair and a tiny table. Stretched out on the bed was a long, thin figure with the dark skin of a man of Gorthon, wrinkled from age. As they entered, he raised his hairless head and slowly pushed himself up. A gray shirt hung loosely from his body which gave the impression of having once been very muscular. The man groaned as he propped himself up against the wall, but Dellea could tell he tried to suppress the sound. His bright eyes regarded the king, then the pair, but he did not speak.

"May I present to you, Hellet," Tollan began, "prince of Su'Meeryn, great-grandson of Jaleph. He was heir to the throne of Su'Meeryn prior to its fall. With him is his betrothed, Dellea, princess of Pathum, though Pathum has been destroyed. They have sought asylum in my kingdom and have offered their assistance as we expect Labyn to be the next target of Mephosh.

"My new friends, may I present to you Wander, the greatest prophet this land has ever known."

# chapter 62

IT FELT STRANGE BEING IN MEPHOSH without Ellaniya. While he was happy to be back within the castle walls and out of the wintery cold, Travyn was not sure what to do with himself. He was now the emperor of a vast area encompassing three cities, but what did that mean? Aniass, the leader of the mercenaries was with him, and Ut had made it clear that Travyn was to defer to Aniass in all situations. Why should such a mighty emperor be subjected to a mercenary? But Travyn would never be able to forget Ut's threats. Despite his disdain for the man, he knew he would have to comply with the orders from the messenger of the gods. Travyn did not know what the ramifications would be if he refused, but he was unwilling to find out.

Upon their arrival to the city, Aniass had announced the return of the emperor to the nobility; however, prior to meeting with them, Travyn said he would retire to his chambers to rest from the trip. While it was true that he was tired, he wanted to spend some time alone, hoping he could figure out what he should do next.

The emperor wandered aimlessly around the chilly, castle hallways as he slowly made his way to his empty room. If he could not rule, and he could not be with his wife, what was he supposed to do? He thought about asking Aniass that very question but decided against it. He knew the misguided opinions others had about himself, and he did not want to risk furthering those faulty impressions by seeming to be so confused. After all, it was not his decision that he could not rule over his insignificant subjects.

Once he had finished the dinner that had been brought to him, Travyn sat down to do some serious thinking. He was determined to devise a strategy for the coming days; however, after a few long, painful hours, he had still failed to formulate a plan.

Rising from a plush chair, he slowly walked to a window. The fire that was burning on the other side of the room was not strong enough to dispel the frosty air flowing in from the opening. The land he saw was covered in snow under an overcast sky, and he was not able to distinguish many features. In the deepening gloom, he was unable to see the sun, and he wondered if he was peering north, towards his homeland of Su'Meeryn. He had been given what he always desired: rule of his home, but was it a hollow victory? Despite what he tried to tell himself, he knew he truly ruled nothing. He was subservient to Ut and to Ellaniya, and even Aniass.

Orrin was dead—along with Jenna—but still Travyn did not sit upon the throne of Su'Meeryn. Had he been the eldest, everything would have been different. He would not have endured the abuse he had received his entire life, and he would not have had to fight and suffer to reign.

Then he thought of his nephew, the only one who had ever treated him well, and Travyn had tried to kill him. Why? Had the mission been necessary? Why had it been put to him to kill the only person—other than his magnificent wife—that he liked? He did not regret killing Darus. Darus and Neffy had always tormented him at every opportunity, but Hellet would rebuke them when he was aware of their teasing. If he still lived, how could Hellet now be his enemy?

Travyn placed another log in the flames then sat back down, close to the fire, enjoying the warmth. Following a few moments in the pleasant heat, he began to feel drowsy. Travyn rose from the chair and made his way to the empty bed. Why did he have to be alone again? Despite all the victories he had experienced since meeting Ellaniya and Ut, the emperor realized that he was more miserable than he had ever been. Had everything that happened since Orrin canceled his engagement to Dellea been worthwhile? Where would he be now if that marriage had gone forward? While he did not like Dellea—or her wolves—might he now be better off? Might he have learned to love her? Would he be alone now in his bed if they had married? But it was too late to question those choices; he loved Ellaniya more than anything, and she was clearly devoted to him. And he knew she was suffering loneliness as well, but what could he do?

Then he remembered the vision of Ut as they stood next to the destroyed kingdom of Pathum. Even if he wanted to make a change in his life, he was trapped. There was no escape for him now. He would have to make do and hope that he would soon be reunited with Ellaniya, and that Ut's promise would come to fruition. The promise remained that he would become one with the gods and all this suffering would be worthwhile.

The bed felt cold with Ellaniya not beside him, and he missed her even more. Despite his exhaustion, sleep eluded him, his mind swirling with thoughts about how he had come to this place. When he finally drifted off, Travyn remained as confused and unhappy as ever.

***

After a fitful night's sleep, Travyn rose late in the morning and made his way to the hall for his breakfast. But seemingly like everything else these days, Travyn's breakfast was cold. He barely managed to choke down a few eggs while the guards standing beside him watched. Travyn glanced about at the empty tables filling the hall while crunching on a hard piece of bread. He thought of the tooth that had been pulled from his mouth and was grateful that he felt no pain while eating. Grateful? he thought, what do I have to be grateful for? He was emperor, but he did not rule. And he was alone. He missed the welcoming embrace of Ellaniya's arms, and he wondered how she was faring.

The door to the dining hall swung open and Aniass strode to his table. "There you are. I've been looking for you."

"Well, here I am. An emperor has to eat, after all."

"We need to discuss your tasks for the day."

Travyn smacked the remainder of his bread against the table then knocked his mug to the stone floor. "You are going to tell me what to do? I rule here!"

Aniass' eyes narrowed, and a smug smile formed on this lips. "Of course you do, sire, but I'm sure I need not remind you of Ut's orders."

Travyn's head dropped at the mention of Ut, and he knew he had no further retort. "What is required of me?"

***

"The emperor has returned for the winter," Aniass declared to the assembled nobles standing before the throne. "He is pleased to see the progress that has been made in his and the empress' absence. All overt traces of the heretic religion have been eliminated and proper temples have been reestablished. However, your emperor wants to make certain that the search continues for any covert worshippers. We do not want there to be any opportunity for the heresy to ever gain a foothold again."

Travyn sat up higher on the throne, watching the nobles murmur and nodded their heads in agreement. Though he had been commanded to acquiesce to Aniass, Travyn would at least present the nobles with an imperial image.

"How are things progressing with the increased taxes and conscriptions for the army?" Aniass continued.

As the various nobles relayed the efforts they had been making, Travyn's mind began to wander. Why should he have to deal with taxes and counting the numbers of soldiers? Should not he have more important tasks to attend to? An emperor has servants for such trivial obligations. He should be plotting the next course of expansion. He should be commanding the military. He should rule. But he was doing none of those things. He was merely sitting on the throne, alone and silent. A pathetic figure for the nobles to gawk at.

This all better be worth it, he said to himself.

# chapter 63

WITH VOR BESIDE HER—and a score of guards behind—the castle gate opened, and a dozen riders entered. Though the frigid temperature persisted, Ellaniya thought it would be best for her to personally welcome her guest as soon when he entered the courtyard. She did not want to risk insulting the prince from Amyon.

How strange to be greeting her future husband with her lover at her side. Vor had finally arrived a few days ago, and it had been a glorious reunion. With Travyn away in Mephosh, the empress had delighted in her personal guard's presence. Ellaniya now wondered how she ever felt any affection for Travyn. He was a complete imbecile and not very attractive. And to top that off, he had been of little use in her plans. Would things be any different now if they had not married? She could not answer that question, but what did it matter? She had Vor, and when she married Mennum, it would be solely a political arrangement. Had she finally, truly, discovered happiness?

Though she found the thought distasteful, Ellaniya knew that, once married to Mennum, they would have to sleep together on occasion to produce an heir. For now, Ut had promised her that she would not become pregnant from her dalliances with Vor until their conquest was completed, but that time was finally nearing its conclusion. As much as she desired Vor, they could never have a child together. Due to his dark skin, she would not be able to pass a child of theirs off as Travyn's or Mennum's. But if her future rendezvous with Vor was the most complicated situation she would have to deal with once Labyn was in her hands, she would find a way to manage.

"Welcome to the empire of Mephosh prince Mennum. It is good to see you again."

"And you, my lady," Mennum replied as he dropped from his horse and handed the reins to a servant. Ellaniya chafed a little at the familiarity of his greeting, but she let it pass. "If I may be so bold, can you take me indoors immediately? It has been a very unpleasant journey."

"Of course, please follow me."

***

Ellaniya sat in a private room, at a small table, with Vor next to her and Mennum across. A fire was lit in the corner, bathing the room in a golden light and pleasant warmth.

"Is it appropriate to have your servant present for this?" Mennum asked.

"Vor is my personal guard and a trusted advisor. We can speak freely."

The empress saw a scowl form briefly on Mennum's face, but he continued with no further complaint. "I was not pleased with the summons to travel here during such a vile winter. My father has begun to weaken again. I wonder if it was wise for me to leave."

Ellaniya took a sip of wine from the goblet before her. When she placed it back on the table, her finger slowly traced the edge while her violet eyes remained fixed on Mennum. "Amyon is certainly of importance to us for our mutual plan, but the needs of Mephosh are paramount."

"Careful, my lady. You are speaking of my home."

Mennum's look of irritation was reasonable, but Ellaniya took another sip before continuing. "I mean no insult to the great kingdom of Amyon, and, as I said, it is very important. However, you must admit that Mephosh is the dominant force in the land. My empire encompasses three former kingdoms, and I will add a fourth this spring. Once Labyn is in my hands, we can be married. The reach of our empire will be unlike anything known in history."

The prince lifted his own goblet from the table before responding. "I grant you that, but what does any of this have to do with my coming to Su'Meeryn?"

"I rule here, while my soon-to-be former husband is in Mephosh with Aniass, the leader of the mercenaries. We have no one in place in Shekul. I discussed this with Ut. I need someone trustworthy to oversee that land. We must make certain no discontent arises while the worship of the gods is being reestablished. You were the logical choice."

Ellaniya saw a grin threatening to sprout at the corners of Mennum's mouth, but he fought it off. She knew he was a petty, vain man, and the thought of ruling a castle on his own was clearly appealing. "Due to his health, my father will not want me away for an extended period of time," he pointed out.

"We can create any number of excuses as to why you are not able to return home until after Labyn is conquered."

"And what if my father dies before then?" Mennum asked.

"What of it?"

"I should be there to receive my crown."

"I am not aware of the internal politics of Amyon, but you are the heir to the throne. If the king does die before you return, who would challenge you? We will have the forces of my empire to deal with any circumstances if one does arise."

Ellaniya watched as Mennum pondered her words, but she could see that he remained skeptical. Thinking back to what Ut had told her of him, she continued. "I hear there are a number of popular brothels in Shekul." While she had no idea if that statement was true, what castle did not have at least a few?

Mennum's countenance brightened at her comment before he replied. "You are indeed a wise woman, Ellaniya. I will travel to Shekul for you. If my father does die soon, the nobles can hold on to my crown until Labyn is conquered. Then we will return to my home to marry and rule!

"It was a miserable trek here, but I see now that it was worthwhile. Soon, we will both have our due."

Ellaniya hesitated a moment. Mennum had assumed they would rule the empire from Amyon after they married, and she realized she had never considered the location of her capital. She had always assumed it would be in Mephosh where she would rule as Empress Lynna from the traditional home of the great queen. But was it a concern? Ellaniya had no desire to live with him as husband and wife. She could remain in the south while Mennum would reign in Amyon. "Very good," she replied, ignoring Mennum's comment regarding their future home. "I will have guards escort you to your room so you can rest and recover from your long trip, and I will have food brought to you."

"Thank you, my lady."

"I don't like him," Vor stated, after Mennum left the room.

Ellaniya's gaze remained on the door, as if she could see Mennum retreating down the hallway. "I don't either, but he will serve a purpose. He will be much more useful than Travyn."

"If you say so."

She turned to Vor, and she thought she saw an expression of hurt on his usually stoic face as his golden eyes narrowed. "Mennum will be useful to further the gods' plans."

"As you say."

"Do not worry," she reassured Vor, resting her hand on his, "nothing will change between us." And for a moment, a look of satisfaction crossed his face, but only for a moment.

# chapter 64

"HOW CAN THAT BE?" Dellea exclaimed. "Wander would have to be dead by now."

"I most certainly am Wander," the old man replied, "and I can attest that I'm quite alive, though I know not for how much longer."

"Why didn't Wairren tell us you still lived?"

"Wairren? I'm sure he doesn't know."

"Why wouldn't your son know you're still alive?" asked Hellet.

The old man's brow furrowed as his still-sharp eyes flashed to Hellet. "Boy, I don't answer to you. I knew your great-grandfather before he was king of Su'Meeryn. I was there at his coronation and his marriage to Kieran. Kieran was a pupil of mine long before she was queen. I knew Sul before his conversion and was beaten on his order. I have seen much and suffered much, and I have no time left or inclination to justify myself to the likes of you!"

"Forgive me. We've endured a lot to get here," Hellet replied. "It's unfortunate that Jaleph recently died. He would have been pleased to see you again."

Wander's face immediately softened. "Yes, I was told of his passing, and I offer my sympathies. Jaleph and I disagreed much, but he was a great man. And Kieran was a remarkable woman. I miss them both.

"My apologies for my sharp tone. Age has not been kind to me; I have pain throughout my body, and it often affects my temper. I strive to remain patient, but it's not always easy."

"I've read much about you," Dellea timidly interjected. "Your son gave me The Book of Sul to study. I have read it countless times. Wairren said it would be vital to us in overcoming the trials we are now facing, but he could tell us nothing more. Do you know what he meant?"

"I'm sorry, but I have no idea. I have read Sul's book a few times, and, of course, I lived some of that story. It is a profound book, but I don't know what it can do to prevent the onslaught from Mephosh."

"If I may, what happened to you Wander?" Hellet asked. "I too am familiar with yours and my grandfather's story. I know you were close friends and a mentor to him. Why did you leave Su'Meeryn?"

Wander sighed and tried to arrange himself into a more comfortable position on the bed. "It's a long tale," he began. "Well, that might not actually be true, but it is a rather involved story. I'm told that Jaleph's disposition mellowed as he aged; however, in his younger days, he was well known for his short temper. Of course, that had much to do with all the suffering caused by Sul, but Kieran was able to soften him. She was extraordinary—one of my closest friends." Wander paused as he glanced towards the ceiling, thoughts of Kieran clearly rummaging through his thoughts. "But I digress.

"Jaleph and I would often argue, but he never took our quarrels personally. I appreciated that about him. Even with all the disagreements, I always felt welcome in Su'Meeryn; however, I had never intended on remaining there for the rest of my days. I figured I should also spend time in the other kingdoms, helping to reestablish the true faith. Jaleph would chastise me regarding these plans. He told me I was being proud and that there were others that could lead in that regard. Maybe he believed that, or maybe he just didn't want me to leave. I don't know. Anyway, at his request, I agreed to remain a citizen of Su'Meeryn, but I would travel to Mephosh, Labyn and the other kingdoms occasionally to help with the congregations. I took a wife in Su'Meeryn who bore me Wairren, but she died suddenly, shortly after he was born. I loved her with all my heart, and her death traumatized me. Sorrow overwhelmed me and turned me into an angry man.

"My disagreements with Jaleph grew in intensity, and there were times when we parted with acrimony. I also found that I was growing resentful of my son. I did not realize it at that time, but I was blaming him for my wife's death. I had transformed into a much different person than you read of in Sul's book.

"It was during one of those arguments with Jaleph that I finally recognized my sin. I recall screaming at the king one day—despite our deteriorating relationship, he still allowed me to speak to him in that manner—then breaking down in tears. What had become of me? I was a shadow of the man I had once been.

"I then determined I needed to do something, though I knew not what. I visited the queen whom, despite my bitter state, remained my closest friend. Talking with her, I realized I needed to make a drastic change. I could not remain in Su'Meeryn. She was saddened by my words, but she did not try to stop me. Kieran told me that she would miss me, but I needed to do as I must.

"When I returned to Jaleph, I told him that I was going to leave; I had to go on a pilgrimage to find the Wander of the past. However, I had no particular destination. Wairren was still young, and I did not think it would be fair to bring him with me, so I asked Jaleph to watch after him. Jaleph initially refused my request. He still did not want me to leave which was a surprise. I wondered why he would want my bitter presence around anymore. Perhaps he thought he could help me regain my former self since I finally understood my problems. I tried to tell him that I needed to leave, I needed separation as too many memories remained in Su'Meeryn. But he continued to refuse.

"It was a conflicting time; I knew I had to go, but my king was declining my request. I returned to Kieran and explained my dilemma. While she too questioned my decision, she said she would see to it that Wairren was cared for.

"I left the next day. Despite Jaleph's order to the contrary, Kieran provided me with a horse and as much supplies as I could take. I then rode away from Su'Meeryn."

Wander stopped for a moment and regarded his guests. "Perhaps it is a long story after all, eh? Well anyway, I first headed east and returned to my homeland of Gorthon. I had left there many years prior under unfavorable circumstances that I will not share. I spent a long time amongst my people, and it was pleasant to be welcomed back, but my time in Gorthon brought no healing to my soul.

"From Gorthon I travelled all over this land—still an angry and bitter man—searching for answers. Unfortunately, I did not know what my questions were. All I knew was that I needed healing and redemption.

"I'm afraid I'm boring you with this long tale, so I will jump to the end. It took me many years before I was able to finally cast aside my bitterness. I often thought of Sul and all he had been through, and all the suffering he had caused my friends and me. Despite everything had done, I had championed offering him forgiveness against Jaleph's desire to see him die. I knew he had a role to play in the conflict against the pagans. Though Jaleph had endured and witnessed much, he ultimately was able to forgive Sul. I realized that my pride first took root there. Yes, I had been beaten, but I had not suffered anything to the degree others had at Sul's hand. I had expected everyone to follow my example. I had convinced myself of my own greatness. But when my wife died, I was not able to follow my own example. Unknowingly, I blamed my son, as well as the creator, for her death, and I wasn't able to find forgiveness in my own heart during my greatest trial. I realized I had become a hypocrite, which had made me even more miserable.

"The revelation of my shortcomings came while I was here, in Labyn, and I was finally able to find forgiveness in my heart for whatever had caused my wife's death. And I was able to forgive myself for my years of bitterness.

"It was then that I desired to return to Su'Meeryn, but many years had passed, and I did not know what I could offer Jaleph and his kingdom anymore. I wanted to return to my son, but I had been away for so long, I was afraid he would turn me away. Perhaps that too was an error on my part. If you get the chance to meet him again, please tell him of this and offer my sincere apology.

"So, I decided to stay in Labyn where the people have warmly welcomed me. I've done all I could to make amends for my transgressions by teaching these fine people as best I can, but I feel my death approaching. While I lament my many regrets, I am at peace. I do not fear death."

Wander stopped and wiped a tear away from his wrinkled chin. "Yes, it was a long story and an uncomfortable one to relive, and I would very much wish there was some wisdom I could offer to help with our current dilemma. One last gesture of service to the creator would not erase my sins, but it would at least give me more of a sense of serenity at my death. Unfortunately, I can think of nothing."

Dellea stood still, staring at the ancient man. She thought of her own parents and the anger she still harbored towards them, even in their deaths. Might she be a different person if she had been raised by a loving mother and father? But perhaps she would have never met Hellet if that had been the case. Was all that pain worthwhile? She turned to Hellet and was certain of her answer. Despite all she had endured in her young life, she could not imagine her life without him.

With the thoughts of her past, the vision of her destroyed homeland returned and the memory of her tears. She still hated her parents, but she also mourned them. It was all so confusing. She felt guilt over her mixed feelings, and she had heard the remorse in Wander's words. That made her think of The Book of Sul she had read over so many times: all the evil he had committed and the guilt he felt. Would she ever be able to overcome all these disparate feelings?

Hellet glanced at her, seeing the distress on her face. He wrapped his arm around her shoulder, and his embrace comforted her. She thought of Wander's words. He had struggled in that he had not realized his own shortcoming. If there was one area Dellea did not toil over was understanding her flaws. Of those, she was well aware.

"Rest assured, Wander, that your usefulness remains, even at your advanced age," Dellea said. "I have learned much, just from your tale."

"That pleases me."

Tollan stepped forward and said, "I suppose we should be on our way. Based on their story, I knew you would want to meet them, but I'm sorry that we were not able to find any answers. I worry for us all."

Wander's weathered face showed the distress at his inability to provide a solution to their desperate situation. "While I regret that I could not give you an answer, it was a welcome visit, and I hope to see you two again. I sense something in you girl, perhaps…" His words trailed off as he glanced up again to the ceiling. "I had not received word that my son continued my legacy as a prophet, but it gives me great pleasure to know that my failures as a father have not hindered him. If he believes the key to our victory over this evil is in Sul's book, I will begin to study it immediately. While I do not have a ready solution for you, it doesn't mean that one does not exist. I understand the threat from Travyn and Ellaniya, and if I receive a revelation, I will send word immediately."

"Thank you Wander," Hellet replied. "And yes, I'm certain we would be happy to visit you as often as possible. Next time, we will bring Neffy and Perrin. They might be… well, they both have very different types of personalities, but they would certainly benefit from spending time with you, as we have."

To her surprise, Dellea approached the old man and leaned down, wrapping her arms around his frail body. "Yes, thank you Wander, your wisdom is of great value."

Wander offered a smile, displaying a mouth of a few rotting teeth, but the sight just increased Dellea's delight with meeting the old cleric. While the threat from Mephosh and Travyn remained, she knew she would be able to learn from the ancient prophet's wisdom, if they survived. Even with Hellet beside her, and her wolves, she still worried about her future. As much as they had already endured, their trials were far from over. What if something happened to Hellet and the wolves? How would she manage if she was left alone? While there was no certainty, she was confident she could avoid the mistakes Wander had made. She might always be the awkward girl from Pathum, but she would avoid turning bitter if the worst happened. At least she hoped that was the case.

"Now, I think it best that you three depart so I may get some rest. Tollan, if you would be so kind as to have a copy of The Book of Sul sent to me, I will begin my study immediately."

# chapter 65

THE WEATHER WAS STARTING TO WARM, if only slightly. A brisk breeze ruffled his hair as Hellet hiked around the castle with Dellea and the wolves. They had been in Labyn for a few weeks, but there was not much for them to do. He had meet with the healers who examined his hand. Despite the imprecise cut of the amputation, he was healing, and though it still ached, they found nothing of further concern. Dellea and he had also visited Wander a few times, but he remained engrossed in Sul's book. The old man seemed invigorated by his new task, and he would say that he was confident there was an answer to be found. He did not know what it was yet, but it must be there.

They saw almost nothing of Perrin. She would rise before dawn and spend all her time training, only stopping to eat. She refused all requests to take a break and spend time with her friends, if Hellet and Dellea could even be considered friends anymore. Perrin had become a completely different person than the woman who had left Su'Meeryn. Her singular focus on revenge against those who killed Darus was unsettling, but there was nothing that Hellet could do about it. Neffy was spending a good amount of time with her, assisting with her training, and Hellet would make sure that Neffy passed along their greetings. However, all she cared about was improving her skills with the sword to exact her vengeance. Neffy reported that her skills were growing far more than might have been expected, and while Hellet was happy to hear that news, he wondered if it was truly for the best. Losing one's spouse is never easy, but Perrin's response was far from anything that he could have imagined.

✳✳✳

"I'm pleased that I finally get to meet you two," the queen said as they sat in the royal library. Despite the recent delivery of Tollan's and her son Gorhum—named after Tollan's father—Adira's beauty was evident. Her flesh remained a pale white, and she had not taken the time to apply cosmetics. Despite that, she looked stunning with waves of golden hair cascading past her shoulders. "It was a difficult delivery, but I'm starting to feel better," she commented as her penetrating olive eyes evaluated the pair standing before her. While her expression was not one of warmth, Hellet perceived no trace of malice either. He got the sense that she was attempting to ascertain their intentions and read their inner most motivations, as if she still needed to determine if they were friend or foe.

"May I inquire regarding the prince's whereabouts?" Hellet asked. "How is he doing? We would be pleased to meet him."

"Gorhum is with his nurses; he's doing well," replied Tollan. "I thank you for your query."

"Are you certain this meeting is wise? We could return later. I don't want to add to the queen's burdens."

"I appreciate your concern, but I've grown anxious for visitors," Adira said. "I've heard much about you two, and the others. I've been wanting us to finally meet."

"Well, it is our pleasure," Hellet responded with a slight bow of his head.

Adira's gaze turned from Hellet as she regarded Dellea. "And what of you princess?"

Hellet could hear Dellea begin to stammer, and he responded again. "Dellea is somewhat nervous meeting the queen. Please forgive her."

"Can she not speak for herself? I've been told of her wolves, and I wanted to hear all about them."

"Please, dear, don't interrogate the poor girl. We have more pressing matters to discuss," the king interjected, and Hellet wondered if Tollan was purposefully turning the attention away from Della. Regardless he was pleased with the change in the conversation as he could sense Dellea's increasing agitation.

"Now, tell us all you can of your uncle and his wife," Tollan continued.

"I wish to help anyway I can," Hellet responded, "but I don't know what information I can provide. Travyn is not a smart man. He could not have accomplished any of this on his own. Ellaniya must be manipulating him, but I scarcely know her. We have no idea where they found the resources to muster such a large army, and I still can't fathom how they managed the destruction of Pathum."

"It seems clear that Mephosh will attack Labyn once spring arrives. How do you think we should defend against them?" Adira asked as she reached out to take Tollan's hand while a slight frown emerged on her face.

"I'm not a military strategist," Hellet replied.

"No, I suppose not. You're still just a boy."

"He may be young, but I'm not much older," said Tollan. "And he's been through a lot."

"We have, and Wairren indicated Dellea and I will be crucial to defend against this burgeoning evil. But we still don't know how that might be." Hellet replied as Dellea began to fidget with a scarf she had pulled from her pocket. "It's not a role either of us desired; however, Wairren's other predictions appear to have been accurate."

Adira took a sudden breath and Hellet saw her frown deepen as a trace of pain crossed her face. Her hand went to her stomach as a servant stepped forward. The queen waved the woman away then continued. "Many of the nobles are asking us to surrender to Mephosh, and for my husband to abandon his crown. They see no reason to subject Labyn to attack. Our spies tell us that the nobles of Su'Meeryn have kept their positions after being conquered. They wonder why we should face such violence and death?"

"The nobles can be a selfish bunch," Tollan remarked.

"What is more selfish, wanting to survive or asking others to risk their lives?" the queen asked rather sharply.

"I'm confused; you want Tollan to surrender?" asked Hellet.

"I want my love to live," Adira answered, "and our child."

"My wife's worry for me is much appreciated," said Tollan, "but Ellaniya is spreading paganism in the conquered lands. After what the pagans did to my parents and Max, I will never surrender to them."

"We have also lost much due to my uncle. Su'Meeryn has been conquered, and I'm told Ellaniya killed my parents," Hellet stated. "Pathum was utterly destroyed along with all of Dellea's family. And I too lost one of my closest friends while fleeing from my uncle—not to mention my finger. I put Dellea and my other friends through extreme risk and much suffering to arrive here. We could have sought refuge in Gorthon, but I refused to hide from our trials. I will fight to defeat Travyn in whatever manner I can. Ellaniya and he must be stopped."

Adira's face turned red, and she began to shake. Hellet thought she was ready to explode in anger, but then he saw the look on her face was that of fear. "Please, my heart. I loved your parents as well. But is this a cause to fight for? I beg you—surrender and live!"

"I'm sorry, my queen, but I cannot. I must fight," Tollan proclaimed. "I will not hand my kingdom over to those who killed my parents."

**✳✳✳**

Over the next several weeks, Hellet and Dellea were able to spend considerable time with Tollan, and the queen when she was not caring for Gorhum. Tollan continued to ask them questions about Travyn and Su'Meeryn, but there was nothing more Hellet could offer. He appreciated the faith Tollan was giving him, but he wondered if it was earned. He still had no idea how Dellea and he could be of any use in the forthcoming conflict. But even amidst the stress and uncertainty they all faced, he was finding that he enjoyed the time they spent with the king, and he was starting to consider Tollan a friend. It was a welcomed relief to have the comforts of a warm bed and regular meals after all the trials they had suffered, but he knew it would be short lived. Winter would eventually give way to spring, and the army of Mephosh would once again be on the move.

"It still hurts?" Dellea asked as Hellet rubbed some of the numbing salve onto his severed joint while they strolled along the castle wall. Though the pain had mostly subsided since the loss of the finger, he was thankful that Labyn also possessed the same ointment that he had been given by the Gorthon soldier.

"It's not bad, but it does ache from time-to-time. I returned to the healers and was told that the bone is likely the problem. They think the cut was not clean and there are some shards still present. The only thing they could do would be to extend the amputation and try to make a clean cut. I certainly don't want to go through that again."

"If the pain isn't bad, I suppose not. I would hate to see you relive that ordeal," she replied as one of the wolves trotted by. Dellea reached over and scratched its head before the wolf darted back out to frolic in the snow with its siblings. It remained a surprising and pleasurable sight to Hellet—watching the wolves romping about and wrestling with each other, free to simply enjoy themselves.

Hellet noticed Dellea's face brighten as her attention lingered on the animals. He was pleased with how she was taking to their new environment. It seemed that with each meeting with Tollan she would talk a little more. She was becoming more comfortable with her surroundings, but they were in a lull. Conflict would be forced back on them soon enough, and they still had no notion how they would resist the armies of Mephosh. Despite his continued studies, Wander remained as befuddled as them, and time was running out.

"I know that Wander is confident he's going to find an answer, but this uncertainty is maddening." Hellet said. "I am not good with a sword, and now I've lost my index finger. What use could I possibly be?" Hellet still remained haunted by the killing of the soldier in the wilderness, and while he knew that action had been necessary, he questioned whether he would be able to kill again.

"That remains a mystery."

Hellet sighed as he squinted up into the distance. A number of billowing, brilliant white clouds contrasted against the deep blue sky. Rays from the sun peaked through and fell upon the snow, reflecting off the crystals and presenting a shimmering prism of color to his eyes. He had never cared much for winter and had spent most of the cold months indoors during his youth, but he had to admit that on bright days such as this, winter possessed many visions of beauty. If only he could freely enjoy them.

"Well, there is not much we can do by continuing to dwell on it," Hellet stated. "Wander still has time to hopefully find a solution. For now, we should enjoy this brief time of peace. And when spring does arrive, we will finally be able to marry."

"Of course," Dellea replied, but he saw the conflicted look on her face. While they both longed for marriage, the reality of their questionable future remained like shackles binding their wrists. She had suffered much in her young life, and he desired nothing more than for her to have a prolonged time of enjoyment. Perhaps Wander would devise a plan to thwart Ellaniya and Travyn, and despite the still frigid temperatures, work on enhancing Labyn's defenses continued. Might they prevail? If not, and Mephosh emerged victorious, he pondered as to their fate. Would his uncle actually have them killed? Again he questioned his refusal to seek refuge within the safety of Gorthon's mountains and starting new lives there. Instead, Hellet had committed himself and the others to fight, but now he wondered if they should just flee. However, he knew that would be selfish on his part. If the two of them were the key to stopping Mephosh, they had to do everything in their power to try.

He looked back at Dellea who had returned her attention to the wolves. If the decision to flee was just about him, it would be no decision at all: he would do all he could to stop Travyn and liberate his home. If he died in that attempt, so be it. But it was not just his own fate he was risking.

Hellet thought back to all the decisions he had made that had brought them to Labyn. Had he made mistakes? Perhaps, or perhaps not. Did he suffer from the sin of pride but not heeding the advice of Neffy and Darus? As long as he could remember, he had been told how exceptional he was, but he was still young. His mother had warned him about his lack of experience. Had he ignored her warnings? Were he and his friends paying the price for his pride?

But there was no point in debating with himself over those choices. If an unwise decision led to further suffering for Dellea, he had no idea how he would respond. Would he morph into a different person, like Perrin? Would he turn bitter as Wander had? The thought terrified him. But at that moment, a wolf pushed its head under his arm, demanding attention, and Hellet could do nothing but smile.

His decision had been made. He had given his promise to Tollan to stand with Labyn, and that provided him some comfort as he rubbed the animal's fur. There still was time for Wander to find revelation, but if he did not, Hellet would not flee. He did worry for Dellea—along with Neffy and Perrin—however, for now, he would try to his enjoy this peaceful time with his bride-to-be—and the wolves.

**\*\*\***

The dining hall was full, and Hellet was surprised that the king and queen had requested their presence at the royal table rather than any of the nobles or leaders of Labyn. While they had spent much time with Tollan, Adira was usually with their son. Now that Gorhum was growing stronger, the queen was venturing out more often from their chambers. Hellet always enjoyed Tollan's presence, and the feeling seemed mutual. However, Hellet wondered if the king should be spending time with his advisors, but that was not Hellet's decision to make.

As Dellea nervously raised a fork of eggs, Hellet remained concerned that Dellea was still uncomfortable. She appeared to be at ease in Tollan's presence, but the queen still clearly made his future wife uneasy. Adira was a pleasant enough woman; however, the queen would speak in short, staccato sentences when Dellea and he were around. It seemed that she equated their presence with the threat from Mephosh.

"It should be warmer today," the king commented. "Unfortunately, we are all aware of what the arrival of spring will bring."

"How are the preparations coming?" Hellet asked.

"As well as can be expected. Travyn will not find Labyn an easy target."

"And what are you two planning for the day? I've still not heard anything about how you're going to save us." The queen's tone was cold, but Hellet could not blame her. Adira loved Tollan greatly, and she believed the only way their family could survive was to surrender to Ellaniya and Travyn. But, instead Tollan was risking everything on this young, inexperienced couple she barely knew.

"We will go see Wander," Dellea said quietly as she dabbed her mouth with her orange scarf.

"That's good," Tollan replied, attempting to keep some cheer in his voice. "I went to the stables today to visit your wolves. They look like magnificent creatures. I was told that they were well fed, but they still were not pleased to see me."

"They don't like men," Dellea responded, "except one."

"I see, well I hope I'll have an opportunity to change their minds. The way they looked at me... they seem to be quite intelligent."

"Yes, we would not be alive if it wasn't for them," said Hellet.

Adira huffed at the comment, and Hellet was able to read the expression on her face. She wondered if Labyn would be better off if the four of them had never made it to their kingdom. Perhaps Tollan could then have been convinced to surrender, and her family would be given the opportunity to survive.

Before another word was said, Hellet was surprised and pleased to see Neffy and Perrin approaching the king's table. He missed his friend as Neffy had been spending all his time with Perrin, and he rarely saw Darus' widow.

"It's a pleasure to see the two of you," Tollan said, rising to greet them. "Please join us. How is the training going?"

Perrin did not respond, and Hellet noticed that Dellea immediately shoved the scarf back into her pocket. "She's progressing faster than anyone I've ever seen, Sire," Neffy responded proudly as two plates were placed before them. "I wonder if she'll end up being better than me."

"High praise," Hellet said as Perrin ripped into a hunk of chicken, seemingly oblivious to the praise or her companions.

"This is good to hear. We will need every warrior we can find," the king said.

Adira then stood from the table. "If you'll excuse me, I should be returning to Gorhum. I'll have a guard escort me to our rooms." As Tollan and the others began to stand, Adira placed a hand on her husband's shoulder. "I know the way, my heart. Stay with your new friends."

The king nodded, then took his wife's hand and gave it a soft kiss. When Adira had left the table, the others sat back down, and Neffy said, "I want to thank you again, Sire, for your generosity and hospitality towards us. I know I haven't had the chance to see you often, with Perrin's training and all. I just want you to be aware of our gratitude.

"You are, of course, welcome."

Hellet noted how Neffy had said 'our gratitude'. He and Perrin had spent almost all their time together since their group had arrived in

Labyn, and Hellet wondered if there was more than just a bond of friendship growing between them. While it was difficult to imagine anyone being drawn to Perrin these days, her beauty was still visible, though it was shrouded by a black aura of hate. However, Darus had been Neffy's closest friend. Hellet was certain that Neffy felt some level of accountability for Darus' death, and he was making himself responsible for the care of his widow.

"She will be an amazing fighter," Neffy continued.

"I'm going to kill them all," Perrin sneered as she spat out a hunk of gristle onto the floor.

"I believe you," Tollan responded.

***

"All the dreams returned," a haggard appearing Dellea said after opening her door to greet Hellet the following morning. "It had been so long, I thought I was finally done with them."

Hellet wrapped his arms around her and pulled her close. He felt a slight trembling in her body as he kissed the top of her head. "I'm so sorry Dellea."

Dellea gently pushed herself away and gazed at him. Her eyes were wide and bloodshot, and he noticed a glistening of perspiration along her brow. He tenderly wiped the sweat away with his sleeve and said, "Come, let's get our breakfast then go see Wander."

With a nod, Dellea took Hellet's arm, and they made their way down the hall.

***

The old cleric was hunched over his table, engrossed as always over Sul's book when Hellet and Dellea entered his home. With a wince of pain, he lifted his head as the pair approached. "Our apologies for entering uninvited, you didn't seem to hear us knocking," Hellet stated.

"No apology necessary, my boy. I was absorbed with my study. It is a sad book, isn't it?"

"Yes," Dellea agreed.

"I know spring is arriving, and I'm growing concerned. I've searched through this book countless times, and I have said many prayers, but it seems I have nothing to offer you, much like my son."

Hellet dropped into a chair as Dellea remained standing, peering down at the old man. "We're running out of time," Hellet dejectedly stated.

With popping from his ancient joints, Wander pushed himself up from his rickety chair, and he began to slowly shamble around his room.

"I wish I could be of assistance, but I don't know what this book has to do with our situation."

"It seems my dreams are going to come to fruition," Dellea sighed.

"Dreams? What dreams? What are you talking about girl?" Wander asked as he turned to them with a speed Hellet did not think possible.

"Nightmares have been plaguing me for months. Thankfully they had stopped since we arrived, but they returned last night. They're terrible."

"Tell me of them," Wander demanded urgently.

Dellea took a seat at the table then recounted all the horrible dreams and grotesque visions she had experienced. Every one of them had returned the night before and they had been as vivid as ever, so she was able to tell Wander every horrifying detail.

When she had finished speaking, Wander's face slowly morphed into a smile. "Now I understand. I know how we will prevail." The smile turned into joy, but then he gazed at each of them in turn, and the joy evaporated into immense sorrow. "And I know what you must do."

# chapter 66

WITH MENNUM HAVING LEFT for Shekul, Ellaniya was finally alone with Vor. She enjoyed their nights together and rarely thought of Travyn. When her mind did turn to her husband, she felt more disdain than anything else. His stupidity now repulsed her. How had she ever found any affection for such an ignorant man? However, she had a more pressing concerning: her bleeding was late. Was she pregnant with Vor's child? Ut had promised her that she would not conceive until the conflicts were over, but had he been wrong? If she was pregnant, she would not be able to pass off a child of Vor's as Travyn's. But she would set that worry aside until Labyn was conquered. She was aware of herbs that might end a pregnancy, but now was not the time to consider such things.

She walked about the castle grounds with only a light coat, enjoying the warmer air as winter had finally begun to loosen its grip. "How are the preparations coming?" she asked Vor, turning her attention back to their immediate matter.

"We continue to have soldiers arrive from Mephosh and Shekul; however, small contingents of warriors are being left behind to maintain order," Vor replied. "The bulk of the mercenaries are already here, with a few more still expected."

"As Aniass is with my husband, are the mercenaries clear that they will be taking orders from you?"

"Yes, that has all been discussed and arranged."

"And the siege engines?"

"We've only be able to build a few due to the harsh conditions," Vor replied. "If we want to embark as soon as the weather clears, we will need to make do with what we have."

"That's unfortunate but unavoidable. I don't think we should spend extra time on construction. Our army will be substantial. Labyn will not be able to resist."

"Yes, but we will lose many good men."

"True," responded Ellaniya. "But most will be mercenaries who will not need to be compensated. And we will gain more warriors once Labyn is conquered."

"You are wise."

Ellaniya offered her lover a smile. "You should probably escort me back to my chambers then return to your duties. I want to make sure all preparations are in order so we can launch the attack once the snow is melted. But I assume I will see you tonight?"

"Of course. I look forward to it."

***

The days were growing longer and warmer—and the snow was slowly melting—as Ellaniya sat alone in her room, the remnants of her meal before her. She rarely ate in public spaces for fear that one of the former citizens of Su'Meeryn would make a foolish attempt on her life. Extra guards were always around, but she felt it was not worth taking any unnecessary risks. Soon all the snow would be gone, and her magnificent army could march. Labyn would be conquered, and she would finally reign in Mephosh as the Empress Lynna with Vor at her side.

Everything was proceeding as planned, but was victory enough? She was delighted that the heretic religion was being eradicated and that Su'Meeryn had been properly punished, but where did it all leave her? While she was pleased, Ellaniya had to admit to herself that she was not truly happy. She would soon be married to a second man she did not love, or even like. And while Vor brought her physical pleasure, she realized she had no joy in her life. Ellaniya desired Vor, and she cared for him. But when she examined herself, she knew that she was not in love with him. What had she become?

Ellaniya chastised herself for her sorrowful musings. She ruled over a vast empire; she commanded the fear and respect of her many subjects. While Ut had orchestrated much of the recent events, she knew it had all started with her: her zeal for the gods, and her disdain for her heretical family.

After pushing her dirty plate and utensils away, she stared at her hands. It had been a long while since she had looked at them and thought of her father and brother. They had been murdered because of her. As time had passed, she thought of them less and less, but she still remembered her blood-stained hands.

How was it that she continued to drift back to these doubts regarding her past actions? She had always been faithful to the gods, and the legacy of Lynna remained strong in her. She knew the abomination of Su'Meeryn was responsible for the hard choices she had been forced to make, so why did her misgivings persist?

She flipped her hands over and gazed at her palms. Her hands were clean, the crimson stains long gone. But so much blood had been spilled in her name, and now she was afforded the comforts of the royal chambers of Su'Meeryn. Soon her empire would expand even further, and many more would die. What right did she have for melancholy while she rested in the luxury of her conquests? Was not she the one who had been blessed by the gods? Not for the first time, she reaffirmed her commitment to them. She climbed into bed and offered the gods a prayer of repentance and thanksgiving.

As she nestled into her bedding—feeling the warmth of the soft blankets the fire crackling in the corner of her room—Ellaniya thought of the promise of her future divinity. Who deserved it more than she? Who else had ever served the gods so faithfully? While the deaths that had surrounded her were sad, all men die. Only the eternal was of true importance. Nothing eclipsed the gods, and she would make sure that all knew of and worshipped them. And hopefully she would join them soon to be worshipped as well.

She then said another prayer, but this time she petitioned the gods for their wisdom and guidance. As she still had not bled, so was convinced that she was pregnant. When the child was born, the rumors of her and Vor would be confirmed. But what of it? she thought; I'll be empress, what do I care what others say about my child? She gave her stomach an affectionate rub and decided she looked forward to the child's arrival.

Plus, the sky was growing dark, and soon Vor would join her. At least she would not be alone this night.

# chapter 67

"YOU MUST BE JOKING!" Tollan cried. "He wants us to attack Mephosh?"

"Yes," Hellet answered, his eyes remaining on Dellea. Her face was still frozen with the same look of shock and despair she wore when Wander had told them his plan. "We came to you immediately once we finished with Wander."

"But this is absurd. It would will leave Labyn unprotected!"

"Labyn will not be at risk," Hellet continued. "Your army will be Ellaniya's concern, not the castle. Once she learns that we are moving to assault Mephosh, she will divert her forces there."

Tollan dropped to his chair, bewilderment dripping from his face. "So we are to leave the protection of our walls and allow Ellaniya to attack us in the open? This is madness!"

"I thought you trusted Wander."

"Trust is one thing, but… to agree to such a foolhardy plan?"

"You haven't heard the entire plan," Dellea finally spoke up in a quivering voice. Hellet knew the old prophet's words rested heavily on her slender shoulders, and he worried that the burden would crush her. But if they were to succeed, there could be no other way.

He glanced at his hand and missing finger. Yes, he could hold a sword, but he was inept with a blade even when he had all his fingers. However, if Wander was correct, his lack of skill would not matter, but it was also a tremendous weight on him. Victory required much of the two of them, and he wondered at the price they would have to pay to achieve that victory. It would be a heavy price, but how steep?

Wander's plan had struck Dellea hard, but what had been worse was when he said they would have to embark prior to Hellet becoming of age. The one bright spot to Dellea through all the turmoil was that they would be able to marry after their arrival in Labyn, but now they would have to wait. And there was no guarantee that any of them would survive. The words had devastated her, both of them, but she rallied herself as best as she could.

Tears streamed from her eyes as she forced herself to stutter out Wander's plan. Tollan's face turned pale as Dellea relayed Wander's words to the king, and he remained dumbfounded when she had finished.

"If Wander's wrong, we all die, but wouldn't we all die if we stayed?" Hellet pointed out. "We might live awhile longer if we remain here, but defeat is not in question. Ellaniya is amassing an army we cannot hope to repel, despite all the preparations. "

"How could he have not known this previously?" Tollan finally asked. "If such a thing is possible, shouldn't Wander or Wairren have mentioned it before now?"

"I don't know. I'm not a religious student. My father thought studying with Wairren was a waste of my time."

"But that doesn't answer my question."

"It wasn't until Wander heard my dreams that he made the connection, then he understood," Dellea stated softly, her voice flat with despair.

"Connection? A loose connection at best. What you're proposing is impossible."

"Sul's book tells us of powers we can't conceive," Dellea replied. "Wander was there; he witnessed them. And my home was destroyed by a power we don't understand."

"As you have made it clear that surrender is not an option. It's our only chance to save Labyn," Hellet stated. "If we stay here, you will lose. Isn't it better to take the chance?"

"But why can't his plan be accomplished here? Why do we have to leave these walls?"

"I asked the same thing," Hellet answered. "Wander was not certain. Maybe the first part is required, or perhaps it's a test? I don't know. But he is convinced this is the only way the plan will succeed."

Tollan just shook his head before dropping it into his hands. "I'll need some time to consider this."

✳✳✳

The pair sat quietly together in the stables; Hellet knew this was where Dellea needed to be after their meeting with Tollan. The wolves would not be able to remove her burden, but they would help soothe her anxiety. The animals whimpered as their tails danced through the air when they entered, sensing Dellea's unease. They circled around anxiously until Dellea and Hellet sat on the straw. The wolves then licked her face until they too finally settled down and accepted the loving strokes from the couple.

"Should we take them on a hike?" Hellet asked.

Dellea shook her head. "I don't want to go anywhere. I just want us all to sit together."

They remained silent for a few moments as they continued to stroke the wolves' fur. "Will you be able to do it?" Hellet eventually asked.

"I have to," she answered softly, "but the task will be difficult for you as well. How can you possibly go through with this?"

"I have no idea. Wairren said we'd face difficulties, but we could never have envisioned this. I suppose we won't be the same when this is over, if we survive."

Dellea dropped her face to the wolf nearest her and kissed its head. "No, how could we?" Her chin remained resting on the beast as her eyes turned to her fiancé. "I just hope you'll still love me," and Hellet heard a question in her voice.

Hellet took a deep breath before he responded; he knew he needed to find the appropriate words. "It will be difficult for both of us, and we will certainly change; however, my love for you will remain. We will marry once we prevail."

Dellea's expression of doubt and concern did not change as she continued to gaze into his eyes. She had been through so much, and just when she thought she might finally find happiness, it threatened to be ripped away. Her experiences left her guarded; she loved Hellet, but Wander's plan put that at risk. Would they still be able to love each other when it was over? Would they be able to love anyone or anything? Her hand caressed the fur of the wolf while her eyes remained glued on Hellet. Hellet had done all he could to be a constant in her life since they had met, but if they survived, they would be different people. There was no guarantee regarding his pledge once this was all over. Would the wolves end up being her only constant? The animals lounged in the stable content and oblivious to what was being asked of their leaders.

"We will get through this, I promise you." Hellet told her. Still her face did not move. Their eyes remained locked together, but tears began to form then slowly run down her cheeks.

# chapter 68

THE HORSES DASHED THROUGH THE COUNTRYSIDE, kicking up showers of mud and slush from the last remnants of snow. The young man in front handled his steed effortlessly while Tollan struggled to maintain pace. Hellet reached the tree the king had pointed out with enough time to turn his horse and grin at his companion.

When the king reached Hellet, he brought his mount to a halt and let out a laugh. "You are a marvelous horseman, my friend," he offered with a smile. On a normal day, the king of Labyn would be able to enjoy the friendly competition and the warmer air that had finally arrived. Unfortunately, Tollan's pleasure was short lived. The break from the worst winter in memory would normally have been a cause for celebration, but with the temperature rising, all knew what was awaiting them.

"I thank you for the kind compliment," Hellet replied as the king's guards pulled up and positioned their own horses back a respectful distance.

"I've not spent too much time with your friend Neffy, but he's told me of your skills."

"Neffy exaggerates," Hellet stated and took a drink from the skin hanging at his side.

Tollan raised his head as he regarded his new friend. "Come now, Hellet. I wouldn't take you as one for false humility."

Hellet remained quiet for a moment, squinting slightly as he pondered his response. "It's not an area I care discussing."

"That may be, my friend, but after what you're asking of me, I believe I deserve a response."

Following another sip of water, Hellet said. "It is true. For whatever reason, I am able to excel at just about everything I try. I've heard how exceptional I am my whole life." Hellet paused for a moment as he looked up at the white clouds dotting the sky. "My mother always told me it was important to be honest with yourself. I understand that I have been very blessed in many areas, but I don't like discussing it."

"I guess we are similar in many ways. While I may not be as gifted as you, I was always viewed as kind of a miracle child after all the struggles my parents had conceiving." Tollan now paused to take a drink himself, wondering if he should share his next comment. Why not? he thought. It seemed silly to worry about revealing his feelings given the fateful task looming before them. "It was a daunting burden for me to be thought of that way. How could I ever live up to being a miracle? And my father was so well loved, how would I measure up to the expectations that would be thrust upon me when I took the crown?"

Hellet's head tilted slightly as he considered Tollan's words. "I never thought of it that way. I was never burdened by the expectations of me." He thought for another moment. "Perhaps I was proud; I don't know. Maybe my mother's counsel helped me more than I realized. But unlike your father, mine was king for only a short time. And while he was a good man, he clearly wasn't as well loved as yours."

Tollan felt his pulse quickening at the thought of his parents, and he replied quietly. "Regardless, both of our parents experienced fates they did not deserve."

"If I may, I don't know what exactly happened to your parents. I've heard some talk, but I didn't think it was my place to ask."

"That's okay. It was a tragic day. My father became a staunch believers in the faith after Wander's arrival. When the pagans resurfaced, my father ordered me to drive them from Labyn. Then on the day of the celebration of Adira's conception, they created a diversion. When my father sent guards to stop a fight that had begun amongst the dancers, attackers stormed the dais. In a moment, they killed my parents as well as my closest friend."

"I'm so very sorry. We've both endured much at the hands of my uncle and the pagans."

Tollan nodded as Hellet pulled some seeds out from his pocket. Recounting the tale of his parent's murder made Tollan think not just of them, but of Max as well. Losing his parents had been difficult enough, but perhaps he had not realized how much he had lost with the death of his dear friend. Maybe that was one reason why he had been so drawn to Hellet. Of course the prince from Su'Meeryn was a charismatic figure, and Tollan could not imagine a single person taking a dislike to Hellet. But maybe there was more to this new friendship. Nobody had been able to replace Max, until now.

"I went again to the stables to see the wolves," Tollan eventually said, breaking the silence. "I brought some meat but they remained leery of me."

Hellet spit out some of the seed's shells then asked, "What did they do?".

"They seemed skittish, which was surprising to me. Eventually they grabbed the meat, but then darted to the back of their stable."

"Dellea always says I'm the only man that they like, although they did seem to warm somewhat to Neffy when we were on the run. And Darus."

"It is a strange thing, but I wish I could have interacted with them more. I pray that they grow comfortable with me one day. I'd like nothing more than to gain their trust," Tollan said.

"For your sake, I hope that occurs. Interacting with them is one of the most pleasurable experiences of my life."

Tollan began to stroke his steed's neck before grabbing an apple from a small pack and gave it to the horse. "Now, if I may be so bold, there has been a question on my mind. You and Dellea? I don't mean to be rude, but it seems an odd pairing."

"I've been asked that question before, and I can't explain it. I was drawn to her since the moment we first met. I remember Neffy daring me to pet the wolves… it seems so long ago. Anyway, Dellea was there and warned me about them. When I was able to approach and pet all three, she was surprised, and a little annoyed to be honest with you." Hellet stopped for a moment and smiled at the memory before continuing. "At that time, she was promised to my uncle, so I put her out of my mind. Then the plans for Travyn changed, and I saw my opportunity. I knew the two of us needed to be together, but I didn't know why." Hellet paused again. "I guess now we know."

Tollan took in a deep breath, and as he expelled the air, he wondered if Hellet recognized the nervousness he always tried to keep hidden. So much was being asked of him, and he still wondered if he would be able to measure up to his father. But he also knew the task being placed on Hellet and Dellea was far greater. "Well, obviously, we need this all to work out, but I worry for you, my friend. It will be a hard road for the two of you, even if we're victorious."

"That is true, but I worry for us all."

"Yes, of course," the king replied, "of course. But for now, let's enjoy this beautiful day. I fear we have few of them left."

A slight frown crossed Hellet's face as he gently nudged his steed, and it began to trot away from the tree, back towards the castle.

**✳✳✳**

Sparring with Neffy was both gratifying and frustrating. While it was always good to test oneself against a superior foe, it was far from pleasant to be routinely bested so easily. While Tollan was more than competent with a blade, he was no match for the large warrior.

Following Neffy's fifth touch in their combat, Tollan signaled to stop and left the sparring area to sit on the nearest bench. The king grabbed a rag to wipe the sweat from his brow then dipped a mug into a large water barrel and gulped down the refreshing liquid.

"You fight well," Neffy said as he joined the king on the bench.

"Ha, I'm no match for you, my friend."

"Most aren't."

"I'd normally take that as a boast, but I know it to be true," Tollan responded.

"It is."

The king glanced at his companion before taking another drink. "You and Hellet certainly have no qualms with acknowledging your virtues."

"Why should we?" Neffy asked.

As Tollan considered his companion again, he noticed that Neffy had not broken a sweat. "Hellet said something similar to me, about acknowledging your strengths."

"Hellet is wise," Neffy replied after a pause. "He learned well from his mother. He told me often about their conversations. She valued honesty greatly, and that included being honest with yourself."

"Did I sense some hesitation in your response?"

As Neffy turned to watch Perrin best another foe, Tollan saw a slight flushing on his face. "It's not my place."

"I beg to differ, my large friend. I'm risking much on Hellet and Dellea. If you have something to say, I want to hear it."

Tollan saw an uncharacteristic quiver on Neffy's lips. "Hellet and I have been friends a very long time," the large warrior began. "Aside from Darus, Hellet has been my closest friend. Everything you've heard about him is true. He's a remarkable individual. However, wisdom and experience are not the same. Had we sought refuge in Gorthon, Darus would still be alive."

"So, you question your friend's judgment?"

"I disagreed with his decision."

Tollan finished off his water as he too turned his attention to the warriors still training in the yard. He watched as Perrin now fought relentlessly against two of his soldiers whom Tollan knew to be very skilled. It was impressive to see the young woman hold her own against the pair. "The death of a close friend is tragic. I experienced the same due to the pagans—along with my parents. Despite your horrible loss, Hellet's decision brought you to Labyn, and as absurd as it may seem, we now have a plan to stop Ellaniya and the pagans."

"I know, but the memory of Darus remains. Regardless, Hellet is my prince, and I will always do what he requires of me. My role is to serve."

Tollan slapped Neffy on the thigh. "You are a good and loyal man, friend Nefalel."

The pair sat quietly for a moment, and Tollan's eyes returned to Perrin. Even in training, she fought with a ferocity he had never witnessed before. After a deftly executed parry, she disarmed one of her startled opponents and glared at the man. "What of her?" the king asked, pointing at the panting woman.

"I've done all I can to prepare her for what's to come."

"That's not what I mean."

Neffy turned his attention from Perrin to look back at Tollan. "If we survive this, I don't know what will become of her. Maybe by defeating Travyn her thirst for vengeance will be quenched and she will begin to recover her old self, but I have no idea."

"If you don't mind me saying, I see the way you look at her."

Neffy shook his head and ran his fingers through his hair. "You are a strange king, Tollan. You talk to me as if we were merely friends."

"I do consider you a friend."

"Perhaps we are, but you are still king."

"I learned from my father. Though he exerted his authority, he never saw a need to speak down to people. He always addressed everyone as an equal. That was one of the reasons he was so well loved."

"As are you."

"I try my best, but you seem to be dodging my query."

Neffy took a deep breath before replying. "Darus was like a brother to me. When he was killed, I swore to myself that I would make certain Perrin was always cared for." He let out a chuckle as Perrin bested the other opponent. "Not that she needs it."

"That's obvious, at least to a degree."

"My desire to watch after Perrin is only superseded by my loyalty to Hellet. Perhaps I will propose marriage to her if we survive, and yes, I do realize being wed to her may be difficult."

"As I said, you are a fine man, Neffy," Tollan remarked as he stood from the bench, "and I'd be honored to have you standing next to me when the fighting starts."

Neffy also stood. "It would be my honor," he replied as he bowed to the king, "as long as Perrin is with me."

"Of course. I can think of no better place for her to be." Tollan reached out and grasped Neffy's large, calloused hand. "I'm glad we had this talk. I just wish we could have found more opportunities prior to today."

"Hopefully we will have plenty of chances once this is all done."

"Yes, hopefully."

# chapter 69

THE SKY ABOVE WAS CLEAR AND DARK. As it was the time of the new moon, the countless stars glistened and glowed brighter than usual. Dellea wondered if anyone had ever tried to count them. Surely some had, but it was certainly an impossible task. It was beautiful sight she wished she could enjoy. Unfortunately, joy was an impossibility now, and she wondered if she would ever experience it again. Whether they succeeded or failed in their mission, how could she ever be the same? How could joy ever enter her life again?

Dellea sat with Hellet, Neffy and Perrin on the hard ground beneath the blanket of shimmering stars. Their journey from Su'Meeryn seemed like ages ago, and they all remained quiet, seemingly transfixed by the fire before them. Though they had been in Labyn for some time, the memory of the miserable winter was strong, and Dellea enjoyed the heat of the flames against her skin.

A pop from the fire sent an ember hurling into the sky, and it seemed to merge with the stars. A puff of smoke rippled in her hair as her vision trailed above. Though the night was warm and peaceful, that peace would soon be broken. Tomorrow the final preparation would be complete, and the army would march towards Mephosh the following day. Their success and the lives of all the soldiers—including Hellet— rested in her trembling hands. Would she be able to do what was required? Wander had expressed his faith in her, and while she appreciated his comforting words, how could she be certain? But she knew she had to make the attempt. Tollan would never surrender to Ellaniya, and Hellet would fight beside the king, regardless of the plan. Despite the seeming implausibility of Wander's directions, she could do nothing but attempt them. The old cleric's plan was their best chance for victory no matter how daunting.

Neffy stood from the ground and placed another log on the fire as Hellet wrapped his arm around Dellea. The fire crackled and more embers flew into the sky as Hellet began to hum. Even without words, Hellet's voice was captivating. The melody seemed familiar, but Dellea could not place the song. She nestled into his arm and closed her eyes, letting his soft music envelop her. For just a moment, the weight of her task was forgotten, and she smiled. When Hellet concluded his song, Dellea opened her eyes, and her smile dissolved. All of Wander's words came crashing back down on her. As her body shook, Hellet's arm pulled her in closer, and she felt some relief.

"That was beautiful," Neffy complemented his friend as he returned to the ground, next to Perrin.

"Thank you."

They remained quiet; all eyes engrossed in the dancing flames. Dellea looked over at Perrin, whose face was blank, expressionless. She had been surprised when Perrin had agreed to join them this evening, but Perrin had said nothing after they left the castle. While Dellea initially was pleased with Perrin presence, even in her silence, Dellea could feel Perrin's fury. That harsh energy which radiated off Darus' widow only added to her anxiety.

"It's hard to believe everything will be coming to a conclusion, for good or ill," Neffy finally said, and through the flames, Dellea noticed that Perrin's arm moved, and her hand came to rest on Neffy's thigh.

"Yes, but I'm confident it will end for the good," Hellet responded. "I have faith in Dellea."

"And you?" Neffy asked.

"I will do what is required of me."

Neffy's head rose at Hellet's response, and Dellea saw a look of pride and determination etched on his countenance.

"You are fine man, Nefalel," Dellea said, surprising herself that she had spoken up. "I misjudged you all those years ago." She felt Hellet's arm tighten again at her words, and a warm smile crossed Neffy's face. However, Perrin's blank expression remained unchanged.

"Maybe you did, maybe you didn't," Neffy replied. "We were all different people back then. I guess none of that matters now. All that does matter is we prevail."

"We will," Hellet said in a steely tone.

Dellea could feel her face flush—but it was not from the fire—and there was catch in her throat. She had more to say, and she knew if she did not speak up now, she might never have the chance again. "I didn't mean that as empty praise, Neffy. It's true that I didn't care for you when we first met, but we don't need to go over any of that now. You are the most trustworthy friend a man—or woman—could ask for. I know that you've disagreed with some of Hellet's decisions, but despite that, you have served your friend and prince faithfully and without complaint." Dellea paused as thoughts of Darus came to mind, but she knew it would be best not bringing him up at this time. "You all know how hard this is for me, but I needed to say it." Dellea wanted to look Neffy in the eyes, but just speaking the words took all of her courage and energy, so she turned her gaze to the flames. "You are what's best in men."

When she had finished, Hellet's arm slowly released her. She looked at him to see the expression of utter bewilderment. Dellea then looked up at Neffy to see a wide smile and what appeared to be tears on his cheeks. Perrin, however, sat like a statue.

The four remained around the fire, none speaking. The pleasant night air was so refreshing so they were not anxious to leave.

As the fire began to dwindle, Hellet eventually rose, stretched out his back and reached down for Dellea's hand. As the others stood, they all silently walked back to the dark castle.

# chapter 70

"YOU CAN STILL CALL THIS OFF," Adira's red-rimmed eyes pleaded. "I beg you, Tollan, just surrender. I can't stand the thought of losing you. Surely Ellaniya will let us live if you do."

Tollan grasped his wife's hand. "You know I can't," he said as gently as he could. "After what they did to my parents and Max, I could never surrender."

"But you don't know that Ellaniya ordered their deaths."

"Directly or indirectly, it doesn't matter. She's responsible for the pagans resurfacing."

"Please, my heart. Listen to me."

Tollan came to the bed and wrapped his arms around his wife, her body trembling with heavy sobs. "The last thing I want to do is cause you distress, but I must follow through on the plan. I realize the risks and that we're putting all our faith in Dellea and Hellet. But I know that it's necessary. I know I must do this."

Her crying abruptly stopped as Adira's body stiffened, and she pushed Tollan away. "Then get out!" she screamed. "Get out and leave me be!"

Tollan was taken aback for a moment at the harsh words, but then Adira collapsed on the bed, and the sobbing returned.

"I'll give you some time," he whispered. "I'll go for a walk, then I'll be back."

✳✳✳

As the king walked through the courtyard, the warmth of the day brought no pleasure. The bustling of activity had ended since the preparations were complete. Tollan would be marching off to war at first light.

He thought on Adira's plea and wondered if somehow there might have been a way to avoid the deaths of Max and his parents, along with the coming conflict. Could anything have been done differently? If he had made the diplomatic visit to Travyn and Ellaniya, might there have been a different result? He doubted it. Gorhum never would have allowed the pagans to take root in Labyn, so nothing would have stopped the attack that fateful day. But this war could be avoided if he were to abide by his wife's desire and surrender. The king gritted his teeth at the idea. After the murders committed by the pagans, surrender was an impossible thought.

Surrounded by his guards, Tollan left the palace grounds to hike his kingdom. He thought of asking Hellet to join him, but he decided he needed to be alone. He normally would chat with his guards, but on this day, with the swirl of thoughts, he remained silent.

While striding down the streets, many acknowledged their king. Some called out his name while others simply waved or nodded. Tollan tried to look at every person and commit their faces to his memory, but he knew it was an impossible task.

As he entered the marketplace, he saw the merchants at their tables or in their shops, but no customers were visible. The whole kingdom knew what was coming, and it seemed that nobody had a heart for shopping.

After leaving the marketplace, Tollan entered the tradesmen's quarter. Blacksmiths were laboring over their forges while leather workers tended to their hides. He heard the banging of the carpenters in their shops and a sad smile crossed his face. Would this be the last time he was amidst these fine people? He had been their monarch only a short time. Had he been a good king to them? If not, would he have the chance to improve?

Tollan waved at all those who acknowledged him, but the smile left his face as he exited the quarter, and his small entourage made its way towards the village. As they continued to walk, all his doubts resurfaced. But perhaps those doubts did not matter. Soon he would be in battle, and he might never return to his home. What would happen to the citizens of Labyn after the battle? If his army emerged victorious, and he survived, he would rule them and strive to be as wise and fair as his father. But if they won, and he were to fall on the battlefield, what would become of Labyn? How would Adira manage as a widowed queen? He did not know, but if Hellet survived, he was certain Labyn would thrive. He was certain Hellet would see to that.

He felt a little sweat forming under his long hair as his trek continued, and his thoughts remained on Hellet. In many ways, they were similar. While Tollan might not be as gifted as the young man from Su'Meeryn, they both had incredible expectations placed upon them. Were those expectations fair? How could they be? They also shared the same tragedy of losing their parents to the pagans at such a young age. Perhaps this was what had drawn the two of them together so quickly. Hellet was such a fine young man, and Tollan knew they would remain close friends when this was all over—assuming they survived.

His thoughts then turned to Dellea and Adira. While Hellet and he both adored their women, those two could not be more different. Adira possessed both stunning beauty and confidence while Dellea was plain and awkward. Even as he got to know Dellea better, she remained uncomfortable around him. Through discussions with Hellet, he was advised it was not a reflection on him. That was just her nature, and he had come to have much affection for her. The thoughts of Dellea brought another matter to mind, and he turned from the village to make his way to the stables.

When they reached the building, Tollan ordered the guards to wait outside as he entered. He went to the stall that housed the wolves and tried to muster his confidence while opening the stall door. The three large animals were lounging on the straw with the remnants of their last meal strewn about.

Tollan took a step in as the three heads raised and dark eyes fixated on him. The king stopped, waiting to see what the creatures would do. He knew they were not dangerous—at least that was what he had been told, but Dellea had said the only man they liked was Hellet. What would they do if he approached them?

The wolves remained on the ground, but their eyes did not leave the king. No sound came from them as Tollan took a tentative step forward. After another step, one of the beasts slowly stood with its head low, the eyes unmoving. Tollan did not move further, and neither did the wolf.

His pulse quickened, and he felt his heart beating in his chest. Another step and a second wolf rose, its head also low while its tail slowly flipped from side to side. "They're not dangerous," Tollan said to himself as he walked up to the first one and arched his back, holding his head high. The wolf's snout dropped a few inches and Tollan heard a slight whimper. Trying to keep his hand from shaking, he reached out and placed it on top of the animal's head. The wolf did not move while Tollan stroked the fur which felt rough against his palm. The whimpering grew louder, as if the beast was signaling it had had enough. Tollan raised his hand and the wolf dropped back to the ground. He then turned to the second, and it reacted in the same manner as the first.

Once the second wolf dropped down, Tollan turned to the third one. It had never risen, but as Tollan approached, it turned on its side, exposing its belly. Tollan dropped to a knee and began to stroke its stomach. As he did, the wolf raised its head and looked at him. Tollan stopped for a moment, but the wolf did not move further, so he resumed his stroking. He then reached over to its head, and his hand was greeted by a tongue. A few short licks caressed his fingers before he rubbed its head a couple times. The wolf then dropped its head back to the straw, and Tollan knew the encounter was concluded.

He got back to his feet and went to the door. Turning around he saw that all three were still staring at him. "Thank you," he breathed as he exited the stall.

When he returned to the guards, he announced it was time to return to the palace.

"Did you enjoy your day, sire?" one of the guards asked.

"Yes, I did," the king responded, "and now I must return to my wife and son."

# chapter 71

SPRING HAD FINALLY ARRIVED. While the budding trees and flowers would normally be a cause for celebration, it brought no pleasure to Dellea. The army of Labyn stood assembled, preparing to march towards Mephosh. Dellea was one of the few who had been given a horse, which was not thrilled to have three wolves beside it. Her steed fidgeted nervously with its head continually swiveling between the three animals while Dellea stroked its neck in a feeble attempt to calm her mount.

Perrin stood beside her, sword in hand, examining its edge. As Perrin sheathed her weapon, Dellea saw the ripple of muscle in her arms that had not been present in the past. Perrin glanced at her with an expression of fierce anticipation. Soon she would be in battle and reaping vengeance on the murderers of her husband. She turned away and Dellea heard a sinister laugh which caused goose bumps to emerge on her arms.

Dellea's horse was finally starting to settle down while the army continued to assemble. She silently went over Wander's instruction, as she had countless times. The task before her—and Hellet—remained daunting, seemingly impossible. But the success of the mission rested on Hellet's and her young, inexperienced shoulders. Wander's plan was an enormous responsibility, and, if they succeeded, how would she change? She was a peculiar person already. What would this do to her—to them? She knew it was a selfish concern as many men were destined to die, but she could not shake her feelings of trepidation.

She had tried to put those thoughts away as they had awaited the spring thaw. The times Hellet and she had spent together had been pleasant, but the inevitability of this day had hung like an anchor around her neck, slowly pulling her down into the depths of a cold, dark sea. It seemed her only solace had once again been the times she spent alone with the wolves, and that only increased her sadness. She wanted Hellet to be with her, but his presence only made her think even more about their forthcoming task.

At least the day had come. The anxiety of preparing and waiting had been the worst: the unknown of what the future would bring. But the future had now arrived. Hellet had promised that their marriage would take place once the conflict was over, and she believed him. There was no doubt in her mind that they would be husband and wife, if they lived. But would their marriage turn out to be like her parents: bitter and vile? Had those two ever even loved each other? She did not know the answer, but that did not matter now. She had the memory of her childhood and now Wander's story. She would not allow herself to fall into one of those pits. But what of Hellet? Despite his deportment, she had to remind herself that he was still young. He had the presence and maturity of someone twice his years, but he was still not of age. How would he change when all this was done?

The army was starting to grow restless as they awaited the arrival of Tollan and Hellet, who had gone off to speak to Wander one last time before departing. Hellet had asked Dellea to join them, but she refused. She had spent a great deal of time with Wander over the last weeks, and she could not bring herself to see him again. There was nothing left to say; she knew her mission and seeing him again would only reinforce her anguish. Instead, when Hellet had departed, she went to the stables with a large portion of meat. She wanted to make sure that the wolves' appetites where fully satisfied before departing.

A commotion began to roll through the assembly, and Dellea looked up to the castle wall. Adira stood there, her golden hair hanging down like a blanket to where a sleeping Gorhum rested in her arms. Even at a distance, Dellea recognized her beauty though it was marred by the scowl on her face.

The soldiers behind Dellea parted and Hellet and Tollan rode their horses under the gate with Neffy following. She noticed that the king had donned his crown, and she wondered if that was the wisest choice as they came up next to her.

"Wander died," Hellet stated in a soft voice. "He wished us well and said he has been praying for you continuously. The king thanked him, and Wander started a final prayer then fell silent. He died in the midst of that prayer."

Tollan raised his head in a nod of agreement. "A fitting ending to great man."

"Yes, it seems as if he survived all these years to bring us to this point. And now that the day is here, he has finally been given his rest," Hellet said.

Neffy took a breath, as if he was going to say something, but he remained quiet. His opposition to their plan was well known, but he would serve his prince no matter his thoughts on the subject. When he spied Perrin, he moved his horse towards her then jumped off. He patted her on the back and offered a smile, which was not returned; Perrin's face remained hard and focused. Dellea then brushed her fingers against the orange and silver scarf she always had with her, a memory of a more pleasant time.

"It is time! Let us depart!" the king ordered, and the army began to move. Soon they would be at war. As they got underway, the cry of a baby could be heard among the marching feet and rattling weapons, but Dellea did not turn to look.

***

"They're marching?" Ellaniya questioned with a laugh. "To Mephosh?" Her army had already left Su'Meeryn and was heading towards Labyn when scouts had arrived with the news. "And without siege engines? I had no idea we would be facing off against fools."

"Do we continue on to Labyn?" Vor asked.

"No, of course not. They have just given us an even easier victory. We no longer have to breach their walls. We will turn to engage them. Once they are defeated, we will be able to walk into Labyn unimpeded."

"Forgive me my queen, but they must know this. They can't be as foolish as some *others*." He paused briefly before continuing. "Surely they must have a plan."

"What plan could they possibly have? They are marching out into the open and won't have time to set traps. It is a move of desperation. They must know we left only a small contingent back in Mephosh and are hoping they can take the castle before we arrive. Well, they are wrong."

Vor's expression showed that he was not convinced, but it was of no matter. Ellaniya estimated her army to be three to four times the size of Tollan's. This idiotic move would only quicken Labyn's defeat. It was a glorious day. Everything was coming into focus for her. Vor was at her side, and Tollan would be easily defeated. Ellaniya was now certain of her pregnancy, and she no longer concerned herself that others would know it was Vor's child. What did the thoughts of anyone else matter? Soon she would claim the title of Empress Lynna and cast Travyn aside. The baby would be heir to the empire of the gods. What could be more fitting? The gods had blessed her far more than she could have ever envisioned.

**\*\*\***

"I still have a hard time believing you are as young as you claim," Tollan said as he rode next to Hellet.

"I've been hearing that my whole life," Hellet replied.

"In case we don't make it out of this, I want to say how impressed I am with you. It's been my pleasure to get to know you, and the others."

"Thank you. I feel the same way. I pray we have much time together when this is all over."

"As do I." After a moment, Tollan continued. "I still worry about Dellea. She is a… unique girl to begin with. She never talked much, and even less since Wander gave us his plan. He is asking much of her, of both of you. Is she ready?"

"I have reassured her as best I can, but it still weighs heavily on her—rightfully so. On myself as well." Hellet paused as he considered what awaited him, and it was a daunting thought. "All she's been through has made her strong," he continued, "stronger than she realizes."

Hellet looked ahead at the vanguard of the army as he removed his glove and pulled out some of the salve to massage into the amputated joint.

"Still painful?"

"Not really, but it does ache at times," he replied, happy to have his thoughts diverted.

"That's good," the king said as he reached over and slapped Hellet on the back. "Those wolves are really something. I'm thankful that they finally warmed to me, but I do worry for Dellea if something happens to them."

"She's concerned too, but she knows their importance."

"True. Now if you will excuse me, I should check on my men."

"Of course, Tollan." As the king trotted away, Hellet enjoyed a rare moment of being left to himself. He glanced about, happy to not have to respond to any questions regarding their plan. But then the thought of what was being asked of him struck him hard as the memory of the man he killed during the battle in the wintery wilderness returned, and he wanted to be with Dellea. She had ridden ahead when Tollan had first approached, and he watched her ride while the wolves loped alongside. He wanted to catch up to her, but he thought he would allow Dellea her own solitude for a while longer.

"There you are," Hellet heard as Neffy brought his horse up. Neffy had spent much of the time walking next to Perrin. He had offered his horse to her multiple times, but she had always refused. She said she was a soldier like all the others and would not be treated differently. No matter how many times Neffy protested, she would not agree. He finally stopped offering when her ire had turned to shouting. The only time he mounted his steed was when he was with Hellet. "How is Dellea?"

Hellet's only response was a raised arm that motioned towards her.

"I guess it's a silly question, just like it would be asking how Perrin is doing."

"We each have our burdens to bear," Hellet replied. "We all handle them differently."

"You know how I feel about this plan, but I will do my best for you. If I die, I will die defending all of us."

"I appreciate that, and I'm glad you're with me… I'm not glad with… well, you know what I mean."

"Yeah, I know."

"I just wish Darus was here," Hellet said. "I miss him."

Neffy sighed, but he did not respond, and Hellet knew that no response was required. Neffy did not need to verbalize his sorrow.

"Soon we will be in battle, and I know at least one person looking forward to that," Neffy said. He then offered his friend a wave before returning to Perrin.

Hellet was left alone again as he returned his attention to Dellea. He wondered if he should keep his distance for a time longer, but he decided she was ready for his company, so he guided his horse forward.

**\*\*\***

"What! They're marching here? What are we going to do?" Travyn bellowed after Aniass had delivered the news, which was as startling as the taste of the not yet fully ripened strawberries he had demanded.

"Relax, *sire*," Aniass replied. "We are protected, and I'm told they have no catapults or ladders. Despite our small numbers, I don't see how they can breach the walls. And I'm certain your wife has the information as well. This will change her plans, and she will be marching here. We will be safe within the castle. Their army will be destroyed; they can't win."

"Then why are they doing this?"

"I don't know, and I don't care. It's a huge mistake, and they will pay dearly. We just need to keep them at bay until Ellaniya arrives. When she does, we will crush them."

Aniass' confidence seeped into Travyn, and he felt his shoulders relax. Victory would be his, and the empire would grow. With this power he would finally be able to enjoy his wife without distractions. Perhaps she would conceive and solidify his imperial legacy. Despite Ut's harsh threats, everything that the god's messenger had promised was coming to pass. His full magnificence was finally at hand.

He bit into another strawberry, and somehow that one tasted sweeter. "Yes, it's all been worthwhile." Travyn then reached down and caressed the edge of his still blood-stained hammer.

# chapter 72

THE CASTLE WALLS LOOMED AHEAD like a wild boar: both a target and a threat. The moment she dreaded had finally arrived. The army stretching out behind her stood silent and still. Dellea could feel their apprehension coursing through her nerves; all the warriors' fates rested in her hands. If she failed, they would die, but how many more would die if she succeeded? She wanted to question again why this obligation had been placed on her, but what good would that do now? In her meetings with Wander, the prophet had tried to soothe and reassure her, but while she appreciated his efforts, those attempts had failed.

All those times reading The Book of Sul ran through her mind. How many had he killed? There was no way to tell. Sul had killed even after his conversion, and those deaths weighed heavily on him. She was not a warrior, just a frail, awkward girl. How could she possibly manage this immense and dreadful responsibility?

She felt a squeeze on her shoulder and looked up and saw Neffy peering at her with sadness in his eyes. "I don't envy you this task, Dellea, but be assured of its necessity." His face gave the impression that he wanted to say more, but no more words came. What else could he say?

Perrin stood beside the large warrior, her sword already unsheathed. Her gaze remained transfixed upon Mephosh, the left side of her mouth raised in cruel snarl. Her body shifted from side to side as the anticipation threatened to overwhelm her. Her glance moved to Dellea. "Don't fail," she commanded then turned back to the castle.

Very comforting, Dellea thought. As she began to prepare herself for her first task, the wolves seemed to sense the change in her energy. They had been resting at her feet, but now they rose and her pack began to howl.

\*\*\*

"There they are." Vor pointed towards the force assembled outside of Mephosh. "And their numbers seem even smaller than we estimated."

"This will be all too easy," Ellaniya almost laughed. Vor did laugh as he rode away to give the final orders for their assault. Her eyes followed him, appreciating the beauty of her lover's dark, muscular body. When her attention returned to the castle of her home, she thought of her husband who was safe behind the walls. It seemed inconceivable that Travyn would perish in this lopsided conflict. Tollan's stupid plan doomed her enemies to an overwhelming defeat, so she would have to divorce Travyn to marry Mennum. But what would she do with that fool of a husband after the battle? What did it matter? She would cast him aside like an old warn out rag, and he could serve the empire somewhere, as long as he was not in charge of anything. She would figure that out later. For now, she would enjoy watching the destruction of Tollan and her enemies.

\*\*\*

"Are you ready?" Tollan asked.

"No. How could I ever be ready for this?" Hellet answered.

"I suppose you're right." Tollan sighed as his head raised to the bright blue morning sky. No clouds were visible, and the sun glowed, casting rays on the first budding wildflowers. It seemed inconceivable that the first part of Wander's plan would succeed. The king was risking everything on his faith in the cleric's words. He felt his self-doubt resurface then prayed that he had not made a terrible mistake.

The beauty of the tranquil scene would be disrupted soon, for good or ill, and he knew that the result of this battle would tell the tale of whether or not he would live up to the lofty expectations he had always placed on himself. "The men are ready. We just wait upon you and Dellea."

"I still wonder if she needs to do this part."

"We don't know how many warriors remain in the castle," the king stated with a tone of resignation. "We can't risk being attacked from the rear."

Hellet nodded sadly.

"I don't envy you, my friend," Tollan continued as he reached out a hand towards the prince of Su'Meeryn. "You are a good man and a good friend. I pray that we will be able to grow closer when this is done."

"As do I."

"Go to her now. Help give her the strength she needs, and I'll see you when it's over."

***

Hellet dropped down from his horse and crossed over to where Dellea stood. As he approached, he saw Neffy leading Perrin away. Neffy stopped and offered his hand to his friend. Hellet pushed the hand away then reached in to hug his large friend. Hands slapped backs, but no words were uttered. When they released their grips, Hellet turned to Perrin. Her expression retained the ever-present stoic determination it had held since Darus' death. Hellet hesitated for a moment before he reached for her also. He wrapped his arms around her, and her rigid body tightened. Her arms remained at her sides, the embrace not returned. He held her for a moment until he felt a slight softening within her. When he released his arms, Perrin gave him a confused look before turning and walking towards the rest of the soldiers, the sword still clutched in her hand.

Now that he was alone with Dellea, the wolves gave him a sniff then returned to their howling. Dellea offered him a mourn-filled smile. He gently took her shoulders and pulled her in for a kiss. When they drew apart, her smile remained, and he noticed a small amount of pleasure in her expression. His fingers drifted down her arms and grabbed her hands. Their fingers intertwined as the howling grew in volume.

"An odd place for our first kiss," Dellea remarked.

Hellet nodded, and their eyes remained fixed on each other. The howling then stopped, and the wolves began to circle the pair. Dellea's smile dissolved and Hellet said, "It's time."

***

The bright sun glistened off the swords of the warriors amassed just outside the castle as Travyn peered out the window. The soldiers of Labyn formed a defensive line against Ellaniya's massive force that was now visible on the horizon., but they did not move forward to attack the castle. "What are they doing?" he asked.

Aniass seemed equally perplexed as he raised a hand to shield his eyes from the glare above. "I have no idea. They're just standing there. Why would they come all this way just to be overrun?"

There was no movement within the castle as Travyn's soldiers remained on the parapet's, bows in hands, prepared for whatever was coming. The emperor peered about, then the silence was disrupted by the sound of howling. As that howling reached his ears, Travyn's anxiety grew. "Why would Tollan do this?"

Aniass fidgeted next to the emperor, his own agitation showing. "Nobody is this foolish. They can't just be waiting to die. This doesn't make any sense."

The fact that Aniass was also confounded increased Travyn's nervousness. He stuck his head out the window and tried to count the enemy's numbers, but he confused himself and lost count a few times. However, he could tell that Tollan's army was small. They were no match for the forces of Mephosh he told himself.

Travyn spat at the ground below. "Let them stand there, then; they will all die." He grabbed his hammer and smacked it against the wall.

The moment he finished his statement, a shadow crossed the sky and darkened the light reaching in through the window. He looked up to see storm clouds rushing towards the city.

✱✱✱

The temperature began to drop and Ellaniya noticed the dark clouds rolling in. "That's odd," Vor stated as their horses continued towards the Labyn army which remained situated before the castle.

What had been a calm day was being disrupted by a wind that was picking up and blowing from the south. Shadows crossed the ground and moved towards the castle as the clouds continued to expand, but only enough to cover the city. Ellaniya sat up in her saddle as the wind swelled. The clouds grew in size and seemed to be reaching down to the castle walls, which were now covered in darkness.

Thunder echoed across the valley as the sky turned black. The empress turned to Vor, but his expression of bewilderment mirrored her own. Since the change in the weather was so tightly localized, and centered over Mephosh, she was certain it could not be natural, but what was the source? Certainly not the gods. She watched dumbfounded. If this storm had somehow been conjured by Tollan and the forces of Labyn, the only thing she could think was that they must attack as quickly as possible. Perhaps by doing so, they could disrupt whatever foul sorcery was brewing.

"Full speed!" she called out. "Engage the enemy!"

Her army seemed to hesitate momentarily while more clouds billowed over Mephosh. Thunder crashed through their ears and lightning shot out in all directions, but with the encouragement of her officers, the warriors bolted forward.

✱✱✱

With the cold wind whipping about and the cascading thunder, the wolves stopped howling and began to whimper. They skittishly circled

Dellea who remained transfixed in what appeared to be a frightful meditation. Hellet attempted to soothe the animals while Dellea struggled to maintain her concentration. Sweat poured down her face as if a dam had burst. The lowering temperature did nothing to quell the flow of perspiration. Her eyes remained half open as she fought to follow Wander's instructions.

Hellet wanted to offer help, but there was nothing he could do. Wander had cautioned them regarding the difficulty of the task, but he had also asserted his faith in her. The cleric was certain Dellea would succeed, but as Hellet watched, he was not so sure. How could her fragile psyche tolerate what she was putting herself through?

The cracks of thunder continued to pummel the valley. Hellet managed to turn his gaze from Dellea for a moment to assess their army. The soldiers had been told what to expect, so they stood poised, ready to engage. If there was any nervousness in the ranks, Hellet could not tell. But they were prepared; soon the combat would begin.

He turned back to Dellea, and her face was a concerning shade of red. The sweating had ceased, but Hellet did not know whether that was a good sign.

The black sky continued to shroud the castle in shadow, but, following a blinding flash of lightning, the thunder suddenly stopped. Then an eerie quiet descended over the valley, and the wind disappeared. The clouds began to descend as if they were a curtain covering all of Mephosh. Hellet heard a rumbling begin which slowly grew in volume, and the wind returned, even stronger than before. Peering into the gloom, he spotted what Wander had promised. A funnel descended from the clouds and raced towards the castle walls.

***

Tollan's long tail flapped wildly in the wind as he spotted the funnel cloud. Even though he had put his faith in Wander's plan, witnessing the growing storm bolstered his spirits. He knew what was about to happen would be tragic, but it was also necessary. While their victory was not assured, he now felt confident that Labyn would prevail. With the wind continuing to rip through his army, it seemed to blow away all his self-doubts. He was truly the king he had been destined to become, and he would lead his army to victory over the pagans.

"She's succeeding!" Tollan heard Neffy call out in the cacophony of the storm.

The king turned to Neffy and Perrin who were standing beside him, Perrin's gleeful laughter drowned out by the roaring wind.

Neffy then pointed across the valley. There was the horde of Mephosh, racing towards them.

✱✱✱

The eerie silence had been replaced by a thundering sound which grew in intensity, threatening to burst Travyn's eardrums. "We have to get out of here!" cried Aniass.

"What, what's going on?" Travyn squealed in terror.

"Now!" Aniass yanked Travyn's arm and dragged him away from the window and towards the stairway. The emperor absently grabbed his hammer, and as the pair rushed down the stairs, Travyn began to hear crashing noises. He had no idea what was happening, but it assuredly was nothing good.

When they reached the ground floor, the stairs collapsed behind them. Travyn felt a fierce burst of wind and was immediately covered with dust. Small rocks pelted his body as he reached the courtyard. He could barely see anything due to the dark clouds and the swirling debris flying in all directions. The wind assailed the castle, and he saw the funnel cloud break through a wall, huge stones collapsing everywhere. As the fortifications fell, bodies plummeted to the ground. Rock and flesh crashed together. If there were screams, Travyn could not hear them. His ears were filled with the sound of the roaring wind along with cracking and collapsing stone.

Travyn stood still, in a daze, his mind frozen, unable to comprehend what was happening. A wall crumbled next to them covering him with a second blanket of dust. His eyes burned as he tried to cough the debris out from his throat. He barely felt a hand grasp his shoulder and pull him away.

They stumbled over the boulders and bodies of the carnage of a devastated Mephosh. Travyn tripped on a rock and fell to his knees. A jagged edge of stone lacerated his left palm, but he hardly noticed it. He grabbed his hammer from the rubble and stumbled forward a few more steps before tripping again. His right knee crashed against a large rock, and he felt a crack. Pushing himself up again, he continued to stagger after Aniass as they made their way from the wreckage.

Climbing over a section of wall, he saw a face trapped beneath the rubble. Blood and dust covered the victim, and he could not tell whether it was man or woman. The mouth moved slightly, and the eyes blinked a few times with tears of blood. He continued on, trying to push the image from his consciousness. There was nothing he could do. Mephosh was being destroyed, and all he could think of was escape.

The sound of destruction still engulfed the air. More stone collapsed as the tornado raged on, circling Mephosh, or what had been Mephosh.

Travyn continued to stumble through the wreckage of the castle. He did not know the destination, but he managed to follow after the mercenary leader. Then the roaring abruptly ceased. The wind stopped as the cauldron of dark clouds rolled away, and the sky began to brighten. As Aniass and he reached the end of the debris, they looked back. The castle was gone; Mephosh was destroyed. Travyn had no idea if anything was left of the city. All they saw was rubble.

***

Dellea's face began to return to its proper shade as the storm clouds receded. While Hellet had been prepared for what would happen, he had never been certain that it would actually come to fruition. Now that it had, he had no idea what to make of it. The devastation was a frightening sight. Mephosh was in complete ruins with countless dead: both soldiers and the innocent. He could only hope that most of the homes of the villagers had been spared.

As the storm drifted away, the wolves rose from the ground, and Dellea sucked in a deep breath. She took a moment to recover, but it could only be a brief moment. Her duty was not yet complete.

"Can you continue?" Hellet asked.

Tears streamed down her face as she nodded. "I must."

Hellet drew forth his sword and motioned to the wolves. Their twitching noses nudged Della, and she stroked each before gesturing towards Hellet. As they left her side, Dellea took another deep breath to gather her strength for the next task. Hellet did not want to leave but he must. While he had only watched the first half of the plan, it was now time for him to fulfill his role.

***

Ellaniya could not believe what she had just witnessed. Mephosh, her beloved home, was destroyed, and the army of Labyn had not even raised a sword to bring that about; they had suffered no casualties. How had it been accomplished? If Travyn was to be believed, dragons had destroyed Pathum, but there were no dragons here. Tollan must have a powerful sorcerer with him. How else could the storm have been summoned? There was no other explanation, but why had the gods allowed this to happen? After everything she had done for them, the only thing left of her home was ruins.

Her rage boiled, but for the moment, it turned from the ineptitude of the gods and was solely focused on Tollan and his army. She had to put the destruction of Mephosh aside and bury her grief. Tollan remained vastly outnumbered, and—unless another storm was conjured—her victory remained assured. She will have paid a much higher price then she could have ever thought, so she would make certain that her foes received no mercy.

"Kill them all," she hissed.

# chapter 73

"KEEP MOVING," ANIASS ORDERED. Travyn did not appreciate the mercenary's tone, especially since he was moving, but now was not the time to chastise his subordinate. He would think on that once they safely reached his wife. For the moment, he would do what he must. If that meant obeying Aniass, so be it.

While he knew they needed to join Ellaniya and the rest of the army, he was also concerned. Would he be put into combat? How would he manage in a large battle? Would somebody else have a hammer?

"Faster!" barked Aniass.

Travyn realized that he had slowed, but catching his breath was difficult. He had been rushing since they spotted the storm. His knee throbbed and dust still filled his lungs, but with a cough, he tried to quicken his pace.

***

Ellaniya's horde crashed into the defending line, and the sound of striking weapons filled the valley. Hellet waited behind Tollan's army, his sword unsheathed, but it did not feel properly balanced due to his missing finger. As his attention was drawn to his hand, he felt the perpetual ache from the joint, but it did not matter. It was not painful, so it would not hinder him in his dreadful task.

Low growls emanated from the throats of the wolves who were waiting beside him. He took a moment to caress each. Did they somehow realize what was about to happen? He thought back to when he had first encountered them, and Neffy had prodded him into petting the beasts. He remembered his nervousness approaching the animals, but for whatever reason they had immediately accepted him. Now they had become more than friends and companions. They had saved his life twice in battle, and they all would have perished in the wintery wilderness without their hunting skills. While he did not have the attachment to them that Dellea did, he realized that he loved them as well.

I hope they survive, he thought.

**\*\*\***

Dellea felt as lonely and distraught as she had prior to finding the wolf cubs, but this was even worse. She had just caused the destruction of Mephosh and the deaths of a myriad individuals. How many were buried under the rocks of the fallen walls? She would never know the number, and she did not want to know. But that was just the beginning. Very soon even more would die because of her, but she knew they were the enemy. If she failed at her task, the army of Labyn would be destroyed. It was a ghastly position to be in, but she had committed herself. Besides, the fate of Hellet and the wolves, not to mention Perrin, Neffy and Tollan rested in her hands.

With Wander's instructions running through her thoughts, Dellea prepared herself. She was already exhausted from the summoning of the storm, but there was no time for rest. The battle had begun, and their forces were severely outnumbered.

Reaching her mind out, she concentrated on Hellet. The sounds of the fighting increased as she realized she was now hearing through his ears. She could sense him sensing her. He quickly looked at the wolves so she could see them through his eyes. Then he turned back to the battle.

**\*\*\***

Once the armies met, Tollan's warriors moved slightly back, into a defensive position. Ellaniya's forces swung swords at spears that kept them at bay. Rows of shields created a barrier through which her warriors were having difficulty breaching. But Ellaniya did not need Vor to tell her it was only a matter of time. By fighting a strictly defensive battle, the shield wall of Tollan's army gave them a temporary advantage. However, the far superior numbers of Ellaniya's forces would soon overwhelm them.

As the empress watched on, swords of the empire continued to rattle against the defenders. Spears shot out from behind the wall of dented shields and caught some of her soldiers. Blood was spilling and more soldiers on both sides began to fall. She could tell that she was losing more men than they were killing, but slowly, the defenses were being pushed back. Soon her men would break through, and when they did, they would rout Tollan's pathetic army. And she would accept no surrender. Every last one would be killed. They would all pay for the destruction of her home.

Her horse bucked as another crash of thunder echoed across the valley, but when she nervously looked up, the sky remained clear. Returning her attention to the battle, she saw the forces of Labyn part in the middle. This is it, she thought; now I have my vengeance.

***

The shield of a defender split in two, and then the man collapsed as a mace smashed against his skull. With his soldier down, Tollan jumped forward, swinging his sword. The blade found its target, ripping through the neck of his opponent. He felt his sword hit bone as the warrior's mace dropped to the ground. Tollan had to yank hard to free the weapon—which left him off balance—while more warriors attempted to exploit the breach. An axe whisked past his face as Neffy pulled the king away. Tollan's foot caught against the body of the dead defender, and he fell.

More attackers pushed their way in, and Perrin jumped over Tollan. Her blade seemed to fly in every direction; three opponents collapsed in pools of blood before she landed on the ground. Neffy was then at her side. Opponents fell to their blades, but there were no other shield men to step in and seal the breach. The two Su'Meeryn warriors presented an impressive sight as they fought. Tollan was then at their side, and they kept the attackers at bay until they heard the sound they had been awaiting.

***

Hellet looked up and took a deep breath when the sound of thunder rolled away. It was time. The warriors of Labyn parted in the middle, and now Hellet would fulfill his task.

He stepped forward with the wolves following. As he moved, everything slowed. The men still fought, but their motions were so sluggish, it seemed almost comical. He approached the front line and spotted Tollan with Perrin and Neffy. The enemy had breached the shield defense, and they were engaged. Perrin's blade was slowly collapsing on the skull of an enemy while a fountain of blood flowed like dripping sap towards her, preparing to douse her skin from the foe she had just slain.

Hellet now could see the massive army of Ellaniya. He had prepared himself for this moment, but still he hesitated. Fortunately, his hesitation would not be noticeable to the others. With a sigh of resignation and despair, he swung his sword.

The first warrior he struck was pushing towards the collapsing line of defenders. Hellet's sword easily drove into the man's chest. He then faced the next soldier and struck again. As he swung the wolves darted away. Fangs reached flesh, and more of the warriors of Mephosh fell.

It was all too easy. He would kill a man, then turn to the next one before the previous victim even collapsed. The blood erupted so slowly from his victims, that Hellet remained unblemished. He killed two more before the first drop of blood reached his cheek.

The wolves rushed about, somehow only targeting the enemy. He had never fully understood how this part of Wander's plan was to be accomplished; however, after witnessing Dellea summon the storm, he now questioned nothing.

Arms reached for him, but they moved so slowly that they were no threat. The only threat was: how would he emerge from this? How many men had he killed? How many more would he kill? What would all this death do to him and Dellea?

***

Ellaniya could not fathom what she was seeing. Her army dwarfed Labyn's and they had breached the shield wall, but there was some sort of shadow, or blur, making its way through her warriors. They were falling in terrifying numbers.

First her castle, and now this? What vile necromancy did Tollan have at his disposal? Had the gods so completely deserted her?

"Ah, we've finally found you!" Ellaniya heard as she saw Travyn and Aniass approaching. Travyn's smile at finding his wife only increased her fury. The fool had nothing to smile about.

"Both of you, to battle," she commanded.

***

Everything was progressing as planned, but this did not quell Dellea's despair. She could see through Hellet's eyes as he continued to unleash his torrent of death. She saw every victim. She felt every sword blow, and she could feel his anguish. Scores of warriors killed by his blade with countless more to follow.

The strain of keeping Hellet and the wolves in this state was beginning to overwhelm her. Wander had said she would only be able to manage it for a finite period of time. With the wolves joining Hellet, her energy would drain more quickly. However, the hope was that the wolves would increase the killing to a degree which would offset the time she would lose.

Hellet faced another soldier, and she felt his blade pierce the man's heart. As Hellet pulled it out, the tears which ran down his face mirrored her own.

She did not see through the wolves' eyes, but she could sense them ripping out throats as they went from prey to prey.

Sweat rolled from her forehead and intermingled with tears. Her body began to shake as streams of liquid ran down her body, soaking her clothes and forming a pool around her. Then a shot of pain seared through her head. She was losing control.

***

A sword grazed his cheek, and another clipped a forearm as Tollan fought alongside Neffy and Perrin. Bodies littered the blood-covered ground making the footing treacherous. A number of soldiers on both sides tripped and fell and paid the ultimate price for their mistakes. The king was thankful to have his companions from Su'Meeryn beside him as they wielded their weapons with such mastery.

In the distance, he saw blurs that had to be Hellet and the wolves. So many opponents fell with no knowledge of what killed them. Confusion was forming in the Mephosh ranks as the casualties increased to a frightening degree.

"Now's our chance!" Tollan called out. "Push forward!"

He heard a cry of glee from Perrin as the soldiers of Labyn turned from a defense posture and counterattacked.

Neffy dashed ahead, his sword quickly dropping two men with Perrin following close behind.

The counterattack caused even more confusion, and the Mephosh warriors scrambled to push back. They had been so certain of an easy victory, they were unprepared for what was happening. Tollan trailed after Neffy and Perrin when he saw a woman sitting atop a large stallion on the outskirts of the battle. She had to be Ellaniya.

"To her!" he commanded. "Seize her!"

***

As Travyn slowly walked towards the combat, some of the forces of Labyn had broken out and were heading towards Ellaniya. The guards who surrounded his wife advanced while two others on horseback remained next to her. Travyn stopped and hefted his hammer; however, the chaos swirling all about confused his child-like mind. He looked up at his weapon, but he did not know what to do.

"Fight!" Ellaniya screamed.

The tone of anger and fear in her voice snapped something in Travyn. The woman he loved was at risk. No harm would come to her while he still breathed. With a cry that engulfed the clamor of the battle, Travyn rushed forward.

He pushed through a line of Mephosh warriors that were keeping the enemy at bay. With frenzied strength, he swung his hammer at his foes.

The hammer crashed through a blade, striking flesh. Travyn spun around and swung again. The hammer pushed through defenses and found targets again and again. Another cry burst from his throat, and he practically danced about the melee.

This is what you get for threatening my beloved wife, Travyn thought as his hammer crushed the chest of an opponent. Blood erupted from the man's mouth, dousing the emperor, while he collapsed.

Raising his hammer to strike again, Travyn noticed that Aniass was beside him. The mercenary leader was covered in a scarlet hue as his sword knocked the weapon from the hand of a Labyn soldier. The man tried to wrap his arms around Aniass, but the mercenary's sword pierced his throat, and the arms went limp.

With his hammer continuing to swing, Travyn noticed Vor crash his horse into group. The dark-skinned warrior's sword struck to the left and right sending crimson showers into the sky.

Travyn was transfixed for a moment until he felt a blow against his left arm. He spun about, his hammer smashing the face of his assailant. Travyn then spotted a woman leap at Vor from a shocking distance. Her left arm wrapped around Vor's waist, pulling the warrior to the ground. They both scrambled to rise, but the woman was quicker. She whipped out a dagger from her belt and plunged it into Vor's neck. A shower of blood bathed the woman as she bellowed in delight. She snatched up her fallen sword and continued to make her way with the other Labyn warriors towards Travyn.

As the group approached, Travyn recognized Neffy, and the woman from the encounter in the snowy wilderness, when he had killed Darus. The woman was a hideous sight, covered in blood and gore. Her eyes grew large when she spotted him. Her body seemed to shake as a wild scream erupted from her hideous sneer. With her sword pointed at Travyn, she sprinted forward.

**✱✱✱**

Hellet's arm ached from countless strikes of his sword. Each swing brought death, and that knowledge caused bile to rise in his throat. He did not know the number of men he had slain, but he also did not want to count. Yet he did not stop his relentless assault. He could not.

He felt Dellea peering through his eyes, and that just saddened him more. How would she survive this? Who could survive being responsible for so much death? He continued to strike as he felt her energy wavering, and he noticed that those around him were beginning to move a little quicker.

Hellet knew he had little time left. He had to kill as many as possible before Dellea succumbed to exhaustion. Once she did, he would be left vulnerable in the middle of the battle, and he was no match for the warriors surrounding him.

***

As with the destruction of Mephosh, the sweat had stopped flowing, and her eyes were dry. She could form no more tears. Dellea's body shook and ached, screaming for relief, but she could not succumb. While Ellaniya's forces had been extremely weakened, Hellet was still surrounded by the remaining warriors; if she lost control now, he would be killed.

She felt a heaving from her gut, but she suppressed it. She must withstand the agony and fatigue. Every second she held out increased Hellet's and the wolves' chances of survival. But Dellea was wavering, and she could see through Hellet's eyes that their foes' pace was increasing. How much longer could she last? She clenched her fists, marshalling her final reserves. She threw forth her last ounce of strength, and the effort gave Hellet a few more precious seconds. He managed to strike down a handful more foes before she collapsed. Her body could take no more strain, and she fainted.

***

Ellaniya's body trembled after seeing Vor killed by the frenzied woman; however, she sat frozen atop her horse, not knowing what to do. Two of her guards waited beside her while Aniass and Travyn continued to fight for their lives, but what remained of her army was now greatly outnumbered. The shadow that had decimated her warriors had finally disappeared, but it was too late. Everything she had fought for and achieved was slipping through her fingers. Vor was dead. Mephosh was gone and the empire of the gods was defeated. Now the only question was whether she would survive. Her entire body quivered in waves of fury and despair, and then she experienced a sharp pain in her gut.

***

Hellet had felt Dellea's valiant struggle and he sensed her resolve to push through her exhaustion. Every second she had held out gave the wolves and him that much more time to strike. She had accomplished the seeming impossible. Though the fighting continued, Hellet could see that the enemy was now outnumbered. She had given him the time he had needed, and his pride in her was beyond words. As he returned to normal time, he felt disoriented, and his sword hung loosely from his hand. He quickly regained focus on the scene. The sounds of combat returned to his ears, and he saw the corpses piled around, but he was also surrounded by warriors; he was now the target. Whether the enemy was aware that he had been the cause of so much destruction, he did not know. But they did know that there was a foe amongst them, and they would show no mercy.

Hellet readied himself as the first warrior approached, but before the man could reach him, a gray shape flew in. The soldier was knocked to the ground and screamed as fangs ripped open his face. The man's sword was pinned under him, and he tried to push the wolf off. But it was no use; the muzzle went to his throat. He gurgled as his life slipped away.

The other warriors turned towards Hellet, but they stopped as he was now circled by all three wolves. Their heads lowered, growling through crimson stained snouts, fangs bared at the enemy.

*** 

The forces of Labyn reached Travyn, as the woman's blade flew towards him. Before it could reach his face, Aniass knocked it away. The mercenary spun about and swung again, but the woman was ready. She blocked the blow, then steadied herself. Aniass and she began to circle each other looking for an opening.

Travyn then saw Neffy racing towards his wife. Ellaniya remained on her horse, hunched over, clutching her stomach. Neffy's sword was drawn, and Travyn could tell that capture was not on his mind. Neffy knocked into him as he passed by causing Travyn to stumble on a corpse. He lost his grip on his hammer, and he knew he did not have time to pick it up. Travyn sucked in a mouthful of air and rushed towards his wife. He jumped and tackled Neffy before his foe could reach Ellaniya. They rolled on the ground, each trying to get on top of the other. While Neffy was large and strong, he was no match for Travyn's wrestling skills. Neffy was quickly pinned, and Travyn's arm was around his neck, cutting off the blood flow. He waited to feel Neffy's body go limp before he released his grip.

He quickly stood as he saw another warrior approaching his wife.

*** 

Ellaniya sat atop her horse, paralyzed but what she was witnessing. She had been certain of victory, but now she was defeated. Vor had been killed, and she did not know what to do. Her instincts were telling her to flee, but she could not force herself to move. Then another painful cramp seized her, and she felt a warm wetness coming out of her and trickling down her saddle.

More enemies were approaching, and her two remaining guards rushed forward to enter the fray. Their horses were quickly surrounded, and the men were pulled to the ground. She could not tell what happened to them next.

Further away, Aniass was in combat with the woman warrior, and they were trading blows. She thought she could see fatigue in the movements of the mercenary, but the woman seemed to have boundless energy. Her sword swirled in a dizzying array that Aniass was having a hard time keeping at bay.

Ellaniya's attention was then diverted to her husband. Travyn had already saved her from the large soldier, but another foe was approaching. The man wore a crown, so it could only be Tollan. His sword was ready too, but she could not move. She was transfixed by her defeat and pain.

***

Tollan raced to the large man who had defeated Neffy. The soldier sprang up and grabbed a sword from the ground. He swung and the blow knocked Tollan to the side. As Tollan stumbled, the man swung again. His blade clipped Tollan's head and knocked his crown away. Tollan regained his footing and struck, but his blade missed its target. The two traded blows, and Tollan realized he had his opponent outmatched. The king's blade nicked the man's face then sliced into his shoulder. Tollan readied his blade for the final strike when the man leapt forward. The king raised his weapon as his adversary's large arm wrapped around his back. The king felt his blade pierce and drive into flesh; however, he still was unable to break free from the strong grip.

The king looked up into the blue sky, and the sun glistened against the steel of his opponent's raised sword. As the weapon plunged down on him, Tollan felt a searing pain and his vision faltered.

The bright sky disappeared, and the pain drifted away. A flash of Adira's beautiful face was his last sight before everything turned black.

***

As the king of Labyn sank to the ground, Travyn dropped to his knees with Tollan's blade imbedded deep in his gut.

With Tollan and her husband both at the feet of her horse, Ellaniya saw the woman warrior finally break through Aniass' defense and bury her blade into his chest. She freed her sword from Aniass' bloody body and turned back towards Ellaniya, and she thought she noticed a look of fury and regret in the woman's eyes when they spotted Travyn on the ground.

"Flee my love," Travyn managed to say through his blood-soaked mouth. "You must survive."

Ellaniya watched the woman approach, and she knew if she remained, she too would die. Travyn's final words had startled her. She looked at him as the last of his life seeped away. Had he deserved this fate? Despite everything, he had sacrificed himself to save his wife. Now he was gone as was Vor, and she feared her unborn child as well.

She kicked her horse and rushed away as she guided the beast north, towards Shekul.

***

The warriors remained at bay, fearful of the wolves, but eventually they gathered their courage and attacked. This time they were prepared, and the wolves would not catch them by surprise. The growls ceased as the beasts pounced. Two of the men were knocked to the ground, but swords from the others reached the third wolf. They pierced through the thick coat and Hellet heard a squeal as the animal collapsed. Blood pooled from the wounds as its head rested on the scarlet-stained dirt, its tongue hanging out to the side. The other two wolves immediately returned to Hellet's side. Their growling returned as their eyes moved from their dead sibling to the enemy.

"Enough!" Hellet commanded as he glared at the soldiers. "Look about, the battle is over. We don't need any more killing." He threw his sword to the ground as he pointed at the battlefield. The fighting had stopped. What was left of the forces of Mephosh had surrendered, and the soldiers of Labyn were gathering up their weapons. His adversaries looked at each other, then at the two wolves and finally Hellet. Their weapons also dropped to the ground as they turned and walked away.

Hellet looked around at the carnage. The number of casualties was sickening. All he saw in every direction was death, and he knew much of it was at his hand. They had won, Labyn was victorious, but at what cost? Who had survived the battle? He had no idea.

He looked at the two wolves, their noses prodding the still body of their sibling at Hellet's feet. Hellet worried over the fate of Neffy, Perrin and Tollan, but he had a more pressing matter to deal with.

"Come," he said, "let's find Dellea." He then turned and strode through the gruesome landscape, the wolves trailing behind. What would happen next, he had no idea. But all he could think of was reuniting with the woman he loved.

# Chapter 74

SHE WOKE TO THE SENSATION of two wet noses pushing against her face and arm. As Dellea sat up, she did not need to be told that one of the wolves had not survived the battle. Hellet was crouching next to her with an expression of grave concern covering his face. She still felt weak from her ordeal when she tried to rise. Hellet reached his hand towards her, and as she grasped it, his skin felt rough. She wondered how many times he had swung his sword; how many had he killed? She had seen the horror through his which still displayed the trauma.

Standing unsteadily beside him, she peered out at the carnage of the battlefield. There was a rippling across the hideous terrain of the crippled and wounded. So many casualties, and more would soon die. Her hands clutched at the two animals, and she would have cried for the third if moisture remained within her body. If only I could have maintained my strength longer, she thought.

"I suppose we won," she muttered as her fingers combed through course fur.

"We wouldn't have, if not for you."

"Both of us." Her eyes continued to rest on the dead and dying. She had been the cause of so much death and destruction. While she had told herself that her role had been necessary, the weight of the dead threatened to crush her. How would she ever get past it?

"It's not your fault," Hellet said, trying to console her. "You didn't kill anyone."

"How can you say that?" she shot back angrily. She wanted to scream at him for the loss of the wolf, and the guilt of all the death surrounding threatened to drown her. But then she saw his ravaged face. She had witnessed every one of his victims, and she recognized the guilt he was feeling. "We did this," she continued softly.

"I know…" His voice trailed off, and she waited for him to say more, but he remained silent as his gentle, yet troubled eyes, looked into hers, and the memories of all her nightmares flooded back.

"I suppose we won't be the same people as we were before."

"No, I don't suppose so," Hellet replied. He grasped her hand again and she felt his amputated joint. She thought of all the trauma that his hand had experienced. First the pain of the frost bite, then having a finger hacked off out in the cold wilderness and finally the countless lives it had ended.

How had this come to pass? And she recalled her last meeting with Wander.

✳✳✳

"Why us?" she asked. "Why Hellet?"

"Hellet is a special boy," Wander's body creaked as he rose from his chair. "Everyone who has ever met him knows this. He may be young, but his age is not relevant, his soul betrays his years. The task before the two of you is a heavy load, but he will be able to withstand it. If anyone can, he is the one."

"That may be, but what about me? I'm nobody special. A princess, yes, at least I was, but that had nothing to do with me. It was a chance of birth. I'm an awkward and damaged girl." Until I met Hellet, she thought. It was still difficult for her to express her full emotions to anyone. Her face dropped into her hands, covering her skin as she felt it flush. "How can I do this?" she whispered.

"You give yourself far too little credit, my girl," the ancient cleric replied. "You have survived much, and it is not for no reason that your wolves follow you. I don't know, perhaps you were chosen for the same reasons you question it. This isn't meant as an insult, but you aren't special. You are a normal girl. The creator needs both: the special and the ordinary.

"The only thing significant about you is that you were chosen. This is what makes you exceptional."

She lifted her face and peered at the prophet. His reassuring expression gave her some solace, but it was not nearly enough to quell her fears. "Perhaps Hellet will be able to live with himself, if we survive, but how will I? I have a hard enough time interacting with people as it is. What will I be like after causing the deaths of so many?" Her thoughts returned to the destruction of Pathum and the fights in the snowy wilderness. Those had been traumatic enough for her, but now she was expected to cause of the demise of countless more. The thought threatened to overwhelm her.

Wander's wise, wrinkled face softened, and his dark eyes drew her in. For a moment, Dellea did not see an ancient man; before her was the great prophet of yore. "All I can tell you is that your task will be difficult," he said. "Make no mistake about that, but it will not be impossible. Remember, I knew Sul. I knew him during both stages of his life. He killed scores of people without remorse. When his life was transformed by the truth, he felt a tremendous guilt for his former deeds. But then he had to kill more; he killed his closest friend. All those deaths weighed heavily on him, but he ultimately was able to forgive himself.

"Of course, your situation is different, but if Sul could experience forgiveness, you will be able to as well. It will not be easy, and most certainly you will not be the same person who leaves Labyn. But I'm confident that you—both of you—will survive."

***

"Come," Hellet said, "let's see if we can find our friends."

They had to step over innumerable corpses, through slippery pools of blood and gore. Dellea was surprised by the smell that assailed her nose. As the deaths were still fresh, the aroma was almost sweet, and she found that sensation sickening.

As they passed by the surviving warriors of Labyn, they were recognized and some cheered. "Please stop," Dellea begged under her breath, but she could not chastise the men. They had prevailed, and Hellet and she had been instrumental in the victory. Instead, she ignored the praise.

Dellea ached to ask Hellet about the missing wolf, but she could not bring herself to do so. She wanted to see the body, but she feared how she would respond. Until meeting Hellet, the wolves were the only beings that kept her sane. Dellea could not bear the thought of seeing the body of her companion and friend surrounded by all this death. It seemed that Hellet could sense her thoughts as he never mentioned it.

After a few minutes of searching through the carnage, they spotted a blood-covered Perrin gazing down at the corpses by her feet. As they rushed over, Dellea heard a gasp from Hellet when they saw the bodies of Travyn, Tollan and Neffy on the ground. A sword hilt protruded from Travyn's stomach, but Perrin's weapon remained clutched in her fingers, so Dellea assumed Hellet's uncle must have fallen to another's hand. Perrin just stood over her husband's killer. Her body trembled, and she did not acknowledge their presence.

Hellet's gaze moved from his uncle to the king of Labyn and then to his life-long friend. Hellet knelt and stroked Neffy's hair while staring at the dead king. The scene was becoming too much for Dellea to absorb, and she dropped to her knees. The loss of one of the wolves was traumatic enough, but now this gentle and wise king who had so willing befriended their small group and led the attack against their enemies had also perished. And there was the still form of Neffy, the brash and boisterous young man whom Dellea had finally learned to love after all the suffering they had experienced together.

Dellea rubbed her eyes as she turned back to Hellet, and she saw Neffy stir. His eyes opened, as Hellet cried out, "You're alive!".

Neffy mumbled something as Hellet helped him to his feet then wrapped his arms around the large warrior.

"What happened here?" Hellet asked after releasing his friend.

"I'm not sure" Neffy replied groggily. "I was wrestling with Travyn then passed out."

"Travyn and Tollan died by each other's blades," Perrin stated flatly, still not moving. "I was not able to kill him, but he's dead. Ellaniya escaped."

"It would have been good to capture her, but after this defeat, I don't suppose she can be much of a threat anymore," Hellet said.

Neffy walked shakily to Perrin. He then gently took her sword from her hand and sheathed it. Putting his arm around her shoulder, he led her away from Travyn's corpse.

"We must take care of the dead, then we'll return to Labyn. We have much to decide." Hellet bent over and found Tollan's crown not far from his body. He gently placed it on the king's head. The huge wound on Tollan's face was gruesome, but at least his body would have some dignity. "We'll take Tollan with us. He deserves a royal burial. He was a remarkable man," Hellet continued, "and a good friend."

Hellet looked at Dellea, but she said nothing. What was there to say? All she knew was she wanted to leave this place as quickly as possible. By the time they reached Labyn, Hellet would finally be of age. She assumed the marriage would still occur, but how would they be with each other? Neither suffered physical scars from the battle, but the emotional scars ran deep.

Would their life together be happy, or would it be as miserable as her parents? She motioned at the wolves—still surrounded by the sight and smell of the dead—and wrapped her arms around their necks. She had not yet mourned the loss of the third, but how could she when so many men had just lost their lives?

She kissed each wolf then rose. "Let the others handle the dead. I need to get out of here. Take me to Labyn."

# chapter 75

WITH THE CONTINUING CRAMPING ACHE and blood flow, Ellaniya knew she had lost the baby. But the pain she felt did not simply reside in her womb. Ellaniya felt a black misery course throughout her very soul. She had lost everything. Her family was gone, and she had watched her homeland be destroyed. She had seen both Vor and Travyn killed. Her army had been routed by a much smaller force; how had all this happened? Where were the gods? It was just a short while ago that she was basking in the full extent of their blessings, and then it had all been yanked away. Had everything she had experienced been a cruel, elaborate joke?

In the end, Travyn had died protecting her, but Ellaniya felt no remorse. She was not pleased that he was gone; though she had never loved him, his devotion to her had been clear. He deserved a better fate, but now he was dead, as was Vor and their child. She would have ruled the empire of the gods as Lynna with Vor and their child at her side. Now she was alone. She had no one and the gods had deserted her. What had it all meant? Had her brother been correct all along?

As she fled from the battle, a half dozen of her soldiers had spotted her riding away. They managed to acquire horses and had joined her on her trek to Shekul, but their presence did nothing to eliminate her loneliness.

Ellaniya had been so sure of herself, and that assurance had allowed Ut to convince her to kill her father and brother. She was to rule and restore the gods; she would finish the work of Lynna, but now none of that would happen. Her whole life, everything she had strived for, was in ruins.

And what of Ut? He had been gone a long time. Was her defeat what he had wanted all along? Was he truly a messenger of the gods? Or was he sitting back comfortably somewhere laughing at her? She shook her head with the assumption that she would never know.

Other than informing her soldiers of their destination, Ellaniya did not speak. Even if she wanted to, what could she say? Despite their proximity, she felt completely alone.

In her mind, she again saw that woman killing Vor. She thought of the nights they had spent together, and she thought of their baby that would never be born. She wanted to cry, but she was unable to, and she realized there was no sadness in her, only rage.

***

"You must be joking," Mennum said as Ellaniya stripped off her clothes. She needed to bathe, and she cared not that Mennum was in her room, watching her. "Why would I still agree to marry you after all this?"

A servant helped her into the tub and began scrubbing the filth from her body. As the warm water dissolved the dried blood from her thighs, she turned an icy glare to Mennum. "Why wouldn't you?"

Mennum unsuccessfully stifled a chuckle. "You are defeated, Ellaniya. Your army is in ruins. What could you possibly offer me?"

While the servant continued to wash her, Ellaniya saw a look of desire from Mennum as he stared at her naked, wet body. "Our goals still remain aligned," she proclaimed.

"How is that relevant?"

His eyes still displayed lust, so she stood, allowing the servant to scrub the rest of her body, giving Mennum a full view. "Mephosh is destroyed, and my empire is gone, but I still have power. The troops here in Shekul remain loyal to me."

"Do you intend to hold this castle?"

Now it was Ellaniya's turn to suppress a laugh. "Of course not. I do not have enough men, and the others would never allow me to remain here after all the bloodshed."

"Then what use are you to me?" and she saw a trace of disappointment cross his face when the servant covered her body with a robe.

"You expect to be king soon. We will return to Amyon as husband and wife, adding my forces to your army. We will most certainly be the strongest kingdom in the north. What other bride could offer you the same?"

"You make a strong point, Ellaniya, but I'll have to consider this."

"There is no time. I cannot remain in Shekul. Should I offer my services to one of your neighboring kingdoms?"

"Do you still intend to reestablish the worship of the gods?"

Ellaniya had to ponder Mennum's question as she donned a fresh gown. Her rage following their defeat included the gods, but during the trip to Shekul, she had had time to consider her anger. Were the gods truly at fault, or did she carry the blame? She did not know how Tollan had managed to orchestrate her defeat, but spies had reported of the arrival of Hellet in Labyn. Was her nephew the sorcerer who brought the storm and the shadowy blur that had decimated her forces? If so, the mistake was hers. She had called off the search for Hellet as she figured he was not a threat. Given her shortsightedness, could she blame the gods for her failure?

"I suppose I do," she finally replied. "Do you have a problem with that?"

"If it helps solidify my power, you can put a temple on every street corner."

"Then we are agreed?"

Mennum nodded. "Let us marry tonight."

✳✳✳

Warm weather greeted the company as they rode out from Shekul a couple days following the wedding. Ellaniya needed that time to organize her soldiers so she could make certain only those completely loyal to her came along. And she had ordered the plundering of as much wealth and items of value as possible from the royal coffers and the nobility of Shekul before leaving. She would have preferred to stay longer to recover from her ordeal and search for even more treasure, but she thought it best not to linger; there were plenty of people in the castle who would have been happy to slice a dagger across her throat.

Soon after setting out, they entered farmland and she saw a parcel of ripening strawberries. She almost smiled when she thought of Travyn, but then Vor and her miscarriage came to mind. She glanced over at Mennum, who rode beside her. At such a young age, she already had a second husband whom she did not love. But she had survived, and she still wielded power. Soon she would be queen of Amyon, and if Mennum spent all his time in the brothels, that was fine with her. He could indulge himself all he wanted. She would rule. She would rule and plan. And she would never forget.

# chapter 76

THE BLACK AND GOLD BANNERS flapping atop the high castle gates offered a welcome and imposing sight. All the conflict was over and Dellea and he—along with their friends—were finally safe. But so many had died, including Tollan. Adira had not wanted her husband to order or participate in their mission, and he was returning as a corpse. How would the queen react? Labyn was safe, as was Gorhum, but her husband was gone. Hellet had made it clear that he would be the one to tell Adira, and he would be the one to receive the brunt of her anger.

Dellea and he had not spoken much since the battle. The loss of her wolf was finally setting in, along with all the death they had caused. Hellet feared that the two of them might be drifting apart after all their experiences. Who could possibly remain the same following everything they had done?

To be truthful, he had little desire to talk either. He remembered the man he had killed in the wilderness. It had been a necessary act to save Dellea and the others, but it had still been traumatic for him. And now he had killed hundreds more; or was it a thousand? Could it have been more? He did not know. Men die in battle all the time, but due to his lack of skill with the sword, he had never thought he would see combat. And what he had done could scarcely be called combat. He had slain men as they stood virtually motionless before him. He told himself those men would have killed him, or Neffy or Dellea, but that reality did not wipe away the memory.

The wolves trotted alongside, and he wondered about the animals. How many men had they killed? Probably more than he. While the animals acted more subdued since the death of their sibling, they were content just to be with Dellea and him.

When they finally reached the gate, Hellet saw the unmistakable form of Adira standing atop the wall, searching for her husband. When she spotted Hellet, their eyes met. He saw her questioning look, and he tried to mask his sorrow. But she knew immediately as she ran from the gate, sobbing.

***

The ceremony to bury Tollan had been the largest regal affair Hellet had ever witnessed. While Labyn mourned the death of their young, beloved king, they also celebrated the victory over Mephosh. Adira stood next to the casket, holding Gorhum, as many of Tollan's warriors recounted his deeds on the battlefield. Next, many of his closest advisors spoke about the king. They told of his humility and his love for the kingdom and its people. He was a king whose primary concern was the wellbeing of his subjects and his family. He truly embodied the memory of his father, and he had proved his worth by making the ultimate sacrifice on the battlefield.

When the testimonies had concluded, all eyes turned to the young prince from Su'Meeryn. Everyone knew how Tollan had befriended Hellet and how close they had become in such a short time. Hellet stepped forward, but rather than speak, Neffy handed him a lute and stool. Hellet knew of no better way to honor such a noble king and friend.

Hellet hated performing to large groups. It was not due to fear or some false sense of modesty—he was well aware of his talents—but he always felt uncomfortable receiving the praises offered in his direction. However, for this occasion, he felt compelled.

He had composed the song the previous night. It was a song of both melancholy and triumph. He sang of sacrifice and duty. He sang of honor and regrets, mistakes and victory. He then ended on a crescendo of hope. After strumming the last chord, there was no applause. The entire gathering remained transfixed until Adira approached him. Her tears flowed freely down her face and, still clutching Gorhum to her chest, she hugged Hellet and whispered, "Thank you."

***

Despite the bright sun that had recently crested the horizon, the castle wall felt cold against his back, and Hellet wondered if the chill was just the result of the stones which had yet to absorb the day's heat. Dellea sat silently beside him watching the two wolves sniffing around some brush. She had been quieter than normal since the battle, even around him, and Hellet was increasingly concerned. His heart remained burdened by all the death, but Dellea seemed like an empty shell. How is one consoled after being responsible for so much misery?

The wolves stopped their sniffing, and their bodies stiffened. Hellet heard rustling then watched them bolt after a brown shape fleeing into the low sun.

He glanced over to Dellea, but she seemed oblivious to the animals' disappearance. Her gaze continued to rest on the lush landscape. The grass glistened a deep emerald and a prismatic mural of wildflowers sparkled in the low sun. Hellet wanted to enjoy the idyllic scene—which was such a juxtaposition to the gruesome landscape they had recently experienced—but how could he after all the death he had seen and caused?

Raising his left hand to his face, he blocked out the landscape and studied his severed joint. Hellet still felt a bit of an ache, but the pain was long since passed. He almost wished that the pain remained; should not he have to suffer following everything he had done?

But he had suffered; he had lost much, and now he wondered if had also lost the woman he had fallen in love with. Yes, Dellea sat next to him, but she seemed so far away.

He lowered his hand and reached over to hers, wondering if she would reciprocate his gesture. His heart skipped a beat when he felt her fingers tighten around his. A sigh escaped his lungs, and the chill of the castle wall seemed to disappear.

"There were times when I wondered if we would ever get to this point," he said.

"I know."

"So many died..." His voice trailed off as he could not find additional words.

"I'm frightened, Hellet. I feel so empty after what I did—we did. I know you are still committed to the marriage, but are you going to regret it? Are we going to end up like Wander or my parents? I had finally become happy once I found you, but now I worry I'll never be happy again.

"I wonder if this was all orchestrated, the two of us. Was our connection just a part of a divine plan for us to work together in the conflict? Now that we've won, will there be anything left between us?"

Hellet released Dellea's hand and grasped her shoulders, turning her to face him. He lost his breath as he saw her horrified face and the tears streaming from her eyes which were almost as red as his father's. "Dellea, I loved you since we first met, and I still do. Nothing we did or experienced will change that."

"But don't you see?" Dellea replied through her sobs, "that's what I'm afraid of. How could you have loved me from the start?" She then pulled away from his grip, leaned back against the wall with her face peering into the sky. "It doesn't make sense."

"Why does it have to make sense?"

She took in a large gulp of air then replied quietly, "I wouldn't be able to stand being rejected again."

"I would never reject you."

"You don't know that!" Dellea practically screamed.

Hellet was taken aback by her harsh reply, and he paused before responding. He first reached down and took her hand again, and it took a few moments before he felt her fingers grasp his. "Dellea, maybe we were unwitting players in some grand scheme, but I don't care what brought us together. Maybe it had nothing to do with us, but maybe it did. I don't know. What I do know is nothing is going to change my feelings. The fact that I feel the same even after everything we went through just makes me even more sure.

"Perhaps this, our marriage, is our reward for what we went through—our blessing."

Dellea's grip on his hand tightened then she rested her head on his shoulder. They sat quietly as the wolves trotted back, seemingly unconcerned that their prey had escaped.

Hellet felt the tension from Dellea's body lessen, and he remained quiet as he figured Dellea wanted to enjoy the peaceful silence. "What happens now?" Dellea eventually asked, and Hellet knew she was not referring to their marriage.

"I've been thinking about that," he said, releasing his grip on her hand and wrapping his arm around her shoulder. "We can't let this all happen again. The realm has known too much war, too much death."

"But how do we fix that?"

"As vile as Ellaniya was, she had one thing right. Too many kingdoms bring about too much rivalry. Pathum and Mephosh are destroyed. Labyn, Su'Meeryn and Shekul have all endured much. Rather than divide again, we should all unite. We could form one kingdom over this whole area, one empire. Then there would be no reason for conflict in the future."

"I'm not sure how Adira would respond to that," Dellea said after a pause.

"I don't expect that she'll agree right away, but hopefully she'll see the wisdom in it."

"And would you rule this new kingdom? You'd be the logical choice."

"Adira will assume that's my intent, but no. I have no desire to be emperor. You and I have been through too much. I don't think we should subject ourselves to further burdens. I just want to return home with you and serve Su'Meeryn. Jaleph counseled me so long ago to be a servant to his people. I can be a regent, duke, whatever we want to call it. You and I don't need more responsibility. We've already gone through more than any two should have to experience."

Hellet felt Dellea snuggle closer to him, and the wolves whimpered for attention, pushing their furry heads onto the couple's laps. Hellet's free hand began to stroke one as Dellea asked, "Who then?"

"Like Jaleph said, a king should be a servant, and we know the perfect person."

***

The kingdom of Labyn remained in mourning for the next few weeks. Adira had rarely left her chambers, but she was starting to venture out more. Hellet and Dellea were spending most of their time together, and their conversations were slowly returning to normal. Hellet wanted to talk about the battle, but whenever he broached the subject, Dellea refused to speak on it. His memories remained filled with all the death he caused, but he was coming to grips with his actions. While he felt jaded and harder, he wondered if his personality had changed much. When he asked Dellea, she would just pat his hand and say nothing.

During their frequent walks about the castle, Hellet was often approached and thanked for the song he performed at Tollan's funeral. Labyn missed their king, but somehow Hellet's song had provided a sense of optimism. While he did appreciate their sentiments—and he was glad he had been able to help the people of Labyn during their time of grieving—Hellet was happiest when they would take the wolves out for hikes so the two could be alone. They were finally talking as much as they used to, but still not about the battle, and Hellet could sense a change in Dellea. She was still uncomfortable around strangers, but she seemed less hesitant, more sure of herself.

Most of their conversations centered on what would happen next. Many wondered why Hellet and his friends had not yet returned to Su'Meeryn, but he had a reason, and Dellea was in full agreement. The time had not yet come to address the subject—as Labyn continued to grieve the loss of Tollan—but it was approaching soon.

***

Once the official period of mourning had come to an end, Hellet determined it was time to broach his plan regarding the future. Pathum and Mephosh had been reduced to a few homes amidst the ruins. Shekul had no king and Adira's son was an infant. He could be named king of Su'Meeryn, but was that the wisest choice?

Hellet sat at a table with Dellea, Neffy, Perrin and the queen. "We need to decide what happens now," he began. "This land has seen much strife. Too many wars are in our history, and despite what we recently endured, I fear we will see further conflicts if we continue down the same path we've always followed."

"What are you proposing?" Adira asked with a tone of aggravation.

"We are currently bound together through our recent hardships and suffering. But what will happen in a generation or two? Might new rivalries surface. No, let's put an end to the cycle. I say we don't divide ourselves back into individual kingdoms. Let's be one nation."

"And I supposed you want to rule?" she asked.

"Hellet is now the legitimate king of Su'Meeryn," Neffy pointed out. "And everyone knows what Dellea and he did to save us all."

"No, I have no desire to rule," Hellet interjected. "After everything Dellea and I have been through, we just want to return to Su'Meeryn to serve our people. I will gladly be regent, with Dellea at my side."

"If not you, whom do you propose?" Adira questioned.

Hellet paused a moment as he expected a strong reaction to his proposal. "I suggest Neffy. He served me faithfully when we were on the run in the cold wilderness. He never aspired to anything like this. He just wanted to serve me. What better trait for a new emperor?

"You will be regent of Labyn, and Neffy can set up in Shekul."

The queen just stared at him, and Hellet could not tell whether she was angered or surprised at his words.

"We are stronger together," Hellet continued, "and we are coming together by agreement, not by force. We have all suffered much. Let's not weaken ourselves now."

"But this would end Tollan's legacy," Adira said, and Hellet could now clearly see the anger in her face.

"While I did not know Tollan for as long as I would have liked, besides his love for you, I know his primary concern was the wellbeing of his people," Hellet replied. "I believe that he would have been pleased with this suggestion and that this will honor his legacy."

"I don't know." Adira's hand went to her face and brushed a long strand of hair away from her eye. "And what do you think about this, Neffy?".

"I'm dumbfounded. I had no idea Hellet was going to propose this. I figured we would soon be returning to Su'Meeryn, and I'd serve him as the new king. If this is what you all want…" Neffy stammered for a moment. "I don't know… If I agree to it, I'd need some good advisors. I was never trained to be a ruler."

"And what of you women? What are your thoughts?" asked Adira.

"I don't care," Perrin stated.

The queen turned to Dellea. "Hellet and I have discussed this many times. I think it is a good idea and what is best for our land."

"Give me a day or two to ponder," replied Adira. "I believe your proposal has merit, but I don't want to make a hasty decision. Let me talk to my advisors, and Neffy would have to agree as well."

***

To her growing aggravation, Dellea had to wait even longer for her wedding to Hellet. After some additional discussion, and bickering with the nobles, the queen had finally agreed to Hellet's plan, as had Neffy. But once that matter was settled, there was debate about what to name the new nation. They did not want any of the prior kingdoms to have priority, so a new name had to be chosen.

In the midst of these discussions, Neffy had announced his intention to marry Perrin. Hellet had cautioned his friend regarding that decision, but Neffy was determined. He had assured Hellet that Perrin was softer when they were alone, and that her rage seemed to be lessening. He had also said that he wanted to make sure that the widow of his closest friend was cared for. A strong bond had grown between them through all they had gone through, and they wanted to remain together.

All had agreed that the wedding should take place prior to Neffy being named emperor and the coronation. A brief ceremony of the marriage of the two was completed in the garden outside the palace. The nobility of Labyn was gathered, but aside from the queen, Dellea and Hellet barely knew anyone. Despite some protests, the wolves stood next to Hellet and her when Perrin and Neffy exchanged their vows. Adira presided over the service, and Dellea could see the anguish in the queen's face as she still mourned for her beloved Tollan.

When the ceremony concluded, Hellet left Dellea's side to congratulate the couple. Perrin stood stiffly, seemingly unsure what to do; she turned towards Adira, but the queen immediately retreated from the gardens without another word.

Neffy was laughing at something Hellet had said, and Perrin remained still, looking uncomfortable. She glanced about, and when she saw Dellea, she left the dais. The wolves' tails began to wag, and Dellea heard soft whimpering as Perrin approached. Perrin rubbed both their heads and Dellea thought she saw a small smile on Perrin's face for the first time since their trials in the wilderness.

"Congratulation, Perrin. I'm so happy for you," Dellea said.

"Thank you. This is all happening so quickly." Dellea was shocked at Perrin's statement. It was the longest sentence she had heard her friend utter in a very long time.

"You know my feelings about Neffy when I first met him, but now I love him like a brother," Dellea stated, though that sentiment was difficult for her since there had not been love with her own brother. "He is as fine of a man as there is."

"That's true."

The wolves continued to push themselves at Perrin, forcing the affection to continue when she had stopped stroking their fur. Dellea pondered for a moment and then decided the time was right. "I have something for you."

Perrin grunted in response; her expression remained indifferent as she continued to pet the wolves. Dellea reached into her pocket and pulled out the orange and silver scarf. It was tattered and there were stains on it, but she hoped it would have some meaning to Perrin.

"I want you to have this back. You were so kind to me when I first arrived in Su'Meeryn, and offered me this gift, thinking it might give me some pleasure. I've kept it with me all this time." She hesitated then handed it to Perrin. "It's just a silly thing, but I hope it might bring you some happiness as a memory of a happier time."

Dellea held the scarf out as Perrin stared at her, unmoving. Dellea had no idea how her friend would react, and she hoped the gesture would be well received. She began to regret her decision as Perrin's entire body began to tremble. But then a shaking hand reached out and tentatively took the scarf from her. Perrin rubbed the fabric against her cheek, and then the wolves howled as Perrin began to sob.

***

A week after his marriage, the ordination of Neffy occurred. Since there was no tradition to crown an emperor, that ceremony—like the wedding—was also brief. Following a blessing by the clergy of Labyn, Hellet placed a crown on his friend's head. "I now present to you Nefalel, the first ruler of the new empire of Xavsyn."

The crowd roared and Hellet saw that even Adira appeared pleased. Perrin smiled and kissed her husband, and Hellet was delighted to see that she was finally starting to mend after all she had been through.

When the tumultuous applause finally died down, the nobles and dignitaries crowded around Neffy to offer their congratulations before they began to mill about. It all seemed odd, as if everyone had forgotten the strife they had been through, but Hellet knew he would never forget.

He still vividly recalled all the death which he had caused. It was a burden that would remain for the rest of his life. But thankfully, Dellea remained at his side.

Now there was one last thing to do before finally heading home.

***

The heat of summer had arrived, and filled Dellea's room as she made her final preparations. The wolves had been brought to her and Perrin sat on the bed while Dellea finished donning her gown. "I so often doubted that this day would ever come," Dellea said. "it's hard to believe it's finally arrived."

"I'm happy for you," Perrin replied with, perhaps, a shadow of a grin. Dellea noticed that her hair was pulled back, tied together with an orange and silver scarf.

"As am I for you. You went through so much; we all did, and I'm glad to see you're doing better."

"It was a difficult time, but Neffy has been good to me. And I'm the empress! Who could have imagined?"

"You know I'm here for you if you ever want to talk about those times. I don't suppose anyone else can understand what we've experienced."

"Thank you," Perrin replied; however, Dellea noted that Perrin did not provide the same offer. Dellea figured that was understandable; while Perrin was slowly healing, she clearly still had a long way to go.

She looked at her reflection one last time. A stray cluster of hair remained stubbornly out-of-place, and no matter the effort she employed, it refused to cooperate. She huffed in aggravation but surrendered to its unwillingness to comply. She would wait no longer.

"It's time," Dellea said, then she opened the door. Neffy was in the hallway waiting, and he escorted the women and wolves away from the room.

As they travelled down the hallway, Dellea still felt some trepidation. All the deaths Hellet and she had caused weighed heavily on her—as did the death of her wolf. But she remembered Wander's words. And she thought of The Book of Sul. If Sul could receive redemption, so could she.

When they reached the hall, Hellet stood waiting. His smile broadened when he looked upon his bride, and she felt blessed. That awkward, plain looking girl, who had been promised to Travyn, was finally marrying the man she loved. And the look on his face dispelled any lingering fears.

# Epilogue

ELLANIYA SAT ON THE THRONE, peering about the royal hall of Amyon. It seemed with each passing day her guards were becoming a bit blurrier. In addition to her declining vision, her hearing was also fading. She shifted in the seat in a failed attempt to ease an ache in her back, but that just caused the constant pain in her hips to intensify. She grabbed a bottle of the salve that she always kept in her pocket and reached under her skirt to rub some on her hips. Unfortunately, the numbing effects of the ointment faded more quickly the longer she used it.

"Where is he?" she demanded to nobody in particular, while running her hand through her thinning, gray hair. She sensed one of the guards turn towards her, but the man did not respond. She wanted to become aggravated that she did not receive an answer, but she decided to let the slight pass. It would take energy to chastise the man, and she had not directed the question to him specifically. "Why must the queen be forced to await her courier?" she grumbled.

The aching in her hips began to slacken as she heard what she knew must be the portal to the throne room opening. Four shapes grew in size as they approached the dais. As they came closer, she noticed one large shape of crimson and another black. Once they reached her throne, she recognized the mute red soldier. Next to him was a slender, but imposing warrior dressed all in black. The pair parted slightly, and Ut strode between them with a fourth individual by his side. That man seemed to resemble Ut, but his appearance was emaciated and hideous. It was as if Ut's reflection was looking back from a mirror, revealing his true nature.

"Ah, it is such a pleasure to see you again, my dear," Ut began warmly. "It has been far too long."

"You haven't aged a day Ut. Why am I not surprised?"

"I told you those many years ago that I have lived a very long time."

Ellaniya huffed at his words. The past decades had given her plenty of time to ponder the events of her life, and she wondered if she would have been better off if she had never met Ut. "And why have you returned to me after all this time?"

"I have wanted to see you these many years, but I was involved in other matters."

She looked at Ut, then at his companions. She wanted to question her self-appointed friend regarding their identities, but she decided she really did not care.

"You've wanted to see me?" she laughed. "Tell me Ut, why shouldn't I have you killed where you stand?"

"You were always my favorite," Ut continued with a broad smile. "There is no need for idle threats."

"It's a question, not a threat. You've caused me much sorrow."

"Come now, my dear. I have done no such thing." Ut remained still, but though it was difficult for her to be certain, it appeared that the emaciated man moved forward a few inches. "I only wanted the best for you, and look, you are sitting on a throne. Perhaps not the one you envisioned for yourself, but a throne nonetheless."

"Why are you here, Ut?" Ellaniya hissed. She would have had no qualms with ordering her guards to plunge their swords into Ut's vile heart, but she questioned if that would be able to be accomplished. So, she resigned herself to letting the messenger of the gods continue.

"I have been given a new task, and I thought we should talk before I embarked upon it."

"You have been assigned a task?" the queen laughed at him. "I thought you ordered tasks."

"We all have someone to answer to, my dear," Ut said with a tone which Ellaniya thought conveyed an honest response.

"Why do you seem so jovial? I haven't seen you since before our defeat. I would have thought you angry with the outcome."

Ut offered a short chuckle. "The outcome of the conflict to which you refer was inconsequential."

"What do you mean by that?" she barked. "I thought your goal was to establish the gods' empire," and Ellaniya again considered having the smug man killed.

"Rest assured, my dear, the goal remains intact. But that was not the time."

Ellaniya's anger grew, but she knew Ut well enough that he would be unphased by her ire. "So what was it all for?" she asked in a level voice. "Was everything you told me a lie?"

Ut's warm grin towards the queen remained unchanged. "Everything? No. A good portion of it yes," and Ellaniya was surprised at the bluntness of his words.

"Yet you stand before me—in my court—and make such an admission?"

Ut continued to smile, and unless her eyes were deceiving her, Ellaniya thought she saw true affection on his face. "It is not a lie when I say you are one of my favorites, my dear."

"And why should I care about that? All your plans, and all your schemes were thwarted."

"Are you certain?"

"I may be queen of Amyon, but I am not empress. Mephosh has been destroyed, and the empire of the gods was not established. We completely failed."

"Are you certain of that?" he repeated.

"What do you mean?" she demanded, her rage growing.

Ut climbed onto the dais, causing her guards to rush forward until the queen waved them away. Ut settled himself onto the seat beside her, and the queen wanted to reprimand him for his insolence. Instead, she decided to indulge him. "Though your empire was not established, we have done much to quash the heretic religion. The gods are worshipped in Amyon, and you have built strong alliances with the other northern kingdoms. Now that Xavsyn has fallen (Hellet's futile vision washed away to history), you can finally have your revenge for the destruction of Mephosh. Su'Meeryn is weak and Jaleph's namesake is a fool. You can destroy that kingdom, and we can finally be rid of Jaleph's and Hellet's line."

"Why should I believe you now, after all the pain you've caused me?"

"Please, my dear. I did not cause your pain. I did not kill your lover or your unborn child. And I did not kill your fool of a husband." Ut paused and gently patted her hand. "As I said, I have another mission to embark upon as there is an item I need to find. I will not be here to advise you, so this decision is solely yours to make."

"And why should I make that decision?" she asked skeptically.

Ut placed his hand on her thigh and rose from the chair. "Yes, you will always be my favorite, Ellaniya. How I wish I could stay here with you." He jumped down off the dais to rejoin his companions who had not moved. "I know you, my dear. Su'Meeryn was instrumental in the downfall and destruction of Mephosh. Now that the kingdom has reemerged, you want nothing more than to see it follow Mephosh into oblivion. After all these years, our goals remain aligned."

With those words, the four figures turned as one to exit the hall, and Ut's shape dissolved into a blur. Then the blurry movement stopped. "The gods will not be thwarted, my dear. Divinity still awaits you."

With that, Ut and his companions were gone. "Divinity awaits," she mumbled. She was certain Ut cared nothing for the gods or for her; if he had, she would have seen him long before now.

While Ellaniya remained convinced that Ut had lied to her about being a messenger of the gods, she could not argue with his logic. She hated Su'Meeryn with every fiber of her being.

Hellet had created the empire of Xavsyn when he defeated her at the battle of Mephosh, but it had taken only two generations for that empire to turn corrupt. Hellet's grandson, Halet, had been instrumental in the final destruction of the empire, which was fine with her. She cared nothing for Xavsyn. But she had been outraged when Halet, reestablished the kingdom of Su'Meeryn and named his firstborn Jaleph. Would she ever be free from the torment of that family? While the untimely death of Halet had given Ellaniya some pleasure, it just meant that she would have to hear the name Jaleph even more.

Though she hated to admit it, Ut was correct. She was an old, bitter woman, who had seen the premature death of all three of her husbands as well as her unborn child, and she had never been able to conceive again. Would she have been happy had she never met Ut? Perhaps, but then the heretic religion might still be thriving. She had suffered much in the service of the gods, and it seemed Ut was the root of that suffering. But, despite it all, she knew if she could relive her past, she would make the same choices. Her devotion to the gods remained absolute, and, just maybe, she might still attain the divinity which had been promised her decades ago. While she despised Ut, she hated Su'Meeryn even more. It was time to marshal an army one last time to strike Jaleph and Su'Meeryn. Finally, she would have her revenge.